Dying for Revenge

ERIC JEROME DICKEY

Dying for Revenge

DUTTON

DUTTON
Published by Penguin Group (USA) Inc.
375 Hudson Street, New York, New York 10014, U.S.A.
Penguin Group (Canada), 90 Eglinton Avenue East, Suite 700, Toronto, Ontario M4P 2Y3, Canada
(a division of Pearson Penguin Canada Inc.); Penguin Books Ltd, 80 Strand, London WC2R 0RL,
England; Penguin Ireland, 25 St Stephen's Green, Dublin 2, Ireland (a division of Penguin Books
Ltd); Penguin Group (Australia), 250 Camberwell Road, Camberwell, Victoria 3124, Australia
(a division of Pearson Australia Group Pty Ltd); Penguin Books India Pvt Ltd, 11 Community Centre,
Panchsheel Park, New Delhi - 110 017, India; Penguin Group (NZ), 67 Apollo Drive, Rosedale,
North Shore 0632, New Zealand (a division of Pearson New Zealand Ltd); Penguin Books (South
Africa) (Pty) Ltd, 24 Sturdee Avenue, Rosebank, Johannesburg 2196, South Africa

Penguin Books Ltd, Registered Offices: 80 Strand, London WC2R 0RL, England

Published by Dutton, a member of Penguin Group (USA) Inc.

First printing, November 2008
1 3 5 7 9 10 8 6 4 2

Copyright © 2008 by Eric Jerome Dickey

Ⓩ REGISTERED TRADEMARK—MARCA REGISTRADA

LIBRARY OF CONGRESS CATALOGING-IN-PUBLICATION DATA
HAS BEEN APPLIED FOR.

ISBN 978-0-525-95086-8

Printed in the United States of America
Set in Janson Text
Designed by Leonard Telesca

PUBLISHER'S NOTE
This book is a work of fiction. Names, characters, places, and incidents either are the product of the author's imagination or are used fictitiously, and any resemblance to actual persons, living or dead, business establishments, events, or locales is entirely coincidental.

For Dominique

In revenge and in love woman is more barbaric than man is.

FRIEDRICH NIETZSCHE, *Beyond Good and Evil*

Dying
for
Revenge

One

crime and punishment

I fought for my life.

The sounds from us trying to kill each other were trapped inside this concrete toilet. My side kick had caught him in the gut, staggered him before he could stab me, and I went after him. We fought for the knife in his hand, a blade that could cut through bones, the knife he had tried to bring down in my back, only I'd seen his reflection. I gripped the wrist he used to hold the blade, threw my knee into his gut, tried to make him bend, then tried to sweep his feet, but he didn't give me space to maneuver. We slammed each other up against the concrete walls, walls built to withstand hurricanes, tussled and crashed into the metal bathroom door, collided with the sink and the unbreakable, reflective Plexiglas.

Violence echoed.

My elbows and knees gave him enough pain to make him loosen his grip on that razor-sharp blade, that moment enough for me to take control of the knife he was trying to put inside my throat, that moment good enough for me to send that sharp blade down across his arm, his DNA spilling in red.

Severe pain resided in his blue eyes.

We struggled, my jogging sandals slipping, his trainers squeaking, battled across the damp concrete floor, wrestled eye to eye, so close I inhaled his rancid breath, breath that stank like he drank nameless black coffee from a paper cup and smoked forty cigarettes a day. The killer's blood dripped down across my arm, splattered my skin and everything in sight as I found leverage and shoved him hard and fast into the concrete wall, that knife still in my control as I threw an elbow into his nose, a good shot with momentum and gravity on my side, a blow hard enough to shatter his face. I expected him to go down, but he surprised me. Still, that blow had stunned him long enough for me to get firm footing. I pressed on, went after him, used my weight and leverage to push that blade toward the center of his soul, his frame muscular, taller than me by at least three inches, his weight mine plus at least forty pounds.

He was strong, swift, as determined to kill as I was determined to stay alive.

I gritted my teeth, grunted and shoved the blade toward the assassin's chest, struggled with him, strength against strength, an arm wrestle that lasted for the better part of eternity, a battle that I refused to lose. I pushed the blade into his sweaty T-shirt, into his skin, inside his body, eased death his way a little at a time, fought and grunted with the killer as I pushed the blade a millimeter at a time, an inch at a time, then, with a rush, pushed it as the blade vanished, didn't ease up as the look on his dank face changed from anger to desperation to surprise to fear, pushed the blade until it stilled his rapid-beating heart.

The Grim Reaper claimed him, pulled him from this tropical world to a hotter place.

He collapsed, eyes wide open, slid down the concrete wall, fell forward, let out his final breath.

His bladder emptied. His bowels would do the same.

Dying was never pretty. Death didn't have the scent of fresh roses.

I went down on one knee, wounded from the fight, struggling to breathe, exhausted, bruised, fists and elbows aching. Midday. Sun at its peak. Sweat drained down my face and neck, the heat from the Cayman Islands now a sweltering oven. I stared at the dead man. A man I'd never seen before.

He was a messenger. And the message from his employer rang like a noontime church bell.

Death's foot was on my shadow.

I took deep breaths, senses on fire, the bathroom hot, the stench of urine strong.

It had happened fast. Less than two minutes had passed since I walked into the bathroom.

Just like that my world would be different. Minutes ago I'd been scuba diving, thinking about the kid, my mind on the kid a lot lately. The kid had been on my mind when I had stepped inside the toilet, too preoccupied to realize I had been followed by an assassin with a blade. A man who, after our quick and deadly fight, I needed to drag inside the stall to hide his body, then let water run from the sink to the bathroom floor to wash away the blood on the tile. I stared at him, a blade in his chest, right in the heart of his University College of the Cayman Islands T-shirt. Once again a dead body was at my feet.

My heart raced. My mind moved faster than the speed of thought.

The peaceful part of my dark life was over, had ended almost as soon as it had begun.

I grimaced at the dead man. Blood dripped from his broken nose.

We'd shared no words, but he didn't come inside this bathroom for conversation.

I went through his pockets, took everything I could find. Copper wire was inside his pocket. The kind made for strangling. Wire I recognized. Anger in my eyes, I pulled the blade from his chest. No choice. Had no weapon of my own. I hurried and rinsed it off, wrapped it in paper towels.

Near the back wall I found a sign that said the bathroom was closed for cleaning, put that on the door as I hurried outside, clear blue waters in front of me, couples and families playing and lounging in the sand, snorkeling, parasailing, Jet Skiing, all unaware of the violence that had happened yards away.

I had stepped inside that toilet less than two minutes ago.

I paused, searched to see if the killer had come alone.

I had been living a hedonistic lifestyle with two beautiful women, had traveled and pretended all of my problems had been resolved. I nodded, understood the significance of that moment. That attack, that bathroom killing, would bring our hedonistic lifestyle to an end.

It was time. I would have to say good-bye. Glad they weren't here. I was glad the women were checking out tourist attractions; the iron-shore landscape of Hell, the twenty-four-acre marine theme park Boatswain's Beach, and Cayman Turtle Farm.

When I felt safe I moved away, unseen, footprints in the sand the only trail I'd leave behind as I hurried toward Seven Mile Beach. I took out my cellular and dialed. She answered on the first ring.

I said, "Lola, where are you?"

"With Mrs. J."

"You okay?"

"We're having a blast."

I told her, "We have to go."

"Where are we going?"

"Not together. I have to go. And you and Mrs. J have to go."

"I don't understand."

"The party's over."

"Wait, talk to Mrs. J."

I told Mrs. J what had happened. Told her to get to the room, pack, and get on a plane.

She understood. I had had that same problem back in London.

Mrs. J. said, "The kid."

"I know."

"Don't forget about the kid. I'm a mother. It would kill me if someone stole my daughter."

She was talking about a kid named Sven.

She said, "Find the truth. You deserve the truth."

"Spoken like an attorney."

"Old habits die hard."

I promised those women that I would talk to them, then I hung up the phone knowing that promise couldn't be kept. That had been our good-bye. Some friendships ended as abruptly as they started.

The hit man never had a chance to tell me who had sent him.

But I knew who it was. I looked at the knife I had pulled from his body and I knew.

His blade had been an MXZ saw knife.

When I saw that familiar blade, when I found the killer had copper wire in his pocket, the same wire I had left on the bed of my enemy, I knew the problem I'd had in Detroit wasn't over.

After I had been attacked in the Cayman Islands, I had returned to North America. Had gone to Detroit. Had gone after her, the woman I had been hired to kill for; our business association had left her bitter, made us enemies until death. Had gone to find my vindictive enemy and put her in the ground before she did the same to me, but she had made it impossible to get to her. Six men guarded her two-level home, hired from a private security firm, the kind where all employees had a license to carry. Those six men were left dead, guns at their sides; at least two of those men never had time to draw their weapons. The one who had shot me had hit my bulletproof vest. My shots had been head shots, in search of bulletproof brains. The last wounded man, as my gloved hand gripped his throat, begged for mercy as I applied pressure to the wound in his knee. Her rent-a-thug had howled and told me that she wasn't there anymore, hadn't been there since the last time I had visited that million-dollar home, that she had sent her kids away, that now she lived in the mayor's mansion but was never there, ran the city from other locations, locations that were well guarded, security better than Al Capone had used back in his day. His face bloodied, his body beaten, his eyes on the silenced gun at my side, he told me the police were on the way. Silent alarm had just been triggered. Before the sirens and flashing lights made it to the scene, I was gone, and he was dead.

I was dressed in all black, but he had seen my face, had heard my voice.

The last face he saw before he met his maker was the face of Gideon.

Part of me wanted to put a plastic bag over his head, let him suffocate, as I had been suffocated. But I didn't do that. His end had been swift, my arms around his neck, then his neck quickly broken.

I had taken out the guards at her mansion, but my anger hadn't lessened, and I did something else. Her children had four private bodyguards and she had two who stayed with her full-time. All carried guns. I went after the four, trailed them as they took her children to private school, watched as those four bodyguards picked them up. Four bodyguards they had found injured beyond repair, that pain and suffering not happening in front of her children's eyes. I had left a typed note with three simple words.

LET IT END.

Now as I moved through London the hairs on the back of my neck refused to stop standing, warned me the way a spider was alerted when an intruder had touched its web.

The kid was on my mind. But that other problem remained with me as well. The storm that had started in Detroit had returned, surrounded me, had me in its eye. I felt its power even though I was back in London. I had avoided this place too long.

I was alone. Inside Thai Square Restaurant Bar, right outside Mansion House tube station. Soft music played, instrumental jazz, music that my heartbeat refused to let me hear. I'd stopped here because of that sensation of being stalked, had ducked inside and moved just behind the door, sat at a table facing the entry and the narrow street that ran down the back side of Mansion House toward Queen Street. Delivery boys on scooters went by. Smart cars that looked like adult toys. Hundreds of Londoners dressed in dark colors—men in dark and depressing suits, women in black dresses and fancy tights—walked the cobbled street, most heading toward the financial district.

Not knowing what I was waiting for, eyes on the door, my hand inside my bag, I waited.

Paranoia had owned me for two seasons.

Paranoia, the first cousin of a bastard named fear.

A chilly day. Overcast, as usual. Dark like the sun was too ashamed to come out.

I'd forgotten how ominous it was in the U.K. For months I had vanished to places where I didn't need too much more than shorts and sandals. This weather was harsh, called for a heavy jacket, Levi's, shoes with soft soles. The skully I wore had the same midnight flavor.

I took to Queen Street, passed Domino's Pizza, headed toward Southwark Bridge. So much noise. So many smells at once. A city filled with red buses and cars and motorcycles. An assassin could be anywhere. I tried to spy into the glass fronts of buildings, tried to see if I could catch the reflection of whoever was so interested in me. It had to be my paranoia. Being this close to where I had died, it was fucking with me, making me think that once again someone had been sent to kill me.

I turned right at the light, took Upper Thames Road and veered to the left, went between Victorian buildings and businesses so I could connect with the footpath that snaked along the Thames River. I moved closer to the Millennium Bridge, then paused, searched to see who was trailing me. Men. Women. Joggers. Kids. Tourists taking pictures with the Tate Modern in the background.

I turned and mixed in with people heading toward the Millennium Bridge.

I paused when I thought I saw a grifter named Arizona coming my way.

But it wasn't her. It was someone else, same height, same complexion.

It wasn't until that moment that I realized where I was, where my mind had taken me.

Last time I saw Arizona, we were close to this spot, surrounded by guns.

It was a day I wanted to disremember, but, eyes wide open, I saw it again, that horrible day as clear now as it was then. Saw the overcast skies, felt the drizzle, saw the Tate Modern and St. Paul's Cathedral. That day, no matter how I tried, I couldn't protect her. We had lost that battle.

On that same day, I was beaten and died a slow and horrible death.

I had died right here in London.

I hopped on the tube and got right back off at Embankment, looked back at swarms of Londoners; no one person stood out to confirm my uneasy sensation. While everyone rushed uphill toward the West End's theater district or hustled back down into the tube, I slowed my pace, my messenger bag on my left shoulder, my right hand inside the bag, my right hand holding a silenced gun, finger on trigger, and hoped my paranoia didn't make me do something I would regret.

I mixed in with a group of Chinese-speaking tourists, left them behind and mixed in with a group of people from India, then broke away from my human shields and stopped at Starbucks, went inside but didn't buy anything, spied outside, did the same at Wasabi, looked in the window at Timpson watch repair, again used that reflection to see who was trying to see me.

A woman glanced my way, panic in her face, the look of a woman concentrating. She searched, then she saw me, her hurried pace faltered, and after she had me in her crosshairs she looked away. What I saw in a glance: hair strawberry blond, dark scarf around an oval-shaped face, generous lips. She could've been Russian, British, Brazilian, Spanish, Polish. Could've been anything.

Her purse was large enough to shelter more than a few weapons.

And her hand was inside her purse, same as mine was inside the messenger bag I carried.

My hand was on the .38-caliber message I had for anyone who came after me.

She was beautiful and I'd have to kill her, without remorse, I knew that; beauty had no value in the world I lived in. At moments getting caught up in physical beauty was the same as committing suicide. On these streets I would have to put her down before she put me down.

I strolled up the incline, moved through European locals and international tourists. Passed by Embankment Café and Holland & Barrett health foods. I paused in front of another Starbucks, the second coffee-house five businesses away from the one right outside the Embankment tube.

People passed by, briefcases, backpacks, and big shopping bags in their hands.

The woman with the oval face and strawberry blond mane was gone.

She hadn't passed me. And she hadn't gone back inside the tube station.

She'd lost me, had turned this around already.

I ducked inside the Arches shopping center, an alley with a strip of businesses that headed toward Trafalgar Square. I took it upstairs and came out of Charing Cross tube station, that woman nowhere in sight. I made it to Covent Garden, took Neal Street through the din of the shopping area, paused at Sunglass Hut to spy back. Did the same at Foot Locker and Aldo. Remained on alert as I approached Shaftesbury. I made a quick left, moved out of sight, and stood inside Neal's Corner Sandwich Shop.

She reappeared. In the middle of a crowd of people. Tried to blend in.

She had breasts and curves, weighed between ten and eleven stone.

Cellular up to her ear, she came out of Neal Street, moved quickly, looked in all directions, searched before she crossed the two lanes that separated this side of the boulevard from the side that housed Forbidden Planet. She was on a cellular. That told me she was part of a team; how large a team I had no idea. Seconds later a European man wearing a long black coat over a black suit came from the other direction, hurried from the Odeon, the cinema on the other side of Forbidden Planet. His stride was deadly. Her stride was just as powerful as she hurried toward him. He could've been any one of a hundred nationalities. Just like her. She went to him, rushed words exchanged, then they both looked around, looked up and down Shaftesbury, before they gave up, held hands, and hurried away, conversation heavy, but they didn't look back. They rushed toward the darkness covering Oxford Circus.

They didn't make contact with anyone else. They weren't on the cellular phone.

This time there were two.

I followed them as they passed by *Les Misérables*, steak houses, and high-end Chinese restaurants on the edges of Chinatown. They remained side by side, doing as I had done, used the reflections from storefronts to look behind them. He bumped her, caused her to pause in front of the cinema; I saw their lips moving as they communicated while pretending to read the marquee. They walked away, their pace telling, not as fast as before; I saw them struggle to not look back at me, their eyes on the reflections. They knew I was there. They used the reflection to gauge our distance apart, moved through the crowd, followed me by leading. I glanced up. CCTV cameras all over.

Still, I needed to pop them and vanish. I would have to kill them here and now.

Before they had the chance to do the same to me.

The well-dressed man stopped the cat and mouse game, turned around, looked in my eyes, and nodded. I did the same, stopped where I was, some distance between us, and returned the gesture.

He had red hair, trimmed short and neat, almost military. Square chin, medium build, about six feet tall. His features were like a combination of a trustworthy schoolboy and a career bad boy, the amalgamation of Brad Pitt and Josh Hartnett, the square chin making him more Josh than Brad. The swank way they were dressed brought to mind soccer star David Beckham and his wife, Victoria.

The strawberry blonde was older than the red-haired man by at least a decade, maybe fifteen years, but he acted like he was the general on the battlefield. Killing was a man's world. He pulled back his trench coat, did the same with his suit coat, revealed he was carrying a gun. I took my hand out of my messenger bag, my restless piece at my side. His peacemaker was in a holster, a threat. Mine was in my hand, a promise.

The strawberry blonde eased her hand out of her coat pocket and let me see a .22 attached to her pretty wrist, her gun hand wrapped in some kind of plastic. I understood. Not because she was afraid it might get wet. She had the gun wrapped up so if she took a shot, no shell would be left behind.

Her eyes rested on mine. Since she had the gun, I obliged the attention.

We stared, evaluated, exchanged energy, anxiety hidden behind cold poker faces.

She was around five-nine with the heels on; that made her about five-six without.

They stared at me like my check had changed into their checkmate.

I'd have to beat her to the draw, shoot her first, then try to pop him before he pulled his gun.

That would be impossible to do, get a clean shot, not without hitting an innocent bystander.

The sidewalks were crowded, busy, people rushing by them and by me. On the streets were red buses, more cars, more black cabs with colorful adverts on the side; all of that added noise to the moment. Nowhere for me to duck or run; same for them.

Nobody in the narcissistic world noticed that we were moments from a shoot-out.

Nobody but maybe *them*, the ones who sat inside secret rooms and worked for Big Brother.

Rain started to fall. A mild drizzle on a street swarming with people, people moving through traffic, people on cell phones, people listening to iPods, people moving like the world was in their way.

I motioned upward, not because of the weather but to indicate that they were in plain view. The strawberry blonde looked up, saw all the CCTV cameras. She did that as if this were her first time in London, as if she had no idea that CCTV cameras were all over, as if she didn't know that Central London was a big prison with no bars, that it was possible for Scotland Yard to track every citizen's move once they entered Central London, that anyone could be tracked from point to point with no interruption. Terrorists had learned that years ago.

The man shrugged as if he didn't really care about CCTV, then he smiled a bit.

Two policemen zoomed by on BMW motorcycles. Then I saw more police were here.

Across the street two of London's bobbies were on Shaftesbury, both of the cops walking this way, those distinctive helmets on their heads, helmets that made them easy to spot from a distance. Not many bobbies carried guns in London. Those two were strapped. This would be interesting.

The man looked back and saw the police cross the street, come toward our side of the road, walk up on him and the strawberry blonde. My red-haired friend mouthed two words to me. "Next time."

My aggravated and exhausted expression said fuck next time, let's do this now.

Then the red-haired man did something that surprised me.

He hailed a black cab. I had expected him to have an exit plan. But he hailed a cab.

He stepped to the curb and hailed a cab without taking his eyes off me. He let his partner get inside the cab first. The strawberry blonde kept her eyes on me, did that like she was trained to always watch her target, her eyes looking deep into mine again, that stare once again connecting us. We shared the stare of death. I caught a better look at her frame. Nice curves leading to a decent backside. Not too thin, but not too heavy. Like her height, her weight wouldn't change overnight. Eyes on me, the red-haired man took his time getting inside after her, pausing to make sure I wasn't about to rush them, my drawn gun blazing.

Both assassins sat in the let-down rear-facing seats.

As sweat and drizzle drained down my neck and back, my attention remained unmoved.

They kept their eyes on mine until their black cab vanished, mixed with a sea of black cabs.

Umbrellas went up all over, pedestrians not missing a beat, light drizzle changing to rain as red double-decker buses spit out carbon monoxide, as the din of cars and motorcycles hummed in my ears.

With a sprint I crossed the street, vanished in the web of streets spreading out into the West End.

Once again Death had been close.

Once again I had outmaneuvered the inevitable.

Two

dark eyes of london

A strong jog took me toward the red-light district, back to the stench of Berwick Street.

When I was sure it was clear, took out my phone, made a call to one of the meanest people I knew, one of my handlers. The guy who'd brought me into the business. The man who had groomed me. Hadn't talked to him in a few weeks, not since the incident in the Cayman Islands.

After that attempt on my life I'd needed someone to supply me with weapons.

He answered on the first ring.

I caught my breath and said, "Konstantin."

"Son of a motherfucking bitch." He sounded like Al Pacino. At least he did to me. "Was beginning to think you were dead and you didn't invite me to the funeral. Feelings were hurt."

I cut to the chase. "Where are you?"

"I am near Krasnapolsky."

That meant he was working in Suriname, camped out near the famous hotel in the center of town.

I said, "I'm in London."

"What are you doing in London?"

"I'm being trailed."

"Like in the Cayman Islands."

"This time there are two hit men. At least."

"You should've put Detroit in the ground when you had the chance."

"My sentiments exactly."

"Never leave an enemy aboveground. Give me the details."

I told him about being followed, described the strawberry blonde, told him she looked like Jaime Pressly with nice legs that were attached to a pair of expensive shoes, those legs moving north into a round backside, said the red-haired man was younger, six feet or so, square chin, Pitt meets Hartnett. My descriptions didn't add up to much. There were hundreds of Presslys and Pitt/Hartnetts out there. I told him about the showdown that almost turned Shaftesbury Avenue into the O.K. Corral.

He asked, "How long ago?"

"Ten minutes."

"My guess is they're still around. It's a contract. They're looking for you."

I looked at the gun in my hand. "I'm looking for them too."

"You're like a son to me, the son I would have loved to have, but I have to tell you this."

"Okay."

"That thing you did in Detroit, you fucked up."

"Yeah. I fucked up."

Konstantin said, "If you had used a handler it could've been resolved in a professional manner."

"I know."

"You never said who gave you that job."

"I know."

Konstantin took a breath, the inhale of a frustrated parent, before he asked, "Need a safe house? I have a reliable contact near Shepherd's Bush Empire. Take a taxi over there."

"I have business to take care of here."

"What kind?"

"It's not a job."

"Let me arrange the safe house."

"Have it on standby."

"How long you there?"

"I'm leaving the U.K. in the morning."

"Anything I can do?"

"Get me some work if you can."

"Short on cash?"

"Not short. Just have a few obligations, bills like the rest of the squares."

"Where you headed? In case something pops up in the direction you're going."

"Heading where they need to change the president."

"God bless America."

"North America."

"I stand corrected. You're heading home."

I didn't have a home. I didn't have a country. I'd been told I was born in North America, but I was a man without a country. Sometimes I felt more European than American, other times more Canadian than European. I didn't know who I was, where I had come from, only that I existed, my life one big lie. I wanted better for the kid. I wanted the kid to be safe and get what I never had, the truth.

I told Konstantin, "Find out what you can."

"Strawberry blond. About five-five."

"Nice curves and pretty face."

"And a six-foot redhead, military haircut."

"I know it's not much."

He asked, "You hear them speak?"

"Just saw their guns."

"No idea what nationality."

"No fucking idea. But I don't think they were locals."

"Why not?"

"The woman. She wasn't aware of the CCTV cameras."

"Maybe she didn't care."

"Maybe."

"I'll make some calls. Hit up some other handlers. We outsource jobs to each other off and on. And nowadays a lot of people in the wet-work business are getting business right off the Internet, finding jobs on Craigslist, so I'll have somebody search that avenue."

"Craigslist. I heard. Advert for hits on the Internet. Those jobs were mostly in Mexico."

"You never know. Anyway, you being off grid so long had me sending work to other handlers. You know how it goes. If you get a reputation for talking you're out of the biz, so most of those sons of bitches won't tell shit. But I'll see who has loose lips. If they have you on a kill list, will hit you back."

I nodded, took a breath, tried to regroup. "How's your health?"

"I am fine."

"I mean . . . got sidetracked with my bullshit . . . the chemo?"

"I'm still doing chemo."

Again I paused. "And you are in Suriname working?"

"Have to keep working. Costs a lot to stay alive in America."

He paused, sounded hopeful. The cancer in his body not making him sound weak.

Konstantin said, "I have to put people in the dirt so I can stay un-buried. Costs me a hundred dollars a day to live. A barrel of oil a day to remain amongst the living. Close to three large a month to stay on top of soil. That means I pay thirty-six thousand a year to stay alive."

"That's a lot."

"Food, mortgage, electric bill, and my wife's hair, nails, and car note not included."

He chuckled, so I chuckled along with him.

He said, "I'm still on top of soil, that's all that matters."

"Sorry to dump my shit on you right now."

"Like I said, I'm on top of soil. And you try to stay the same way."

We disconnected.

My heartbeat refused to slow down.

My paranoia refused to let me breathe.

I had nightmares about the man who had killed me. Still got that horrifying sensation I owned as Death claimed me and I suffocated. A man I hadn't been able to kill and get my own revenge, that moment of my life never getting the closure it needed for me to relax, for me to rest, for me to not feel hunted. That had left me uneasy, feeling incompetent, more vulnerable than I'd ever admit to anyone breathing.

I was a man who did wetwork; admitting that I had cracks in my armor didn't work in this business. I had to remain as professional and removed as the rest of the people in my trade.

I was a gun for hire trying not to get killed. A man trying to stay on top of the ground.

Because of the kid.

Still, I searched the landscape, that foreboding sensation refusing to wane and let me go.

The kid; had to make sure the kid was okay. On my iPhone, I clicked on an icon for software I had installed, entered the I.P. address, and looked in on a house in Powder Springs for a moment. Catherine was in the kitchen. The kid was sitting at a table, book in hand. Fourteen cameras were hooked up. I saw every move they made in the shared spaces. No cameras were in bedrooms or bathrooms. Saw what was outside the house. In the kitchen. Watched footage of them moving from room to room. It was like having my own CCTV. Big Brother was watching.

Everything was fine. No one had reverse-engineered my life back to them.

Not yet.

I spied the streets of London again, in search of a strawberry blonde and a redheaded killer.

Killed them.

I should have killed them like I had killed the assassin she had sent after me in the Cayman Islands. But that message had not been strong enough to end this. No matter how many morticians I kept in business, Detroit would send more hired assassins, would send killers until she succeeded.

Eventually she would.

She lived to finance my death.

I spied Berwick Street, let droves of people go by before I blended into the morose crowd, stopping at a vendor and buying a dark, over-sized hoodie, stuffing my black jacket in my dark bag, buying a dark cap and darker scarf, putting them on, changing as much of my wardrobe as I could change in less than three minutes. The midnight colors I wore made me a moving shadow amongst moving shadows.

If I were smart I would be on the way to a safe house.

I would be on the way out of the U.K.

Right now I had another mission. I'd resurfaced and come back to London for another reason.

This reason more emotional than logical.

I'd come back to the U.K. because of the kid. This mission was as personal as it was urgent.

I rushed through the center of the whores' district, hurried by vendors selling fruit and clothing as upstairs international women sold their bodies, moved by strip clubs that were advertising American-style pole dancing, big guys who looked like they were Russian mafia guarding the doors.

One of the Russians posted outside a den of sin caught my eye and said, "Hello, my friend."

Making eye contact, hand inside my bag, I replied, "*Zdorovo*, my friend."

He smiled. "*Hochesh poglyadet na golyh devok?*"

"*Spasibo ne nado.*" I shook my head. "I don't want to look at naked women."

A dark-skinned African boy was kicking a worn soccer ball. He'd grown almost a foot taller since the last time I saw him. He paused when he saw me, looked at me as if he knew me, remembered who I was, what I had done in the name of anger, and his mouth opened like he wanted to sound an alarm.

I put my finger to my lips before the fear in his eyes made its way to his mouth.

That hushed him.

He had seen me once, a year ago, when I had come here in search of my own revenge. I had come here to put the woman who had corrupted me in the ground. But that hadn't happened.

With a kind smile I asked, "Are you Nusaybah's son?"

He nodded at me, soccer ball underneath one arm, his free hand creating a fist, my smile not trusted.

I asked, "Where is Nusaybah?"

He pointed upstairs to a dirty window. His mother's red light was off. I understood that signal. She had a customer. While her son played in the streets she was busy getting pounded for the pound.

I couldn't talk to Nusaybah, not right now. Wasn't sure if she would talk to me at all.

So much hate was in her eyes the one and only time I'd ever seen her, rightfully so.

I'd hurt her friend on that day, my anger deep and never-ending, out of control.

But when money was on the table, people would sell their souls, would sell out their friends.

It wasn't for Nusaybah but because of another woman that I had come back to this sordid place.

A woman who used to be one of her coworkers, her red light glowing in the gloom on this street.

I paused and stared up at what used to be her red-lit window. Hundreds of people were out, not nearly as many as the numbers walking Piccadilly Circus or Oxford Circus, but more than the number needed to make the street feel crowded. In the din of the afternoon children were out and about, playing on streets that smelled like piss and sex, the neon signs from the strip clubs high overhead. Men were on lunch breaks, some slipping into the narrow doorways that led to leased pleasure, some leaving those dens of satisfaction, checking their watches as they adjusted their white collars and black trench coats, heads down as they mixed in the crowd and hurried back to work, wedding rings untarnished. Children, vendors, women passing on bicycles, shop owners lining Berwick Street, all unaffected, none noticing or protesting the XXX video store that had pictures of hard-core gay sex in its windows, this world desensitized to prostitution and amoral acts. As was I. I had grown up like this, had lived in brothels from North Carolina to Montreal, had visited whores from Rio to Amsterdam.

I took out a picture I had in my inside pocket. Thelma and Andrew-Sven. Only her name was Catherine now. I had come back to the red-light district to knock on some doors. To talk to the whores who had been here over a year. I needed to talk to the ones who were here when Thelma first arrived with the boy. *Thelma.* In my mind she was still Thelma, even though she no longer used that name.

My heart knew her only as the woman who I had killed for, the woman who made me this way.

It remained a struggle to accept that she had shed the skin of a whore and become Catherine.

This was like being an archaeologist. I came to dig for answers to the past. I saw the edges of bones buried underneath a world of dirt, but I had to remove the dirt to find out what type of skeleton was being hidden. I wanted to ask those who knew her when she was here, find out if she'd arrived in London with the boy. Or without the boy. I had returned to the land of Charles and Camilla to ask questions.

Pinned to the dilapidated wooden doors, taped on the stained walls, all over the red-light district were handwritten signs advertising models. Russian models. African models. Polish models. French models. Asian models. Some here as part of the slave trade, their pimps in the avenue guarding the doorways. Some here because of the economics in their homeland, this being their best option.

They were all here to model—*model* being the euphemism whores used in the U.K.

A rail-thin girl appeared, cigarette in hand, her brows dark, her hair the same color. She was young, barely a woman. She stepped out into the street, her eyes on me.

The whore inhaled her cigarette and as she exhaled she asked, "Blow job or full service?"

Her accent was Yugoslavian, clothing simple jeans and trainers, her sweater modest and red. I followed her into the piss-smelling hallway.

I asked, "How long have you been working here?"

"Long enough to be better than the Africans. And I am better than the Asians. Come to my room and we can talk. No pressures. Tell me what you need and I will tell you how many pounds it will cost."

With Death on my heels, I didn't have a lot of fucking time.

I showed her a picture of Catherine and the kid. My bête noire and my life's only concern.

She inhaled her cigarette, her expression not changing, my problems not being her problems.

I asked, "You know her?"

"Maybe I remember her."

"Either you fucking remember her or you don't."

"My memory . . . sometimes it gets to be really bad."

I pulled out three hundred pounds, the equivalent of six hundred U.S. dollars. The equivalent of more rubles than that Yugoslavian had ever made standing up or with her legs closed. Wanted to get to the point, didn't have time to bullshit, not with trouble stepping on my heels.

"Don't fuck around with me. Understand? You know her?"

"My memory, it is getting better now."

"Fuck you."

I turned around, headed away.

She called out. "Wait, wait."

I faced the whore again.

She dropped her cigarette, crushed it out on the concrete stairs with the bottom of her worn trainer, the scent from the cigarette blending with the aroma of old orgasms, with the stench of layers of piss and cologne and perfume that had permeated the chipped and peeling paint on the tattered walls.

She took the picture, looked at Catherine, looked at the kid, sighed, took out another cigarette.

She said, "This is Sven."

"Andrew-Sven. That's the kid she had with her while she was here."

"I remember them." She nodded. "And I remember you. You beat her with your fists."

My jaw tightened. "That wasn't me."

"That was you. I gave her my gun to shoot you with if you ever came back to try to harm her."

"I need to ask you about the kid." I took a breath. "The kid that was here with her."

"And if I do not tell you, will you beat me too?"

I paused. "No."

The whore lit her smoke, then motioned for me to follow her, her pace aggravating and slow.

Hand in my bag, I spied behind me, searched and made sure no one was following me.

No one other than them, the ones who watched every step that everyone made.

The ones spying down on the world through the eyes of CCTV.

Three

a thousand lies

Frustrated and anxious.

I took Cannon Street toward Bank, hiked across the bridge toward London Bridge tube, walked Borough High Street, and stopped in front of a row of flats and businesses. I had died inside one of those rooms. I wasn't sure which building, but I had met Death in one of those rooms. Standing there haunted me. But I had to face that fear. That other stress. There was a lot in London I had to face.

My cellular rang and my uneasy hands grabbed my phone. It was Konstantin.

He said, "The safe house is ready."

"Might not use it."

"You okay?"

"Have another place in mind. I'll keep you posted."

"Do I need to head toward London?"

"You finished your work in Suriname?"

"Problem solved."

I paused, staring across the Thames. "I can make it here another day."

"Stay on top of soil."

"Doing my best."

I took a black cab to Bloomsbury, had the taxi drop me off by the museum. After I was sure no one was following me I doubled back, made my way to a hotel called Myhotel. Fake I.D. and credit card in hand, I checked in, requested the same room I had stayed in months ago with my friends. Hedonistic lifestyles were good while they lasted, but they couldn't last forever.

I went online, read *The New York Times*'s theater section. Checked out the mixed reviews for *Cat on a Hot Tin Roof*. Directed by Debbie Allen. Starring Terrence Howard, Phylicia Rashad, James Earl Jones, Giancarlo Esposito. And Lola Mack was filling in for Anika Noni Rose.

Lola Mack.

We had been in this room months ago. I stared at the bed, remembered what we had done that night I had rescued her from being broke stranded. And what had happened when the knock came at the door. I remembered Mrs. J. Remembered the invaluable lesson she taught Lola. Six months since I had heard from her too. She had a daughter who needed her attention and I had bigger issues.

My enemy in Detroit, I had her name in Google Alerts, had her set at Comprehensive and As-It-Happens. As soon as news about her hit any newspaper, any blog, the Web, any video, any article, any mention anywhere in the world, that information was sent to several of many e-mail accounts.

I clicked the link that came up in the alert, and that link led me to a Web page for the *Detroit Free Press*. Did the same for *The Detroit News*. I'd had the chance to shut her down before her power had grown, taxpayers' dollars lining her pockets. Now I wished I had taken her out, should've been smart and put her in the ground, just for the peace of mind. She had learned too much about me. Too much.

In between killing her husband and ordering assassinations, she had been busy.

The widower. The single mom. The working woman. The new mayor of a threadbare town.

The woman who hired hit men to do what she was afraid to do herself.

Immediately after she had gone home and found her husband's dead body, she had turned up at a press conference in a bloodstained blouse and told the story of how she had come home from a religious retreat in Seattle and found her preacher husband assassinated in her basement, told how she had held her dead husband's cold body in her arms and prayed to God. She had manipulated the assassination she had financed, showed up on the news with her husband's blood on her blouse. Had dipped her hands in his blood and smeared it on her blouse and went to talk to the media, tears in her eyes.

Another self-absorbed opportunist.

Said she vowed to find out who killed her husband and would pick up the torch and continue his work, would continue to help bring Detroit back to what it used to be. She had won the people over.

She lived for the press.

When she walked into a room people crowded her and all hell would break loose; people begged and yelled to be acknowledged with a simple hand wave or nod of the head. Atlanta. New Orleans. Detroit. Chicago. Anywhere she walked she was surrounded by security guards and bodyguards, like she was more popular than the most popular. But I knew that security was because of me, because of the war she refused to let end. That husband killer was a combination politician and televangelist, the new face of change and tragedy, twice as popular as another woman who was the new face of domestic abuse. Detroit had a publishing deal to put out a nonfiction and a spiritual children's book, was set to release those two books and a CD that was supposed to be confrontational, inspirational, moving, and unexpectedly humorous, trying to outdo her competition for media attention. She was going to start her own cosmetics line and create a line of hats for women. She had been a bona fide media whore.

Fame and money changed people. Could make good people bad. Made bad people worse.

I read about the new mayor of Detroit and her rumored affairs, alleged sex with a married member of her staff. There was a lot of talk about her preferring her bed partners to be married. Said she belonged to an elite group of swingers. A lot of talk, but no confirmation on her sexual habits. Rumors she went on television and addressed, asked her god to forgive and heal those who chose to spread falsehoods, chastised her invisible enemies for saying despicable things that could damage her children, and moved on. It also said her elite protection group had run amok. She had become more than a preacher's wife, her husband dead because she had had him assassinated. She was the mayor. She had position and power. She had access to taxpayers' money and a police staff. Both newspapers said there were lots of cover-ups, just like with her predecessor. Her bodyguards making over 100K a year, somehow magically padded up from their 40K-a-year salary. Any suspicions over her husband's death were answered by outrage and a reinforced alibi; she let the world know she was at a church conference in Seattle when her husband was assassinated, the blame being thrown on the politicians in the city.

The rumor was that anyone investigating any of her alleged wrongdoings was immediately fired. Anyone in a position of power who asked too many questions was relieved of command. Whistleblowers vanished overnight. Some said they went into hiding. Some said they were somewhere in Kalamazoo or Flint, buried in the ground. Some said her enemies had been dismembered and buried all over.

She was quoted: "Don't get me confused with the last mayor. We allowed him to spend over nine million dollars of our taxpayers' money to hide his mistakes. And on a trial that cost the city millions of taxpayers' dollars. That was a lot of jobs we could have had for the people in our city. More police officers and more firefighters. Sexual text messages on city-furnished cellular phones can end a lifetime of dedication and civil service. Extravagance can destroy the city I love the most. I am not that mayor."

She was right. She was worse.

Next I plugged into accounts I had in the Cayman Islands. I'd gone there with my hedonistic traveling companions to check on my money. Last year I was close to being a millionaire. Now more than half of that was gone. Getting rid of real estate in a buyer's market had cost me. But I didn't have a choice. I'd been exposed. Taking care of Catherine and Sven, being on the road living an exotic and first-class hedonistic lifestyle, all of that dug deep into a man's pocket. I could survive with what I had left, could make it a long time if I moved to an island and resigned myself to a simpler lifestyle, maybe moved to Barbados and got a small condo in the St. Lawrence Gap. But that would take up at least half of what I had left.

Rain falling, I was up, heart racing like my thoughts, sweating to the point that I had a bout with nausea and the shakes. Every time I closed my eyes it felt like someone was in my room. No one was there. Kept getting up, checking the locks, and spying out the window, my mind moving like a tornado.

I spent the darkest hours sitting in a chair, facing the door, gun in my hand, finger on the trigger.

Exhaustion covered me but I couldn't sleep. Didn't sleep much. Never slept more than five hours at a time. Was up before dawn, logged on to my computer, entered the I.P. address of a computer inside a home in Powder Springs, Georgia, took control of that computer without the owner ever knowing the system had been compromised, connected to a surveillance system, reviewed some footage.

After being followed I wanted to look at a day's worth of footage.

I saw her walking around the house, already up. The woman who had been my mother. The woman who had come inside my room and abused me. The woman who had called herself Thelma.

Separated by the Atlantic Ocean, I could see her, saw all of that history in her eyes, eyes that were soft and brown, fingernails short and clear, her eyebrows arched thin, like the American women, her hair in a motherly and chic bob, like the American mothers. A rough life hadn't stolen her beauty. Her clothing was modest; today she had on soft pinks, very girlish, nothing cheap, clothing that came mostly from discount stores, her tastes conservative. She moved from the laundry room to the living room, folding clothes, doing laundry as she cooked. A world away, I saw everything she did.

Anger in my heart, I dialed her number.

I said, "Thelma . . . I mean, Catherine?"

I had called her by her old name, then corrected myself, called her by her new name, the name she had taken when we had run away to Montreal, after the first time I had killed a man.

She said, "Jean-Claude, how are you?"

Her accent was French. Years ago when we were on the run, living hand-to-mouth in Canada, she had told me she was a Yerroise, meaning she was born in Yerres, France, a commune in the southeastern suburbs of Paris, about eleven miles from the center of the City of Light and its Eiffel Tower. She had run away from a land of culture when she was a young girl. She said that she had been abused, had found her way out of Europe, working on her back to pay her fare, lived in America, had been all over the world working the same way, spoke many languages, but her French accent remained.

I heard all of that history in her voice.

She sounded excited. "I'm so happy to hear from you, Jean-Claude."

She called me by that name and memories of Montreal, Canada, came and went.

I said, "I'm coming to see you and the kid."

"Where are you now?"

"London."

She paused. "Are you working there?"

"That's not important."

There was guilt in her voice whenever she talked to me. Guilt and fear. It was hard for me to not sound annoyed, a little angry, whenever we spoke. She knew a blood covenant existed between us.

I made myself smile when I talked to her; smiling while talking made the voice sound happy.

She was running her fingers through her hair. "My son . . . he asks about you all the time."

"Sven is afraid of me. He doesn't admit it, but I see it in his eyes."

"He's Steven now. Andrew-Sven is now Andrew Steven. Likes being called Steven."

"Two-letter difference. Why did you get a new name for the kid?"

"Wanted him to have a nice North American name. Something they can say. People are nosey. So I wanted his name normal. Kids in North America, very racist. So hard on kids who are different."

I had my own issues, issues that followed me wherever I went.

Wisdom was knowing what to do. Skill was the ability to do it. Virtue was doing it.

When wisdom didn't subdue anger, anger destroyed everything.

I had planned on going back to North Carolina, back to where she had told me I was born, wanted to go back and pull up some old newspapers, search for birth certificates, do what I could to find out about the murder of a prostitute named Margaret, a murder that happened when I was a child, and then find out what I could find out about my father, find out what I could about his murder as well. Get his name. Reverse-engineer his life. But I wasn't ready. Too much guilt. I had only seen him once.

Even then, like now, he wasn't much more than a shadow in my mind.

Margaret was my mother, a woman who was less than a shadow. There was no memory of her.

I wanted to ask Catherine about my deceased father, find out what she hadn't told me. She was a beautiful woman who told a million lies. Her lies were sweeter than any truth I had ever heard.

I kept the conversation on the kid. "How is he holding up? America is not like Europe."

"He misses the few friends he had. He misses playing soccer with the friends he had in London."

"He's a tough kid. Tougher than I was."

"You were teaching him to fight."

I had put a sixty-pound boxing bag up in their basement, suspended it from one of the beams, then spent some time showing the kid how to throw a punch, how to pronate when throwing a punch, then showed him a few combinations. After that I showed him some basic grappling. I told him boxing was cool, but in a real fight he needed to know how to work from the ground. Most fights were with knees and elbows, forearms, palms of the hand, sometimes head butts. Most fights were brutal and ended up on the ground; most battles were won or lost on the ground, not standing like two boxers.

There was no referee in a real fight. All about the last man standing. Last man breathing.

Like it had been inside the bathroom down in the Cayman Islands. When it had been about a strong side kick to take an opponent down to the tile, the years of studying mixed martial arts, submission wrestling, muay thai, wrestling, and boxing all coming down to a life-and-death battle that lasted less than two minutes. No gloves covering my hands, no shin guards, no soft mat to fall on. A battle in a toilet made of concrete and steel, a battle where I had been the last man standing, the last man breathing.

I said, "A boy needs to know how to take care of himself. And he has to take care of his mother."

"He loves our home. He loves having his own room. And the basement. He says that when he gets older he's going to finish the basement, move down there and have his own house. Said his wife would move in with us and they would stay down there. I've never had a house. He's never had his own room. This is . . . it's like a miracle. For both of us. He'd hate to have to leave here. So would I."

She said that as if she were afraid her new life would be taken away.

The same way things had been taken away from me.

I said, "I will see both of you soon."

"Be safe, Jean-Claude. Be safe."

We disconnected. And I wondered if we had ever truly connected.

I took the picture out of my pocket again. Once again I stared at the picture of Catherine and the kid, both of them smiling and laughing at Six Flags over Georgia. My attention remained on the kid, the boy she told me was the son of her flesh.

They had a nice home, a place to rest their heads, stability and normalcy.

The blood on my hands made sure they had no blood on their hands.

I was homeless, living on the run, sleeping in rented beds, no stability whatsoever.

I needed a base, a place to live, a familiar bed with a comfortable pillow, a closet with clothes. I had grown tired of living with what I had on my back, tired of discarding my life on a daily basis.

Every day, everything was new; I wanted something to remain, something familiar.

And maybe a steady woman for a change. At least for a while. Had never had a steady woman. My loving had always been on the run, on the move, unexpected chances at intimacy accepted because I never knew when I would have a chance to defeat loneliness again. Every man needed a steady woman. But behind this man lived the boy who had wanted to become a man named Jean-Claude.

Again I rubbed my eyes, tried to rub away the burning sensation that came from lack of sleep.

A headache attacked me, made me cringe, rub my temples.

I dug in my bag, found a B.C. Powder, took it dry, washed the grainy powder down with tap water.

The whore on Berwick Street told me that Catherine had arrived with the kid, that no one had seen her pregnant, that no one had ever seen pictures of Catherine pregnant. The kid and Catherine, in the picture I had, I couldn't see any resemblance. That was all I got for three hundred pounds.

That and an offer to get my dick sucked for another sixty pounds.

That last offer was passed on.

I had come to London to keep from confronting Catherine about the kid.

But the information I had obtained left me living inside that same darkness.

I needed evidence. I had to go see her and the boy because I needed conclusive evidence.

My every breath, the rise and fall of my chest, told me she could not be trusted.

Not with a child.

Not with the horrible things she had done to me when I was supposed to be her son.

Four

the woman hunter

She had fucked up in London.

Seven days ago they had not killed the man called Gideon and the client wasn't happy.

She had been distracted, had lost the target, then the target had outmaneuvered them.

No, outmaneuvered *her*. Matthew reminded her of that a thousand times. *He* was where *he* was supposed to be, *he* was doing what *he* was supposed to do. *He* was ready to dispose of the target.

She was the one who had fucked it all up.

She had been outmaneuvered, *she* had blown her cover, and *she* had fucked up the job.

Not today.

She didn't fuck this one up. She had gotten it right. Forget about London.

Fuck Gideon.

That was what she thought as she watched the sun begin to rise over the lush mountains.

No longer in London.

Now in the West Indies.

Working alone.

Like she used to work in the beginning. Before Matthew. Before all the goddamn criticism.

She took a deep breath, the smell of cordite in the air, covering her skin.

Sunrise on the island of Antigua was the most beautiful she had seen. The sunlight expanding over the hills and reflecting on the waters, spectacular. It was as if there was a different sun in the heart of the Caribbean. It paused her. This was her first time witnessing sunrise as she stood on a yacht.

She could see herself walking that deck wearing a bikini and Blahniks. Or naked wearing Blahniks. With Blahniks, clothing was not necessary. With a yacht, all a woman needed was a pair of Blahniks.

Falmouth Harbour Marina, north of English Harbour, this was a rich man's playground.

From what she had seen, it was a dark man's point of labor and a white man's paradise.

She lowered her .22, stepped over dead bodies, and stared at the bullet hole lodged in teak.

She cursed. She had missed once. Countless hours had been spent at the shooting range.

First the screwup in London. Now this.

She had flown Heathrow to JFK, then JFK to the airport in San Juan, San Juan to Antigua.

Eighteen hours of flying on American, including the downtime between the two connections.

Five thousand three hundred and sixty-one frequent flier miles from her fuckup in the U.K.

But that error weighed on her mind. This was supposed to be perfect.

To prove a point, this was supposed to have zero mistakes.

She had tracked the target to cricket matches on Friday and Saturday, then on Sunday she followed him and his crew high into the hills over Nelson's Dockyard to the party at Shirley Heights, almost killed him as he sipped rum punch and watched the glorious sunset, a steel-pan band onstage, but the place was too crowded, one narrow road in, one narrow road out, no way to get away clean. She had followed him down Fig Tree Drive, had trailed him when he went to look at land out at NonSuch Bay. His friends were with him at all times. If he went food shopping at Epicurean, they were there. If he went to the YMCA to watch young men shoot basketball, they were on both sides of him at all times. If he went to the Sticky Wicket to eat, if he went to Kings Casino, if he ate at Coconut Grove, they protected him like he was the prime minister of the island. They were always there, those men he called his friends.

Friends who carried hidden guns as he played golf at Jolly Harbour. Men who looked out for him as he went to Heritage Quay to eat lunch upstairs at Hemingways. Men who remained around him as he walked Redcliffe Quay shopping. Following him she had fallen in love with that area in St. John's parish, with Redcliffe Quay, with all the restaurants and shopping on Redcliffe. She had trailed her assignment as he went from Blue Diamond, to Diamond Ice, to Skells, to Jam Dung, and had followed him into the red-light district on the edges of Heritage Quay, on Popeshead Street, watched him go inside Wendy's with his four friends, watched them all leave with a Guyanese stripper-whore, watched his gun-carrying friends escort him to a house up the road, all of them with a Red Stripe or Wadadli or cups of Coke and Mount Gay rum in hand, watched his light-headed friends wait for him to finish with the whore.

She started to chance it then, started to creep down the streets that smelled of oil, refuse, and fresh sewage, was tempted to try to find a back way into that Caribbean-style house of sex, knowing the one-level homes weren't air-conditioned, hardly any were on the islands, and on a warm night the windows had to be open. All she had to do was tiptoe through the darkness and find the bedroom window, one shot to the head as his rented lover gave him head or rode him, or as he fucked her from the back, then, after that pop that came from a silencer, as her sponsor's head exploded and before the whore could scream, one shot to her head as well. But so many people were out in the red-light district at night, the two-laned street with no sidewalk, barely room for cars to pass each other; Popeshead Street was crowded with locals liming and eating, whores out and about in their shorts and flat shoes, a sex shop openly selling condoms and Viagra, snowy faces in shorts and T-shirts pussy shopping like they were in Amsterdam, nonstop traffic like this was their version of the Las Vegas Strip.

Her instincts told her to remain patient.

She had wanted it to be perfect.

And it was frustrating. Everywhere he went, even to fuck, he took his four friends.

Now the target and four of his gun-carrying friends were dead.

But the job hadn't been perfect.

She took the plastic off her hand, tucked that and the expended shells inside her purse.

Fingerprints were on shells, not on bullets that missed their target, not on bullets that were left inside their target. She ignored the smell of death: bladders and bowels releasing their final loads.

She pulled her jacket back so she could return the gun to her abdomen holster, then looked down at her outfit, a pristine First Caribbean bank worker's uniform, one that reminded her of uniforms she had worn to Catholic school when she grew up in Chicago, and hoped no bloodstain had spoiled the fabric.

She turned, looked out at the yachting marina, the tropical hills and the other yachts in the harbor changing from silhouettes to being easily seen. The *Alfa Nero* was in the distance and in good company: *April Fool, Maltese Falcon, Gliss, Esense,* and *Skylge* being the most impressive of the superyachts.

She wondered what it was like to be that rich, to be filthy rich and own a yacht that leased for a million U.S. dollars a week, to have the kind of money to afford a life of diamonds, gold, and emeralds.

And a closet filled top to bottom with every creation by Manolo Blahnik.

With that much money, she could live out her *Sex and the City* fantasy every day of her life.

She had to hurry, had to collect things, had to finish this job, darkness losing its battle with light.

This job should've been done at least thirty minutes ago. While this world was still a shadow.

Actually it should have been done days ago.

Matthew had told her it should have been done days ago.

Since London her husband had completed a contract in Bogotá, Colombia. A midlevel mobster who had fled the U.S. and went back to his homeland. A man who lived and died for soccer. Matthew told her he'd knifed the target during a stadium brawl at a soccer rivalry game, the target dying in the middle of almost eighty people who had been wounded in the riot, added him to at least twenty of the soccer lovers on the ground with stab wounds. Matthew had stumbled into a riot, and that festival of hate had been the perfect cover for his job. He had completed his job the same day he had arrived.

And now he was back in the U.S. waiting for her to come home.

He had offered his help. She had refused. She had to do this on her own.

She was doing this before she met Matthew. She didn't need any man's help.

She had trailed her target for most of the week, searched for the perfect moment.

Last evening, while the men were out liming at strip clubs, she had snuck onto the megayacht. Boarded in the darkness. Waited for hours. Waited until they came back with girls. Waited until they had fucked the girls. Waited until they had paid the girls. Waited until the girls left. Waited until the men slept. Five men were dead. Death, like a bad lover, had come quick.

From what she had overheard, all the men had been bad lovers.

Very bad, very selfish. And the women had been cheap as well. Amazing what a woman would do for thirty dollars, how they let men trade them and degrade them in the name of orgasm.

She returned her gun to its holster. The holster she had on now wasn't like the standard holster most police departments issued; her holster was made for her body, more agreeable to the frame of a woman. She hurried out the door, wiping down all she had touched as she retraced her steps, looked out at the deck, saw no one was looking her way, then, umbrella in hand, left the yacht unseen, its British flag waving in the gentle breeze.

She took to Rhodes Lane, a dirt road peppered with cozy and modest one- and two-level homes.

The distance had been measured. After she exited the dockyard she had to walk a quarter mile, about as far as she could jog, the equivalent of one lap around a track field. She had walked so she would leave no tire prints. So no one would notice the license plates on the scooter that had been rented in the dockyard at Big Ed's. So no one would remember her transportation being there all night.

The items in her oversized purse, she felt their weight. A MacBook, a Canon camera, three Rolexes, iPods, wallets, cash in both British pounds and Eastern Caribbean dollars.

It would look like a robbery.

Six shots, five of those kill shots.

That one missed shot troubled her, weighed down her stride.

She shook her head as she walked. The umbrella wasn't needed at sunrise, but she kept it up to hide her face, in case anyone was watching her casual stroll up Rhodes Lane, in case anyone was leaving Harbour View Apartments, or outside working at Antigua Rigging, or coming out of La Boheme, or outside D's car rental service, maybe spying out one of the windows at the half-dozen Caribbean-style homes that lined the dirty and rocky and tattered lane, this area reminding her of rural parts of Arkansas or Mississippi—agricultural in smell, goats and horses on the sides of the road, unprocessed goat manure and unprocessed horse fertilizer seasoning the tropical air—only there were palm trees, and at the end of the narrow, uneven road were condos and yachts, a juxtaposition of blue-collar living and wealth. As if she were on a road of poverty that led to wealth. She thought that was a good sign, being on that road.

Hit complete, something inside her relaxed. Once again she felt normal.

Once again she thought about how Matthew had gone off on her after the London job.

Killing was easier than loving. Killing involved no emotions; loving involved too many.

Marriage hadn't been like she thought it would be. Monogamy was hard. Too fucking hard.

Same meal every day with the same seasoning, always served on the same plate.

She thought it best that she marry a sensible man, someone to save her from her money-spending ways. But she had been wrong. She was who she was, and that was who she was.

Hot. She was so damn hot. Her heart beat fast as she tried to control her pace.

Amazing.

She was almost back at the main road, weighted down by her bag, sweat rising on her neck.

Soon she would be ten thousand dollars richer.

Ten thousand dollars. A lot of money, but not nearly enough to suit her needs.

The thing she had to do in New York. That would cost twenty-four thousand.

So the ten thousand would soon be gone. Soon she would need more to survive.

She thought about her other problems, felt a stress headache coming on just like that.

Fucking IRS. Fucking mortgage company.

Fucking credit card bills. Fucking note on her Range Rover and Maserati GranTurismo.

And a fucking husband who kept tabs on every fucking dime she spent.

Always chastising every little thing she did. Could never do right by him.

Her husband. Matthew. The assassin known as El Matador.

But to her he was just Matthew.

He had been orphaned at three months, grown up in foster care like her, shuffled around more than two dozen times, just like her, had run away when he was a teenager, just like her, everything so simpatico. Meeting was kismet, and she was with him because she hoped he would understand her in all ways.

In a system where they aged out and lost most of their financial benefits when they turned eighteen. Where more than 50 percent of the people she had known became homeless within two months of their eighteenth birthday. A broken system where half of the kids earned a high school diploma. Where 2 percent obtained a bachelor's degree or higher. Where 84 percent became parents.

That had been her world. That was the world she ran from.

Growing up without made her want to have things, all things, no matter what the cost.

Dying rich was as stupid as shit. Working hard, dying, and leaving money for lazy fucks to have, for free, becoming someone else's lottery ticket, that was the dumbest shit she'd ever heard of.

Well, maybe the second-dumbest thing.

The dumbest thing was the way her husband was always asking her to stop shopping.

He might as well have told her to stop breathing. She'd be shopping on the day she died.

That was what had happened in London. That was what went wrong.

That fucking Gideon.

She was following the target down Neal Street, had Matthew on the phone, directing him to cut off the target, Matthew's plan being to put a knife in the contract, leave him dying on a side street. The target had spotted her. She had wanted to be spotted. She wanted the target concerned with what was behind him, not paying attention to what was in front of him. It was going according to plan.

Her only thought was it would be such a shame to kill a man who looked so ruggedly handsome.

But in a few minutes it would be done.

That was her only thought, until she passed by that window, saw what she saw in the corner of her eye. *Blahniks.* She had looked in a window and saw a collection of *Blahniks.*

All sisters and cousins to the Blahniks she had on at that very moment.

She stopped at the window no more than five, maybe ten seconds.

Buckled sling-backs. Mesh leopards. Snake low-heel slides. Pointed-toe suede pumps. Jacquard halter sandals. In her mind she was buying them all, spending every dime of the money she was going to make on the London job.

She trembled a bit, sighed, the sight of Blahniks giving her a shoe-gasm.

When she looked up the target had vanished in the crowd.

Neal Street ended at Shaftesbury; she didn't know if the target had gone left or right.

She had taken off, moved as fast as she could, come up on Matthew, and Matthew hadn't seen the target. She had stopped, frantic, began looking in the opposite direction. If he had gone that way, there was no way to find him in that crowd. He could be on a bus, in a cab, gone down one of the hundreds of lanes that ran like parts of a spider's web. With an angry smile Matthew told her she had done a nice fucking job, a real nice fucking job, cursed her for blowing it, chastised her, asking her what the fuck had gone wrong within the last sixty seconds. One second *she* was on the target, the next *she* had lost him. People didn't vanish. People you had your eyes on, they didn't vanish like in a magic act. She had no answer. No way would she tell him about the Blahniks. He wouldn't understand. He had grabbed her hand, grabbed her hard and pulled her along the street, cursing her, no longer searching for their prey.

Because they had become prey.

Matthew had seen him first. She looked up and there the target was, walking a few yards behind her, his reflection in the store's window. The target had ended up behind them, was following them.

"*Two against one,*" Matthew had whispered to her. "*Don't worry.*"

"*He's too close, Matthew. Close enough to pop one of us.*"

So they stopped and faced the target, two hunters facing a growling lion.

Matthew moved his coat, brandished his weapon, the gun, his knife still in the sleeve of his coat.

Matthew. In the business he was called El Matador. The man who loved to stab, kill as if he were in a bullfight. Matthew was a knife man but used a gun when he had to. Only when he had to.

The target had a gun in his hand, the devil in his intense eyes telling them he would shoot them right then. She had never seen eyes that intense. She had never felt the energy that came from the man she had followed in London. He scared her. She put her hand inside the plastic bag, took her gun out. In public she had taken her gun out. She didn't feel as if she had much of a choice. Matthew wasn't a great shot, could hit only from point-blank range, couldn't hit a moving target, not like she could.

The next thing she knew Matthew was shoving her into a taxi and they were speeding away.

Matthew called in, told the handler what happened, told the handler what his *partner* had done.

His *partner* had fucked up London. He had no blame. His *partner* had fucked up the deal.

She had fucked it up.

She stared out the window, lips pulled in, leg bouncing, wanting to cry, knowing she wouldn't.

At the hotel room at Knightsbridge, arguing, shouting, then he walked out, left her on the verge of tears, had vanished for hours, then came back with bloodstains on his clothing.

She had asked him if Gideon was dead.

He cursed her out, told her Gideon wasn't dead. Gideon had vanished.

But someone was dead. The blood on his clothing. The way he scrubbed himself clean.

She knew her husband. She knew El Matador. She knew his temper, his rage.

All because she had been hypnotized by a pair of mesh leopard pointed-toe Blahniks.

Therapy. Maybe she should go to a rehabilitation center. She had tried to go once. But she'd passed a sale at Nordstrom and just couldn't seem to make it. Spent her therapy money in a matter of minutes. Was depressed after. But the E brought her back up, made her happy enough to hug a tree.

As she walked and held her umbrella up high, sweat dripped down the back of her neck.

She dabbed her forehead and cursed. She felt so out of shape. So heavy. Her ideal weight was around one forty-five, but she was closer to one sixty. All the traveling and the hotel eating. The weight had changed her from a B cup to a C cup. Now she had a twenty-nine-inch waist. Five-five and a half. Forty-one inches around her hips and ass, most of it being her rear, not much to the hips. The weight gain had been proportional, made her handler tell her she put the *ass* in *ass-assin.*

Everyone else in the business had a sobriquet: El Matador, or Mutt, or Crazy Shank, or Bull's-eye.

She was *the Assassin with Ass.*

Whatever.

Said her backside was so nice she put two asses in the word. *Ass ass in.*

What the fuck ever.

She wanted to get back on the diet: cayenne pepper, lemon juice, and honey for twenty days. Maybe she'd shed a few pounds, lose that weight before she spent the twenty-four thousand dollars and went to New York. Maybe. Maybe not.

Finally. All Saints Road. Her umbrella up high. More sweat dripped down the back of her neck.

She stumbled, her heel caught in the roughness of the road. After the stumble she cursed. Lowered her umbrella. Looked down at her heel. Hoped she hadn't ruined her Blahniks, this pair black patent leather. Open toe. D'Orsay sides. Hook-and-loop ankle straps. Heels over four inches. Not made for this road.

She paused at the intersection, vans and buses and cars zooming by.

Then all traffic ceased. Not a car or bus in sight. The world became quiet.

She closed her umbrella, crossed All Saints Road, and faced Sweet

T's Ice Cream Parlour and Snackette, a colorful wooden structure, rustic like most of the buildings in the islands, greens and oranges and shades of purple, licking her lips and craving. The morning was so warm it took her mind off death and put her mind on ice cream. Made her wish Sweet T's was open. She wanted a scoop of ice cream. Hell, after the job this morning, she was ten thousand dollars richer. She could afford two scoops in a waffle cone.

Her scooter was parked behind a green lattice fence at T's, that fence around three feet high, tall enough to shelter her scooter all night. She had left it by a sturdy tree, a kid's stage and other children-type playing equipment adding to the camouflage. Now she would ride near St. James's Club, an area no more than ten minutes away, and get the clothing she had stashed there, change to jeans and sandals, and drive back to her hotel. That missed shot continued to plague her mind.

She told herself she had missed because she was hungry, hadn't eaten for almost eighteen hours. She'd make it back to her hotel in time for breakfast. Maybe head to the other side of the island.

Before she could get her scooter started, there was a *pop* sound. The sound of a silenced gunshot. Purple wood in front of Sweet T's exploded. Then the wooden fence that supported the green lattice erupted, then the ground near her feet did the same, kicking up gravel and dirt.

She jerked, dropped her umbrella, and looked back in the direction she had come from.

One of the men she had killed, or thought she had killed, was staggering down the dirt road, blood draining from his face, covering his white T-shirt. A gun was in his bloodied hand, six-inch barrel dressed in a silencer, that gun raised and aimed at her as he staggered toward All Saints Road. He had staggered after her for a quarter mile. Bullets flew her way, missing by inches, all hitting the front of T's.

Adrenaline rushed. Heartbeat accelerated.

She was in that zone where the distance between living and dying was measured in seconds.

Shoot and move. The voice inside her head reminded her to shoot and move. In a fight, front and sight. Keep the target in sight. Never turn around, never run. Keep the goddamn target in sight.

That information moved around inside her head as she did as she had been trained to do, as she had learned ten years ago when she had longed to be part of Chicago's police department. She moved to the right as she went for her holster, removed her gun with quickness, knowing any hesitation would put the scent of her death in the air.

The bloodied man came in a straight line like an amateur, growling, shooting, and refusing to die. She moved in an arc and closed the gap on her attacker, shooting and still moving to her right, smooth steps, never crossing her feet, bullets whizzing by her as she remained focused, everything else blocked out, tunnel vision, her gun shooting a police double, *pop*, hitting her target twice, bull's-eyes in the center of his forehead, popping three more before he fell.

Her prey crumpled to the battered road, dust and gravel rising up around his lifeless body.

First London. Now this. She looked up All Saints, traffic starting to come her way.

A man left dead on the edges of All Saints Road. No way could she drag the body off to the side. Too much dead weight. An impossible task. Matthew would never let her hear the end of this shit. She hurried to the scooter, sped away, sweating, Antigua's sunrise warming her suntanned skin.

Inside her room. Trembling. She called her husband. No answer.

She left him a calm message. The job was done but it wasn't as clean as she had anticipated. Big sale. Five bags for the price of one. He knew what that meant. She didn't tell him about the shoot-out on All Saints Road. She made the job sound, for the most part, perfect. She said the weather was nice but the island was *hot*. Too *hot* to go to the airport right now. She needed a few days to cool off. Small island, only one airport, basically one way in and one way out of Antigua's one hundred and eight square miles of floating paradise. Couldn't drive to the other side of the island and find another airport, not like in Jamaica. Do a hit in Kingston, drive a hundred miles of bumpy roads north, fly out of Montego Bay. In a sexy voice she told her husband she loved him, missed him, and purred that she would see him soon.

Then she hung up the phone, cursed, and screamed.

Five

pain and pleasure

Powder Springs, Georgia.

Formerly Springville, a city with seven springs, water with over two dozen minerals that made the sand look like gunpowder. Six square miles with a population under twenty thousand. Sixty percent white, thirty-eight percent African American, the rest mostly Native American and Pacific Islanders. The perfect place for Catherine and the kid to blend in with the rest of North America. Median income for a family about thirty thousand British pounds, which was about sixty thousand U.S. dollars, the amount I made sure Catherine and the kid had for the year. That didn't include making sure the mortgage was paid. The car she drove, a two-year-old Mini Cooper, was paid for, the title in her new name. That was the car she had wanted, something cost-effective, sensible, and European, refused to let me buy it for her new, refused to let me get her a convertible. The same for the city she had chosen to live in. She didn't want to live in Los Angeles or New York, wasn't interested in being put up in a condo or home over in Buckhead or in Virginia Highland, wanted a smaller, quieter community. I never asked her why she chose Powder Springs, but maybe it was a place that reminded her of the commune she grew up in outside of Paris. Out of London's red-light district, no longer having to live the life that the friends she had left behind still lived, she and the kid lived in a small town where gold had been found in the 1800s and the Cherokee people were forced off their land and marched to Oklahoma on the Trail of

Tears. Not too far from the Civil War's Battle of Kennesaw Mountain. American Revolution. War of 1812. Civil War. All of that carnage happened in this part of the greatest country in the world.

No matter where a man put his foot in North America, there was blood in its soil.

Same went for most of the rest of the world. Whoever had the biggest bomb ruled their land.

When I was the kid's age I had longed to have a house with a yard. Now he had one, two stories and a basement, the house sitting on three quarters of an acre, plenty of room to play British or American football in the backyard. Same for baseball. Him having the life I wish I had had, that made me smile.

But him having that life with Catherine, at times that terrified me.

The memories were too strong. Forgiving was not forgetting.

The weather was cold. Forty degrees. Partly cloudy. Rain due late tonight or tomorrow.

I was in a rental car I had picked up at Hartsfield, a car Konstantin had arranged to be waiting for me. One that came with all the latest options: navigation system, Sirius, and a few loaded weapons.

I took the kid for a drive. Catherine was driving her car to Publix to go food shopping.

It was time for some male bonding. Just me and the kid riding the highways.

His frame was strong, shoulders broad, could see where he was going to fill out as he got older. He had a severe ruggedness about him. He had on jeans and tennis shoes, a pair of Nikes with AIR JORDAN on the side. Up top he had on a golden Old Navy hoodie underneath an oversized blue jean jacket, a worn jacket he would grow into. For the most part we were both dressed the same way.

He had his soccer ball with him, but he knew we weren't going to play European football.

I asked, "How's school?"

"Good."

"How are your grades?"

"Good."

He wasn't the best conversationalist in the world.

Neither was I.

We stopped by Titan Games & Comics on Spring Road, near Cumberland Boulevard. The kid wanted to go there. *Sin City. All-Star Batman and Robin, the Boy Wonder. Golgo 13.* I bought him a dozen manga graphic novels and comics. That reminded me of when I was about his age, sitting on an urban stoop in Montreal, reading comics I had bought from a bookstore on Sainte Catherine West.

We went by a gas station, filled up, then took Barrett Parkway toward Kennesaw, made a stop at Costco, and loaded up on canned sodas. After that we got on I-575 and went out past Woodstock, Georgia. I took the kid to an abandoned farm I knew about, a place a long way from civilized life, an area that had no traffic and no spectators. He took cans of soda and headed for a wooden fence, lined the cans up along the edges, set them about five feet apart. I opened the trunk of my car and took out my four handguns. Two .22s and a .380. Then I took out ammunition. I went over the proper way to hold a gun with the kid, then went over the proper way to load a gun, then we did some target practice.

The closest home was probably a mile away, the report of the guns insignificant. This was NRA country, pictures of Charlton Heston in every home, a gun rack in the back of every truck.

He did okay; hit about 30 percent of his shots from thirty feet, much better than the last time.

I needed to make sure he knew how to handle a gun, knew that it wasn't a toy.

I wanted to ask him if he had ever shot anyone, but I was afraid to ask him, not sure if I wanted to know the answer. Now I wanted to make sure he would be able to protect himself and Catherine.

I asked Steven, "Does Catherine ever touch you?"

"Mum touches me all the time."

He didn't understand what I meant.

I said, "In the areas . . . your genitalia . . . does she touch you on your private parts?"

He still didn't understand what I meant.

I said, "She ever talk about your father?"

"No."

The kid picked up the .380, the smallest of the weapons.

I said, "Support the bottom of the gun with your left hand. That way you can control the kick. Squeeze the trigger. Don't pull it. What they do in movies is bullshit. Always squeeze."

The kid fired six times, a three-second lag between each shot, hit two cans.

My cellular rang. Konstantin's number. I answered.

By then the kid had reloaded, was shooting again.

Konstantin asked, "You getting shot at?"

"Out on a range."

My Russian friend told me he had assignments in the States. One was on a real estate mogul who had swindled people out of millions. The second job was in the heart of Dixie.

I said, "That's down in Hawks's territory."

"Hawks. That's one mean son of a bitch."

"Yeah. Mean as a pit bull on gunpowder."

The kid had lined up more cans. Shot at them like he was shooting at his problems.

Konstantin asked, "You talked to Hawks?"

"Not since that time we worked together."

"How long ago was that?"

"Fort Hood. Right before I did a job in Chapel Hill."

"For me?"

"The Chapel Hill job was for . . . someone else. Close to two years ago."

Another job was in Miami, a contract that paid well. The third one was in Birmingham, was a contract on the type of person I hated the most. A pedophile who had escaped justice.

Konstantin said, "Have to run and pick up some things for the wife."

"You have the best wife in the world."

"A wife who hands me a computer-generated honey-do list when I walk out the door."

"Your wife has gone high-tech."

"Printed the list off from some Web page. Has low-, medium-, and high-priority boxes, but she only checks the high-priority box. Toilet paper, high priority. Paper clips, high priority."

We laughed.

He said, "Sounds like you're back on grid."

"Guess so."

"Welcome back."

I hung up. Back on grid. It was as if I had never left.

The kid was standing to the side, waiting on me.

Then I had him set up more cans and load the gun, again six shots, this time hitting four cans.

I said, "You ever ask about him?"

"Ask about whom?"

"Your father."

"No."

"You ever meet him?"

He shook his head.

I fired six times; deliberate one-second lag between shots, hit five times. Not good enough, not from this distance. I had to be better at close range. I flexed my fingers a few times, popped another B.C. Powder, washed it down with soda, reloaded, took a breath, imagined I saw Detroit, and fired again.

The second time there was no lag, sounded like one continuous shot.

Like in a war.

The kid was watching me. Studying me. His eyes telling me he was amazed at what he saw.

Even though I was pissed because I'd hit only five of the six shots, part of me smiled.

I cleared my throat. "Were you living with someone before Catherine?"

"We lived different places."

"Yes, but do you remember a time when you lived with someone else?"

"I don't understand."

"Do you ever remember having . . . having another mother?"

"Another mother?"

"Before Catherine, did you live with someone before . . . did you have another mother?"

"What do you mean?"

He didn't understand my concerns. So I let them go. Decided to do what I was planning to do anyway. This felt like a fool's move, like a betrayal, but I had been lied to since I left my mother's womb.

And my heart told me the same had happened with the kid, that his life was built on lies.

He asked, "Are we going to throw knives?"

"Not today. No knife throwing today."

"Next time?"

I nodded.

He asked, "Will you show me some more fight moves?"

"Next time."

"When is next time?"

"Soon."

"When is soon?"

"Soon is soon."

No, with the kid I wasn't the best conversationalist in the world.

He said, "I ran two miles."

"When?"

"On Saturday morning. While Mum walks at Piedmont Park, I run in front of her."

"Two miles?"

"Without stopping." He smiled. "My mum couldn't catch me."

Most of the time his accent was very European. I rubbed his head, smiled too.

He said, "Then we ate breakfast at Thumbs Up."

"I like their biscuits."

"Me too. My mum likes the catfish and eggs."

When we were done we loaded up what we had left. I had the kid come to the trunk of the car. Inside was a box, a kit I had bought. Three kits were in my possession. Opening the kit, I was trying to convince myself to change my mind. Everything was perfect. This was his Montreal. This was the kid's chance at peace and normalcy. I didn't want to mess that up for him. He had what I never had. But I had to be sure that the kid was supposed to be here, that no one out there was missing a son.

I had the kid open his mouth. I opened the DNA kit and took out the cotton swabs, ran one on the inside of his left cheek, then did the same on the right. I sealed his DNA in the container enclosed.

The kid didn't ask what that was about.

The kid never asked too many questions. He just answered questions the best he could, English still being his second language and the ways of North America foreign to whatever he was used to.

But I had so many questions that had never been answered, not to my satisfaction.

He asked, "Can we play soccer for a few minutes?"

I smiled. "Sure."

We messed around in the open field, first doing ankle dribbling and toe touches, then spent some time kicking the ball back and forth, switching between being goalkeeper and field player.

We played and laughed and sweated.

As I drove back toward Powder Springs, one question was burning a hole in my guts.

I took a deep breath, swallowed before I asked the kid, "Have you ever shot anyone?"

He answered without hesitating.

Catherine had cooked dinner, had set the table, and was waiting for us to get back. Baked chicken. Macaroni and cheese. Greens. Apple pie. I didn't remember her cooking for me when I was a kid, not like this. But our life was so different. I used a guest bedroom and showered, put on dress pants and a nice shirt I had bought, looked presentable. In the mirror I saw a decent man named Jean-Claude.

We sat at the table and Catherine said grace. We ate together. Like family.

The kid said, "I want a dog."

Catherine shook her head. "No dog."

"Please?"

"We have had this conversation, Steven."

I said, "Every boy should have a dog."

Catherine frowned at me.

I backed down.

She looked at the kid and shook her head. "No dog. I have allergies."

"But, Mum, I can get a dog that does not have long hair."

"No dog."

"I looked them up on the Internet. I can get a Chihuahua mix."

"No."

"What about a pug?"

"No."

"A Japanese chin?"

"How will you take care of a dog? You don't clean your room two days in a row."

"I'll keep my room clean."

"I am tired of cleaning up behind you. Now you want me to clean up after a dog?"

"I promise to take good care of the dog."

"No."

"I'll walk it every day. You said you need to walk more so we could walk with you every day."

"Please stop asking me about a dog."

"I want somebody to play with. I get bored. I promise to take care of the dog."

"Do not go to anyone else when I tell you something, do you understand?"

"Yes, Mum."

When I was homeless in Montreal, on Sainte-Catherine East, I remembered seeing a homeless man who had several dogs. Back then I had wanted to have a home and buy a dog.

I said, "I never had a dog either."

The boy looked at me. So did Catherine. I didn't look at either of them.

I said, "But I used to have a horse."

"Did you?"

"Sure did. When I had a home in California. Had a horse."

"Where is your horse?"

"Sold it. Had to sell everything."

After dinner was done I almost let it go, but I couldn't.

The house was so clean, so well put together. She had painted every room, earth-tone colors that replaced blandness with life, knickknacks from discount stores, paintings and sculptures; things that made a house look like a home were all over. I had no idea Catherine could paint and decorate that way.

The kid asked, "Can we go in the basement and hit the boxing bag?"

Catherine told him, "Not today. You have responsibilities, young man."

"Okay, Mum."

Mum. Not Mother, not Momma, but Mum. Like the British.

While the kid loaded the dishwasher, I pulled Catherine to the side. She had a broad smile, looked happy. But that smile went away when I showed her the box with the DNA test.

She asked, "What is this, Jean-Claude?"

"I need you to do this."

"Why?"

"The kid . . ."

"What about my son?"

"I have to be sure he is yours."

"Are you serious?"

My answer was etched in my face. This had troubled me for too long.

Tears formed in her eyes.

I said, "I have to make sure he is your son, that you're his mother."

"I am his mother."

"Where were you pregnant?"

"What are you asking?"

"Who saw you pregnant?"

"Why are you asking me that?"

"No one on Berwick Street saw you pregnant."

"I was pregnant before I went to London. I told you. I was pregnant in Amsterdam. I was pregnant then . . . when you . . . when you came there . . . so angry . . . when you came to hurt me."

"Why didn't you tell me then?"

"You terrified me."

"I terrified you."

"And you still terrify me now."

I took a breath, rubbed my eyes, shook my head, refused to back down.

"I have to make sure that no woman out there is dying because her kid is missing." My voice trembled enough to make me pause. "And if you are not the kid's mother, and if the kid's mother is dead, then I have to make sure that there isn't a man out there grieving and wondering where his son is."

She trembled and whispered, "This is about Margaret. This is because of Margaret."

"I don't know Margaret."

"She was your mother."

"You were my mother."

"I only did what I did—I took care of you for Margaret."

Margaret. The woman who was supposed to be my mother. The woman I never knew.

Whatever warmth should have existed between me and her memory, Catherine had never nurtured that; she had lied, had never given me the truth, and now Margaret was but a name, but a word.

Margaret was but a faceless noun.

My throat tightened, cheeks felt flushed.

I nodded. "This is about me and you. This is about North Carolina. This is about what you did to me when you came into my room. Can't let that happen again. Can't let that happen to the kid."

"Don't do this, Jean-Claude. Everything is perfect. Everyone is happy for once."

"I have to."

"I am his mother."

"Then you have nothing to worry about."

She glanced toward the kitchen, toward the kid, then she looked around at her home, at the pastel walls, at the nice furniture, at the new life she had. Maybe she remembered London, living off Berwick Street, that red-light district that smelled of piss and paid-for sex.

She said, "What kind of horrible person do you think I am, Jean-Claude?"

"I knew you when you were Thelma."

"That was a long time ago, another life."

"I know what you're capable of."

"Look in my cabinets. Look everywhere. Do you see alcohol in this home?"

"This isn't about alcohol."

"Do you see men coming in and out of my door? Do you see any men here? Do you want to go ask the neighbors what they see? Would that put trust in your heart? Would that make you feel better?"

"I have no idea what you do, Catherine. I have no idea. This is about the kid, not you."

She trembled, shook her head, sounded like she was begging me. "I've changed."

"Have you?"

She closed her eyes, opened her mouth so I could swab the insides of her cheeks.

I swabbed her left cheek. More tears flowed as I swabbed the right cheek.

I said, "The results will come here. Do not open them."

When I was done she walked away, her head down, crying, trying to not let the kid see her being upset, and headed up the stairs with a quickness, went inside her master bedroom, and closed the door.

Growing up, my world had been anything but five-star. It had been poverty and pain.

My early years were hand-to-mouth, always on the run, hardly with a roof over my head.

I would've killed a thousand people to have a resting place like the one they had now.

I would've killed to have been able to live in a place like Powder Springs.

I went to the kitchen, stared out into the darkness awhile before I told the kid good-bye.

Soccer ball in hand, he asked, "Will you come back soon?"

"I'll come back soon. Real soon."

"Can you take me some of the places you go?"

I smiled a false smile. "One day we'll take a trip. We'll go to Disneyland in California."

"Me, you, and my mother?"

I hesitated. "We'll see."

His face didn't smile, but there was a glow in his complexion and a shine in his eyes.

He began kneeing and chesting the ball, a lot better at it than when he was in London.

I said, "Not in the house. You might break something."

He stopped right away and nodded. Then the kid said, "Jean-Claude?"

I looked at him. I'd never heard him call me by that name before. He'd never said my name.

He said, "You had a horse?"

"Sure did."

"If you get another horse can I come ride it?"

"You sure can."

"If you get a dog can I play with it?"

"Okay."

He smiled at me. I ran my hand through his hair, then he walked me to the door.

He asked, "Did you tell my mum you were leaving?"

"She knows."

"Where are you going?"

I paused. "Back to my hotel."

"You could stay here. We have an extra bedroom."

I smiled a heavy smile. "Maybe next time. Maybe."

I reached into my pocket and took out a piece of paper, wrote down a phone number. Then I reached into another pocket and gave him a cellular phone and a phone charger. It was a throwaway phone that had a couple hundred dollars on a SIM card, enough to last awhile.

I told him, "If anything happens, if anybody comes around here and they look like bad people, I want you to use this phone and call this number. It's my emergency number."

"You mean like if bad guys come here, call your number?"

"Yeah. Bad guys. Or bad women too. Call this number."

"Like calling a superhero."

I smiled. Wanted to tell him I wasn't a superhero. I wasn't bred to be one of the good guys.

He asked, "Are you like the men in the comic book *Golgo 13* or *Batman*?"

I knew Batman but wasn't familiar with *Golgo 13*. I'd seen him grab the manga at the bookstore but hadn't paid any attention to what the comic was about; again, too many other issues on my mind.

Before I could leave he ran to his brand-new comics, came back, and gave me two. Said he wanted me to have something to read. When I got inside the car I saw that he had given me his *Golgo 13* and *Batman* comic books. Batman. The man whose mother and father had been murdered when he was a child. A man with more darkness inside him than the night.

The jacket for the other manga said that the Golgo 13 character was a hit man, his origin unknown, his attitude toward sex hard-core, as amoral as they come. The first part of Golgo 13's name sounded like it had a religious origin, was probably related to Golgotha, the hill where Jesus Christ was crucified. Jesus had twelve disciples. With Jesus added, the number was thirteen.

I read a few pages of *Batman*. This Batman was different; gritty, unshaven, much darker, unhinged, and on the verge of being a psychopath. Hurting people in ways the television Batman and movie Batman never did. The Dark Knight was obsessive and had deep psychological problems. Like the Joker. This version was more realistic than any comic I had read when I was a kid in Montreal, this Batman a loose cannon and ready for men in white suits to put him in a psychiatric ward.

In the kid's eyes I was a demon. A demon he had befriended, a demon he admired.

I opened the third DNA kit, ran swabs inside my cheeks, collected my own deoxyribonucleic acid, my genetic instructions, my information, my blueprints, my truth.

I labeled each kit. Catherine was X. The kid's was Y. Mine was Z. Each on swabs that cost thirty U.S. dollars, another one-twenty U.S. to process each one. Four hundred and fifty American dollars to put values to X, Y, and Z and solve the unknown values in an algebraic equation.

I was an unknown. It felt as if I had always been an unknown.

Some days not knowing who I was bothered me. Some days it didn't.

When I was the kid's age it didn't bother me, never thought about it, never cared.

At some point the kid would care. The kid would want to ask his own questions.

When I had asked him if he had ever shot anyone, his answer had left me shaken.

Buckhead.

An area that had Atlanta's most important business districts and wealthiest neighborhood, the Beverly Hills of the South. An area that got its name from a story about a man who killed a large buck deer and placed the severed head inside a local tavern.

The same area where Sir Elton John lived part-time, somewhere off the famous Peachtree Road.

The DNA kits I had, I took them to FedEx, stared at them, hesitated before I dropped them in.

Soon that mystery would be answered via DNA Solutions, Incorporated.

It weighed on me but I kept telling myself it was the right thing to do.

If someone had done that for me when I was a kid my world would've been different.

I wanted to talk to somebody about it. Maybe reach out to an old lover, maybe call Konstantin, but I wasn't the type of man who called up others just because the weight of the world was on his shoulders. I stopped on Piedmont Road and valet-parked at Sambuca, a place with good-natured doormen who ushered me inside the lush, Moroccan-influenced décor, a place with dim lighting and lots of animal prints, art for sale on the walls by the bathrooms. Lights so dim a man could go blind trying to read a menu. A good place for a man who didn't want to be seen to become a shadow. I didn't come to eat, wanted to sit and think while the jazz band added a soundtrack to my thoughts. I wanted to be alone but I didn't want to be by myself, not this early. I needed to be alone in a crowd of people and music.

As alone as I could be with a loaded gun tucked in the small of my back.

Detroit was still out there.

This hot spot was the cousin of the place I had hung out in on a date down in Dallas, Texas. That had been two years ago. Right before that life-changing fiasco in Detroit.

A beautiful woman who had auburn locks that hung down to her tailbone went onstage and joined the band. The featured saxophonist. She began playing David Sanborn's "The Dream." She wore a black dress, a fitted number that showed her slender frame had dangerous curves. A brown-skinned woman with cinnamon freckles on her face. I wanted her. I wanted to fuck that pretty woman and leave my problems inside of her. Just because I wanted it didn't mean it would happen.

I went to the open bar, found a seat where I could watch the door at all times. I had been conditioned the same way soldiers who had gone off to battle had been conditioned, those who had a hard time leaving the battlefield and fitting into the regular world. When I ordered I watched the person making my drink, knowing that a drop of poison could be put in my beverage on Detroit's behalf, and while jazz filled the air, I'd find myself dying a slow death, like the Russian spy did not long ago, his death slow and painful, his dying worse than death itself. For the past six months, since the Cayman Islands, I had stopped drinking at bars—didn't matter if I saw the bartender making my drink; I knew the poison could already be spread in the glass he had chosen to serve me. Anyone could be on the enemy's payroll.

But tonight I needed a drink. I needed a Jack and Coke without the Coke.

A beautiful woman came in and sat next to me. A beautiful woman with long blond hair, hair that was full and wavy and styled in a Veronica Lake peekaboo-bang number, that World War II hairstyle that covered one eye and almost half of the face, leaving half of her beauty hidden behind a falling curl of hair. She had on black calfskin boots with about a five-inch stiletto heel, tall fuck-me boots with sexy stitching.

I sipped my liquor and complimented her on her boots, asked her who designed those.

She gave me a half grin, said, "Christian Louboutin."

"Nice style."

She smiled. "Bought them at Phipps today."

To go with her boots she wore black jeans, those, too, designer, jeans that fit her as tight as a grandmother's hug, and a black blouse that was fitted and open enough to expose the swell of her breasts. Big hoop earrings revealed themselves inside her wavy mane. I don't know who said something to whom next, but we ended up sitting elbow to elbow, talking while the band played.

The smell of cordite was in my flesh; I smelled it despite the shower I'd had.

I was wearing gunpowder like it was my favorite cologne.

The woman next to me asked, "You from Atlanta?"

I shook my head. "Montreal."

"Never been there. How is it?"

"Cold. Two seasons. Winter and almost-winter."

"Sounds like Minnesota."

"Minnesota's two seasons are winter and still-winter."

She laughed.

I was once again a hired gun struggling to fit into the regular world. Her voice and the way she articulated her words told me she was a professional woman; her wide smile told me she was in the mood for chitchatting with the opposite sex. Since our moods were similar, I obliged. The wine she was sipping gave her manner a sexiness that reminded me of a beautiful attorney I had met on a flight to London.

She motioned at the band, at the beautiful woman playing the sax.

She said, "She used to be in the news business. Think she's from North Carolina."

We fell into general conversation and an hour passed like seconds. Obama's speech on racism, she thought it was one of the most important speeches of the millennium and wanted to know what I thought about it. Guess she wanted my perspective. We talked about how Canada controlled American oil so the politicians talking about being tough on NAFTA was nothing more than a joke.

Conversation evolved from politics to travel. Talked about London. Other countries. She hadn't been to Amsterdam but wanted to go. She had gone to Barcelona and loved it there, had stayed at a wonderful hotel near La Rambla, the Apsis Splendid, a small hotel with big rooms, situated in the central area, a very safe area. We talked about a few other places. She told me she had roots in Jamaica but was brought up in a small town in Georgia. She didn't question me or my past so I didn't have to lie. She did most of the talking and sipped red wine while I nursed my dark liquor and listened. She had a wedding ring on her left hand, a nice number that sparkled in dim light, but the way she leaned in and touched my hand over and over as she chatted didn't make it seem as if that diamond ring mattered.

She said, "You're well-traveled."

"I've seen a few places. More than some, less than others."

She sipped her wine, bounced her leg, her flirtatious smile telling me she was feeling restless.

I hadn't had a nice conversation in months. I hadn't been this relaxed in just as long. Had been a while since I didn't feel as if Death was tiptoeing behind me, trying to tap on my shoulder.

I hadn't come there for chitchat, but part of me needed this. A man always needed a woman.

Her aroma was magnetic, held me where I was, made me want to inhale her.

She asked, "Do you know who I am?"

"You're that newscaster on all the billboards."

"That's me."

"Jewell Stewart?"

"Jewell *Stewark*. Not *Stewart*."

"You don't wear your hair like that on the air."

"I'm forced to be a conservative lady on the air."

We shared a small laugh.

We drank and listened to the sax player. Alcohol was amazing. Magnified every need, every emotion. Made people feel invincible. Made people not care that Death was stalking them. Made people attractive. Made people want to connect with strangers. Jewell Stewark touched me, smiled as I smiled at her. She bit the corner of her lip, paused, contemplating her next question.

She asked, "How long are you in town?"

"One night."

"Where are you staying?"

"Ritz-Carlton."

She hummed. "Maybe we should leave when she finishes this song."

She rubbed her finger on my hand, smiled an anxious smile, all of her professionalism giving way to desires magnified by alcohol. I put my hand on her upper thigh, ran my finger up and down her leg.

Five minutes later she was inside her convertible Jaguar, following me toward Peachtree Road.

Jewell Stewark moaned.

She was upside down, in my arms, her blond hair hanging to my feet, her thighs on both sides of my neck, squeezing my neck as my hands held and squeezed her soft ass. I savored her while she took me inside her mouth, sucked me and made it a vertical and simultaneous exchange of pleasure.

She weighed between nine and ten stone, weight that felt light in my arms.

I eased the Jewell of the South onto the soft bed, pulled her shivering body and moans toward me, did what I wanted to the woman who made love with her five-inch-heel black leather boots on and her black fitted shirt wide open: twisted her, sucked her, pulled her hair, moved her around the suite, from chair to dresser to wall to window, fucked her with her sweaty face against the tinted glass. My double suite looked down at Lenox Mall and the office lights creating stars in the darkened city. She wanted it from behind, told me she loved being taken that way, to take her and fuck her like I wanted to come. Her Veronica Lake mane bounced, sometimes covering her face until she pulled her hair out of the way.

I stared beyond our reflection in the darkened window just in time to see her smiling face on the side of a bus as it went by down below. That bus created a strange moment, because the Jewell of the South's smiling face was in a news advert on its side while Jewell's orgasmic expression was in the window's reflection. She remained ambitious with me and I remained rough with her.

Jewell Stewark loved it all. Loved it so much she wouldn't let it end. Told me to take her back to the bed. Her wish, my command. When I was on top she had her hips thrusting up to meet every stroke. When I was behind her she pushed back into me. I moved her blouse and grabbed her soft breasts, fucked her as hard as I could, felt sweat gathering on her neck and back, fucked her the way she kept telling me to fuck her, and when she told me she wanted me to come down her throat, I did that too.

She swallowed and panted, looked up at me, my erection filling her mouth until it slipped away. Then she wiped her mouth and hid her face in her hands, turned her back to me, and cried.

She said, "I make love to *him* like that . . . I please *him* like that . . . and it's *never* been enough."

I sat on the edge of the bed, everything turning cold, not knowing what to say, so I said nothing.

Right then that part of me that wanted to fix all things almost rose to the top, almost made me ask the local celebrity if she wanted me to fix her problems, like I had fixed so many problems for so many people. Those words stayed on the inside of my lips, rested on my tongue until I swallowed them all.

She ran her hands through her tousled mane and said she had to get home.

I gave her a brief nod that said I understood, that her wedding ring spoke volumes.

Black boots still on, she hurried inside the bathroom, heels clicking on tile, closed the door.

The Jewell of the South washed up, did her makeup, gathered her clothing from where it was scattered all across the suite, stayed in the sitting area as she dressed. I left her alone, remained in the window.

Back to her, I waited for her to leave. Waited to hear the door open and close without a farewell.

I stood there until I was interrupted by the sound of a slightly inebriated woman standing at my door. I faced her. She was a gorgeous woman, the kind you looked at and wanted to keep for your own. The kind of woman some men would kill to get and kill to keep.

She said, "Didn't mean to become so emotional and break down like that."

With every woman I came in contact with I think I understood women a little less.

She asked, "Would you mind if I stayed here a little longer?"

Stay or leave, at this point I didn't care one way or the other. Still, I remained cool with it, my voice kind, told her she could have the bed and I'd take the couch in the other room. I grabbed one of the extra pillows and made myself comfortable, gave her some space.

I was in the mood to be alone until the next sun; my thoughts were enough to keep me company.

A few minutes later she came in the front room, her steps slow, stopped about three feet away, leaned against the wall, her head slightly tilted downward and her wavy mane falling across her left eye. I sat up, looked at her silhouette. She was naked except for the high-heeled boots. I wasn't surprised.

She smiled but I saw the need in her brown eyes, saw the pain in the corners of her lips.

Lips that were painted red. Lips the color of blood. The hue of pain.

I'd been raised in brothels. Where people exchanged pain for momentary pleasure.

At times I wondered how much of me was like my unknown father.

And how much was like my mother, the woman whose commerce was pleasure.

I chastised the womb I had come from for being the womb of a whore, but I had failed to realize that I had inherited half of my mother's DNA, that whatever was inside of her was inside of me, along with whatever was inside my old man. By nature or nurture, this was who I had become; fighting it was futile.

Jewell said, "I'll go home to my husband in a little while. And I'll never see you again. So before I go back to my unhappy existence, I want to have something for me, for myself, a stolen moment."

I put my hand on Jewell's beautiful skin, touched her like I was a miracle worker, some sort of a healer, then moved my hand to her narrow hip, squeezed her modest backside, pulled her closer to me.

She trembled under my touch, trembled like I had never touched her before.

She was exposed now. It wasn't the undressing that made her naked. It had been the tears.

Jewell took to her knees. Her painted mouth found my weakness and made it rise until it became strong. Her hunger was strong, more powerful than before. She made me moan like I was dying.

Jewell looked up at me and smiled her wide celebrity smile, the same enthusiastic smile that lived on billboards around the city. Her peekaboo bangs loosening, looking wild and postcoital, her voice tinted with the timbre of much-needed attention and her skin tanned with the glow of extreme orgasms.

She whispered, "Do that freaky, nasty upside-down thing to me again."

I did what she asked, took her in my arms, flipped those stones as if she were as light as a feather, gave her my tongue and lips as she moaned and took me in her mouth again, anxious to please her the way she wanted to be pleased, anxious to fall inside her and forget about my problems.

Not long after that we were on the carpeted floor. I no longer saw Jewell. I saw Detroit; it was her I tried to kill with my every stroke. It was the woman from Detroit I was giving my unbending rage.

While the woman under me put her nails in my flesh and moaned like she was dying, while she held on to me and begged me to go faster and deeper and not stop, three things remained on my mind.

X.

Y.

Z.

Six

the woman chaser

Still in Antigua, the front door to paradise.

Her heartbeat was back to normal. She was on the beach at Sandals.

Lounging in an area populated by colonists who were pretending they were no longer colonists.

Sandals was the grand resort, couples only, same-sex or traditional marriages, all inclusive, security at every entrance, and property that stretched along at least a mile of top-shelf beach. Hundreds of women who looked like her were all around her. No way the police would come here and disturb paradise. Dickenson Bay was as it had been described in the brochure. Silky white sand, incredibly clear turquoise water that went on forever, and never-ending golden sunshine like a gentle lover.

After the shoot-out on All Saints Road, she had lain low, had gone back to her room at Antigua Yacht Club, never left the area, didn't go any farther than Mad Mongoose and Seabreeze Café in the daytime, never ventured beyond English Harbour at night, hardly able to relax, overwrought and fearful.

Until today.

She had rented a Jet Ski and ridden out to the quay that was no more than a mile outside the strip of beaches. Other Jet Skiers were out, but she rode awhile, working on her skills, separated herself from anyone who was trying to follow her. On the back side of that quay, where no one Jet Skiing or riding on one of the catamarans could see her, she had dumped her .22 and all the goods she had stolen in the name of making a hit look like a robbery. After the problem on Rhodes Lane she hadn't had the time.

She had been trapped with the stolen goods and guns in her room.

Now that was off her chest. Now she could breathe. Now she could relax.

Her mind on New York. On Carrie. Samantha. Charlotte. Miranda.

Her mind on red carpets and diamond mink eyelashes.

She was on the crowded beach, resting on a beach chair, sipping a cosmo, hair slicked back, yellow bikini wet from Jet Skiing, suntan lotion on her skin, a novel, *The Winter of Artifice*, in her hand, a novel she'd picked up at Skullduggery Café. She tried to fit in with the crowd. All around her people were reading. Novelists she had never heard of. R. J. Archer. Thomas Greanias. Jeremy Robinson. Dale Brown. Lee Child. Douglas Preston. Matthew Reilly. The reading thing wasn't working for her. Maybe if they made the book into a movie, some sexy actor playing the part in an R-rated film. No, make that NC-17. Something like *Lie to Me*. Movies, exciting, visual. Looking at words all day, too fucking boring.

She finished her cosmo and eased her novel down, put on more suntan lotion as she stared at the miles of people lounging behind Sandals, snowy-faced people who were paying between five hundred and two thousand U.S. a day to sit out on white sands and read novels while they cooked their pale flesh golden brown. Other tourists were buying T-shirts and jewelry from the local men and women who walked the white sands, strolled the beach from end to end selling their inexpensive wares.

The swarthy men in the islands fascinated her. Their accents intrigued her. Their energy so sexual and strong. The ones with the locks, the ones with the short haircuts, the ones with the long nappy hair, the ones in security uniforms, the ones working construction at the casino on the other side of Sandals, the ones tending to horses on the dusty road outside of Siboney. She stared at them all, tingling, wondering. A woman was entitled to two things. A husband. And a lover. The lover was most important. The darker, the more untamed, the more she tingled. Antiguans. Jamaicans. Men from Dominica. Barbuda. Men from Suriname. Guyana. St. Lucia. Even some black Brits. So many different types of exotic men from the Bahamas, Greater Antilles, and Lesser Antilles.

She had settled down, gave up having torrid sex with swarthy men when she married Matthew. The sex with her dark-skinned lovers had been taboo and remarkable. Before two months ago, she hadn't been with a black man in almost five years. Two months ago in Barbados, her first relapse.

Everyone had secrets. No one had more secrets than women.

She was a cougar.

So many cougars were prowling in the jungle. Being a cougar was about being busy, having fun, looking great, and feeling great. A cougar wanted to have fun, was always on the prowl, always hunting, too long since the last kill. Relationship-wise, before Barbados, she hadn't had a victory in too long.

Some days the need for a victory was too strong.

She had planned on grabbing a bite to eat at a restaurant called The Beach later, maybe lime in St. John's at the club called Coast, or go dancing at Rush, or just tan awhile and then head back to Falmouth Harbour and chill out in her room, get a massage and relax before making that long flight back home.

Back to her husband. Her cheap-ass, always-getting-on-her-nerves husband.

The man she loved.

Her mind went back to the shoot-out on All Saints Road.

She cursed, tension rising as she shook her head, biting her bottom lip.

She had missed a shot.

She picked up a local paper she had bought at the market inside of Antigua Village, read the local headlines. This land appeared too congenial and utopian to imagine transgressions ever took place here. *The Daily Observer* said crime was getting out of control and the locals posted letters that said the police were incompetent. Bombing at the Mansoor building. Serial rapist. Home invasions. Roti King burglary. Payroll heists. Mother and sons guilty of murder. Black Antiguans outraged by snowy-faced policemen from Canada hired to fix their crime and murder problems, the white foreigners demonized as being the Four Policemen of the Apocalypse. From what she had read, maybe some help was needed. A Jamaican was stabbed on Redcliffe Street, a ten-minute walk away from the police station on Newgate Street, and the police didn't show up for over two hours. An ambulance was called but an ambulance never came. Marijuana had gone missing from the police station. Car rentals had been robbed.

All of that information printed in the local paper made the island sound like Little New York.

Not that she wanted it any better than it was right now, not at the moment.

Yesterday dead bodies on a yacht and a shoot-out on All Saints had been the front page.

Like everything else that went bad in the islands, the Jamaicans and Guyanese were blamed.

She put the paper down, again shaking her head, biting her bottom lip, and cursing.

A tall native, his hair long, locks like ropes, came her way, smiling, swimming pants hanging a little low. Black T-shirt with yellow lettering on his slender frame. RUDE BOY followed by DON'T BE SILLY . . . She smiled at his smile. His mustache struggling to grow. Strong chest and toned arms. Nice. Suitcase by his side. Selling incense, jewelry made with sharks' teeth, bootleg CDs and DVDs. Most of his movies were African movies. Films made in Nigeria. Nollywood, as they called it; the Nigerian Hollywood. *Beyonce* parts one through four; *Blood Sister* parts one and two.

None of his goods interested her. But she could tell that her goods interested him.

His stare made her self-conscious. She dabbed her forehead. Compared to his frame, she felt so out of shape. But the young boy stared at her mostly naked body with awe, like she was the most beautiful woman he had ever seen. That made her tingle. That made her smile. Made her happy.

He said, "A who an' you ya?"

She adjusted her bottom, chuckled. "I don't understand what you just said."

"You come wid somebody?"

She loved the dialect. Not watered down by the British or American influence. She paid closer attention, trying to listen to the words, trying to capture and learn as he spoke. She'd been pretty good at mimicking the Brits, the Irish, Southerners, New Yorkers, Creoles, a few others. She found the islanders' accents interesting, harder, challenging; not all were rooted in Latin, not all followed the rules of linguistics.

She answered, "I'm by myself at the moment."

He nodded. "You does smoke? You does get high?"

She hesitated, licked her lips over and over, finally asked, "You have E on this island?"

"You wan' me source some E fu you?"

"Maybe. Just checking out my options. I'll let you know."

She stared out at the Caribbean Sea as the handsome boy sat next to her on the sand, his body a wonderland, wondering how old the boy was as he struggled to do the small-talk thing. He was young; if his body didn't reveal his youth, his awkward conversation did. He looked all of seventeen, young enough to make her feel like that old woman out of that movie with Dustin Hoffman. He had to be at least twenty years younger than she. He could've been younger than that. But he wore a wedding ring.

The forbidden said, "Yuh looking sweet, miss."

"It's *Mrs.*"

"Yuh looking sweet, *misses*."

"Mrs. Robinson."

She loved the sound of the boy's voice, his patois, his swagger that said he was confident and virile, that he owned the world as he knew it. Wanted to listen and learn as much as she could.

He said, "Yo, baby, me nar lie, you looking fly."

"Enough already." She motioned at his wedding ring. "Where is your wife?"

"Me hab one wife, but if dat no bodda you, e alright wid me."

She said, "Might *bodda* my husband. That crazy bastard. I'm married to a very jealous man."

"You alright wid he?"

"What you mean?"

"He tek care a you like how you want?"

She laughed, sweat and suntan lotion scenting her golden skin.

She asked, "So what's really on your mind?"

He smiled, rocked back and forth in the sand. "You wan' me deal wid you case?"

"I have no idea what that means."

"You want arwe go fuck?"

"Well, I know what that means."

He smiled, his smile attractive and wide.

She said, "What's the legal age for sex on this island?"

"I'm legal. Don't stress. Jus' cool."

She smiled, found the young boy's directness amusing. But she had heard about what went on in the islands, had heard about women coming in search of suntans and befriending the rent-a-dreds.

She hummed. "Go fuck where?"

"You hab somewhere fu me stay?"

"Maybe."

"Uh-huh."

She said, "And what do you plan on doing when we get in that room?"

"You wan' me nyam out you subben?"

She smiled, chuckled a little. Never had a man just walked up to her and asked for sex.

"Me can fuck you right."

She laughed. He did the same.

He asked, "British?"

"American."

"You sound British."

"American."

She glanced around at all the people in bikinis and swimsuits, most tanning and reading novels. Cornwell. Grisham. Roberts. Young or old, fat as hell or rail thin, all of the women lay out like they were demigod bitches. Nothing wrong with being half-god. More tanned girls were walking the beach with swarthy natives. She wondered how many women came to the islands to get their batteries recharged. She leaned forward, looked down the beach, spied beyond Antigua Village to the quieter, less populated beaches, her eyes looking in the direction of Siboney Beach Club. Less people. Very discreet.

She asked, "How much do you usually charge? How much do women usually pay?"

"Thirty American dollars." He shrugged. "Eighty E.C."

"Really?"

"But 'cause you look so sweet, me can gee you fi twenty U.S."

"Twenty dollars."

"Jus' hook me up wid some weed and couple beers an me nar charge you more than twenty U.S."

"You buy your own weed and beer. I'll share some E."

"Okay." He chuckled. "Twenty U.S. Fifty-two E.C."

Twenty dollars. Less than the sales tax on a pair of Blahniks.

She paused, thinking. She was on an island. A beautiful island. Next to a beautiful young man.

She loved men. And she loved sex. And she loved sex with swarthy men.

No one would know. What happened on the island, what happened before she left, her secret.

She said, "There is a red phone booth down at Coconut Grove; it's right where Antigua Village ends and Siboney begins. One hour. I'll look for you by the red phone booth. I'll have a room by then."

She slipped on her Blahniks. Flesh-colored. Nappa stitching detail. Scalloped edges. Flat heel. With a smile she gathered her things and headed toward Coconut Grove, feeling nervous, anxious to rent a seaside room at the Siboney. A woman deserved a husband and a lover. She had the husband.

It was the other part she needed to work on.

She called Matthew again. He didn't answer. She paused, wondered why he didn't answer, wanted to know what he was doing. He hadn't answered for two days. Jealousy lived with insecurity. She did love him. Did miss him. That wasn't a lie. A woman deserved to have a man who loved her. But marriage had become a dungeon. She just wanted more. She needed more.

Life was too short to sleep with one man.

She finished her call and glanced back; the slender rent-a-dred was on the beach, hustling his wares. The boy was so damned handsome. A natural beauty. So unspoiled in his own way. She continued toward the Siboney, moved up the narrow, sandy footpath behind Antigua Village, and took steps closer to a more private, more discreet hideaway. Again she stared out toward the quay.

Then she remembered the yacht, the fabulous view, how magnificent it had been at sunrise.

She wished she were about to have a rendezvous on a superyacht.

Another fantasy came to mind.

Blahniks on her feet, getting fucked good on the deck of that superyacht.

Then she remembered the bodies she had left behind.

The bullet left in the wall.

She had missed a shot.

And one of the men she had failed to kill with one shot had tried to kill her on All Saints.

She replayed it all in her mind, remembered everything she had done, what had gone wrong.

And she remembered how she had lost focus and fucked up in London.

If only she had killed Gideon.

Maybe that's where Matthew was now.

Back on that Detroit contract that had them stressed the fuck out.

She nodded. That had to be why her husband hadn't called her back.

Gideon had been located and her husband had to be on the move.

She imagined that El Matador was somewhere killing the target.

Putting his knife in the heart of the handsome man who had the eyes of a devil.

That made her angry.

That made her jealous.

Seven

seven doors to death

Huntsville, Alabama.

Last night had been a stormy night, tornado warnings in Rocket City and the surrounding areas.

With the weather like it was, I didn't want to chance it on the highway, so I stayed at the Embassy Suites across from the Huntsville-Madison library, got some much needed rest, and now I was back on the road, GPS guiding me toward the land of Jack Daniel's, country music, and Super 8 motels.

A two-word message popped up on my iPhone: FUNDS TRANSFERRED.

Konstantin had sent me to the Bible Belt and I had taken my trade to a section of America heavily invested in aerospace, education, health care, banking, and various heavy industries, including automobile manufacturing, mineral extraction, steel production and fabrication. The news on the radio was about a fourteen-year-old who'd flushed her newborn baby down the toilet. Did that in a school bathroom. Then they let the world know nine third graders had conspired to torture and kill their teacher.

Third graders. Killing. About the same age I was when I first pointed a loaded .22 at a man.

I changed the station, focused on driving, the smell of cordite rising from my flesh. Rain was coming down hard. Sixty degrees, gray skies, strong winds, and an aggressive downpour turning the city into

Southern soup. Stopped tuning the radio when I made it to a morning show, jokes in progress.

"Do you happen to know the most popular pickup lines in the South?"

"Okay, Bubba. What's the most popular pickup line in the South?"

"Hey, babe, looking sexy. Is this your first family reunion?"

"Uh-huh."

"We's cousins but we can move this relationship to a new level."

"That's sick, Bubba."

"Heck, it works. That's how I met my wife."

I took Jordan Lane, also known as Ardmore Highway, also known as Highway 53, passed by Grainger Industrial Supply and a Conoco gas station. I was coming up on Woody Anderson Ford when it looked like I had picked up a tail. I wasn't sure, slowed down and almost turned off into AutoZone, but if it was a tail I'd box myself into a parking lot, and that was a major no. It was best to keep moving, stay in front of whoever it was. Had seen the same car leave the Embassy when I had pulled out of the lot.

I told myself it was nothing. Highway 53 was a main road, everybody took this route.

I slowed down. The car behind me did the same, but not before I saw that two people were in that car, one in the backseat, right side of the vehicle. Two people. Like in London. I took it up to the speed limit. That car did the same. Two in that car, that could mean a driver and a shooter. I could be outpositioned and outgunned at this point. Again I slowed, again they did the same, sped up, the same.

Cat and mouse; cat and mouse. Man against man in the heart of Dixie.

I slowed again. That car did the same. I sped up. That car did the same.

That dark car with the unknown occupants stayed about an eighth of a mile back. A few cars moved between us, each car or truck exiting at some point, but that sedan was still there.

I searched the landscape for some way to get off of this route. Two-lane road, some housing developments on the edges of fields, larger homes at Mountain Cove. At Burwell Road, off to my right, were open fields that led to tree-covered hills and mountains, almost spring, trees still barren. That area was too wide open, too isolated to take a chance, not when I didn't know the land or what kind of trouble was following me. The car on my tail slowed down like it was about to turn off the road, but it didn't turn, adjusted and remained a good distance back.

I took 53 out of Huntsville toward Nashville.

The car behind me did the same.

I double-checked my widowmaker, made sure it was loaded to the teeth. It was a new gun, had been supplied with this car, had been left in the car in case I needed it for the job.

Nothing changed but time, and soon I cut to the right, took I-65 heading north; the rain came down harder, the storm sat on top of me, speed limit seventy miles per hour but was barely able to do fifty in the madness. I took my trepidation deeper into Tennessee. Eighty miles away from Nashville. Storm wouldn't let up. Visibility decreased with every second. Forced my speed to do the same.

Hard rain turned into hail; terror came down from the skies so hard my windshield wipers worked overtime and didn't make any difference. Was as effective as using a paper cup to throw water off the sinking *Titanic*. Visibility diminished rapidly and soon I couldn't see behind me at all, looked like that part of the world had been erased and the world in front of me no longer existed. I was surrounded by wetness and whiteness, fogged over and barely able to see ten feet of reality, just as impossible to see the horror driving behind me. Man against nature in the land where Civil War pitted brother against brother.

My car jerked when it was rammed from behind. I gripped the steering wheel, turned the wheels the opposite direction of my skid; my heart pumped as I brought it back under control. My gun slid away from my grip, moved across the seat, and fell between the passenger seat and the passenger door. Slamming into my car had caused that driver to struggle for control while I did the same.

I cursed and accelerated, the wall of fog and rain refusing to give me any reprieve.

Again I was rammed from the rear, caught off guard and forced to deal with my skidding car, the layer of water between the tires and the road making it almost impossible to keep the car on the road.

I tried to speed up, didn't know if I was about to crash into the back of a stopped car, truck, or eighteen-wheeler. I was driving blind, eyes wide open, whiteness and hail clogging my vision.

My rear window exploded, the din from the hail and storm covering the wanting sound of death, the report of an unseen gun smothered by the forces of nature as it fell like thousands of golf balls.

They had sped up, afraid they were going to lose me when visibility wasn't in their favor, had raced through fog and hail, and now they were on top of me, the gunman firing shots, the driver swerving toward me in the middle of the hailstorm, slamming into me as I struggled to keep my car on the road.

They had waited to get me off the two-lane road, into the in-between land, the open highway offering them instant escape, especially now, when the forces of nature were on their team as well.

Again they rammed me, made everything jerk when they hit me with a police-style maneuver.

My car lost control, hydroplaned, began spinning.

I gripped the steering wheel as the car took flight and left the road.

Eight

five minutes to live

My car crashed through a series of smaller trees before coming to rest at a larger one.

Whoever was after me wasn't with the police. Their car had skidded out and they had to park and rush down into the mud, mud that was almost powerful enough to suck off shoes with each step.

The hail. The poor visibility. It was like driving through an endless cloud.

The storm roared like a demon, a monster breathing its frigid breath.

They came through the mud and hail shooting, no hesitation between shots. Two men emptied their clips and then reloaded as they walked toward my car, fired like they were professional killers paid to kill someone thirty times over. Gunshots, the psychopathic roar of tough guys. They put bullet holes in the car, shot the driver's side the same way the officers from Texas and Louisiana had shot up Bonnie and Clyde's car in 1934, killed those desperados on a desolate road near their Bienville Parish, Louisiana, hideout. And now I was being gunned down in the mud, somewhere between Huntsville and Nashville.

They were up on the car, emptying their clips into the air bag. The storm had the same effect as a silencer, hid the sounds that created death, swallowed all noises, their shooting so rapid and fierce that it sounded like one elongated sound of terror. They shot and shot while the skies coughed and wheezed. One of the men was tall, at least six-seven, the other at least six feet tall and almost as wide.

Dimming visibility cloaked them until they were right up on the car.

Shooting, reloading, shooting, reloading.

They were meaner than the notorious Kray twins.

Not until then were they able to slosh through the mud and get close enough to pull the destroyed air bag out of the way, not until then did they realize there was no blood in the driver's seat. No blood, and no body. And the passenger-side door was open; on that side footprints were being filled with rainwater.

I wasn't in that crippled car that had its front end wrapped around a one-hundred-year-old tree.

I was twenty yards and ninety degrees away, my body covered in a chilling rain; the season was spring but the rain and hail belonged to the coldest winter. I was muddied up to my chest, mud on my body from where I had fallen down when I fled the vehicle as fast as I could. Eyes squinting as hail changed into a freezing rain and made a river across my face.

Gun in my hand. Trigger pulled back.

Blunt trauma from the air bag made holding a gun feel as if I were supporting a forty-pound weight in the palm of my hand. And it felt as if hot gases from the air bag had burned my skin when that air bag had deployed. Teeth clenched, controlling my breathing, I aimed, arm trembling. It was kill or be killed, fight or flight, flight from a fight not encoded in my DNA, the DNA I had inherited from an unknown warrior.

Those were the lies I had been told. Those were the lies that haunted me.

Those were the lies that had become my truth.

The pain from the air bag smacking me resounded, echoed, had almost deafened me.

My first shot missed them both, the bullet hitting the car, creating awareness of my position.

Then they both turned my way.

I aimed, shot, missed, adjusted for pain, compensated for the weight of the gun.

Water dripped across my eyes as my enemies tried to move in the mud, but the mud had them glued where they stood, made them stumble in a torrential downpour, man versus man as man fought with nature. One of them dove in the mud and yelled as the other fell against the car, reloading his gun.

I focused on the one with the gun. From my angle he was the closer of the two. He was the taller of the two. The other one, the heavier one, was slipping and sliding in Mother Earth.

The head of the tall assassin was in my crosshairs. That head, as the rain fell across the world as I knew it, exploded when a bullet from a .38 turned his head into an instant convertible.

Before his body could hit the ground another shot created redness across his torso.

Two shots later his friend had bullet holes in his right arm and left leg, shots that took him to the ground and filled his chubby face with mud and earth. He struggled to sit up, took a desperate look at his friend, the wildness in his eyes saying he didn't want the same convertible hairstyle, didn't want a hole where he processed foolish thoughts, didn't want Tennessee rain putting puddles where his brain used to be.

A third shot put a hole in his liver.

I took no chances, not with my life. Not when I was on a battlefield in an unwanted war.

Soaked with rain, battered by hail, muddied all over, more mud sloshing through my soft-soled shoes, I kept my gun trained on the wounded man as I took steps through the mud and trees. I stopped at the tall, dead man. Asian man in a gray pinstripe suit and black shirt, Italian shoes that told me he hadn't planned on hiking through mud with the viscosity of quicksand.

Rainwater diluted redness, created a pink death, his matter mixing through mud and grass.

I went through his pockets, gun trained on the wounded man, his swollen face showing he was in more pain than he had felt since birth.

No words were exchanged. Done collecting a wallet, a cellular phone, and an iPod, I moved past the dead man and made my way toward his partner in crime, offered a deadly grimace to a man who had tried to cease my existence, went inside his pockets, fished out anything I could find, jammed all of that in my jacket pockets, pain from the crash nonexistent, all of that smothered by the adrenaline rush. White hair, white goatee, a young version of Kenny Rogers in gray pants, black suit coat, and crisp white shirt, all of that soiled by this storm and mother earth.

I asked, "Detroit?"

He nodded. "Contract . . . came outta . . . Detroit."

"How many with you?"

"This is it. Just us."

He was both living and dying, blood draining away as mud glued itself to his final moments. I remained next to him, mud splattered from my feet to my waist, an artistic and woodless wainscot that looked like it had been designed by a third grader who had had too much sugar in his diet.

I asked, "Were you in London?"

"Never been . . . to London."

I took a handkerchief from his suit pocket, wiped water from the dying man's eyes.

He thanked me for that moment of kindness.

I looked at the car I had been driving. Fiberglass and metal and tires and glass filled with bullet holes. Around me rivers of blood being thinned out by what felt like a never-ending storm.

My voice and disposition were as cold as the rain when I asked, "Do you know who I am?"

He coughed, then spat to the side. Panted as he said, "You . . . are . . . Gideon."

We looked into each other's eyes. Coldness glaring at coldness.

I hit him across his face, knocked teeth from his mouth, beat him with my gun until he collapsed facedown in the mud. I put my foot on the back of his neck, pressed down with my weight as he struggled to breathe, flailing and splashing mud, trying to kick free, held my foot there until his struggle ended, until gurgling ceased, his lungs clogged with the same earth they had been sent to bury me in.

I had taken my backpack and messenger bag out of the wrecked car, was rushing to make sure I had all I had, when I thought I heard someone call out. I moved through the mud, almost stumbling, had a feeling it was highway patrol. Wiping filth from my face, I looked through the falling water and saw someone coming down the pathway the dead men had taken. The hail had become a steady rain, visibility good enough for me to wipe my face, see forty yards away. I moved through the mud toward whoever it was. Didn't see flashing lights. Didn't hear sirens. That didn't mean that flashing lights and sirens weren't on the other side of my opaque world. The rain was still the blanket that covered us.

It was a woman. Slender like a model, borderline anorexic with an alabaster complexion, hair dark. Jeans, black jacket, black blouse, black umbrella up high. A woman with good bone structure and lovely skin, didn't need to gild the lily by wearing makeup. Saw that in the blink of an eye. The rainfall hard but slowing down, visibility increasing, allowed her to see just as much of me as I could of her.

The woman paused when she saw me, a man soaked from head to muddied shoes, behind me a wrecked car that was riddled with bullet holes. Add to that carnage two dead men sleeping in the mud.

I shot her in her heart. Her death so immediate her expression never had time to change.

As I passed her, I saw the umbrella she had held in her left hand was at her side.

So was the gun she had held in her right hand; it too rested in the mud at her waist.

Her weapon of choice had been a stainless steel .357.

Sludge still sloshing in my shoes, cold and shivering, wiping water from my eyes, I struggled up the slippery hill, anticipated another assassin, maybe more than one, guns aimed.

There was no fourth shooter. There was no fourth death.

I had been surrounded by a violence that would've made Sam Peck-inpah stand up and applaud.

I was the one who had survived the beautiful catastrophe, wind and gunshots its soundtrack.

Muck dripping from my body, I hurried back to the interstate, got into their sedan, and sped away.

Nine

lady gangster

The same horrendous weather that had worked against me now worked in my favor, washed away footprints at that new death site. That layer of water left no tire marks on the highway as I fishtailed away and dark clouds rolled in. Would be at least a day before that death site was found.

That was what I hoped.

I ached.

I trembled from both anxiety and the chill of the cold rain.

Everything in my sight pulsated, the world swelling and shrinking. A new wave from the rainstorm deafened the rampant heartbeat inside my chest. For a moment the world was on mute, the shadow of death all over me. That was how I had felt when a plastic bag had been placed over my head.

It passed. It took a long moment, but it passed.

I dug through my muddied clothes, fished out my cellular, and dialed a number in the 615 area code. It was a number I hadn't dialed in at least two years. I hoped the number was still good.

Three rings, then we were connected.

I said, "Hawks."

"Who is this calling this number?"

"Gideon."

"Gideon?"

"Yeah."

"Well, well, well."

"How are you?"

"I was feeling supercalifragilisticexpialidocious until I heard your voice."

"Didn't mean to turn your mood in a negative direction."

"You're bad news."

"People say the same about you."

"What do you want?"

"Konstantin told me you were still down south."

"So you managed to call Konstantin."

"I'm coming out of Rocket City."

"Rocket City."

"Huntsville, Alabama."

"I know what and where Rocket City is."

"Hawks, you in the area?"

"Maybe."

"Are you in the area?"

"Where have you been?"

"Abroad."

"Is America the only country with telephones?"

"I guess not, Hawks."

I looked at the mud that covered my clothing, at the smoldering gun at my side.

I said, "I need help right now."

"Where are you again?"

"I'm on 65 . . . I'm . . . let me see. . . . Looks like I'm not too far from exit 22."

I told Hawks to meet me, didn't want to chance driving a car when I didn't know its history. The front end was damaged and I had one headlight. The side of the car had fresh damage as well.

"Better be careful, Gideon. The Bubbas down here that work law enforcement aren't the types that live on coffee and doughnuts. These fools eat anabolic steroids for breakfast, lunch, and dinner."

"I'm not in the mood for sarcasm."

"That wasn't sarcasm, asshole."

"Hawks. Look . . . I just had three motherfuckers on my ass."

Hawks said, "I'll see what I can do."

"And bring a lot of plastic. Industrial plastic."

"Enough to wrap up three bodies?"

"Enough to cover your seats top to bottom."

"Yeah, enough to wrap up three bodies."

I ended the call, anxiety rising, gun within reach, as focused as I'd ever been.

Exit 22 fed into Highway 31A.

Rain battered the car as I turned left and found shelter at Country Store & Restaurant. It was a nice-sized building that looked like it was filled with country music, three DVDs for ten bucks, and honey buns. The type of place that stocked B.C. Powder.

The crew that had been sent after me had been riding with the radio on a country and western station. My mind cleared up enough to notice the voices coming out of the speakers. A comedian who sounded like former president Bill Clinton was telling Hillary, McCain, and Obama jokes. I wiped as much mud off me as I could, did that while Stevie Nicks and Don Henley sang a love song, a duet called "Leather and Lace." Even in my agony and anger the song made me pause when it got to a line about wondering if a woman could love a man like me. That hit home. Took me back to London, to the West Indies, to South America, to places I had traveled with two women, Lola Mack and Mrs. J. But in the next hour those thoughts had changed one hundred times and I was restless, listened to James Brown telling everybody that Poppa had a brand-new bag, Lola Mack and Mrs. J. no longer a part of my world.

No woman was a part of my world for long. Came with the territory.

The storm was still on my side. No reason for the dead to be discovered, not as of yet.

The I.D.s from the men identified one as Ronaldo Lysaght, the other as Thomas Goetzman.

A purse was on the backseat. I grabbed it and looked inside. It was the woman's identification. Pieronzetta Lupe Rosalyn Marquez. I.D.

said she was from Ashland, Ohio. That was seventy miles from Cleveland, that strip of Interstate 71 surrounded by farmland, tractors, and barns, mostly agricultural, this time of year trees barren and grass the lightest of browns, almost like fields of wheat.

She was a long way from home, her moral compass not working at all. I scrolled through the text messages on her phone. Lots of sexual messages. A stone freak. And a player. Her messages told me she had a boyfriend in Akron named Fred Guidry. But she also had another boyfriend in Toledo.

Two men would have to buy black suits and carry her coffin to its final resting place.

I'd taken cell phones from both men. Goetzman had the most recent call, to area code 313. Detroit. I pushed redial and the call was answered in the middle of the first ring.

Someone was more anxious than a child on Christmas Eve.

Without greetings or salutations, her tone intense, she asked, "Is it done?"

"It's done."

She hesitated, "Goetzman?"

"No."

"Lysaght?"

"One more try. And it's not the woman."

There was a pause of disbelief. She heard my voice, for the first time without my using a filter. I had never contacted her without a filter. But there was so much anger inside me I didn't care.

I said, "They're dead. All of them."

Another pause.

Her voice trembled. "You've been running."

"You've been hiding."

"I hide from no one."

"Why don't you show up for your dirty work? Fucking coward."

"You're the one running, not me."

"You've increased the guards at your home and now you travel with a dozen bodyguards."

"You got rid of your properties. You moved the money from those sales several times, moved it from bank to bank, island to island, did that until I could no longer keep up with you."

"I should've cut your motherfucking throat, should've left your head hanging from your neck. My mistake was thinking you were smart enough to let this go. Soon your head will hang from your fucking neck. I'll try not to mess the face up so they can keep that casket open for friends and family."

I heard her swallow, her breathing becoming filled with a fiery anger and extreme panic.

"Son of a bitch . . . you came inside my house. Threatened me. Threatened my children. This will end when *you* are dead. Whatever it takes, *no matter how long it takes*, this will end when you are *dead*."

"Or you. When you are dead, this will be over."

"Stay out of Detroit. Keep away from my children, you son of a bitch."

"I don't give a fuck about your children. This is between me and you."

"Jesus is on my side."

"Tell him that when you see him."

"Blasphemous bastard."

"None but the righteous. And I doubt if you are in that short line."

"Whenever you sit down to take a *shit*, have toilet paper in one hand and a gun in the other."

"You do the same. And don't forget which is which."

There was a pause.

She said, "Wet your hand and wait for me."

"You do the same."

The call ended in the middle of her hostile breathing, disconnected on her end.

Her war against me made as much sense as the war against Iraq.

But it was a war that had momentum.

In her eyes I was the terrorist who had invaded her home; now there had to be retribution.

I'd tried to end this in a kind way. In my own way I had tried to make a deal.

It was impossible to be logical with someone who was running on emotion.

I rubbed my eyes.

If it wasn't for the problem I had in Detroit, I'd still have my homes in Seattle, in Stone Mountain, and on the outskirts of Los Angeles. She'd tracked me down, forced me into a state of homelessness.

She was the type of woman that a man couldn't make deals with. She didn't have enough sense to understand when she should be terrified. She didn't know she should be pissing where she stood, that piss running down her legs into her high heels. She was a churchgoing Bible thumper who had killed her own husband, the father of her children, had done that using her husband's money and my hands.

She was a bloodthirsty psychopath who believed she was righteous.

Nobody stopped her from getting what she wanted.

And she was dying for my death. Dying for revenge.

Ten

under the skin

I slipped out of the car long enough to spy inside the trunk. Needed to see what they had in the vault of the sedan. There was a suitcase and another purse; the woman had left her designer bag. More guns. Ammo. Duct tape. Knives. And gasoline. Somebody had planned a torture party that would end in the guest of honor becoming a human barbecue. They had everything but the barbecue sauce.

There was a black briefcase. Inside was around sixty thousand dollars.

I took out the briefcase and closed the trunk, wiping away my fingerprints.

Back inside the car, I went through the papers I had taken off them. I.D.s. Lysaght was from Cincinnati, Goetzman from Dayton. The pretty woman had been from the same part of the country. Pictures of a wife and children were in both wallets. Could've been real or fake. Never knew in this biz. But I was betting these were real. Death was like a spider's web, moving in many ways, touching many.

Their money was in a combination of C-notes and Jacksons. Worn bills. Out of sequence.

It smelled like the same money I had returned to my enemy was being used against me.

I should've finished her. Should've killed her on my last visit to Detroit.

Hindsight, twenty-twenty.

If she'd had her way I'd have been in a wrecked car, my body riddled with bullet holes, cooling to the touch.

Soon after that a dark gray Excursion pulled into the lot. My cellular chimed.

Hawks was there. I had Hawks pull over to the side of the car closest to the store, had Hawks back in so when I jumped out of one vehicle and climbed into another, that and the rain would cover me.

I began wiping down everything I had touched inside the car.

Then I got out of the car, the smoking gun in one hand, briefcase in the other.

Hawks got out dressed in a short black leather jacket, dungarees with a big belt buckle that had an oversized red heart with a knife going through its center, Lucchese crocodile cowboy boots, and a simple black T; burgundy hair with highlights, pulled back into a ponytail that hung down the curve of her butt. Before I had worked with her, some years before, she told me her hair used to touch the floor.

She had grown up in awe of Crystal Gayle's long mane. But Hawks had grown into her own style.

Hawks was a woman who wore Levi's as if she were made to fill them out, a woman who wore cowboy boots like they were stilettos, another stunning woman with good bone structure and lovely skin, another woman who didn't need to gild the lily by wearing makeup.

The assassin known as Hawks. I'd forgotten how beautiful she was.

Chic, hip, and cool, with a romantic mane of hair that swept down below her waistline.

Rain fell on her hair and round cheeks, but she moved like the chilly water didn't faze her.

She faced me. The rain on her cheeks looked like tears.

Hawks's eyes were green, haunting, the kind that testified to a life of pain. Intriguing eyes, like that Afghan girl on the cover of *National Geographic*. And her scent was subtle and exotic, like eucalyptus and rosemary mixed with sandalwood and lavender.

She looked me up and down, shaking her head, frowning.

I said, "Hawks."

"You look like the Creature from the Black Lagoon."

"I know."

"I don't know if I should slap you or kiss you."

"A kiss would be nice."

Hawks slapped me. Then she went back to the driver's side of the Excursion and got back inside.

Hawks's Sheryl Crow CD played as we rode toward the area known as Music City, USA, because of that industry. And known as the Athens of the South because of all the colleges.

A few good-old-boy trucks passed going in the other direction, F-250s and F-350s and pickups with wheels so large passengers would need an escalator to get to the doors, a parachute to get out.

Hawks shook her head and mumbled, "You have a lot of nerve calling me."

"I know."

"Just because I came to help you, don't think I'm happy to see you."

"I can tell."

"You look stupid. Wrapped up in industrial plastic like a mummy. You look as stupid as I feel."

Hawks was driving, her eyes on the road ahead and checking her rearview. Seventy miles and no conversation whatsoever. Sheryl Crow serenaded us. I kept my eyes on the passenger-side mirror, always looking back. We sped into Nashville. Jefferson Street. Jackson Street. Went by B. B. King's Blues Club and Schermerhorn Symphony Center.

"Gideon?"

"Yeah?"

"Stop shifting around."

"I'm not shifting."

"You are shifting and that plastic keeps making that irritating *crinkle-crinkle* sound over and over and it's getting on my nerves right about now. So stop shifting around before I start screaming."

Hawks drove around the river port and railway city formerly known as Fort Nashborough, her lips tight. Her mind worked the same way my mind worked. She made sure there wasn't a second team on my heels. James Robertson Parkway. War Memorial Plaza. Tennessee Tower. Freedom Center. Had been a long time since I had been to Nashville. West End. Over by Vanderbilt University students were jogging in the rain, some walking with umbrellas, none intimidated by the sixty-degree weather.

Vanderbilt, in an area built by gunrunners and bootleggers. Corruption at its best.

I shifted a little, tapped my leg, and asked Hawks, "How's Nashville treating you?"

"Nashville is evolving."

I moved around, plastic crinkling as I sweated. "What does *evolving* mean?"

She took a breath, struggled. "Hispanic and Laotian gangs have moved into the 'Ville."

"I take it not all evolution is for the best."

"One of the hazards and joys of being multicultural; the good comes with the bad."

I struggled to get comfortable, and the cab was filled with the sound of plastic moving against plastic. Hawks had strips of industrial plastic covering my seat, like I had asked, every drop of the mud and sludge being captured.

I said, "Hadn't heard from you."

"I think it's the other way around."

I nodded. "Thought about you a lot since then."

"Thinking ain't dialing."

"No, thinking ain't dialing."

"You mocking me?"

"Not mocking you."

"You had my number, obviously."

"Just saying."

She took a deep breath, swallowed. "Thought you were dead. For a while I did."

I said, "Thought you were out of the business."

"Konstantin calls every now and then. When he has something that fits my build."

"Something easy."

"Not always easy. I do what I'm paid to do. No matter how ugly. Or sadistic."

"That we do."

She paused. "Does it ever bother you?"

I shifted a bit, uneasy with the conversation. "Try not to think about it."

"You keep count?"

"Nope."

"I keep count. But then again, I'm a woman. And we keep count of everything."

Another pause as I checked the mirror, made sure we were riding unaccompanied.

Hawks asked, "You tell anybody what happened? You tell what I did in Killeen?"

"No. That was your job. I was just your wingman."

She quieted, sucked her bottom lip, and drove, looked like her mind was in the past.

The job we had done together. That played in my mind too.

Eleven

invisible ghosts

Back then, two years ago, the day I met the hired gun known as Hawks.

We had connected in Texas, a state so wide it would take a man three days to drive across that part of North America, the better part of two weeks to walk across barren plains covered with dust devils. You could sit the U.K., Holland, Paris, and a few other countries in the middle of Texas and the supersized state would swallow up those nations and still have room to have Austria for dessert. Those were my thoughts as we left Dallas, where Hawks had picked me up at DFW, that marker being the start of a three-hour drive east so we could go handle a contract Hawks had picked up. She had called Konstantin and asked if he could arrange for her to have some backup. He recommended me. I needed the money.

I said, "Too bad we couldn't get our hands on a Cessna."

"You fly?"

"Small planes. Time to time."

She said, "Your diction . . . you don't sound like you're from the South."

"I've lived all over the world."

"At first I was going to say you were from Europe."

"Not from Europe."

"I can tell. Your teeth are too pretty."

"Tell me about the job."

The job was in the city called Killeen. The target was an enlisted man who lived at Stone Hill Apartments. When the target opened the door, I was about to rush in and take him down, my mind in pit bull mode, but what Hawks saw made her have a change of heart. She had grabbed that soldier, her teeth tight, her gun at her side, and forced him to come with us. She did the same with the rest of the people in that apartment, made them come along, no questions asked, everyone trembling.

I sat in a cheap hotel room with a nervous soldier, a jittery and sweaty enlisted man from South Carolina, a man who had been to both Iraq and Afghanistan, a man who had spent almost three years away from his family. He had left his home with what he had on, left his car, and got inside the SUV Hawks was driving, and we sat in a La Quinta. *We* being me, that man, and his family.

Gun in the small of my back, I kept an eye on that twenty-year-old man and his twenty-two-year-old wife. Their kids were there too: one in diapers, one barely walking, one who acted like he had ADHD.

The man's wife looked like motherhood and debt had aged her ten years. Looked like the soldier had made a baby before he left to go overseas and had made one every time he came back home.

Toys in hand, posted in front of the television, the kids had no idea what was going on. I did what Hawks paid me to do and did it without asking questions. I wasn't comfortable with what was going on, was taking a big chance on her anger backfiring in more ways than one.

Hawks had left the family with bags of junk food from Wendy's, food she had paid for, then had gone to visit the man who had hired her, wanted to have a conversation with him. What she was going to do wasn't wise, but she knew that. She didn't say what she was planning, but it was in her eyes. I saw that anger and asked her if she wanted it the other way around, for me to go while she babysat, and she said no. She had no problem looking a man in his face and telling him how she felt.

The soldier had marks in his skin, shrapnel from almost being blown up defending the country. Two of his buddies hadn't been so lucky. Not all Iraqis were thrilled by the American occupation.

He rambled, "I know I messed up. I know I did, just . . . please . . ."

I gave him a look that made him shift and rock.

He stared at his feet, left foot bouncing, rubbing his hands hard enough to start a fire.

He said, "She looks like one of the singers. The woman you're with. Looks like one of the country singers. The Judds. Wait, not one of the singers. The one that's the actress, she looks like her. Forgot if that one was named Naomi or Wynonna. Same cheeks and shape of head and—"

"Shut up."

He stammered, "Yes, sir."

"Go play with your kids. Make them shut up too. Especially that little one."

"Yes, sir."

When Hawks came back she gave that soldier an envelope. Inside that envelope was some money. She put it in the soldier's hands, told him to get his shit together because next time he might not be so lucky, then we left, told the soldier he would have to get his own way back to the apartment he was living in with his family. The soldier asked her what he was supposed to do with that money. She snapped, told him to get out of debt and take care of his family. Told him if she heard about him gambling or taking out loans from another loan shark she would come back, and next time she would not be so nice. Hawks was angry as hell. Told him if he was wise he'd look into getting a vasectomy because if he went back to Iraq he might not be so lucky and leaving his wife with a house full of kids wouldn't do anybody any goddamn good, because he knew that when he died they would be on their own, never depend on Uncle Sam. He trembled, asked her what about the loan shark. She told him that he didn't have to worry about that problem anymore. That loan shark had lived seventeen miles from Fort Hood.

We were riding toward Dallas, Hawks driving with a tense expression, both of us in silence until she popped in a CD, the best of Elvis Presley, his thirty number-one hits, looking at the flatlands as the King began singing about blue moons, suspicious minds, being in the ghetto, and blue suede shoes. We passed R.V. parks, truck stops, Dairy Queens, graveyards, salvage yards, Harleys, and vintage cars.

Hawks turned the music down and asked, "You think I'm stupid for what I did?"

"Depends. What did you do?"

"I went to see the man who hired me."

"Depends on what you did when you went to see the man who hired you."

"I killed him."

"What happened?"

Hawks told me that the loan shark would be found dead in his bath-tub the next morning, all of his records, every trace of every single debt, gone.

I said, "Bathtub."

Hawks had knocked the loan shark out, then filled the tub with water. Undressed the man and put on some Motown. The Four Tops sang and drowned out the gurgles that came from a drowning man. Hawks had held the loan shark upside down by his ankles until water filled his lungs.

Accidental drowning. That was her specialty.

She said, "I can use a gun but I don't like to. And I don't like using a knife. I can and have, but I don't like the mess. Water is better. And it's quick. No bullets. No knife. No bang and no blood. Nothing but a little water to mop up if I'm in a mopping mood, and today wasn't a mopping-mood day."

That was what would've happened to the soldier if his apartment hadn't been filled with crying babies. But then again, Hawks had been a military brat, so maybe the contract was too close to home.

In the end the soldier was alive and his debt was erased.

She asked, "Do you think that was just plain dumb?"

"The envelope filled with money."

"Took that from the loan shark. That no-'count, worthless jerk."

"Do you always do that?"

"You think what I did . . . letting the soldier go . . . you think that was wrong?"

"Was that your first time?"

"I broke the rules of the business."

"You were paid to do a job."

"And I made you my accomplice."

"You did."

"So you think what I did was stupid."

"You did what you did, that's all I can say."

"Don't worry, you'll still get the money you were promised."

"That's not the point."

"I don't always do something stupid like that. I was out in Bakersfield last month, did this thing for Konstantin off Highway 99 out on Buck Owens Boulevard with no problem. Flight attendant for Continental. Got inside her room at the Doubletree Hotel on Camino Del Rio, did it good and quick. Contracts I did at Fort Meyers, Hilton Head, Raleigh, Louisville, and Indianapolis, all good and quick."

"Konstantin spoke highly of you."

"He sent me on another job up in Memphis, made sure this guy did a T-bone into a semi. He hit the trailer and the trailer took the roof of his car off. Needless to say he was too busy screaming to duck, so he lost his head and lost his head. Official ruling was brake failure. Double-indemnity clause kicked in, wife got paid a million dollars, I got paid my fee, happy ending for everybody. Except the poor guy."

"Thought you liked doing the bathtub thing."

"Can't drown everybody. Have to pick and choose."

"T-boned into a semi."

"Which wasn't easy to make happen."

"He lost his head and lost his head."

"That's what I said."

It sounded like she was trying to convince me she was competent, had what it took to work in this cold business. I didn't help her with that part of the conversation. Didn't bother me one way or another.

My mind was on the whore who had raised me. I wanted to find her and finish our business. That was before I knew about the kid. Before I had found her on Berwick Street in London.

A moment passed. The temperature was mid-sixties, skies partly cloudy, sun bright.

I shifted in my seat, stared out at the edges of nowhere, this drive taking us toward its middle.

Hawks took a deep breath. "Do you think I'm nice-looking?"

"Where did that come from?"

"First it was in my head, then it slipped across my tongue and came out my mouth."

"You're kinda pretty."

"Kinda?"

"The soldier thought you looked like one of the Judds."

"Ha."

"The actress."

"If I had a dime for every time I heard that one. I do not look like Ashley Judd."

"When I first saw you, the cheekbones, I thought you looked a little like Janet Jackson."

"Well, if you hold up a picture of Momma Judd and Janet Jackson side by side you see they almost have the same face. Same cheekbones, same smile. All that is to say, I have heard the Janet thing a time or two."

"Doesn't matter if you look like a Judd or Miss Jackson, you're pretty."

"Pretty is for little girls and women who will never be nice-looking."

"You look sexy, if you don't mind me saying so."

"Oh, now I'm sexy."

"And mean."

"I am not mean."

"More mean than sexy."

"Is that right."

"You PMSing?"

"That was mean. Sexist and mean."

"Looks like you need sex real bad, if you ask me."

"That was evil."

"Maybe that's why you look so tense. Your hormones are out of control."

"Stop being evil."

"You have a boyfriend?"

"That's none of your business."

"You need somebody to make you smile."

"Why do men think that is all a woman ever needs?"

I closed my eyes, chuckled a bit.

She said, "So you think I'm sexy."

"Of course."

"Liar, liar."

"Yes, I do."

"I have on brand-new jeans and my best Tony Lamas and you haven't looked at me once."

"We were going to kill somebody."

"So what?"

"Trying to be professional."

"When has a man ever been *that* professional?"

"So you don't have a boyfriend."

She took a breath. "I'm tense. What I just did . . . geesh . . . really tense."

"Want me to drive?"

"I said tense, not sleepy."

"Was trying to help."

"So you think I need somebody to make me smile."

"Face in the pillow, ass in the air."

"Oh really."

"That's what I said."

"Well, I don't have a boyfriend, if you must know."

"Which explains the tension."

"Jerk."

"Vibrator?"

"I'm not into that. Can't imagine putting an inanimate object inside me. I'm into flesh and blood, not into plastic and batteries. A vibrator can't hold you and kiss you and get on top of you."

"So you have tried it."

"Couple of times. Felt stupid."

"What do you do?"

"Nothing. Ride it out the best I can. Been riding this so long I'm about to get bucked off."

"No wonder you're acting the way you're acting."

"And how am I acting?"

"Like you need somebody to make you smile."

"Bet you've made a lot of women smile."

"A few."

"What kind of smiles?"

"Big smiles."

"You are so full of it."

"Are you calling me a liar?"

"Maybe you could . . ."

"Could what?"

"Nothing."

"What?"

"Nothing."

"Chicken."

"What you said, face in the pillow and booty in the air, that image done got stuck in my head."

"That's what you need to make you smile."

She laughed a little. "Since you think that's what I need, you want to try to make me smile?"

"I don't think you want to go there with me."

"Kind of figured that would make you shut your trap."

"Keep it professional."

"Now who's the chicken?"

"Not chicken."

"Well, maybe I want to see if you can back up all that yack talk."

"I'd be more than happy to do my best to put a smile on your face."

"Maybe we need a little less conversation, little more action."

I thought Hawks was just shit-talking, but she took the next exit. Walked into Motel 6 and rented a room. Stepped into the room pulling off her cowboy boots and T-shirt. I pulled the legs of her dungarees, tugged her pants off her, and she climbed on the bed naked. She didn't wear panties or a bra.

Some women look good dressed up. Hawks looked better undressed. She had been camouflaging paradise with boots and jeans and a T-shirt. What I saw made me pause like I was at a museum admiring a work of art. Her body was beautiful, the right combination of softness and firmness, her breasts full and round, her nipples erect. Had no idea that sensuality was hiding under those dungarees and T-shirt. What I saw on that bed could make a man feel like a goddamn god.

She asked, "You going to stand there staring at me or strip and get down to business?"

I undressed and went to Hawks, the center of my chest throbbing, an aching down below.

She said, "I don't know if this is a good idea, but I'm sure I've had ones worse than this one."

I kissed Hawks, did that to shut her up, and that kiss was probably the best kiss I had ever had. It surprised me. That kiss led to me being on top of her, her soft breasts pressed on my chest, her legs wrapped around me, backside moving as her hand reached for my hard-on, put me against her wetness.

I went inside her, went in slowly, came out just as slowly, went in as deep as she would let me.

Hawks was a moaner. A woman who dragged her short nails across a man's skin and rose up to meet what was being given. Never would have thought she could gyrate her ass the way she did.

Twenty minutes later Hawks was catching her breath, sheen of sweat on her reddened skin.

"Good Lord."

"Smiling?"

"Like a baby with a lollipop."

We laughed a little.

Hawks asked me where I was from, the start of her asking personal questions. With a woman personal questions were inevitable. With most women. That had never happened with Arizona.

I searched for a lie but settled on what I knew, had no choice with her whispery and soft breathing on my skin. I put my fingers inside her hair and told her I was born in Charlotte, North Carolina.

She asked, "Who are your people?"

"My people?"

"Family. Where is your family?"

Again I went on a mental safari. Again I stopped searching for a lie and gave her my truth. All I knew was what I had been told, that I had been born in North Carolina. I'd never seen a birth certificate.

I told Hawks the lie that had become my religion. I told her that my father was an army man. That he used to jump out of planes, took sniper training, made Delta Force. That when I was a child he had been sent to Latin America, had been shipped somewhere in Honduras and Nicaragua, so he could deal with arms traders. He met my mother on his sojourn in South America. He had stopped at a brothel in Montego Bay, where my mother was working at the time. Told her that my mother had been the prettiest woman in the whorehouse. And nine months after my daddy eased his load I was born in the city named after King George III's wife.

When a lie is repeated enough, it becomes the truth.

I didn't tell her the other things that Catherine had told me, that my father was strong, used to fight bulls bare-handed, beat them every time. I just knew that after I told Hawks as much of my history as I could bear to repeat, I felt strange. Strange because I had always known that my mother was the queen of lies, and that meant that my entire history, everything my mother said, could have been a lie.

She asked, "You done unloading your wagon or you ready to head on to Dallas?"

"I'm good for another one."

"Good, because when I get heated up I can go awhile."

"Me too."

"Hard to find a man who can keep up with me."

"Oh, I can keep up with you."

"Little less conversation."

Hawks's legs opened for me and I eased on top of her. We kissed, touched, started off slow, ten toes up, ten toes down. Lots of kissing. Lots of nibbling. Lots of soft biting. Lots of soft noises. Soon I had Hawks upside down, her long hair coming loose and tickling my feet as my tongue massaged her clit.

She shivered and moaned for Jesus.

I took her to a chair, put her on her knees, made her hold the back of the chair. I took her from behind. Her hips moved, her ass coming back at me. She was beautiful. Hawks let out a spiritual hallelujah chorus. We had intense sex and had a short nap. There was no cuddling in between. We'd had sex like we were whores to each other, and when it was done, we each moved to our side of the bed, boxers going to their corners, then when it was time the imaginary bell rang and we went at it again.

Hawks said, "You over there asleep?"

"Not asleep."

"Well, are you going to ask me anything about me?"

"Where are you from?"

"Just like a man. Can get some and not care who he's getting it from."

I slapped her ass. "Where are you from, Hawks?"

Hawks told me that she was born in Pittsburgh.

I said, "Three Rivers."

She nodded. "Where the Monongahela and Allegheny rivers kiss and form the Ohio River."

She was proud of Pittsburgh, a city with a skyline of one hundred and fifty-plus high-rise buildings, four hundred and forty-six bridges, two inclined railways, and a pre-Revolutionary fortification. Never would have guessed she was from that part of North America. Hawks had a mild Southern accent and deep Southern ways, but she told me that she had been born a Pittsburgher at St. Francis Medical Center.

She said, "My mother was half and her father, my grandfather, was full-blooded."

"Heard there used to be a lot of Indians in Pittsburgh."

"Native Americans have been here since the Ice Age."

"Can't argue that."

"And we lost the whole country. We never have been good at real estate."

Hawks leaned over, kissed me awhile. My fingers ran through her long hair as I stared in her face, looked at her features. She was beautiful in clothes, but absolutely stunning in the raw.

Her hand was on my erection, her body shifting, moving to climb and mount me.

She moaned. "Mind if I put this big piece of meat back inside me for a while?"

"Go right ahead."

She did, closed her eyes, and bit her lip, put me inside a warm and friendly place.

Hawks moaned as she moved up and down, her movements slow and intense.

I stared up at her beauty and eroticism, moaned, then whispered, "So you're part Indian."

"Native American." She took a ragged breath. "That bother you?"

"Turns me on."

"Glad something about me turns you on. Lord knows you had me turned on when I first looked at you. I was like, good Lord." Hawks moaned a little louder. "I love your voice, the way you talk."

"You love my diction."

"Everything you say makes me tingle all over."

"My diction turns you on."

"Right now just hush and keep giving me the diction without the *-tion* part."

I pulled Hawks's hair as she rode me, looked at her as she moaned, stared into her haunting eyes.

Hawks moved up and down, going up easy, coming down hard, did that over and over. I held on to her, let her move, let her roll and gyrate, move up and down on me, her moans severe.

She slowed and kissed me, sucked my lips, sucked my neck, bit my skin.

She moaned. "How long you gonna be around this part of the country?"

I moved deeper inside her, held her waist, made her sit, tried to fill her up.

I caught my breath. "Leaving Dallas tomorrow . . . spending the night at the Adolphus."

"Always wanted . . . to stay there . . . heard it was beautiful . . . all kinds of fancy-shmancy things in it."

I moaned. "You're more than welcome to stay with me at my fancy-*shmancy* hotel."

"Stop mocking me."

She laughed, the walls of her vagina tightening around me as she laughed.

"You staying at my fancy-shmancy hotel?"

"Sure this won't be enough to unload your wagon?"

"Won't be enough."

"You are one frisky man. I have to be in Houston tomorrow."

"When you leave Dallas?"

"My flight is . . . is . . . is . . . at three . . . on American . . . to George Bush International."

"You coming?"

"About to come . . . about to . . ."

"To the Adolphus."

"Uh-huh uh-huh if you want if you want mmm I can stay mmm I can I can stay the night."

She closed her eyes, her breathing intense, her body trembling, panting.

When she slowed down she swallowed, took a few deep breaths before finally opening her eyes and looking at me, glowing, smiling, her expression vulnerable, her expression sexy, a different Hawks.

She moved and moaned and came, rocked her hips back and forth.

When she was done moaning she stayed on me, caught her breath.

I said, "Maybe we can get cleaned up, go to Sambuca, take in some dinner and music."

"Like on a date?"

"Yeah. Like on a date."

Hawks moved again, became a rocking chair, slow at first, then a little faster. "Damn."

"What?"

"Oh god this is so amazing so amazing so damn amazing."

When we made it to Dallas, Hawks marveled at the suite. Two bathrooms. A living room. Two televisions. Dining room. Then I took her to Crimson in the City on Commerce, bought her some nice clothes to wear, some things by Matt & Nat, Ronen Chen, Lilith, and Independent Art, designers out of Canada, Israel, France, and Japan. I sat to the side and let the owner, a beautiful woman named Stefani, treat Hawks like she was a top model. Hawks loved it. The way she did the girl-talk thing with Stefani, another side of Hawks was being witnessed. Only a few hours back she was visiting a loan shark, bringing his loan sharking days to an end. We put people in the ground, then went on with life as if we were getting off a regular nine-to-five. I shopped, bought myself a few things to get me through the next few days. I usually bought my gear at someplace that ended in *mart* or at the low-end store owned by the Gap.

I thought about how Arizona liked her men, all dressed up. But that day I dressed for Hawks.

Hawks dressed country with an edge and I dressed the same.

Guess I was like tofu, took on the flavor of whatever was around me.

Hawks was the kind of woman who had one drink, that drink being Johnnie Walker Blue on the rocks. She would rarely swear but she laughed at dirty jokes, could close down a bar, and would prefer to listen to Brad Paisley rather than Miles Davis, but she enjoyed listening to Miles just the same.

Later that night, after the jazz and dinner, after foreplay and sex, she had put her head on my chest, the windows open, the lights in downtown Dallas shining like stars. The sex we had that night was different than before. She made love to me like she was my girlfriend. Hawks's Elvis CD was playing like it had been her good-luck charm. We talked about the places we'd been. I was still angry back then. Not that my anger has gone away now, but it was greater back then, not as controlled. No one was following me when I met Hawks, but I had been searching for the whore who had turned me into an assassin.

I was searching for the woman I wanted to put in the ground for the things she had done.

Hawks whispered, "You work a lot, if you don't mind me saying."

"Trying to get a million dollars."

"Why in the world you need that much money?"

I had almost told Hawks, but I didn't reveal my motivation. Lying in bed naked with the scent of one woman on my dick wasn't the right moment to talk about another woman. Didn't tell her about Arizona, the Filipina grifter I had met in a pool hall in Sherman Oaks, California. Kept that to myself.

I said, "I just need a million dollars."

"I don't know what I'd do if I ever had that much money at one time."

Hawks was the opposite of Arizona. That wasn't a bad thing. Just an observation.

She said, "Maybe I can help you out. Throw some work your way."

"What do you have?"

"I have this other job that came through yesterday. I turned it down but you might want to check it out. I can put you in contact with the woman who's ordering the hit. She's a bitter, angry woman."

"Where is the job?"

"In Detroit."

"What do you know so far?"

"Some preacher always in the news, about to run for mayor. Wifey already has her alibi set up and the money is in place. Supposed to be a real easy one. She's been planning her husband's demise for some time. Supplying codes to the alarm. Floor plans. From walk-in to walk-out, five minutes."

I asked her how much the job paid. She told me. The sum was right. I'd pick that job up.

And that would be the job I regretted the most.

Hawks kissed my chest, rubbed my skin, whispering, "This has been the best day of my life."

"Mine too," I said, not knowing what misery was down the road. "Has been a great day for me."

"Don't take my number and promise to call me and don't call."

"I'll call."

"I mean, if you're just unloading your wagon, tell me that you're unloading your wagon and that will be okay, because I needed to unload my wagon too. Been a while since I had this wagon unloaded."

"Hawks, I'll call."

Her voice softened. "Don't leave me waiting like a little girl waiting on her daddy to come back."

I kissed her again. Didn't do much more because this wagon was empty. By the way she moved and touched me, the way she moaned, I could tell she wanted more, wanted it all night.

I put two fingers inside her, touched her on that swollen spot, massaged that magical button.

Not knowing that my life would become convoluted, not knowing I wouldn't call. My own issues had consumed me then, as they consumed me now, left me unable to focus, unable to sleep.

Twelve

death in the shadows

Outside Nashville. Rain still falling, skies dark.

Soaked in mud. Covered in plastic. Checked behind us. No one was following me.

Again Hawks asked, "This trade we're in, does it ever get to you?"

"Let it go, Hawks."

"Have you ever done a job that just messed with your head?"

"Hawks."

"Being a gun for hire. When the cowards hire us to be executioner, does it bother you?"

I didn't care for the direction the forced conversation was going. I gave Hawks some ambiguous answer, then took the reins of the conversation, asked her what work she'd done, tried to understand what had put her in that frame of mind. What we did, if we thought about it, pondered it, if we became too human, if we became less than soldiers on a battlefield, that was no good. So I moved from that conversation into another one. Did that so we wouldn't have to go down that bumpy and uncomfortable road. Hawks was smart enough to know what I was doing.

"Well, you can't mean-mug me and stop me from asking whatever I want to ask. You might not answer, but that sure as hell won't stop me from asking. So it will be revisited, even if that visit is a wash."

Again I asked her what work she had done, trying to find out what had changed her.

She didn't answer. Something about Hawks had changed.

I said, "If you have problems with the work, bail out before you end up having to post bail."

"Can't."

"Why not?"

"It's called food, clothing, and shelter."

"You short on money?"

"Made some bad investments."

"As have we all."

"Had no choice but to come back and pick up a few jobs."

I nodded, let a few seconds move between us before asking, "What did you do in between?"

"I picked up a job working at the Caterpillar office, West End."

My face showed my surprise. "You got a job?"

"Administrative assistant."

"You serious? You work a nine-to-five?"

"I like the job."

"Hold on, you're a secretary?"

"Administrative assistant."

"Same difference."

"The pay is for the shits, but I like the job."

"You work with squares?"

"Like the people. Pittsburgh, remember. I'm hardworking and blue-collar to the bone."

"You're looking good."

"I've put on ten, fifteen pounds."

"It settled in all the right places."

"Go to hell."

She drove to some lofts on the edge of downtown, a place where two bedrooms went for one hundred and ninety thousand, high for Nashville. With the value of the dollar now rivaling the value of the peso, that price was a steal to anybody from overseas dealing in European currency.

She parked and led the way, left me following her like the Creature from the Black Lagoon.

The beauty and the beast.

Hawks started talking again. "Corporate outsourcing. Autism. Strokes. Epilepsy. Tornados. NAFTA. Subprime loans. Makes me wonder what kind of god would allow for all of that mess. I wish Jesus would come back, maybe have a Bible signing over at Barnes and Noble. I'd get in line just to ask him a couple of questions. And to take a picture of us with my camera phone. Put it on my MySpace page next to the ones of me and Keith Urban and Kenny Chesney."

I didn't respond, just walked behind her, sloshed in my shoes.

Then she whispered, "But I'd really want to ask Jesus a question or two. The way the world is now, all this hate, if Jesus decided to come back—he thinks he had it bad the first time. If I was him I'd stay right where I was. Which is probably what he's doing."

After that Hawks took a deep breath, most of what was burning inside her now gone.

She put down some more plastic and I stepped inside her loft, a place with earth-tone walls, exposed brick, fireplace, hardwood floors, and colorful artwork. I took all of my muddied clothing off, let her roll it all up and take it to the Dumpster. By the time Hawks came back I was inside the shower.

Had my head down, rubbing the back of my neck, stress as thick as rope, angst as hard as concrete.

She said, "That's a lot of money."

I'd left the briefcase on the table in the living room, left the case wide open.

I said, "Didn't count it."

"Do men count anything?"

Her sarcastic words aggravated me. I made myself smile, said, "Not really."

"Yours?"

I took a breath. "It is now."

"Where did you get it?"

I took another hard breath, let the water hit my face. "Took it off the crew who was after me."

"Contract money."

"I guessed the same."

"Do I detect a flippant tone?"

"Was just saying that that's pretty obvious."

"Never met a jerk so ungrateful."

"I'm a little stressed at the moment. A few people just tried to kill me."

"And how is that my problem?"

"Yeah, it's contract money."

"They're dealing in cash, no wire transfers."

I mumbled, "Looks that way."

"Somebody wants you in the ground pretty bad."

Again I mumbled. "Give the lady a door prize."

Hawks walked around a moment. "You need temporary transportation?"

"Hard to fly with my wings this wet."

"I'm going to take some of the money. About a thousand."

"Most women try to take half."

"Imagine you can see my middle finger."

"Take a joke."

"What size you wearing?"

I told her.

She asked, "Shoe size?"

I told her that too. She told me she'd be back.

I asked Hawks, "Whose place is this?"

"My husband had it when I met him."

"Husband."

"That's what I said."

"You're married?"

"Was married for a while."

I paused. "When did you get married?"

"About eighteen months ago."

I paused. "Congratulations."

"Don't you sound happy about it."

"You kind of caught me off guard."

"That makes two of us. Never expected to hear from you again."

"Where is he?"

"Don't worry yourself too much. I'm divorced now."

"He in the business?"

"You sure are full of questions all of a sudden."

"For what it's worth, sorry to hear about the divorce."

"My heart wasn't between my legs. Not with him it wasn't."

"Okay."

"He was worthless. Good-for-nothing. He made promises he couldn't keep. Just like my daddy did. Seems like I try to get away but I keep meeting my daddy over and over. Not keeping a promise is the same as lying, if not worse. I hate men who lie whenever they breathe, and most do."

I didn't say anything. Part of me wished I had called her long before now.

But a grifter named Arizona had been in my heart.

Hawks said, "But at least I got this loft in the settlement."

"Real nice place."

"Ain't much, but it's mine now. Well, not really *mine*. It *belongs* to the mortgage company and thirty years of payments belong to me. I have a roof over my head so I guess the divorce wasn't all bad."

"Like I said, sorry to hear."

"But the dumbass got a subprime loan, so the mortgage payments are through the roof."

"Real sorry to hear that."

"Whatever." Hawks moved across the room, her boots clacking against the hardwood floor. "He was half Coharie, part Native American like me. Guess we didn't have enough in common to make it stick. He wasn't much in bed. Not at all. Sizewise or timewise, not much at all no matter how you hold it up and look at it. Can't miss what you can't feel. But at least he knew how to make a damn phone call."

The front door slammed behind her, echoed like the report from a .38.

Yeah, part of me wished I had called her before, but another part of me told me I never should have called Hawks at all. The last part would have been the best voice to listen to.

I hurried into the living room, water dripping from my body, and grabbed my gun.

Then I went back to the shower.

Gun at my side.

Representative of Detroit or an angry ex-husband, I was ready for whoever showed up first.

An hour later Hawks was back with bags from T.J. Maxx. For a moment the name on the bag looked fake, because across the pond the store was *T.K. Maxx*. Either way, same discount clothing store. Hawks had three bags filled with clothes for me. Levi's and a black T-shirt, a button-down collar shirt to wear over that, a light coat, socks, black Calvin Klein underwear, a pair of steel-toe boots.

The change from the money she took was dropped next to the briefcase.

She said, "There is a blue Honda downstairs. Five years old. Dent on the left rear panel."

"Okay."

"It's a worthless piece of crap. Sorry like my ex-husband."

"Okay."

"Leave it at the airport when you finish doing whatever you came here to do."

"Okay."

"Send me a text telling me where you parked it."

"I'll call you."

"I don't need to talk to you. Just send a text."

"Okay, Hawks."

"Lock the door when you leave."

"Okay."

"And lose my number."

"Okay."

"And if I ever call you, please don't answer."

"Hawks."

"Can't stand a man who can't keep his word. Man who can't keep his word ain't no man."

Then Hawks was gone, the door once again slammed like a gunshot, her anger reloaded.

Thirteen

the killer inside me

I didn't take Hawks's Honda.

I cleaned up the mess I had created and left, walked by the Tennessee Performing Arts Center, headed toward Gaylord Entertainment Center, walked down to historic Second Avenue and Printer's Alley, changed directions a few times, and let my paranoia take me toward War Memorial Plaza and Freedom Center. When I was satisfied I doubled back and checked into the Hermitage Hotel. I needed rest, had to get off my feet. Didn't need Hawks caught up in my drama with Detroit. And I didn't need the drama Hawks was issuing. I'd left five thousand on her dining room table, left the money and no note, just sent her a text telling her I was gone, told her thanks. Same as I had done the last time I had seen her. One day. We had been together twenty-four hours back then.

I saw it as something pleasant that had happened, intimacy with no strings, no need to get emotional over one day of fun and one night of liquor and dancing to jazz; if we connected again, cool; if not, cool. I guess Hawks saw that night a different way.

The same way I had seen my nights with a grifter named Arizona in a different way.

Arizona had seen it as intimacy with no strings, necessary maintenance for the body.

One thought of Arizona and memories tried to take root.

Inside my room at the Hermitage I popped a B.C. Powder, washed it down with a Canada Dry, looked at my bruises. The air bag had done a number on me. I cleaned up a little more; the muddied sensation and the rage refused to let my skin go. I wiped down the gun I had, went for another short walk, the skies still ominous, headed toward one of the bridges that went over the muddy Cumberland River. When traffic was at a pause, I tossed that gun into the murky waters. I hurried back toward the Hermitage, felt naked and vulnerable. Cellular up to my ear, I made a call to Konstantin as I moved through wetness. It was a rushed call, one that cut right to the business without giving any details.

I knew they were out there. Somewhere.

Just like the man with the broken nose had been waiting for me at Millennium Bridge.

Just like the man who had attacked me in the Cayman Islands.

Just like the strawberry blonde and the red-haired man had been waiting for me on Shaftesbury.

Just like the team had been in Huntsville.

Each time they did a little better. It was only a matter of time.

Within the hour another car had been delivered to the Hermitage, one that came with wonderful options, like new hardware in the glove compartment. I moved like a man with a vendetta, trying to prove myself worthy. The sting from Death, that agony, never went away.

Same as the sting from when Hawks had tried to knock the left side of my face to the right.

A few hours later I paid a visit to an exec at Sony BMG, fulfilling that contract over on Seventeenth Avenue in Music Square, an area filled with Victorian-style mansions, students from Vanderbilt jogging in the rain, women pushing strollers, and men walking dogs under gray skies with their umbrellas held high. The customer wanted it to look like an accidental overdose, another cocaine binge. And in the end it would look just like that, the end result a heart attack, an adverse effect of ingesting too much snow. I closed that account, then drove to the Malls at Green Hills, the area that was Nashville's Buckhead, a come-to-life fantasyland where housewives spent their days shopping and getting their nails and hair done while a full-time nanny raised their two-point-five children, staying busy while their hardworking husbands spent their extra time with escorts, clandestine meetings at the Hermitage.

I headed down to a Joseph-Beth bookstore, sat near the children's section, not reading, just thinking that a few hours ago I was being run off the road and bullets were being sprayed into my vehicle like I was public enemy number one. Problems plagued my mind, angst and old fears rising up. For a while I looked over real estate brochures, focused on that crumbling economy to take my mind off other things. Read about the homes in Green Hills and Spring Hill. That added stress. I wanted a home. Giving myself roots had caused problems. I'd been on the move so long I had grown weary, tired of the nights spent traveling down darkened roads, sleeping in beds in Hiltons, Super 8 motels, and every type of hotel or hostel in between. I dropped the brochures, put that need aside, and watched families, saw the kids who were with their parents, kids being read to by their real mothers and their real fathers. A chill attacked me, made me wonder who my mother was, made me wonder who my father was.

X.

Y.

Z.

I put in a call to my contact at DNA Solutions. A woman. An old friend. I left her a message, told her the package was a rush job, asked her to give it top priority. I knew she would. Some old lovers were priceless.

I wanted it rushed because I didn't know how many more sunrises I might survive.

I stared at my latte. Sipping the latte would be a big deal for me. It would be a big deal to just take one sip. As I raised the cup my cellular rang. I put the cup back down without tasting a drop. It was Konstantin. I answered with strength and confidence. Konstantin told me he was in New York, down at Park Avenue and Eighteenth, had just finished working a contract and had just crawled inside a Yellow Cab.

Konstantin told me he was calling because another job had popped up in Nashville.

I took a deep breath, rubbed my eyes, and told him, "Call Hawks."

"Hawks turns down a lot of work. Had good work in Columbus; somebody at Victoria's Secret was pissed at some upstart lingerie company, wanted to take out the competition's CEO. Had three or four jobs in Buckeye territory. A Nationwide thing. A White Castle contract. She passed on them all."

"She's hurting for money and passing on work."

"Her choice. To be honest, I'm beginning to become a little concerned about her."

"I'm listening."

"There was one at Ohio State, parent wanted to put her own kid down, kid was a major slacker and disappointment and the parent paid a mint to initiate a retroactive abortion on the boy. The kid was in his seventh year of college, living off his mother, hanging out on Buckeye Nation Lane with the college grads and the population that was gentrifying the neighborhood. I mean, the kid was a loser, but I didn't see it as a reason to put a kid in the ground. But that was what the customer wanted."

"Lots of people dead for no good reason. Wouldn't be the first, won't be the last."

"Kid was a liberal arts major at OSU. The mother was a surgeon at McConnell Heart Hospital."

"Familial hate. Nothing new there either."

"Job paid well. Told Hawks there was a safe house in Short North on High Street, another at Heartsbridge condos, had whatever she needed next door to Luigi's Pawnshop. All she had to do was walk in and walk out, no more than three days to do it all. She could've blown time, could've had a beer at the Elevator, or gone to Gaswerks and had drinks with the Buckeyes, or gone to a concert at PromoWest. Those are the kinds of things Hawks loves to do. Long story short, Hawks turned it all down."

"Sounds like you know the area."

"Oh yeah. Whenever I go there I go to the Mug N Brush and get a shave. Down in the college area, right before Clintonville. Great place. The guy there, he does a shave like a work of art. And if you ever want to get some tattoos, I mean real nice artwork, this guy Jeff, his work is phenomenal."

My mind was on what Konstantin had said before.

I asked, "The kid, his mom put him down?"

"Don't know who she used, but she had the kid euthanized."

"How?"

"An explosion."

"Car."

"Just so happens there was a faulty gas line at the kid's apartment."

"Yeah, that will make an explosion."

"Blew the kid into kibbles and bits. Whoever did it made it look like an accident."

I nodded. "Cold-blooded."

"Cold-blooded world out there."

"Sure is."

"And the coldest of the cold come to us cold-blooded motherfuckers to do business."

"That they do."

"Strange thing happened after that kid was killed in that *accident*."

"What was that?"

"They found the kid's mom dead. Drowned in her bathtub. Ruled an *accidental* drowning."

"*Accidental*."

"That's what I said. Healthy, rich woman found *accidentally* drowned in her own bathtub."

"No sign of forced entry."

"All doors and windows were locked from the inside."

"Suicide?"

"She had cruises and vacations in Switzerland planned."

We paused, a lot being said in the silence.

Konstantin said, "Almost as strange as the time I sent you down to Texas to work with Hawks. She gets there and the guy who ordered the hit was found drowned in his bathtub, so there was no hit."

"Oh, yeah. I had forgotten about that one."

"Well, I haven't. Then this doctor thing, *accidentally drowning* in a bathtub the same way the guy in Killeen *accidentally drowned* in a bathtub, needless to say that got me to wondering."

Another pause.

Konstantin asked, "Have you talked to Hawks?"

"Called her." I swallowed, pushed my lips up in a smile. "Had a problem after Huntsville."

"What kind of problem?"

"Detroit again. An ambush that ended in my favor."

"How did Detroit know where you were?"

"She's good."

"Don't tell me the same ones from London trailed you across the pond."

"New people. Two men and another woman."

That was all I said, didn't tell him they had tried to gun me down, kept it rough and rugged, remaining the Gideon who owned no doubts or fears.

I asked, "The other job here in Nashville, what is it?"

He said it was a fresh contract on the board president of a condo association, a woman who had turned into a dictator, and the neighbors wanted her removed. The target was controlling delinquency reports, a bitch in high heels when challenged. Somebody had passed the hat and taken up a collection.

I took the job.

Konstantin said, "Gotta run. Have to make a stop. Wife wants me to pick her up some things from this health food store. Have to make a quick stop and take care of my honey-dos."

We disconnected, ended the call, and I stared at the world, eyes wide open, seeing nothing.

My mind on the shit I needed to let go of. But I couldn't.

None of them knew I had died in London. None knew I had failed. No one but me.

More than a few nights that failure returned to me in my dreams, modified in its own horrific way. I felt the plastic bag over my head, my hands and legs bound by duct tape. Plastic was over my head but I could see, with a clearness that rivaled HDTV, the clearest of all horrors. The woman from Detroit was there, standing over me. And as I died, she danced. In my dream I could feel the capillaries breaking in my eyes, light receding toward a moment of permanent darkness. I'd wake up panting, sweating.

Anger rose inside me, the kind that made veins rise as hands became fists and trembled.

I had died. I had failed. I wasn't invulnerable, invincible, or perfect.

I had been lucky. It was nothing but fucking luck. A rabbit's foot. A horseshoe.

That failure would haunt me forever, that ghostly sensation going with me to my grave.

That was what I was thinking as I left Joseph-Beth, sipping on my latte, on my way to visit the board president of a condo association, a woman I would go after like she was my problem from Detroit.

Fourteen

the damned

Her moans were long and winding, her swarthy lover's stroke ambitious, steady, and intense. Red Stripe beer, weed, and E in her bloodstream, every sense magnified in a wonderful way. Her young lover went deep inside her, and that depth felt good. His strong hands squeezed her backside and he pulled out to the edge, went deep again. His stroke made her moan as she grabbed the edge of the bed, released falsetto sounds. He moved his hands to the bends of her knees, pushed her knees back up to the sides of her head, went in and out of her so fast, so deep, his stroke steady.

He slowed down, smiled at her as he talked dirty to her in dialect. She moaned loud, talked erotic in English. He stroked her like he wanted to get nominated for a porn award.

She cursed.

She was losing it, so messed up.

Her young lover hit spots that caused tears to flow. So turned on.

He sucked her nipples, put fingers in places fingers shouldn't be; all of that badness felt too damn good. He gave her chills. Everything felt so surreal. So damn wonderful.

In bed she was so weak. So submissive. Sex made her feel so fragile, so dominated.

"Yuh wan' me fuck you sweet like dis nuh?"

"Yeah, yeah, shit yeah."

"Dis black dick sweet you nuh?"

"Yeah, yeah, shit yeah."

"Tun ova you pan you belly so me cyan fuck you backway."

"I don't . . . I don't . . ."

"Me wan' pull you hair an' reach right up inside da pussy dey. Me wan' ride you, wan' drive me cock right up and lef it dey, den fuck you long and hard, drive me skin up 'gainst you."

"I don't . . . don't . . . understand a word you're saying."

He flipped her over, put her breasts and face deep into the white pillow. She caught her breath, got comfortable, turned her face so she didn't suffocate, anticipating pain and pleasure. Her young lover positioned himself behind her, eased back inside, gripped her short hair, and stroked hard, rode her, moved in deep and held, filled her up, drove her insane as she cried and moved against him. He made her beg. She begged for him to fuck her. He gave her long strokes, his skin slapping against hers.

Her cellular rang. The ringtone she had given her husband.

The call went to voice mail.

Her young lover changed positions, grabbed her and pulled her rear up high, did some move that had him squatting over her, went inside her at a brand-new angle, stroked and grunted. So damn intense. Like he wanted to crawl inside her. She let her young lover twist and turn her; he took her in so many positions, positions she had never been in, went inside her at angles that made sex feel brand-new, moved her around until she ended up on top of him. She squatted over her young lover. Made sure his condom was intact before she took him back inside. Her lover, a bona fide condom filler. Slim, toned, all muscles and dick. She moved up and down fast and hard, caught her breath, turned and rode him backward, moaned when he slapped her ass, wanted to scream when he put a finger of his left hand inside her ass, trembled, her lover finger-fucking her as she fucked him as hard as she could.

Her cellular rang again. Same ringtone.

She couldn't stop coming. When one orgasm ended another took control of her. She moaned and cursed and held on to whatever she could hold on to. Her young lover moaned and cursed and said things in dialect she didn't understand, his back arching as his dick stretched her open.

She held him until she stopped thrusting. Held him until she stopped coming.

Her lover came and she was glad, glad he would stop making her come like that.

She rolled away from him, rolled too far, began falling off the bed, and released a yell. As she tumbled his strong hands caught her, hands that were rough from years of hard work and labor. His callused hands pulled her back to the bed, hands that reminded her of the life she had left behind, her life as a little girl, a life of poverty and endless struggling, more pain than pleasure. Her heart raced as her young lover touched her sweaty side, pulled her toward him, panting and laughing, talking in his dialect. He moved up and looked in her eyes, his smile so wide. He sucked the fingers on his right hand.

"Me min haffu lick me fingas; cyan' waste de juice."

She caught her breath, looked at her watch. Almost three in the morning.

He had been pleasing her off and on since the sun went down, had been fucking her into the middle of forever, her rented lover a young man who had the stamina of a horse, a dick like one too.

He sat up, held his pride and joy in his hand, still hard enough to make her come again. She reached over, held it in her hand, measured its girth with her thumb and finger, and then measured her wrist. Becoming soft he was still larger than the circumference of her wrist.

She asked, "How you manage to stay that hard and fuck so long?"

"Me get some pills."

"Viagra?"

"Dem betta dan Viagra. Mek me last forever."

She closed her eyes, her insides still trembling. Nipples and clit swollen.

The fan blew across sweaty flesh. She was on a modest bed in a modest room in a modest hotel surrounded by a never-ending tropical garden that was a strip of sand away from the Caribbean Sea.

She said, "You'd better get home to your family."

"Soon."

"Where does your wife think you are?"

"Up de road. Club Rush."

"If you give your woman sex like that, I know she will be up waiting for you."

He laughed. "Party no get hot 'til tree. Dem party 'til de sun rise up."

She moaned. "Damn. You have a steel pipe in that thing or what?"

He laughed harder.

"Goddamn, you have one hell of a cock."

She opened her eyes, heard birds flitting through the foliage, moonlight shining through the palms, the song of the tree frogs and waves lapping on the beach. Trade winds rustled through the foliage. Her cellular rang again. Her husband's ringtone. Calling over and over. At three in the morning.

Matthew was calling her back. Probably pissed that she hadn't left the island as planned.

She didn't answer. The sound of E and Red Stripe and sex would be in her voice.

Her rented lover passed her the joint; she shook her head, had had enough.

She scratched her legs, felt the irritation and swell of multiple mosquito bites.

Her lover was on his back. His chest rose and fell at a fast rate. The condom was still on. The condom was full and heavy with the fluids of life. She took it off her young lover. Inspected it.

She said, "Is this leaking?"

"Ee neva use."

"What does that mean?"

He looked up. "It brand-new."

She said, "I think this condom is leaking. It's milky on the outside. Come milky."

"One new condom haffu good. Ee safe. Ee nar go break. Guaranteed."

"It's brand-new."

"Me sure a fu you cum pan de condom. You does cum hard and plenty. When you start fu come, you mek one man feel real good. You fuck good bwoy. Me shoulda gee you subben fu how good you fuck. White woman doesn't fuck so. You move dem hips and you ass real fucking good. You know how fu wine like one island gyal."

"I have no idea what you just said."

Her young lover chuckled, closed his eyes, and nodded, a big smile on his face.

A small fear rose inside her. The biggest fear of all.

She staggered to the bathroom and flushed the condom, made sure his DNA was gone bye-bye, turned, sat on the toilet, grabbed a *Daily Observer*, read it as she waited for her water to flow. *Daily Observer*. Was looking for shoe sales, but saw a personal ad in the back. White British man had an ad looking for a very attractive black female; she had to be able to live in with him, no ties, no kids, and help manage his hotel in Dickenson Bay. The Brit wanted to pay between two thousand and four thousand E.C. depending on her attractiveness, that price negotiable. She did the math in her head. Divided by 2.7. That was between 740 and 1,480 dollars a month. Roughly one pair of Blahniks every full moon to move in and be an old British man's day worker and nighttime bed warmer, sex-for-hire not mentioned, just reading between the lines.

She whispered, "No wonder they hate you tight-suit-wearing bastards."

Foster care. Being shuffled around. Abused. Men who wanted to pay her to suck their dicks.

She did good, got out lucky. Considering. Could've been worse.

She flushed the toilet, turned on the shower, hopped in, and cleansed herself.

She ran water over her hair, her face, did that with warm water, then made the water cold.

Her husband was on her mind.

When she made it back to the bedroom her young lover was sitting up, wide awake and tipsy.

"So many damn mosquitoes. They didn't bite me all day, now they are all over me."

He shook his head, spoke slower. "Dem na like day or col'. E dark an' warm in ya."

His dialect didn't sound so foreign now. She understood most of what he said. *They don't like the day or cold. It's dark and warm in here.* She grabbed some repellent, closed the windows, sprayed the rooms with Baygon, turned the air conditioner on high, and as the unit rattled to life, she sprayed OFF! on her legs and arms, sprayed her ankles, between her toes, repeated that two more times.

Her young lover said, "Misses Robinson."

She didn't look up, not at first, and then she remembered that was what she had told him to call her. *Mrs. Robinson.* The name of that character from that movie with Dustin Hoffman and Anne Bancroft. She couldn't remember the name of the movie. Only that the song from that movie was about the woman who had bedded a boy young enough to be her son. She smiled. Almost broke out singing. *Here's to you, Mrs. Robinson, Jesus loves you more than you will know.*

He touched her skin, touched three spots, spots that were not mosquito bites, one on her left arm, one on her right shoulder, another on her right hip. She felt self-conscious, but she didn't jump.

"Dem look lakka tree bullet hole. Ah who shot you?"

"Nobody living."

He rubbed her healed wounds, touched where three memories had pierced her skin.

She reached for his penis, began stroking him in slow motion, made him thicken in her hand, made him moan, did that to take him away from her injuries, did that to get away from her memories.

He asked, "You wan' fu go one nodda round?"

"How much?"

He laughed, raised the joint, and grinned. "All inclusive."

She laughed at the way he imitated her accent. "Let me use the bathroom first."

All of this for twenty dollars U.S. This was a bargain, mosquitoes and all.

When she was done she stood at the foot of the bed, admiring her lover. He was naked, body young and toned, firing up another joint, sipping his warming beer, and smiling at her like she was perfect. Her husband used to look at her like that, before they had married.

Then her young lover sat there, beer in one hand, joint in his mouth, wood rising.

She wanted to take him to America with her, hide him away, have him to herself.

She turned the television on. *Sex and the City* was on.

She said, "I'm going to meet them. All of them. Carrie, Miranda, Charlotte, and Samantha. I'm going to the movie premiere. It's in New York. I'm going to meet everybody on the show. I'll be wearing diamond mink eyelashes. And Blahniks. Can't wait. Already excited. Bet it'll be the best day in my life."

Her young lover wasn't paying attention. Too busy nursing his burning tree.

She said, "Take a quick shower with me. Let's get cleaned up. Let's go to the beach."

He did as she said; walked to the shower, allowed her to wash him down, cleanse him from head to toe as he continued sipping his Red Stripe. She kissed his chest, sucked his nipples, held his firm ass.

He had the nicest ass. Taut and round.

She made sure he was fresh and clean, old lovemaking washed away.

All DNA sent down the drain.

She dried her skin, put on the black linen pants she had in her bag, slip-on sandals, a dark T-shirt, did that while he pulled on his shorts and sandals and tugged his RUDE BOY T-shirt over his head.

She smiled at him, a little nervous, as she grabbed a hotel towel, stuffing it inside her bag.

She said, "Enough with the bed. I want to do it outside. I've never done it on a beach."

Holding his hand, sneaking past the red phone booth, she paused and stared back at the front office of the hotel. It was dark, the office having closed long before midnight. The restaurant, Coconut Grove, that sat on the edge of the Caribbean was pitch-black as well. She didn't see a light on in any of the hotel rooms. Most island businesses were closed now, all but a few employees at home with their lovers and families.

She looked out toward the quay for a moment, where she had Jet Skied and dropped everything she had used or stolen, then led her anxious lover up the footpath, sand getting inside her sandals, exfoliating her once-perfect pedicure. She held her lover's hand tighter with each step, not talking, the cool breeze and sound of the ocean like music. It was as if they were the only people in the world.

She asked him what the people who lived here did for fun, not the tourists.

He told her there were a lot of political protests, some about the roads that had been built around the cricket stadium, a stadium that was built by the Chinese and not maintained, lots of marches, barbecues, parties, going to clubs, visiting friends, church, raffles, fund-raisers, going to the cinema in the evening.

She wasn't listening.

She was tingling.

Thinking she had never been fucked like that.

She wanted to keep him. Have him for her selfish needs, no matter what it cost.

She kept to the edges where the water met the sand, where the water washed over her footprints, the edges so dark nothing could be seen, they couldn't be seen. The couples' resort was as dark and quiet as Antigua Village. They walked close to a mile to where that stretch of the beach ended, beyond another section where Jet Skis were rented, beyond another restaurant on the beach, walked to where it all ended at the base of a cliff. Holding hands, fingers tracing palms, she let him lead her deeper into the darkness.

She wondered what it was like to do it in the sea, waves smashing into her body.

The constant roar of the Caribbean waves stealing all sounds.

She smiled at her young lover. A slice of heaven for twenty U.S. dollars.

Felt like he had given her a year of therapy in a few hours. The E had helped. But the flip side of taking E, she hated that part. Suicide

Tuesday. When the E began to wear off, the crashing, the depressed feeling, the sadness, being scared to death, feeling empty. On E, sex was so incredible.

Then the dehydration, how her body temperature soared, the way her brain felt fried.

Her young lover put his tongue on the palm of her hand, sucked her fingers.

He touched her, kissed her neck, again rising like wood, pushing against her as he pulled her linen pants down. She took the towel from her bag, put it on the sand. He eased her down on her back, spread her legs, his locks tickling her flesh as he kissed her knees, her legs, and sucked her toes.

In his dialect he told her he wanted to take her to a special place to-morrow, said he wanted her to rent a Jeep so he could drive her across the roads behind Falmouth Harbour, past a basketball field, Falmouth's cricket fields, and beyond the horse stables, a journey that would take them up a rocky hill past homes that were isolated and situated on the edges of the bush, leave civilization behind and take to treacherous and natural roads steep and worn by rain, no road signs, just a rugged path-way going deep up into the mountains, the view of the sea and harbors magnificent from up there, before descending into country that looked like the land before time, a section of Antigua that was unspoiled, parts of it still occupied by wild boar, a difficult ride that would end thirty minutes later at Rendezvous Bay, a hidden treasure along the southern shore of the island, a place few had ever seen, sand so pure and undis-turbed that each step in its softness would allow her feet to sink into the sand up to her ankles, to her shins in some spots. He licked her orgasm, told her Rendezvous Bay was a place people went to escape the world.

She moaned.

He told her it was a beach they could go to and be naked all day. He kissed her skin and said they could make love in the sun, have sex out in the open, beach towels and the sand becoming their mattress. He put his tongue against her flesh and she imagined her lover eating her out on the shores of Antigua with the Atlantic Ocean lapping at their feet. He put many more kisses on her skin, whispered that he would give her sex from morning until night, give her any kind of sex she wanted, make her come over and over, pleasure her through the night if she wanted to stay there, camp and sleep under the stars.

She asked, "How much would that little fantasy cost me?"

"One hundred."

"Eastern Caribbean?"

"U.S. 'Round two seventy E.C."

She hummed. "All day?"

"Whole day."

"Are you serious?"

"Whole night if dat a wha' u want."

That made her tingle. Imagined her young, enthusiastic lover pleasing her. Sex from morning until night, coming over and over, receiving pleasure throughout the night, underneath the stars, camping and sleeping under the constellations, the roar of waves, maybe riding him and coming with the rising of the sun.

He went down on her like he owned her, licking her, making her moan, tears trying to rise again.

Her young lover was a damn good salesman.

He licked, told her he was free all week, licked, said he could show her around the island, licked, said he could take her out on peddle boats, licked her with a fast-moving tongue, then told her they could scuba dive, swim with stingrays, licked figure eights and said they could go into the rain forest and do a zip-line adventure. All she cared about was what he was doing at that moment, the way he used his mouth.

She moaned. "Love the way you are eating my pussy . . . damn, you are eating my pussy."

It felt like he was making love to that part of her with his mouth, lips, and tongue, so meticulous, licking her as if he knew her, taking his time, not at all what she had expected from a boy so young.

Her hands held his strong hair; she sent her hips up into his tongue, a tongue that went deep. She gazed up at the sky. A million stars. Had never seen that many stars at once. Not while coming. Had an orgasm and imagined the same thing happening all day and night at Rendezvous Bay. Getting like she was Heather Graham in *Killing Me Softly*. Helen Hunt in *The Waterdance*. Halle Berry in *Monster's Ball*.

She could get fucked repeatedly like Halle Berry in *Monster's Ball*.

Taboo and intense. Sunrise to sunset. Naked on an uninhabited beach.

All for one hundred dollars.

She whispered, "Take your clothes off. Let me get some protection."

Her teeth chattered, her eyes fluttered.

As he undressed she reached inside her bag.

Lying back, eyes closed, a tree rising between his legs, her lover never saw the gun.

One soft pop and a small hole opened in the center of his head.

Death came quickly.

She hurried, pulled her linen pants back on. Sand stuck to her damp skin. She grabbed the hotel's towel. Had to push his dead weight away. Rolled him over on his erection. Gathered the hotel towel. Picked up her bag. Stood in darkness. Listening. Heard nothing that caused alarm.

She whispered, "*The Graduate.*"

The name of the movie with Mrs. Robinson had been *The Graduate*.

She walked back through the darkness, heart racing, but her pace as casual as it had been on the initial journey. She kept to where the water met the sand. Waves erased her footprints. Darkness concealed her. The only noise she heard was the same din that had masked the sound of her handgun being discharged, the sweet sound of Caribbean waters as they crashed into the shores.

She went over everything in her mind. He didn't leave the beach with her. No one had seen him come to her room at the Siboney. In the shower she had washed all of her DNA away from his body.

Weed, lager, and ecstasy in his bloodstream. Bullet in his head. His wares missing.

She walked back to the Siboney, picked up the inexpensive briefcase her rented lover had left behind, wiped down all he had touched, then carried his merchandise to the property on the other side of the hotel, Buccaneer Cove. She listened again, looked around again. No one in the world but her. She threw the contents of the briefcase into the sea, wiped the briefcase down, dropped it in a trash container. She wiped down her backup gun and threw it as far into the darkness as she could.

It hit a roaring wave and went to the bottom of the sea, emerald waters sparkling in the moonlight.

Again she looked up at the stars. She folded her arms, held herself beneath the constellations.

London. The missed shot on the yacht. The unnecessary shoot-out on All Saints Road.

Now this mess. This couldn't be justified. This wasn't a contract. This had been murder.

But she didn't want Matthew to find out she had cheated on him.

Just like she had done in Barbados.

She got ahold of herself, slipped back inside her rented room, wiped everything down twice, gathered her things, and left the room key on the dresser. Then she looked at the key again. It had the number twenty-nine attached to it. This was room 8. She had the keys mixed up. She found the right key and left it, took the key to room 29, and put it back in her pocket. She cursed, ran her hands over her hair. Again she'd almost fucked up. Almost. She crept downstairs, took to the dirt and gravel parking lot, and got on her black scooter, this tropical part of the world having very few streetlights, this part of the world so dark.

Down the road at a club called Rush there were a lot of cars, people still partying. But where she was there was no traffic. No headlights. Antigua Yacht Club, where she had another room, was a long way away. There was no GPS on the island and not many streets had their names posted, so she had to drive by landmark, hope she remembered how to get to the bottom of the island from where she was.

She shivered and sang, "To the left, to the left . . ."

She sang Beyoncé's song as a reminder to keep to the left side of the road as she turned right and went away from Sandals, passing the

Anchorage Inn, one of the three KFCs on the island, Percival's Texaco, down Popeshead Street and through the red-light district, passed Wendy's and Burgers 2 Go, then got lost when the street ended, saw a big church up to her left, but turned right, made her way through downtown, again at Heritage Quay, recognized the area, headed up St. Marys, found her way toward Independence Avenue. She knew she would have to fight darkness and narrow roads that had potholes, had to travel from town through areas that had herds of goats, livestock that might run into the streets without notice. And compete with cars that raced by her, others that came right at her at lightning speed, zooming like they wanted to run her off the road. She was driving through a pitch-black obstacle course, nervous and shaking as she maneuvered from the northeast to the southern portion of the island.

A pond was to her left, then she passed by Sir Vivian Richards Street, Acme Preschool, some place called City Motors, and a Latter-Day Saints church, became nervous, and pulled off to the side for a moment, had to because someone was riding her back tire.

Her cellular rang.

Again her husband was calling. His calling was relentless. She didn't answer.

She let traffic go by, then pulled back onto the narrow road, nervous because of the drugs in her body, nervous because the sides of the roads were uneven and open; the drainage area to the left was like a small ditch, but to her the opening looked cavernous.

She pulled out, zoomed into the wrong lane, the American lane.

She screamed at herself, *"To the left . . . to the left . . ."*

Heart thumping in her chest, she swerved back into the left lane as headlights zoomed at her.

She had to keep away from the edges so her back end didn't drop off the road and have her sucked into a concrete ditch, had to swerve to the right into the bright lights of oncoming traffic because of stopped cars, people who had pulled over to chat, no turn signal being used to warn they were about to park and obstruct traffic, then she had to swerve back into the left lane, shivered and tensed and did the same zigzag dance all the drivers before her had done. A stream of headlights tried to blind her, remarkable traffic as she came up on Antigua Plumbing and Hardware, then she curved to the right back toward All Saints Road, people practically walking in the middle of the streets, forcing traffic to move into the other lanes, passed a rum shop with a Heineken front, came up to Texaco, a familiar landmark.

"To the left . . . to the left . . ."

She made it to All Saints Road, took that snaking road through sleeping village after sleeping village, her speed down so she didn't get thrown by a speed bump, finally came up on Our Lady of Perpetual Help, steered to the left, headed toward Liberta, passed a tranquil police station. Cold air made her shiver. She focused on making her way downhill, the darkness and the ride terrifying. More cars zoomed around her, her eyes straight ahead, focused on getting back into Falmouth. She sped by Rhodes Lane, the spot where she had left a man dead in front of T's Ice Cream Parlour. Where she had almost been killed because of her mistakes. On top of her fear, from St. John's to Clarks Hill to Buckleys to Swetes, she had smelled the scent from her young lover rising from her flesh. From Liberta to Falmouth to Cobbs Cross to Falmouth Harbour she felt her young lover between her legs, opening her up, moving her around the bed, going deep, fucking her like he had fifty years of sexual experience.

She made it back to Antigua Yacht Club, parked underneath the orange and yellow sign in front of Sunseakers, sat on her scooter facing the row of multimillion-dollar superyachts resting comfortably in the marina.

Red Stripe, weed, and E were dancing in her system. All senses magnified.

The wind was blowing hard now, so hard that the national flag that stood over the docks was flapping with a fervor that made noises, echoes like people running across a wooden floor.

She took a thousand deep breaths, did her best to shake off the buzz.

The boy.

She thought about the boy.

And she thought about her husband, the man she wanted to get home to.

Then she called Matthew. She called the assassin known as El Matador.

He answered, "Where the fuck are you? I've been calling you for hours."

His voice was deeper than most, very masculine, very powerful, always threatening.

She said, "I was asleep. Just woke up. What's the problem?"

"Don't tell me you're still in your hotel room in your bed."

"Didn't I say I just woke up? Still in bed. Needed some sleep. Just waking up. Was up all night doing that job over in Falmouth Harbour. Had to hide out. Closed that contract at the crack of dawn."

"Is that right?"

"Where are you? I called you and got no answer."

"I was at the airport. Was getting on a plane."

"Where did you go?"

"Antigua. It's in the damn West Indies. You heard of that place? Island about an hour south of Puerto Rico. Three hundred and sixty-five beaches. That's where my wife has been all damn week."

She paused, then let out a nervous chuckle. "You're . . . joking, right?"

"I'm here. Been here walking around in Falmouth Harbour for hours."

"Where are you right now?"

"Antigua *motherfucking* Yacht Club. Room twenty-*fucking*-nine. Sitting on a *goddamn* four-poster bed that has a *damn* mosquito net pulled back so I know I can see what the *fuck* I see. And I see an *empty* four-poster bed, an *empty* bathroom, an *empty* patio, and an *empty* kitchen. But hell, maybe I'm wrong, because I know I didn't marry a *goddamn* liar. So I guess if I'm in your room and *you're in the goddamn bed*, just waking up, then either I am blind as a *fucking* bat or you must be *fucking* invisible."

Fifteen

the world gone mad

Cuts and bruises were on my swollen hands.

Pain in my ribs, wondered if one was cracked. Or if a lung was punctured. An abrupt wave of chills arrived to keep my pains from feeling lonely. My weakness was both abrupt and intense, only magnified a thousand times. Red streaks and pus, a lot of swelling on my injuries.

I looked over at my passenger. My contract. A man I had captured in Birmingham. He moved like he was waking up. In my lap was a stun gun. I zapped him again. He jerked and his lights went out.

Somewhere between Georgia and Alabama, I was a bird in a $140,000 plane. Skies smooth, stepping at ninety-five knots, airspeed that translated to about a dime over the century mark on a car's speedometer, but with the tailwind I could easily add forty miles per hour to that number.

I took my eyes away from the instrument panel long enough to glance at the terrain; snow, winter-brown grass, and barren trees down below. Weather at about forty Fahrenheit on the ground. Up here at twelve thousand feet, much colder. I was flying a Cessna Skyhawk, one of the few things in life that gave me joy.

My passenger was stirring again, disoriented, moaning like he was in severe pain.

My chills were getting worse, the pain doing the same; both had me in a bear hug. Sweat dampened my clothes. Underneath my jeans and sweatshirt I had enough bruises to show that my life had been a war. No matter how many B.C. Powders I took, the pain wouldn't let me go.

I didn't zap him again. He could wake up now. He groaned like a bear coming out of hibernation.

My attention went back to the Cessna. The Lycoming engine was running perfectly. I kept the two-seater straight and level, identified waypoints, kept track of timing the distance between them. Had been a while since I took to the air. Had been too long. I loved the way the 172 responded to my whims, like a woman after she was two drinks deep, willing and ready to do whatever I asked.

Smooth moans, very responsive, like Hawks after a glass of Johnnie Walker Blue.

Then I thought about her. The one I had tried to get a million dollars for.

I'd never been able to control a grifter named Arizona the way I could control a Cessna.

Garmin G1000 flat-panel avionics suite. Leather seats. Air bags.

Was like being inside a BMW Z4 with wings. Defying gravity, the ultimate high.

My passenger struggled, finally opening his eyes, opened them with a dreamy surprise.

I struggled with my pain, fought back, and stayed focused.

My passenger coughed and spoke in disbelief. *"I'm in a goddamn airplane."*

"Don't scream."

"This is unlawful kidnapping."

My passenger was an actor, short and thin-framed, old enough to be my father. Not a movie star, one of those Broadway actors. His last and greatest work being the lead in a play based on Steinbeck's novel *Of Mice and Men*. I'd never heard of him, but most people hadn't heard of those working on Broadway. He'd left New York in a hurry, left ahead of the police. I'd trailed him to Birmingham, where he had gone to hide after committing his crime; found him walking in Five Points, his smooth face now covered in a beard, his black hair now dyed blond;

trailed him into a pool hall on Twentieth Street. He was with friends but stepped outside to smoke, went outside alone. I had walked up behind him and introduced him to a stun gun, lugged him to the car I had waiting. Before I could dump him inside two of his friends had come out. We battled a short and brutal battle. They took me to the ground in the alley, but in the end, after a flurry of elbows and knees, they were both left in that alley, neither alive. My passenger in the car, I had headed for the airport where Konstantin had this plane ready, my exit strategy to get me out of the epicenter of the area that held some of North America's most heinous history. Bringing the passenger was improvisation. He was secured; duct tape was on his wrists and feet. And between the duct tape on his feet and hands was more duct tape, enough to keep him immobile.

He said, "They sent you to find me."

I told him his sins. "Sexual abuse and sodomy."

"Fine." He shifted in his discomfort, almost smiling. "Take me back to New York."

"Rape by use of drugs, rape of an unconscious person, sodomy by anesthesia or controlled substance, and sodomy of an unconscious victim."

"Don't believe all you read in the funny papers. Doesn't matter. I will do like James Barbour, strike a deal, enter a plea of misdemeanor counts of endangering the welfare of a minor."

I opened and closed my aching hands. "Is that right?"

"Precedence has been set. I'll get two months in jail. If I go to jail at all."

"Over twenty counts of having sex with a minor."

He huffed. "Reduced to soliciting a minor for child pornography."

"Ten counts of videotaping the acts."

"All thrown out."

I echoed what he said. "Two months."

"Two months in jail and a few years of probation."

"The girl was fourteen."

"I'll make a public allocution. We had a relationship, for Christ's sake."

"You're forty-five. How could you possibly have a *relationship* with a fourteen-year-old?"

"She gave me the clap. Did you know that? The whore was a walking communicable disease."

"You have no shame."

"Christ, you make it sound like I urinated on the girl."

"Answer my question. How can a forty-five-year-old man—"

"Oh, spare me. They are inhaling shoe polish, rubber cement, getting high before they make it to middle school. Kids from the suburbs are having oral sex before they learn how to French kiss. Blacks and Latinos are in the backseats of cars smoking weed and copulating before they can spell *condom*."

"With each other." Sweat rolled down my face. "Not with old men."

"Kidnapping me. You think this little stunt will matter?"

"You think it won't?"

"I have money. Jail is for the poor. I'll be out of New York before the week is up."

"That kid . . . what you did fucked that kid up." I panted. "Self-esteem issues. Panic attacks. You abuse a kid and you never know what the kid will turn out to be. Are you listening to me?"

"All this will go away as if it never happened. It's not like I'm a damn politician."

I whispered, "You have no remorse."

He scoffed.

I said, "I'm going to do you a big favor."

"Is this the part where you tell me your outrageous price to let me go free?"

"They do horrible things to child molesters in jail. Fuck you like you're a bitch. Shove brooms up your ass. You're a small man. They might turn you into a bitch and pass your asshole around."

"Is that threat supposed to terrify me?"

"It should. If you had any sense it would."

"I will never see the inside of a jail. Do you not understand that?"

"God will judge you."

"God judges no one because there is no God."

"In your bio from the Broadway play, I read it, read the last line, read where you thanked God."

"That, my friend, is mockery at its best. Why? Because it means nothing. *Everyone thanks God.* Actors do coke and rappers do drive-bys, then get onstage and thank God."

"I see. Mockery at its best."

"The best way to pull the wool over the public's eyes, the best way to get a world of fans, the best way to get the sheep into that ludicrous cult and buying tickets, is to pretend you're one of them."

"So it was a business move."

"A wise business move. A *brilliant* business move. The same way politicians claim God in order to get votes. Mentioning a fictitious God makes me money." He chuckled, his chortle ostentatious. "I know the Bible better than many Christians and I enjoy pointing out the cruelty and caprices of the Old Testament Jehovah, as well as the side-show carnival nature of Jesus's supposed miracles."

"You make Jesus sound like David Blaine."

"Blaine has *more* talent. If Blaine had existed two thousand years ago, existed and did the same carnival tricks he does now, rose from being underwater for fifteen minutes, he'd be praised by the masses and those barbaric soldiers would capture him and leave him stuck on a cross." He chuckled, laughed as if his words, his diatribe, were sheer brilliance. He added, "Quote me on that if you must."

"You thanked God."

"That line in my bio, that's me flicking a booger at religion."

"I see. You were flicking a booger at God."

"At the stupidity of religion. 'There is no God. There's no heaven. There are no angels. There's no hell. When you die, you go in the ground, the worms eat you.'" He smiled. "Madalyn Murray O'Hair said that."

I coughed. "Never heard of her."

"The most hated woman in America."

"Hadn't heard about her. Will Google her first chance I get."

"Well, you have heard of Albert Einstein?"

"I have."

"Would you not say he was brilliant?"

"Goes without saying."

"A letter in which Albert Einstein dismissed the idea of God as the product of human weakness and the Bible as pretty childish was sold at auction for more than four hundred thousand dollars."

"What's your point?"

"One day they will pull the cover back on religion, the same way the cover gets pulled back on Santa. Adults will once again realize how they have been bamboozled and hoodwinked, deceived, all in the name of collecting ten percent of their beloved income, all to help finance the greatest lie ever told."

I was talking to him so I could remain alert, my pain and illness magnifying with my every word, sweat draining down my back and face, licking my lips, dying of thirst, maybe just dying. Tried to remember all I had eaten, all fluids I had ingested, head was too foggy to remember what I had done, the world cold and opaque, my body feverish and weakening, like I had been poisoned.

I asked, "Have you heard of Newton's Second Law?"

"I never studied law."

"It's physics, not a law in the legal sense."

"*I'm a goddamn actor.* You son of a bitch."

I nodded. "His Second Law . . . force equals mass times—"

"*Who are you?*" he barked.

I paused. "My name is Gideon."

"Well, *Gid-e-on, you will regret this moment.*"

He struggled in vain. I wondered if pedophiles ever stopped being pedophiles.

"You mocked my name. You haven't heard of me."

"*What does that mean?*"

"Means that if you had, then your tone would be different."

"Whoever you are, you are nothing, nobody, zilch, nada, bullshit on a saltine cracker."

Male or female, I wondered if they ever changed or just became better at hiding their sickness. Or if they all went off and carved out spaces, cults where they could brainwash and impregnate children.

He growled out his pain. *"Who are you working for?"*

"Pentkovski. Konstantin *Pentkovski."*

"Konstantin Pentkovski. Konstantin?" That name brought fear into his eyes, paused him in a way that made me think he had died instantly, eyes wide open. "The man in the white shoes?"

"Konstantin Pentkovski. The man in the white shoes."

"No . . . no . . . *noooooooooooooo* . . . please . . . no . . . I will do anything . . . *not Konstantin."*

"You've heard of him."

"He is an assassin. Everyone in Hollywood . . . everyone on Broadway . . . they know Konstantin."

"He trained me."

"You are a . . . you're not . . . a bounty hunter? Please tell me you're taking me to New York."

I coughed and shook my head, my breathing shortening, the world glazed over.

There were hundreds of poisons, easy to slip in food, on the surface of cups and glasses, poisons I'd used before, poisons that had no antidote, like the slow-acting poison that had killed a Russian spy.

The latte I'd had back in Nashville. That could've been drugged.

I fought with the illness.

My passenger's breathing accelerated, panic in his eyes. "Force equals mass times . . . *no, no."*

He struggled with his binding. Struggled and yelled and cursed, his tantrum that of a three-year-old child. He did what others did, begged and offered to pay me more than the original contract. I reached for the stun gun, held it against his neck as he screamed, zapped him unconscious.

I struggled with my own pain, again chills weakening me, like a slow-acting poison.

Seconds and altitude were lost when I faded out, came back with a jerk, struggled with the plane, my battle to stay alive ongoing. It was true. Dying was a lot harder than killing. I had learned that firsthand. I looked at my unconscious passenger. I zapped him again for good measure.

Ten thousand volts made him dance deeper into unconsciousness.

The iconoclast would wake up to freezing air, the grip of gravity pulling that pedophile toward earth, his impact calculated by Newton's Second Law: force equals mass times acceleration.

The same formula that, as I struggled with consciousness, pulled the Cessna toward the earth.

Sixteen

an unpardonable crime

Matthew snapped, "You're lying."

"I'm not lying."

"First you said you were in the goddamn hotel room, sleeping; now you have a new lie."

"I told you what happened."

"Tell me again."

"I was sleeping, then I had to get up and go to the other side of the island, had to get rid of the stuff from this morning. Wanted to wait until the sun went down. Spread everything over eight beaches."

"So you say."

"Then I stopped at this place called Beehive Sports Bar, down at St. John's Heritage Quay. It's this place right under a huge clock tower. Then I ate and walked around, did some window shopping at the diamond stores, had a drink at Cheers, played the slots at Kings Casino before I went to the Coast."

"It's not adding up. Your lies make one plus one come out to three."

"Where else would I be on this fucking island?"

Room 29, third floor, high on a hillside facing the marina. Across the way, more yachts and a two-level structure that had the Seabreeze Café, Slipway Chandlery, Dockside Liquors & Supermarket, Lord Jim's Locker, a place that sold yachts, a little bookstore called Jo & Judy's Delightful Bookstore, other shops and boutiques. She noticed it all because as Matthew stood off to the side questioning her like she was an Iraqi fugitive, she stared out at the shops, glass of wine in hand, and took it all in, every light in the rolling hills that surrounded the dockyard for what looked like 360 degrees, looked down at every person who walked or drove down the narrow road in front of her room on their way to the restaurants in the harbor.

She said, "You talk to me like I'm some man off the streets."

"When I talk to you like that it's because you're my fucking partner and I talk to my fucking partner that way, especially when my fucking partner is fucking up."

"I'm your wife."

"Not during the course of this fucking conversation. Not at this moment. Me putting my dick inside you from time to time won't change the language I choose to use while conducting business."

"But it might change the chances of you getting to put your dick inside me from time to time."

"What, you think you can stop me?"

"Well, I'd suggest you remember who the fuck you're talking to."

"I suggest you do the same."

Silence.

He said, "So, tourists are getting robbed by masked men at gunpoint, women are getting raped by a serial rapist, and you were out until this time of the night alone, dressed like that, all by yourself?"

"That's what I said."

"You're a liar."

"What is there to lie about?"

"We'll come back to that later. Let's get back to the job."

"I told you, it's done."

"This was a simple job. Five body bags? A bodyguard left dead on the side of the road?"

"It's done. What's important is that the job has been completed."

"You had a goddamn shoot-out in the middle of All Saints Road."

"Pop a fucking Xanax and get off my back."

Matthew gave her a cold stare. A cold, threatening stare that looked through her and at her all at once. His hands became fists. He stared at her, his jaw tight. Then he nodded and walked away. His depression; she knew that he hated when she mentioned his depression.

Matthew. Her husband. Catholic, with French-Canadian roots. Said he went to high school at Agincourt Collegiate Institute, same high school Jim Carrey went to, years after Carrey had dropped out. Matthew had dropped out too. Carrey had left to go work comedy clubs. Matthew left to work for a guy named Brick. A guy who did bad things to people for a price. A guy who had double-crossed Matthew. A guy Matthew had killed in Ottawa, left a blade running from his chest to that thing in his chest that made his blood circulate.

Nobody fucked over Matthew and lived to brag about that victory.

The television was on CNN. Matthew had been watching that when she had panicked and hurried inside the room. The talking heads on CNN stopped yapping about the American dollar being down and the yen being up and went back to yapping about a tornado that had destroyed parts of Atlanta.

She turned the television off. She called her husband's name. He didn't answer.

She went to Matthew, put her arms around him from behind, said she was sorry.

He said, "One more time, tell me what happened. What kept you out all night?"

Always so focused.

Instead of feeding him the same lie, she got on her knees, undid his cargo pants, reached inside, and pulled out his penis. He tried to push her away. She struggled with him, struggled until he gave in, until she had his dick in her hand. She smiled up at him, sucked him as he stood on the deck with his hands gripping the wooden rail, sucked him as people walked by down below, sucked him as she heard people in the next unit come out on their deck, sucked him as that group of people fell into conversation, sucked him as a yacht sounded its horn in the darkness, sucked him as he held the back of her neck and pushed his swollen cock down her throat, sucked him as he shivered, sucked him until he came, sucked all the questions out of his body. She sucked the hell out of him and sent him to a dreamy-eyed heaven.

She left him on the patio, panting and sweating, and rushed inside, hurried to the bathroom, and spit into the sink, turned on the water and poured mouthwash in a plastic cup. She gargled long enough for the liquid to burn her throat. Spat. Gargled again. Spat three times, wanted to get the taste of come out of her mouth. She didn't mind giving a blow job but never had the taste for come. It made her retch.

Even when she spat it out, some remained, some was always swallowed.

She hated that.

When she looked up Matthew was behind her, face dark, watching her.

She said, "You didn't come that much."

He waited for her eyes to meet his. "Where were you all night?"

"Why didn't you come as much as you normally do? You take all those pills that make you come like a horse. You always come more than that. Want to tell me what's going on?"

"You sure this is how you want to play this?"

"And why did it take you so long to get one?"

"Don't think sucking my dick is going to make this problem go away."

He walked away.

He said, "If I made you come, would you come enough?"

She cursed him, cursed and thought of the swarthy boy on the beach. She felt him inside her.

Her husband said, "You smell. You know that? I can smell you. You smell different."

"You smell your insecurities."

"I should stick my finger up your pussy and see if I smell the scent of another man's dick."

Matthew's BlackBerry rang. He hurried and took the call, said a few words, then he hung up.

She asked, "Who is calling you at this hour?"

He nodded. "We have an unexpected meeting."

She didn't question where the meeting came from, just asked, "With whom?"

"The Lady from Detroit."

"You're joking."

"Wants to meet up the road by the Cockpit."

"She's on the island?"

"In Antigua. Her grandmother and aunt have homes here. Hodges Bay."

"That other island?"

"That's Jumby Bay."

"Where is Hodges?"

"North, not too far from the airport. Doctors, lawyers, Caribbean rich people live up that way."

"Thought the Caribbean rich people live in Cedar-something by the golf course."

"There too."

She paused, thinking, feeling uneasy. "You knew that Detroit bitch was going to be here."

He nodded. "I knew. Thought we would meet tomorrow sometime. She wants it now."

Then she understood why Matthew had allowed her to do the solo job. She understood why he had come to Antigua. Detroit had hired them to do the job in London. The job she had fucked up.

She asked, "Does she want her deposit back?"

"We can't afford to give her back her money."

"Why not? Minus expenses."

Her husband stood in front of her, confronting her once again. "Let's talk about expenses."

"What now?"

Matthew said, "We need to talk about your little shopping spree."

She rolled her eyes and released an irritated sound. "It's under control."

"If it's under control, why did somebody call the house asking if you still wanted to purchase a set of diamond mink eyelashes? Diamond mink eyelashes. Five thousand each. Ten large total."

She sighed and rubbed her forehead but didn't respond, not with words.

He went on, "After that phone call, I went inside your closet."

"You broke the lock on my closet?"

"I picked it."

"How dare you . . . that's violating my personal space."

"Saw all the shit you had hidden."

"What the fuck were you doing in my closet?"

He went into his speech about the mortgage, the new Sub-Zero refrigerator that cost fifteen grand, her two brand-new vehicles, both high-end vehicles, his two vehicles, both five years old, modest and inexpensive, the insurance on their fleet of cars, ranted about how he had paid off all of her charge cards before they married only to have her sneak and get new charge cards, all of those cards already maxed out, a whopping thirty thousand in brand-new debt, and he had yet to see her buy one thing for him.

He said, "You don't understand debt, do you?"

"Of course I understand debt."

"I don't think so. You had leased a Mercedes, and what did you do? You put over one hundred thousand miles on the car in two years. In two years. It's twenty-five thousand miles around the world at the equator and you put one hundred thousand miles on a brand-new car that your lease told you was good for fifteen thousand miles a year. Then you had to pay for the overage, which came out to be about twenty thousand dollars, and what did you do? Instead of keeping the Benz you took the loss and came back home in a brand-new Range Rover, another down payment. Never mind the fact that you had a six-month-old Maserati sitting in the garage. Without talking to me, just did what you wanted."

"It was my money, dammit."

"Marriage means it's *our* money. Like *your* fucked-up credit became *our* fucked-up credit."

She sucked her lips and looked away, her autonomy suffocating.

The conversation terrified her, made her heart race, made anxiety swell inside her.

He said, "You made so many promises. If we get married then I'm going to do this, if we get married then I'm going to stop doing that. We were supposed to be a team. A team. I think you were pretending to be who you thought I wanted you to be, act right until you got what you wanted—"

"I wanted to get married, just like you."

"You wanted the wedding, the party, the ring, the dress, to be Cinderella at the ball in front of your friends, but you didn't want anything that came after that. You don't want the hard part. After marriage, that's when the relationship starts. We're not dating anymore. We're married. I put twenty-five percent down on a house that cost seven hundred thousand dollars. A brand-new house. You didn't want to look at resales. You had to have a brand-new house. Your credit was so fucked-up you couldn't afford to buy anything larger than a Dixie cup. I had to buy down the interest rate because of your credit. Then you had to have all the upgrades, had to have the hardwood floors, the leaded windows, the plantation shutters and designer curtains, had to upgrade the kitchen, had to have better carpet."

"And you had to have the house wired for sound."

"Which cost nothing compared to all the shit you had to have. Marble in the foyer, all the cabinets upgraded, all those overpriced closets put in by Closet World. Thirty thousand for particleboard closets."

"They're pretty."

"You paid for them, had them installed without talking to me."

"I needed closets. You know I need closet space."

"That's not the point."

"What's the point of this conversation, Matthew? Just get to the point."

"So in the end a seven-hundred-thousand-dollar house became damn near a million-dollar debt."

She snapped, "Why did you marry me?"

He snapped, "Because I loved you."

Silence.

He had said because I *loved* you, not because I *love* you. Past tense.

He said, "You know how many people I had to kill to pay for all that shit?"

"We."

"You have worked, but your money hasn't gone to the house or the cars."

"You think I can't survive without you?"

"You'd be on skid row if it wasn't for me."

"Is that what you think?"

"Your money ends up on your ass or on your feet."

"I did jobs before you. I was working long before you got in this business."

He ran his hand over his red hair, rubbed the stubble on his chin. "We met on the job."

"The job we did at Disneyland. That time we killed that big-ass mouse."

"Goofy."

"Thought we did the mouse."

"We did Goofy. We killed the mutt."

"Either way, we had fun after. All the rides. We had a lot of fun after that job."

Again silence.

She said, "I still want to have fun, Matthew. Just want to have a little fun."

"We can have fun and I want to have fun, but we have to be realistic about where we are."

She tightened her lips, stared at her wedding ring.

Matthew. Ten years younger than she. The Guy Ritchie to her Madonna. The Gabriel Aubrey to her Halle Berry. Talked to her like she was a goddamn child. Talked to her like he was her father.

She asked, "What do you think we should do?"

"Counseling and a financial planner."

"Is that an option?"

"Not an option." His eyes darkened. "And this time I expect you to make it to therapy."

She rocked and pulled at her hair. Just the thought of meeting with a financial planner gave her angst. All that talk about hedge funds, twenty-five managers, oil stock, short the financial sector, net-worth requirements, buy and hold, shorting the marketplace, absolute return, S&P, Dow Jones, a share mutual fund, June and December no penalties, surrender penalties—all of that was gibberish to her.

He said, "No more shopping."

"What do you mean no more shopping?"

"I mean you need to wear what you have. And we both sell one vehicle."

She rocked faster, pulled her hair harder.

He asked, "How much did you drink tonight?"

She took a deep breath. "Not much. I was stressed. Somebody tried to kill me today."

"Comes with the job."

"I know. Was just saying. Had a bad day at work, that's all."

"I smell weed in your hair. And your eyes . . . your eyes are red. What else you take?"

She didn't answer, sat there rubbing a dozen mosquito bites, all of them itching at once.

He said, "You rode a scooter from one side of the island to the other, loaded."

Still no answer. Didn't sound like he needed one.

He grunted. "Stupid. So fucking stupid."

"Don't call me stupid."

"I'm not talking about you. I'm talking about me."

He walked away from her, left shaking his head, went and stood on the balcony.

He chuckled. "I guess I'm the best investment you ever had."

She sat on the bed, her leg bouncing, hands rubbing over her hair.

He said, "I'm a damn fool. A damn fool."

She imagined poisoning him with antifreeze, watching him die a slow death, vomiting and diarrhea and stomachaches weakening him to the point of wishing he had been nicer to her.

She said, "You want a divorce?"

"For better or worse, fat or thin, sickness and health."

" 'Til death do us part."

He nodded. "Until death."

He said that as if there was no other option, no other way for the marriage to end.

That terrified her.

Again he stared at her, his eyes dark enough to make her want to run to the sea, swim away.

His cellular rang again. He answered and went outside.

He came back inside and said, "Time to go."

She stood up, Matthew standing over her, staring, his face rigid, the look of death in his eyes. She was afraid. Trapped in a hotel room, no gun in her possession, a killer a few feet away.

Then her husband smiled, his grin small but so sweet and loving, so boyish.

He said, "You have a little dried-up come on the side of your mouth."

Panic rose up inside her. At first she thought it was the young boy's come on her lips.

She hadn't tasted the young boy.

It was her husband's flavor drying on the edge of her lips.

She went and washed her face, took her time, staring in the mirror, not blinking, her mind in another place. Weed, lager, and ecstasy still in her bloodstream. She remembered the first contract. A decade ago. A back alley in Tijuana, the sun going down on a day so hot it had felt like the sun was sitting on top of her skin, flies buzzing, taco smell in the darkening desert air, stench of mules, mules that were painted to look like zebras, the chatter of automobiles and motorcycles, drunken and horny tourists all over. Women and Corona, sex and alcohol, those were the reasons people went to Mexico. Streets lined with young women wearing short dresses, women stationed no more than every ten feet, leaning against concrete walls, offering insincere smiles and themselves for twenty dollars. In the background, on the same street punctuated with Spanish and broken English, strip clubs were on every corner, the women inside offering the same dispassionate sexual healing for twice, maybe three times the street price, as if what they had between their legs was so much better than what was being whored curbside. God bless third-world countries and their old-fashioned bartering. On a sunny day in Tijuana there were plenty of people around. At night there were ten times as many. She had followed the boy she'd been sent to handle. He was a young man. A man who met a bullet and didn't live to get old.

You never forgot the first time. The fear. The rush. That first face never left you.

Like sex. Or adultery. You never forgot the first time.

Matthew was watching her, that dark and deadly look again; then the boyish grin followed.

She said, "What are you looking at?"

"The Assassin with Ass."

She smiled.

"You have Betty Grable legs. Jayne Mansfield tits. Add that up and you're a damn Bettie Page."

She chuckled. "What do you want to call me now?"

"My beautiful wife. I want to call you my beautiful wife."

He came over, kissed her on her neck, squeezed her breasts and backside, became hard.

She whispered, "Somebody's tense."

"Yeah."

"Want another blow job?"

"We have an appointment."

"Make that arrogant, stuck-up Detroit bitch wait."

"Stop."

"I want to please my husband."

"What, you're going to take it?"

"I want to suck my husband's cock."

She got on her knees, unzipped his pants, took his penis out again, smiled up at her husband. She wanted him depleted, didn't want him to need sex later, wasn't going to sleep with two men in a matter of a few hours. She wasn't that kind of girl. Suck Matthew dry, no penetration, not today.

She took him in her mouth. Felt his hands in her hair, his penis at the back of her throat.

Again her husband grunted, pushed deeper as he came. Again he didn't come enough.

She ran to the sink, gargled again, her mind on the same thoughts.

No shopping. Counseling. Neither of those was an option.

Women needed clothes, shoes, and jewelry.

Not just clothes, shoes, and jewelry, but *new* clothes, *new* shoes, and *new* jewelry.

New hairstyles. *New* accessories.

A woman *needed* a husband. A woman *needed* a lover.

A lover on the side was the ultimate accessory.

Matthew had found out about the diamond mink eyelashes.

But he didn't find out why she was buying them. He hadn't found out that she was spending more than that to live out her *Sex and the City* fantasy. A want that would cost another twenty-four thousand dollars. Matthew wouldn't understand. That it was a bargain to be able to spend ninety-six hours living out the existence of characters from the best show ever created, a show that had ended and sent her into depression, as it had done so many other cosmopolitan-sipping, Blahniks-wearing women. Spending that twenty-four thousand to live like Carrie, Charlotte, Samantha, and Miranda, a life filled with luxurious shoes and handbags, being pampered at luxury spas, and sipping cocktails at the same nightspots featured in the show, places where she might be able to sit in the same chairs the women from the show had sat in, ordering the same drinks; that was all the therapy she needed. Matthew would die if the people from Destination on Location ever called and left a message. Matthew didn't understand the global phenomenon, didn't understand that Blahniks were not shoes, that Blahniks were *Blahniks*, what Picasso and Rembrandt would've designed if they had not wasted so much time painting canvas and wall. Van Gogh didn't have the brilliance of Manolo Blahnik, that was the real reason he cut off his ear, did it so he didn't have to listen to the artistic sound Blahniks made when a woman sashayed across a tiled or wooden floor. Matthew wouldn't understand why she was so angry when she hadn't been the *first* to book her tour, how enraged she had become when a woman from Singapore had managed to book the tour *two minutes* before her, a bitch from another country was first in line, a bitch from a fucking third-world country where the show was banned. The bitch couldn't watch the show and she was going to be known as the first. She had almost booked a flight to Singapore, would've if she could've vanished from her marriage for a few days, long enough to make sure her competition was no longer her competition, and she would be first in line, the first to be chauffeured to Saks, Barneys, and Patricia Field. She was dying to meet the designers and stylists whose imaginations gave birth to the creations the characters wore, clothes to die for, and if she had made it to Singapore, to kill for.

But if she had been number one, then there would have been a lot of attention, a lot of press, maybe interviews, things she didn't need to chance Matthew seeing.

Not only that, that type of press could be bad for the business she was in.

Still.

Twenty-four thousand was nothing to be able to enjoy all of that and dine where the characters ate, Balthazar and Pastis, get chauffeured around and party at Bungalow 8, leave there and step across the velvet rope at all of the exclusive nightclubs, moving by people in her Blahniks, the envy of the world.

To top it off she would get to spend an afternoon pretending to be her favorite characters. She had it down to two: Charlotte and Samantha. If she chose Charlotte her spree would take her to Tiffany & Company, then a tour of some art galleries—galleries didn't thrill her, never saw anything she would want to buy; if she chose Samantha her excursion would be Madison Avenue and a trip to a high-end sex shop, hopefully one that had some of the toys Samantha had owned.

So Samantha it was.

Samantha. The ultimate cougar.

And included in the twenty-four-thousand-dollar package was the chance to see the movie on opening night. She would walk on the same carpet, be in the same room, breathing the same air as the stars.

She would witness history hours before the regular people lined up to see the film.

Not before the bootleggers sold it curbside in every ghetto in America. But bootleggers couldn't get her seats next to Carrie Bradshaw, Samantha Jones, Charlotte York, and Miranda Hobbes. Bootleggers couldn't get you in the same room as Mr. Big, Aleksandr Petrovsky, Aidan Shaw, Steve Brady, Harry Goldenblatt, Smith Jerrod, Jack Berger, Stanford Blatch, Anthony Marentino, Trey MacDougal, and Richard Wright.

Only twenty-four thousand dollars could get you to live that fantasy.

Only twenty-four thousand dollars could enable a woman who had grown up in foster care to be accepted by the upper echelon of society.

She was glad Matthew didn't know about that. His understanding didn't matter.

Nothing and no one was going to extinguish her chance to live out that fantasy.

Nothing was going to stop the woman who had endured everything from becoming one of them.

What mattered most was that she would be one of *them*.

Fifteen minutes later.

She had on jeans and sandals, a sleeveless top, her body sprayed with more OFF!

They left their room and headed down the steep bricked walkway that led to the guard shack sitting on the main road. Matthew held her hand. Like husband and wife. Like lovers.

She took a breath. Matthew understood money but didn't understand women. Most men didn't. Men thought the fight was over, but the woman still held the grudge and remembered every fucking word that had been said. He was a leader. A control freak who talked like he was in the movie *Goodfellas*.

He asked, "You have a gun?"

"I'm naked. Everything is in the Caribbean Sea."

"I'm not naked."

"You have a gun?"

"A blade."

She swallowed. Matthew had a knife on him. She had no weapon. But he had a knife.

All he had said, all of his unhappiness, every negative word echoed between her ears.

She had not been a good wife. She had fucked up London. She had not been a good partner.

He'd be in a better financial position without her. But she knew he couldn't divorce her. She knew all of his secrets, just like he knew all of hers. She knew where the bodies were buried, the type of information that would have a man sitting on death row before the next sunrise.

As they moved up the road, passing La Perla real estate offices and Sunseakers, her scooter parked where she had left it, then coming up on Tiki Car Rental, she wondered, if this meeting was unexpected, why Matthew had come to see her here, why he had shown up unexpectedly with a knife.

She wondered about the Lady from Detroit being in Antigua. It didn't make sense.

And Matthew never told her he was coming to the West Indies. Not one message.

Like he had wanted to surprise her.

She wondered if her husband had come to her room and waited for her as her husband.

Or had been in her hillside room, waiting in the darkness, lurking, as El Matador.

His BlackBerry rang again. Again he answered. Said a few words, hung up.

She felt the swarthy lover's heavy penis inside her. Tasted Matthew's come on her tongue.

Matthew said, "Change of plans."

"What now?"

"She wants to meet at Pigeon Point. Said this is too close to the police station in the Dockyard. Doesn't want anyone to see us meeting. So she wants to meet at a private area."

"We can take the scooter I rented."

"No scooter. She wants us to walk."

"That will take at least twenty minutes."

"Then we better keep moving."

Her mind raced.

Now he wanted to turn around and walk up a hill and down roads too narrow for two cars to pass without someone pulling to the side, an area with few homes, plenty of tropical foliage, emerald waters, and white sand, wanted her to leave all she had behind and walk and have a meeting at a beach away from the rest of the harbor, a secluded shoreline that very few went to, a place not many knew about.

A place like she had taken her swarthy lover not that long ago.

El Matador.

His being here had surprised her; his barrage of questions never gave her time to think.

She hadn't asked Matthew how he got inside her hotel room. Or how he knew what room she had been given when she checked in. He had no luggage with him, there was no job, but he had a knife on his person. Wasn't adding up, not the way she wanted it to add up. It added up another way.

She wondered if the Lady from Detroit was really here or just a lie to get her out of the room.

Sweat grew on the back of her neck.

Nervous sweat that made the scent of a dead lover rise from her flesh.

He had permeated her being.

They hiked up a ragged road, past a construction site, new condos being built, a tattered road made for a Jeep, a road few cars would brave, a road that turned left and led to darkness and isolation.

Matthew could've killed her in the hotel room.

She knew killing her in the hotel room would be a problem that would have to be explained.

He led her over a gravel road that went uphill past where they were developing new properties.

She licked her lips, uncomfortable.

When she slowed down, Matthew pulled her hand, made her keep moving. If he took her to Pigeon Point Beach, killed her, locals would get blamed. This was a small island that had plenty of places to dump a dead body. E in her system, weed and lager still in her bloodstream, a sobering fear in her heart. She held her husband's hand tighter. She noticed he was holding her just as tight.

Like he wanted to make sure she didn't get away.

At the top of the first hill she glanced out at 360 degrees of lush mountains, looked down at yachts and dinghies in the marina, stared at all the British flags waving from the superyachts docked in the Antiguan harbor.

She wondered if that was the last time she would see that beautiful sight.

Seventeen

mysteries

Matthew said, "You're trembling."

She didn't respond, just wiped sweat from her forehead, did that using her free hand.

She was out of breath, sweating, feeling uncomfortable.

Matthew said, "You're out of shape."

She didn't reply to that either, his list of disappointments growing every time he spoke.

She asked, "Are there snakes in these woods?"

"No snakes on the island."

"How do you know?"

"They brought in mongooses, did that years ago; the mongooses killed all the snakes."

"Mongooses, those things that look like rats?"

"Same family, I suppose."

"Do mongooses bite people?"

"Keep walking."

Every little noise she heard made her jump.

Matthew led her down the rugged street that ended at Pigeon Point. The downhill walk moved from an area covered by trees to where it opened up at the edges of the beach. There were two vehicles there, both small four-door Nissans with the steering wheel on the right-hand side. Both license plates started with the letter R; R was used to designate those vehicles as rentals. Eight men were standing by those cars.

Eight men of various sizes, all clean-shaven, all dressed in jeans and colorful shirts that only a tourist would wear. They wore hats. Expensive, stylish hats, not baseball caps. Borsalino. Panizza. Peto. Henschel. Biltmore. Capas. Scoini. Goorin. Hats that took the look of a man to another level. She knew hats, knew fashion. Each man had on a different-style hat, wore those the way women hated to have on the same dress or meet a woman who wore the same shoes. The only thing about them that was the same was the shades, same brand and style, like there had been a clearance on Ray-Bans. Or they shopped at Costco.

Two of the eight came toward them as they made the left turn and moved toward the cars. The man wearing the Peto and a man wearing a Goorin.

She looked around. Nothing but Caribbean Sea and palm trees in front of them. She thought that she should tug on Matthew and have him back away from this meeting, maybe pause at this point and have them bring the rest of the meeting to them. It was too late. She heard something, looked behind her. Matthew did the same. The sound of rubber rolling over loosened gravel. Another car came down the road, moved slowly, dirt rising under its wheels, the first letter on its license plate the letter R as well. It crept and stopped a few yards behind them. The occupants got out and stood by each of the four doors. Four more big guys, clones of the ones who were in front of them, same standard-issue Ray-Bans; those men put their distinct hats on as they exited the vehicle.

Twelve men of various complexions, shapes, and sizes. Waiting in silence. Not a smile in sight.

The Lady from Detroit wasn't in sight either. Maybe she wasn't here.

Maybe this was a West Indies setup, payback for the fuckup in London.

She felt the men staring at her more than they regarded Matthew.

She asked Matthew, "What's this?"

"Looks like an affirmative action reunion."

"Or a hat club meeting."

The way one of the men tilted his hat and gawked at her, the way he licked his lips, she felt the heat. In silence she imagined she heard his thoughts, *their* thoughts, about her body.

Matthew said, "What's up, bro?"

"I'm not your brother, white boy."

Just like that hate filled the Caribbean air; the man's eyes blamed them for the degradation and abuse of slavery. She had seen that same hate so many times, race hate, and the hate due to complexion. Not just black and white race hate, but as she traveled she had seen the same internal hate in the South Asians, in the Pakistanis, had seen that same stupidity in the Bangladeshis. They hated different complexions in their own race and they hated the complexion of people with snowy faces.

The bodyguard's eyes came to her, those eyes lingering on her backside as a wicked smile grew. At the moment she felt uncomfortable with what she carried.

The bodyguard looked her up and down, frowning deep. "You a sister or Puerto Rican?"

Matthew said, "You're disrespecting my wife. You're disrespecting me."

"That onion got a serious hook to it. You rocking ass like Kim Kardashian."

"Motherfucker, you hear me? This is my wife."

She squeezed Matthew's hand, that single squeeze telling her husband to let it go, for now. They were fucking with them. What was the shrinking minority in the States was the growing majority here.

Twelve well-dressed, hat-wearing men moved through the moonlight, fanned out, and they were surrounded. It felt like what she had read about in history books, only in history it was reversed, the night lit up by a burning cross. All the love she had for swarthy men, it became fear, the cousin of hate.

One of the men broke ranks and went to Matthew first, patted him down, found nothing. Another man came to her, the same one who had been looking at her in that wanting way, motioned for her to raise her arms, began patting her down, put his hands on her body, touching everything longer than necessary, his hands moving across her breasts and tracing her bra, moving up and down her thighs.

She snapped, "What the hell do you think you're doing?"

Matthew snapped, "Get your hands off my wife."

The bodyguard ignored her, ignored her husband, patted her again as if he had missed something the first time, did that like he was showing her who was running this show.

She cursed the bodyguard when he backed away, cursed him and adjusted her clothing.

Matthew nodded. "Molesting my wife like that, disrespecting me, you think that was wise?"

The bodyguard sneered, then the tough guy walked away, her husband not worthy of an answer.

Another one, this one wearing a Stetson, a goatee on his square chin, said, "Follow me."

None of their accents were Antiguan. They were from the States.

They followed two of the arrogant men as four of the others followed them.

Matthew's jaw was tight; she saw that, knew that meant he was in a killing mood.

Her mood was the same as her husband's, multiplied by a thousand.

All the shit she had been through growing up in foster care, now being abused by strangers.

One of the bodyguards said, "When you get to my boss lady, you speak when spoken to. She talks, you listen. She asks questions, you answer right off the bat. That understood, white boy?"

Matthew said, "Whatever you say, black boy."

The bodyguard stopped walking and faced them.

A stare-down, this bodyguard the size of the Hulk, making Matthew look like Bruce Banner.

She wanted a gun. Any gun. Any kind of gun. She wouldn't miss a shot. She would be perfect, would fan out like she had been taught, would take down six before the other six realized their numbers had been cut in half. But there was no gun. She wasn't a fighter. And she couldn't run.

The scent of adultery rising from her body, she moved closer to her husband.

Matthew said, "Either get on with this shit, or we're going back the other way."

"Think you can get off this island unless she says so?"

"You think I give a shit what she says or you say or what anybody else says?"

The stare-down continued, the bodyguard's hands becoming fists.

Matthew smiled. "Call me white boy again. I dare you."

"What the fuck you gonna do?"

"Find out, motherfucker."

She cringed; her heartbeat sped up when Matthew said that.

There were twelve of them.

She stepped between the bodyguard and her husband, said, "Let it go, Matthew."

The bodyguard shook his head and walked away, again leading them toward the waters.

"Follow me, *white boy.*"

Matthew did something she didn't expect; he smiled. "No problem, boss man. No problem."

To her ears the word *boy* had sounded more offensive than the strongest racial epithet, more demeaning. She stayed close to Matthew as they were led over the ruptured road, across the white sand, through the trees, and then to the edges of the Caribbean Sea. To their left, across the sand, about fifty yards away, was a wooden jetty that went from the shore out twenty yards into the emerald waters.

At the end of that jetty was a tall woman dressed in sun-yellow linen.

The Lady from Detroit.

Eighteen

a tattered web

By the time they made it to the start of the jetty, she saw the Lady from Detroit was on her cellular phone. Still at her husband's side, watching the politician, she waited behind the bodyguards.

Yellow wide-leg pantsuit over yellow top. Movado on her left arm, one that went for five thousand dollars. Her hair dark and shoulder-length, parted on the left side, as if that was some statement of her political preferences. But the shoes, those were beautiful yellow shoes she had dangling in her hand, designed by Bottega Veneta, three thousand a pair. And a Bottega Veneta bracelet and Bottega Veneta pearl ring that added close to another four thousand to her wardrobe. The David Yurman oval Figaro chain around the politician's neck cost another four thousand dollars.

Her eyes went back to the politician's shoes. The Bottega Veneta shoes.

The city of Detroit may have been struggling, but the woman standing in front of her was not.

Over the waves, through the wind, as the politician talked into the cellular phone she held up to her right ear, she could hear some of the conversation the Lady from Detroit was having as they were forced to wait.

They were late, had made the Lady from Detroit wait. Now she was returning the favor.

"It is beyond wicked. What is happening to my city is an atrocity.

What I love is going up in flames, and nobody is doing anything to put out the fire. Every radio station host who was willing to discuss the facts about the city I love second only to God and my family has been replaced with more music, there are no people going on television outside of Detroit discussing the depths of economic despair that are rising at an alarming rate either, and do not get me started on the schools that they shut down in my city. As John Lee Hooker sang, 'the Motor City is burning'; it started on Twelfth Street back then, and this destructive fire started long before sex text messages. We're on fire and nobody can smell the smoke and they are ignoring the heat from the flames. What? Told you, I am about rebirth. I want people to be able to sleep at night and rest assured because I care, and I want to send the message to Washington because we need people outside of Detroit to know there is something rotten in Denmark. A country is only as strong as its weakest city. What? Detroit isn't the weakest, not what I'm saying."

Corrupt politics, religious bias, God, sex, bribes, extortion. A declining population, safety issues, limited public funds, and scarce land. The well-dressed politician ranted about all things American, the same things that plagued the world, the things that kept her hired guns employed.

The politician went on as if they were unimportant. "What? Why does that keep coming up? I'm sure he had his hand in my husband's assassination. All of his rhetoric about me being the one who had my husband killed is and always will be an attempt to hide his own wrongdoings, his own misconduct, his own lies. I loved my husband; he was a good man, pillar of the community, my best friend, my faithful husband, and the father of my children. Missing money? My financial statements have been presented to the public. I have no missing funds. Maybe you should ask him about the dead stripper. What? Of course. We need to focus on uniting our party, on facts and not lies, because America is crumbling."

She watched the elected official as she frowned and flipped her phone closed.

They viewed the woman who had summoned them in profile, the

left side of her face. A small keen nose, full lips, auburn hair that hung like she had the perfect perm. A haircut of power and money.

Then came another voice. *"I should've cut your motherfucking throat, should've left your head hanging from your neck. My mistake was thinking you were smart enough to let this go."*

It was a recorded voice; it came from the phone the Lady from Detroit had in her hand.

She watched as the politician took her time. The winds picked up, made the politician's yellow linen outfit flutter and tighten against her figure as sand danced on the beach. The politician had on close to ten thousand dollars' worth of clothing and jewelry, whatever she had on underneath not included in the sum. The politician had a nice figure, size twelve, maybe fourteen, waist small, well-defined, not beautiful, but money had kept her looking extremely attractive. Money and power were aphrodisiacs. Money and power had a way of making the ordinary look extraordinary. Hair done, well-manicured; nothing about the politician stood out as being ordinary. She stood strong in the winds, not a hair out of place.

"Soon your head will hang from your fucking neck."

The politician stood as if she were a thinking sun, solving the problems of the world, or just the problems of Detroit, her face for a moment showing a deep fear and a weighty concern, before she took a shuddering breath, and after that deep breath she took her time, maybe staring out at the lights from the yachts in the distance or staring at the lights in the hills, then turned away from the emerald waters and faced them. This was the politician who had sent them to kill a man in London. Then what she saw as she stared at the hypocritical politician, what happened in the next moment, unnerved her.

The politician smiled.

Not the generic, welcoming smile of an elected official.

And the smile was not aimed at her.

The woman dressed in the colors of the sun yielded a soft, almost girlish smile that came alive when she saw Matthew. The stoic Lady from Detroit had smiled a soft smile for her husband. The smile of familiarity, followed by the Lady from Detroit's eyes coming to her, and that softness vanished.

Maybe it wasn't the fact that the politician had smiled that bothered her.

For a moment, as he held her hand, she thought she had seen her husband smile too.

They were directed to walk a few more feet along the jetty.

The bodyguards moved away, stepped back down the wooden structure, and stood where the jetty met the sand. The only escape was to dive into the Caribbean Sea and swim toward the harbor.

The politician looked at Matthew, then her, then again at Matthew.

"There is no one here but us. I will deny knowing you. I will deny ever meeting you."

She nodded at the politician, not caring if Matthew did the same.

Matthew said, "Likewise."

They had exchanged smiles. Smiles that had made her heartbeat and breathing accelerate.

She took her hand from Matthew's, stared at a political woman whose attention had returned to the hills and waters.

The politician addressed Matthew, asked, "A wha' tek you so long?"

"Me walk wid me wife."

"Me tink you min ya wid you partna."

"How you mean? Me wife a me partna."

"I didn't know that."

"Now you do."

"You no 'fraid you ketch worm?"

That last sentence was delivered to Matthew, to her husband, with a hint of sarcasm, the exchange so fast, so deeply rooted in dialect, that she had no idea what the politician had said, but the body language, the direct eye contact, that told her what she wanted to know.

The Lady from Detroit turned away from them, shaking her head.

Twelve bodyguards had them blocked in. Like twelve disciples. Like she was their Jesus.

When the Lady from Detroit was done with her thinking, done pretending she owned time, she faced them, again staring at her and her husband, before she took a step toward them, ready to speak.

"I hired an assassin who now calls himself Gideon. My first mistake. He did a job for me in the Midwest. He claimed he almost lost his life during the job and he blamed me for his incompetence. Then he extorted me. Demanded money, a lot of money, threatened to kill me if I didn't pay. I had no choice. He has broken into my home, stolen information from my computer. He has violated me over and over. A man who I had paid to kill; for all I know he could go to the authorities, turn it all around. He is corrupt, has no morals or ethics. I want this finished. I want my children safe. I want to be able to sleep at night."

She didn't say anything. Matthew nodded.

The politician said, "I want my vengeance. You're the third ones I've sent to handle this. This first one . . . I have no idea what happened. He sent me confirmation that Gideon was dead, *visual* confirmation, then he vanished. Without a trace. Without collecting . . . the rest of his fees."

Matthew said, "That means he failed."

"The second worker was sent to the Cayman Islands. Paid him half. Never heard from again."

"I take it that whoever you sent there failed too."

"Failure means death." Her voice trembled. "Gideon came after me and told me himself. The man rose from the dead and came inside my home, touched my things, terrified me. Nothing scares me. But this man does. I hate to admit that, but he does. God told me that this must be done."

She said that she spent her days surrounded by bodyguards, hadn't been alone for almost a year, not one minute, since Gideon had broken into her home, threatened to assassinate her and her children. She said that Gideon had threatened to kill her friends and family, kill everyone she knew, repeated and emphasized that he had stolen information from her computer and BlackBerry, had left her in a state of paranoia.

A state of paranoia that had never ended.

The politician looked directly at her, said, "Now, tell me what the fuck happened in London."

She stared at the woman dressed in fluttering yellow. Stared and said nothing. The center of the politician's head now looked like a bull's-eye. The spot that marked her heart looked the same way.

Matthew said, simply, "He got away."

"That's no excuse, Matthew."

"Then walk the fuck away."

"I've invested too much money in this to not have this resolved as of yet."

"You put down half and if you don't like how the fuck this is progressing, walk the fuck away."

"Respect me."

"Give to fucking get. Go hire some-fucking-body else and we'll be fucking done with each other."

"And you will return the monies I have invested thus far."

"Not a dime."

Silence moved between them, as if that answer wasn't good enough.

The politician said, "Respect me."

"As soon as you throw some respect this way. Give to get."

Matthew, pissed. Her husband sounded like he was having a lover's quarrel with the woman.

The politician raised her hand, but not to them. It was a motion to the bodyguards at the end of the jetty; the raised voices had them coming that way. With that simple wave, they backed away.

Now, as her husband faced the Lady from Detroit, her own jaw tightened with anger.

She said, "What other information did you get for me in London?"

"They didn't talk."

"How many did you interview?"

"Two women, both whores."

"Where are they now?"

"I did what you paid me to do. Left no trail behind. They can't warn anyone."

Matthew had vanished in London, had left her at Knightsbridge, had dropped her off and stormed out of the hotel. She had taken her anger on a walk, become distracted when she saw she was in a shopper's paradise, ended up shopping at Hermès and Chanel along Sloane Street; the same orgasmic sensations came at Harrods, then she calmed down, visited Buckingham Palace and Jimi Hendrix's flat.

Matthew hadn't told her about doing any more work for the self-important politician.

The politician said, "I sent others after London."

"What happened?"

"They failed."

"What happened?"

"They failed."

"So you came running back to us."

"I want this resolved. For my children. For my sanity. I want it resolved yesterday."

Again the politician paused, pondered, once again in charge of time and the world.

"This is about honesty and integrity, truth and honor. This is my calling. I am the Roman goddess of justice. I carry the scales of justice and a double-edged sword. My husband was corrupt. He had to be dealt with in the way he was dealt with, his crimes personal, the pain his lies caused so very deep."

She paused.

"And Gideon is no better than my husband. I'll spend what it takes to put this to an end."

Matthew said, "We can foster a plan."

"Whatever it takes."

"It takes money."

"Money?"

"You said you would do whatever it takes. At this point it will take money."

"You want more money. Like Gideon."

"No, our contract stands. We get our other half when the job is done."

"I'm at a loss here."

"Can you access any more money? Simple question."

She took a deep breath. "I can manipulate things so I can have access to funds."

"About two hundred thousand. Maybe less."

"That's a lot of money."

"Worst-case scenario."

"I'm listening."

"We pay Gideon to come to us."

"What?"

"We get to whoever is handling him. Put a contract out on someone else."

"Who would the contract be on?"

"Can be real, can be bogus."

She frowned. "I'm listening."

"The point being to get Gideon where you want him. Hopefully he will take the work, then he will show up and never know we'll be there waiting. He thinks you're chasing him. Don't chase, lead."

"Ambush."

"Stop chasing the bastard and lie in wait. Like Kennedy riding by a library in Dallas."

A moment passed before she asked, "Can that work?"

"I don't see why it wouldn't. Put enough money on the table, he'll come."

There was a long thinking pause before she nodded. "Where?"

"Here is as good a place as any."

"My grandmother is from here."

"My grandmother is from Germany. Your point?"

"Antigua has enough going on at the moment, more than enough negative publicity."

"Well, see, we're already here. We don't have to race to some location and beat him there. Here they don't have CCTV cameras all over the place. That was the problem in London. We would've had collateral damage, and there was no clear exit. The only cameras here are in the hands of tourists. We're here, so we have time to set it up. We have time to get the hardware we need. Here is good."

"A contract on whom?"

"You can make it on the prime minister or Stanford for all I care. Hell, half of the islanders are mad because all the Brits are over here buying up land the locals will never be able to afford, so throw the Brits' names up in the air and pick one. Pick one of the rich fucks over at Jumby Bay. Pick a worker at Roti King. Taxi driver, bank worker, fisherman, baker, farmer, hairdresser, AUA student, hotel worker, it doesn't matter who you pick. The point is you make the contract look legit, pay the fifty percent up front."

Another thinking pause, as if she were considering her career, as if she were considering the possibility of this scheme failing and her spending the next fifteen years in jail because of a felony.

She nodded. "My children, they have to be protected. He threatened my children."

Matthew nodded. "You're just doing what a good mother would do."

"Don't patronize me."

Matthew seemed unfazed.

She said, "Thirty thousand people have fled my city in its time of need."

The sound of the Caribbean Sea absorbed the silence.

She said, "I'd be forced to . . . the city is bankrupt and . . . I'd have to use taxpayers' money."

"Not my problem."

She paused. "I've done a lot for the city I love. I have given that city my blood, sweat, and tears. If the city can be foolish enough to spend eight million dollars . . . on sexual text messages . . . they can contribute to my cause, to make this end. What I do, I do for those I love. Because in the end, when Gideon is dead and this is behind me, when all is said and done, I will make Detroit rise from the ashes like a phoenix. My city will become the envy of America."

The politician looked at Matthew.

"This is larger than Detroit, Matthew. This is my assignment from God."

"If you say so."

"I want to see his body. No photographs. No duplicity. I want to see him dead."

"Is that right?"

"Cut his head off. Send me his head."

"I'm not going to decapitate the son of a bitch and mail his head to you. If you want to see his dead body as confirmation I'd suggest you stay here until it's done."

The politician shuddered. "I want to see you kill him. I want to watch that bastard die."

"Think you can stomach that?"

There was a pause before she answered, "I want to see his head hanging from his neck."

Then the politician's eyes came to her. The subject changed, became something else.

Nothing was said, nothing Matthew could hear, the silent language of women.

Matthew told the politician, "I think I can save you a little money. Not much, but some."

"How so?"

"I have an issue with a couple of your bodyguards."

"Which ones?"

"Let's start with the big one. The one who has no idea who the fuck I am."

"That's Charlie. He said you were incompetent. A disappointment."

"Because of London."

"Yes. Says you're incompetent and overpriced and he could do better."

"He wants the job."

"Maybe I should give it to him."

"Let me have two minutes with Charlie."

"He's a former marine."

"Then if he is right, let him do the job."

Again the politician went into deep thought, and again she nodded.

Meeting over, they walked down the jetty; this time she walked behind her husband, no longer walking side by side like they were equals, following him by ten feet, doing that as if she were in a Muslim country that oppressed women.

The bodyguard the size of the Hulk waited for them, had never taken his eyes away from them.

Matthew's pace had quickened, had changed to a fast walk, that fast walk to a slow jog, that jog to an all-out sprint. His speed took him on a direct path, on a collision course with the huge man who had insulted him. Matthew leaped at the man, struck him in the face and neck before the bodyguard realized he was under attack, sent the man's stylish hat flying into the sand.

Matthew stepped away. Waited for the big man.

The big man grabbed his neck and yelled out in pain, the sound swallowed by the sea.

He had been cut. He bled from his face; blood spurted from his neck as well.

Matthew faced the big man. "I told you that was your last time calling me white boy."

Like he was a matador. El Matador had risen from inside her husband.

A knife was in Matthew's hand, its blade dripping blood, a blade no more than an inch long. A knife she hadn't seen. A knife that the bodyguards had failed to find. A short blade that, based on the way the bodyguard was bleeding, was sharp enough to perform surgery.

The politician did another hand motion, told everyone else to stand down.

The bodyguard who had been cut ran after Matthew. Matthew didn't run. El Matador never ran. As the big man tried to attack El Matador, he was cut again, and again, cut as El Matador did smooth moves around the huge man, each cut weakening his prey, each cut on a specific artery, spots that made blood flow like a river. The big man never touched Matthew, went down on his knees trying, became a crippled bull at the mercy of El Matador, redness pouring from his body and mixing in the beautiful white sand, sand that had risen up on the man's face and body, sand that covered the big man as he fell.

She had heard that there was only one hospital on the island. Holberton Hospital on Queen Elizabeth Highway. It was near town, at least forty minutes and two thousand potholes away from this secluded beach. It would take an ambulance much longer than that to get here, if one came at all.

And all that would be left in the sand was the remains of what used to be an arrogant man.

Matthew stared out at the rest of the bodyguards, tropical heat putting sweat on eleven swarthy faces.

She knew who her husband was looking for. And the man backed away, saw when the politician signaled to leave it be, meaning he had no help, and the big man started running. It was the one who had patted her down, the one who had touched her breasts and thighs in that disrespectful way.

The man didn't make it far. He looked stupid trying to run in the sand. His hat left his head as he bolted. The man stumbled and fell like a woman in a horror film. Seconds later he too was in the sand, hat blowing and tumbling in the wind, his blood flowing like an undammed river.

Breathing heavily, Matthew faced the remaining men.

With his right foot he drew a line in the sand and waited, blade in hand.

No one crossed that line. No one answered his call. Ten men stood like statues.

There was a difference between men who hurt people and men who killed people.

There was something in their eyes that hadn't been there before.

Some would confuse it for respect. But she knew it was fear. Unadulterated fear.

Matthew strutted toward them and they all parted like the Red Sea, some stumbling to move. As her husband marched away, she looked back at the politician. She stared at her with her teeth clenched.

Then she walked around the dying men, sand getting inside her sandals and between her toes.

While the men shivered at the sight of El Matador, she stared at her husband.

That smile he had shared with the beautiful politician burned inside her brain.

She wasn't going to look back at the woman dressed in yellow. But she did. Like Lot's wife she did look back. Looked back at the well-dressed woman who was looking down at her.

Men lay dying, blood on the tropical floor, but none of that mattered.

She didn't care about the politician's perfect hair or the beautiful yellow shoes designed by Bottega Veneta. She didn't see the Bottega Veneta bracelet and Bottega Veneta pearl ring. Didn't see the David Yurman oval Figaro chain around the politician's neck. She didn't see a woman hiding behind more than ten thousand dollars of top-shelf designer gear. All she saw was the face of her enemy.

She saw a woman who, if the wrong word was said at that moment, she would battle in the sand.

With a curt sneer that came from the streets of Detroit, the politician told her she saw the same. It was almost a battle between Chi-town and Motown.

There was a difference between women who hired people to kill people and women who would walk up to you and put a bullet in your head. A big difference that she was ready to teach the politician.

The politician turned around, did that as if all other women were insignificant, and walked back down the jetty, went back to staring out at the Caribbean Sea, did that as if nothing else mattered.

Did that as if she were not surrounded by the dying and the dead.

Again she raised her cellular, clicked a button.

"Soon your head will hang from your fucking neck."

Then the cellular rang. The politician looked at the number before she answered.

She watched the Lady from Detroit for a while.

Hypnotized by power.

Then the politician turned and saw she was still there, the politician's eyes moving up and down her body before she, with the flick of her wrist, made a dismissive motion, a motion that made her feel so small, so unimportant, so nothing, so much like she had felt as a child.

With a simple motion the master had told the slave she was no longer needed.

She moved away from the politician, jogged through the killing fields, passed two stylish men's hats that no longer had owners, moved around two dead bodies that no longer were the shells of egotism, passed stunned bodyguards, sand flying from her sandals as she hurried to catch up with her husband.

Nineteen

doomed to die

"Gideon?"

It was a woman's voice, soft and strong all at once, mild Southern accent to her speech.

The room was dark. I was on my back. Throat so dry it ached to swallow. The winds were strong. Sounded like Armageddon was happening, like I'd woken up in the middle of a hurricane.

"Gid*eon . . . eon . . . eon.*"

Her voice echoed as pain moved through my body.

"Open *up up up. Take take take* these pills."

I tried to talk, but the words refused to form. Tried to focus on her. Couldn't.

That throaty alto voice stopped reverberating, repeated, "Drink."

Long hair. Haunting eyes. Deep frown on a pretty face. It was Hawks.

"*Damn it, drink. Take the pills. I would let you suffer awhile longer, but I'm not that evil.*"

I did what she said.

"*Konstantin sent me to babysit you.*"

My mouth opened. First there was a chalky taste. Water on my lips.

Her hands were warm. Scent sweet. Same as it had been in Dallas.

I tried to look at her. Light was behind her head, making her look like an angel with a halo.

I remembered letting close to fifteen stone of arrogance fall from the Cessna. My fever had magnified, body aches had done the same, turbulence, ground had rushed up at me, I had struggled to land.

After that, all was a blur, no solid images, snapshots from an opaque world.

I asked, "What's going on . . . all that noise . . ."

"Tornadoes."

I mumbled something. Pain and fever stole my words.

She said, *"Don't think I'm doing this because I care. Owe Konstantin a favor, that's all."*

Then I was unconscious again. Covered in a nightmare.

Imprisoned.

My hands were tied, a plastic bag was over my head, and I was being suffocated.

I was on a filthy floor of a flat in London, an assassin dancing over me as I died.

She was there too. The woman from Detroit. She was there, arms folded, smiling.

I jerked awake, grogginess on me, mind heavy with a thousand thoughts, my body in pain.

The skies boomed.

My eyes tried to focus and make out the shadows in this small, stuffy room. The T.V. was on and I made out a familiar voice. Heard her say a tornado had carved out a pathway through the center of downtown. Windows blown out at the Omni and just about every skyscraper in the area. Trees were uprooted. Skies boomed. Rain fell harder. Sounded like someone had slit open the heavens.

I took a hard breath. Rubbed my temples. The bedroom was barely a six-by-nine. I looked at the digital clock. The numbers were flickering, first digit hard to read. It was either eight at night or three in the morning. Room smelled like a cross between an old folks' home and an abandoned building.

Lightning. Then another boom that echoed like the report of a twelve-gauge.

The bed squeaked as I shifted around and moaned. Back ached. The mattress was prison thin, the pillow not much better. The pillow was damp with the sweat from my face and neck.

"You up?"

I jumped at the sound of the voice.

Hawks was by the window, watching me. It took me a minute, but I pushed up on my elbows.

Hawks had a newspaper in her hand; it rustled as she snapped it closed.

"Hawks . . ." My voice was gravelly and slow, each word thick. "What are you . . . doing here?"

"You should be on your knees thanking me."

A glass of water was on the nightstand. My dry throat and dehydrated body begged me to reach for that and drink. I did. Swallowed hard and coughed. Put the glass back and asked, "How bad?"

"Plenty of bruises, nothing broken."

I practiced breathing for a few. "Doesn't feel that way."

"Could have chipped bones. Can't tell without an X-ray. Your knuckles are swollen."

"Had to deal with a couple of problems."

"Both of your hands and arms are cut up like you were dragged across concrete."

I grunted. "Alley fight in Birmingham."

"Figured it was someplace where there was garbage or urine or rat feces, because you've got a real nice infection. You have to wash cuts like that in a ten-minute time frame. You could've died."

There was a jolting triple boom that rattled the room, made the lights outside flicker.

"Your temp was a hundred and two when I got to you," she said when there was a break in the thunder and lightning. "You were as feverish and delirious as a North Korean POW."

"Swing by a gas station or a drugstore and get me some B.C. Powder. You can go back to Nashville. I don't need you sitting over me looking like you need some Tucks. I'll be okay."

"Look, you have excessive swelling. Redness from the cuts all up and down your arms. Pus. That means the infection has gotten through the skin barrier and into your tissue. Moved from there into your bloodstream and caused a systematic reaction. Immune system breaking down."

A chalky taste was on my lips. I asked, "What did you give me?"

"Cyanide."

"Hawks."

"Theraflu and a broad-spectrum antibiotic. Don't know what you're allergic to, so I'm taking a chance. My guess is that you're going to need to be on antibiotics for at least a week."

Bed squeaked a hundred times while I sat up the best I could. Hawks had on nice dungarees and green cowboy boots. Black turtleneck. Black leather coat on the small table.

My wardrobe was simple: gray boxers and white socks, my socks dirty on the bottom. I reeked like the day before yesterday. Licked around the insides of my mouth. Tart and dry. Tongue felt thick, swollen. My jeans, boots, jacket, backpack, all my clothes were piled up at the foot of the bed.

She said, "You took a serious ass-whooping."

"I gave better than I took."

She went on, "This room probably has just as many germs."

"Probably."

"Sheets are atrocious. Stained. Wouldn't doubt if that bed kept you infected."

"How did I get here?"

"I brought you here. I came from Nashville, got you from the airport. You were unconscious when I got to you. Guess you got in just before the storm hit. You called Konstantin and passed out in the plane from what I know. As sick as you were when I got there, I'm surprised you landed the plane."

All she said seemed like a dream. The room was stuffy. Wasn't sure if I was awake yet.

Hawks said, "You doing okay over there?"

"Still breathing." I nodded. "What time is it?"

"Three thirty in the morning."

"You've been here the whole time?"

"For the most part. The storm was too bad to go anywhere for a long time. Once I got you situated and the winds eased up, I took a chance, came and went, had to get your meds."

A dry cough came on hard. Nose was stopped up, started running. Bladder was full. Stomach rumbled. All systems woke up and cried for me to get to the bathroom before liftoff. The covers on my legs were heavy, weighed down by my own sweat. I groaned, struggled to get to my feet.

She said, "You're welcome."

I nodded. "Thanks, Hawks."

"You're one ungrateful bastard."

"Hawks."

She folded her arms and took a hard breath. "Should've picked up that cyanide."

A moment later I asked, "Where am I?"

"Alamo Motel."

"What part of town?"

"Metropolitan Parkway."

"Safe here?"

"If you call being surrounded by whores, drug dealers, and bottom-feeders safe, yeah."

"Why here?"

"There was a safe house over at Fulton Cotton Mill Lofts. Good thing we didn't go there."

"It get raided?"

"Tornado hit it. Direct hit. Tore the roof off. Ripped down the brick walls."

"Last night?"

She nodded. "CNN building and the Congress Center, all the windows blown out. Trees down and in the middle of houses. Looking like Cambodia out there. You slept through it all."

I took a step and almost went down, my legs feeling like wet noodles, embarrassed for a moment.

Hawks stepped closer to me, but I waved her away.

My limp made me have to hold the wall as I moved on to the bathroom. Small space. Shower over the tub, and a toilet. Barely enough room to close the door. I sat and let nature do its thing.

Poison passed through my body. Everything about my insides felt wrong.

Hawks called out, "Everything all right in there?"

"Yeah."

"Solid or runny?"

"Can I have a moment to myself, please?"

I flushed. Then damned whoever invented one-ply tissue. Then flushed again. Washed my hands and face in the dark. Went back into the other room at a slow, wounded pace. Still dark. Rain steady and hard. Winds blowing like they wanted to rip us up and send us to the other side of Kansas.

I took my iPhone from my bag. Logged on long enough to look in on that house in Powder Springs. Catherine and the kid were home. Didn't look like there had been any tornado damage, they didn't look like they were afraid. Saw they were okay. I turned the phone off, put it away.

Then I looked at Hawks. Her long hair, Native American features, and haunting eyes.

She pulled a chair up to the television, motioned for me to sit. I did. She pulled another chair up next to me, took one of my arms, looked it over, did the same with the other. Her hands were warm.

Her touch sent electricity up my arm.

She said, "Don't think I want to touch you. You just need some hemming up."

"My own Florence Nightingale."

"Do us both a favor and this will be less painful for the both of us."

"The favor?"

"Speak when spoken to. Keep your trap shut unless you're answering a question."

A big black purse was on the table. Darkness had hidden that from me. She opened her bag and took out six or seven cellular phones;

sounded like more were inside her bag. I assumed they were clones. She put those phones aside, then took out silk sutures, a straight needle, some xylocaine to numb the area, and betadine to clean the wound before she started sewing me up.

Hawks looked up long enough for me to see her haunting eyes.

She asked, "Why are you looking at me like that?"

"No reason."

Her scent was subtle, eucalyptus and rosemary mixed with sandalwood and lavender.

She said, "Just because you're half-naked and we're in a hotel, don't get any ideas."

Again, thunder boomed. Lightning flashed. Winds roared without mercy.

Hawks used the television as her light and focused on fixing me up. She worked without a word, sewed me up in two places, one on each forearm, both taking three stitches, did that without flinching or being squeamish. While she did that I looked at the images on the news. Downtown looked like a war zone. When Hawks was done, she put the chairs back at the table, went over to the window.

I went to the dresser and looked in the scratched mirror, checked out her patchwork.

"Thanks."

"And one more thing." She nodded. "I don't need your charity."

"What are you talking about?"

"Five thousand dollars."

"Nobody said you were a charity case."

"I came up here to tell you that face-to-face. And to bring you back your money. It's over there with your filthy things. I took out enough for gas money, which was a lot, and I took out enough to pay for the medicine, and I paid for one night at this skanky motel, and I bribed the guy at the airport to hear no evil and see no evil, and . . . oh, and since you cost me two days off work, I took enough for that. I think that just about covers it. The rest of the money is tucked in with the rest of your stuff. We're even."

I nodded, not in the mood to argue, not strong enough to reply.

The lady on television was tracking the tempest. Said that the windstorm had crossed through Cobb County into Fulton County. Trees were being ripped up and streets were flooded.

The next round of thunder and lightning sounded like a series of nuclear explosions.

She said, "The Jewell of the South is reporting today."

I glanced over, saw Jewell Stewark's face on the television, her hair down and straight, her clothing conservative. No longer Veronica Lake. She looked different in person, looked much better.

I said, "She sounded different in person. Guess that's her television voice."

"You know her?"

"Ran into her once."

"You worked for her?"

I shook my head. "Used to live down here."

"You stayed in Georgia?"

"For a while."

"When?"

"Up until last year."

"I imagined you always lived someplace exotic, Paris or Italy, someplace overseas."

We silenced ourselves and let Jewell Stewark do the talking.

Landmarks had been damaged. Cabbagetown took a hit. Trees uprooted. Pets were missing.

The winds picked up and lightning flashed as thunder boomed.

Hawks said, "So you lived in the South up until last year."

"Had a place here."

"Well, that's good to know."

"Had homes in Seattle and right outside of Los Angeles too."

"And you lived right here in Georgia."

Hawks turned the television off and that left us in the dark. Guess she was scared all of that would attract the lightning. It was just me, her, and the forces of nature. She went to the dresser. Bottles of medicine were lined up near a Bible. A Bible furnished by the Gideons. For a moment, in my mind, I was back in Detroit, in the basement of a million-dollar home, a hollowed-out Bible at my feet. Hawks tore a disposable thermometer from a strip, opened one, and put it inside my mouth. Had me hold it under my tongue for a minute. Clicked a light on long enough to read the result. Temp was down to a hundred.

"Take your temp every hour. It hits one oh two, it will be time to pack up and go to Grady. Agreed?"

I didn't answer her. In my mind that meant there was no agreement.

She went on, "You're a mesomorph, so I think you'll be okay, but you never know."

"What's *mesomorph* mean?"

"Surprised I know a couple of ten-dollar words, are you?"

"Nothing about you surprises me."

"It means you're athletic, solid, and strong. Gain and lose weight easily."

"Mesomorph."

"Worth a few points playing Scrabble. Eighteen with no double- or triple-letter scores."

I limped to the bathroom, came back, and crashed on the squeaky bed. Mattress was as soft as a slab of concrete. Hawks sat in the wooden chair. Crossed her legs, her hands on the knee of her dungarees, a sigh etched in her face. She leaned back into the darkness, became that silhouette once again. Every now and then the sky rumbled and lit up and I had a better view of her.

We stared at each other for a while, her green eyes magnetic and haunting.

I said, "Sometimes."

"Sometimes what?"

"It gets to me. Sometimes. Only when I stop and think about it."

"Now was that so hard to say?"

"Did this job down in Tampa. Took out a few men with sledgehammers."

"That rapper? You did that job? Good Lord, that was you?"

I nodded.

Hawks made a nasty face. "That was plain old disgusting."

"That was the one that got to me."

"Talk about some nasty work. They had that on the news for weeks."

"That's the one that stuck with me."

She shook her head, took a deep breath, slapped her thighs. "Want to talk about it?"

"No. Just answering your question."

I limped to the bathroom again, came back, and crashed on the slab of concrete.

I told Hawks, "Sorry I didn't call you."

There was no reply.

She asked, "Will you need anything else?"

"Food. Water. B.C. Powder."

"You'll need more drugs. I can get a prescription called in."

"Just tell me what I owe you, Hawks."

"Doing this for Konstantin, not for you."

"For Konstantin."

"And I wanted to bring you back your money. I'm not a charity case."

"You drove up in a thunderstorm to tell me that?"

"I called you and you didn't answer your dang phone."

"You told me not to answer your calls."

"So now you can do whatever I ask you to do?"

"I can."

"Good. Go to hell. Could you do that for me? Don't see you moving."

"Give me the directions."

"Jerk."

"Stop being cheeky about everything."

"And *cheeky* means what exactly?"

"Stop being rude. You're pissed off, I get it. You're vexed at your old man. He abandoned you. I didn't call you. Don't take it out on me. Now let it go. Move on. Or leave. Let it go or leave me alone."

Hawks huffed. "You're a real jerk, Gideon. The jerk of all jerks. A worthless jerk."

She quieted, leg bouncing at an easy pace. Don't think she was paying attention. Her body language told me that she had drifted, was processing a thousand thoughts. Moans. Grunts. In the room next door, a sex therapist and her client cursed and called out for Jesus, tried to bang a hole in the wall, the headboard hammering at an uneven rhythm, like he was fucking her in Morse code.

"Because the heathens next door are unloading their wagons, don't get any ideas."

"Not getting any ideas, Hawks."

"And stop looking at me."

"Hawks, you can stop looking at me too."

"I'm not looking at you."

I asked, "Then how do you know if I'm looking at you?"

"Get your mind out of the gutter. Those memories are no good."

"I didn't say they were good."

"Oh, it wasn't good?"

I took a breath. "It was good."

"Not good enough to make you want to pick up the phone."

"Hawks."

"You were a mistake."

Hawks picked up her newspaper again; it rustled as she snapped open the pages, now done arguing. I closed my eyes again, my stomach calming down, the pain easing up, the medicine settling in.

Darkness pulled at me. I struggled, a tug-of-war with consciousness. Darkness won.

Twenty

the stranger beside me

Antigua Yacht Club.

She snapped at her husband, *"It's a yes-or-no question."*

Matthew walked away, went across the room, again putting the television on CNN.

She followed him across the room. "Did you sleep with that bitch?"

Matthew went back on the patio, hands on the rail, staring at lush hills and yachts.

She stormed inside the bathroom, turned on the shower, hands in her hair, her head down.

She knew about Matthew, knew of some of the women before her. Spanish woman, Native American woman, East Indian woman, an occasional Asian girl, women who flocked to European men the same way men of African descent, Asian men, and Spanish men were fascinated with European women. She knew Matthew had been with many types of women, women he had met at art museums, smart women, older women who were good with their money, women who had taught him to be good with his money. Before her there had been so many different types of women.

But she was the one he had chosen to marry.

He had told her that when it came down to the time for a man and woman to settle down, no matter how much fun he'd had with women of other races, most times he picked someone from his own tribe. Everything else was just practice. Everything else was just pussy.

The way she saw it they were all the same race, the human race, and if God didn't want what man had defined as being different races to procreate, then God would've made it so mixed races couldn't have babies, or the offspring would be unable to procreate, like a horse and a donkey making a mule or a hinny, the end result being ugly as hell and sterile. If that were true then the arguments to not mix races would make some sense, but in her mind it was stupid. People had the same number of chromosomes for a reason. That was part of the plan. Whatever was here now was part of millions or billions of years of evolution, every day a fight to not become extinct. To her the mixing of races was as natural as evolution, and people were afraid of evolution because people were afraid of change.

People were afraid of change.

That was how she had felt, before today, before that meeting at Pigeon Point Beach.

All of her liberalism had been destroyed; all she could imagine was Matthew fucking that woman.

Fuck liberalism. Fuck broad-mindedness, fuck open-mindedness, fuck goddamn freethinking.

Fuck horses, donkeys, and mules.

She stepped back out of the bathroom, tried to keep calm, failed terribly, anger out of control.

"And tell me, Matthew, when did you learn to speak this patois they speak here?"

"Long time ago."

"What did she say when I walked up?"

"Nothing you need to know. She's always had an attitude like that."

She snapped, "So you fucked her."

"For somebody who was out all night and couldn't answer one or two simple questions—"

"I was working."

"Then why did you lie and say you were here sleeping? You are full of shit."

"Did you?"

"Yeah, I fucked her. I fucked her *good*."

That halted her, her anger expanding. "When did you fuck her?"

"Before I met you."

"Have you worked for her before?"

"Worked for her husband before. He had some problems he paid me to fix."

"Never for her?"

"She wanted to hire me a few years back."

"To do what?"

"A contract on her husband."

"Such a devoted wife. Did you take the contract on her husband?"

"It was a tight time frame. I wasn't available that weekend."

"Why not?"

"I was in Costa Rica on vacation with my wife. So it was farmed out, went to this other guy."

"The guy we followed in London. The guy she called Gideon."

"Yeah. The guy who calls himself Gideon."

"When did you fuck her?"

"Before we married."

"When before? The day before? The night before? Five minutes before? How long before?"

"Before before."

"Where?"

"The Omni in Detroit."

"While you were working for her husband."

"Is there a point to this inquisition?"

"She suck your dick?"

"Don't ask if you can't handle the truth."

"Did she swallow?"

"Get out of my fucking face."

"Did she?"

"Don't fucking push up on me."

"You're thinking about that *bitch* right now, aren't you?"

"Move. Last time. *Move.*"

"That's why your dick is so fucking hard."

"Does it fucking matter?"

"Stop, Matthew. Take your hands off me."

"What's your fucking problem?"

"What're you going to do? Beat me up or fuck me?"

"If you want me to fuck you just say so."

"*You fucking pig.* I'll *never* let you fuck me again. Never."

She wrestled with him as he yanked her pants off her, tried to get away as he lifted her and threw her on the bed, squirmed as he pulled his pants to his knees, moaned as his dick went inside her.

She was sore. Tender. His harsh penetration brought tears to her eyes.

He asked, "Is this what you want? What's the matter? Okay when you take what you want but when it's the other way around, you don't like it, do you? Stop trying to be a fucking control freak."

"Answer the question, Matthew." She put her nails in his skin. "Answer the goddamn question."

His moan covered her as he moved, as her dampness spread, as she began to tingle with fire.

She moaned as well. "Answer . . . answer . . ."

She cursed him, his fucking like thunder and lightning.

She grunted, panted out her words. "You fucking . . . me . . . or you fucking . . . that bitch?"

His hand moved around her neck, choking her, shutting her up as he manhandled her.

She stared at him, unable to breathe, glowered at his intensity.

He was killing her. It felt like he was killing her. 'Til death do us part. And this was death.

Then his choke lessened. She gasped, coughed, felt him growing inside her, his stroke faster.

She grabbed his hand, put it back on her throat, his grip cutting off the blood supply to the brain. Everything intensified, every sensation; she felt his every stroke. Anger was erased, replaced with light-headedness, an overwhelming exhilaration.

The Red Stripe. The E. The weed. It was all there, lingering in her system.

Her orgasm came hard and fast, a series of waves, a tsunami that displaced all other emotions, a devastating orgasm that destroyed all in its path. She was drowning, gasping, her breathing so labored.

It was as if time were skipping. As if she were experiencing a temporary loss of consciousness.

His hand slipped away from her throat; she gasped back to life, sweating, dizzy.

It felt as if she were blacking out again. Everything so stretched out and so far away. Everything so blurred, the world melting. Her breathing was short and quick, rapid, hyperventilating.

Then it felt as if she were being pulled away from the world again.

In that transcendental state, she saw him. She saw his swarthy skin clearly. Saw his locks.

She left that nightmare, came back a little at time, life creeping back into her body.

Matthew was over her, jaw tight, yanking her back into him over and over.

He was going in and out of her so fast. His face as red as his hair.

Her hands went up, touched his face, grabbed his throat, choked him as hard as she could.

She struggled, growling as she strained against his strong neck.

She panted, "Come, damn it . . . will you fucking come already . . . shit."

He bucked hard as he struggled to breathe. Bucked hard, swelling inside her.

"That's it . . . that's it . . . come . . . come . . . get your nut."

She cringed as he pounded into her, fucked her with no mercy.

"Come on Matthew that's it that's the shit come on damn it come come Matthew come."

Then he gripped her, letting out a roar as he exploded.

She held him as he came, her mind back at the Siboney, back on the lover she'd had hours ago. Back on the boy she had killed. In the throes of autoerotic asphyxiation, she had seen him.

She held Matthew as long as she could, panting, not wanting him to roll away and see her face.

In that moment she thought about the first time they had had sex.

Right after a job on the East Coast. A fight between bookstore co-owners. Successful business. But money was the dividing line in a lifelong friendship and partnership. One partner threatened the other, brought an ax to a meeting, demanded a showdown. The other picked up his cellular and called their handler. Took out a contract on his business associate of twenty years. Wetwork, a twisted aphrodisiac. After the job. Sheraton. Rittenhouse Square. Philadelphia. The next week he had taken her to Place Pigalle, Paris's sex district. Matthew had needed her to fulfill a contract on a Parisian woman. A whore who was about to step up and go to the media and expose a very important politician, destroy his career and his family. Matthew took contracts on women, had no problem walking into a house and taking out an entire family, adults and children, if that was what the contract called for, but he had called her in on the job.

The start of teamwork.

She'd done the job, then went shopping; he had bought her a present, that being unexpected, the first present he'd ever given her, a pair of brown suede Blahniks, tonal topstitching, three-and-a-half-inch heel, had given her a fifteen-hundred-American-dollar *shoegasm*. A bonus for doing such a damn good job. Brand-new Blahniks in her hand and a pair of cobalt-blue satin Blahniks on her feet, silver-tone hardware, crystal broach detail on the vamp, stilettos that made her four and a quarter inches taller.

She'd held his hand, her pussy tingling, the shopping making her so damn wet as they walked by sex shops, went inside peep shows, had drinks at strip clubs. Then back to Jays Paris for sex in a five-star room. New Blahniks on her feet. Matthew let her turn the experience into a sex-filled fashion show. Sex that lasted for two days. Sex that made him run out and come back with a new pair of Blahniks for her to wear as she fucked him, the new pair silver metallic leather with a grosgrain trim, button strap across the vamp, open toe, four-inch heel. Blahniks inspired her and her inspiration drove him mad. The madness made him give her rough sex that made her dizzy, nonstop sex that made her nose bleed, S&M that rocked her world, sex that made her give up dating all other men. And her sex made him stop and shop before they left the ecstasy on Champs-Elysées, inspired him to buy her another pair of Blahniks, black with red lining, gold-tone hardware, perforated detail, buckled ankle strap, four-inch covered heel.

Matthew was her Prince Charming, her shining knight, her Mr. Big.

She sucked his dick inside the crowded store. Had taken him inside the tiny bathroom and sucked his dick until he couldn't stand it, made him moan as she sucked the come out of his dick, the new Blahniks on her feet, so inspired, so fucking inspired, so damn horny, willing to do anything.

Except swallow.

They were a team. A hardworking team. Fucking like maniacs and killing like crazy.

Bookstore owners. Drug dealers. Rappers. Politicians. Wives. Soccer moms. Children who wanted to accelerate the date of their inheritance, parents who were disappointed in their children.

Everybody wanted somebody to cease existing.

Everybody wanted someone to be unborn in order to make their existence a little more pleasant.

Money was always a dividing line.

And hate. Hate was a dividing line as well. Not all work was about money.

Some was simply rooted in hate. Like Detroit. The bitch Matthew had fucked.

Staring at the ceiling, she swallowed and managed to say, "Asshole."

She let her husband go, pushed him away. A dollop of come leaked out of her, stained the covers on the four-poster bed. She saw Matthew was barely sweating. Her sweat was a raging river. When she positioned herself to look at him, he was already staring at her, intense El Matador eyes.

Matthew said, "At least this asshole can be honest and answer a question."

"Fuck you."

"That's good, real good."

"And now you have me working for her."

"Money is money. If I had a wife who wasn't a shopaholic and understood the value of a dollar . . ."

"Is she good with money? Is that what you like about that embezzling bitch?"

"Obviously, when it comes to finances, she's better than you are."

"She's nothing more than a thief. Stealing from her precious city to pay for this shit."

"Takes a smart woman to pull that off."

"Anybody can embezzle."

"You should know. You've had your hands so deep in my pockets my net worth has dropped. We are worth two hundred thousand. That's all we have to last us the rest of our days. And if I let you, you would spend that much next week. The house we bought has decreased in value and the new cars you bought will never appreciate in worth. We're in the middle of a recession; that means we have to save more than we spend, but you don't get that. My credit score has taken a serious hit, one I will never recover from in this lifetime. I was worth a lot more before this marriage. A lot more when I was solo."

"Maybe you should've married Suze Osmond."

"Suze *Orman*."

"*Like I give a damn.*"

Her clit throbbed. Her pussy ached. She still felt his hand around her neck.

Her thoughts remained the same.

Soon a dead boy would be found on the beach.

Across the room, on CNN, they kept yapping about a crumbling economy, the housing crisis, cosigning all the depressing shit Matthew had said, as if Gerri Willis had teamed up with her husband.

Matthew was up, heading for the bathroom, rinsing himself off, then pulling his pants back on.

"How many times did you fuck her?"

"Never fuck a woman once, because she'll feel like a whore. Never fuck a woman three times, because she'll think you're in a relationship. How's that for yet another answer?"

"So you fucked her twice."

"Worry about where you were last night."

"Did you fuck her more than two times?"

He ignored her.

She cursed him and moved from the bed, picked up her pants, come draining down her leg.

He said, "If this Gideon job doesn't work for you, feel free to hop on a plane and leave Antigua."

"What did you do for her in London?"

"Something that I decided did not require your assistance."

"Was she in London?"

"She was not in London."

"She hired you for a side job and you couldn't tell me."

"I could've told you, but I chose not to tell you."

"Why?"

"Because I didn't need you there to fuck it up."

"I thought we were a team."

"That was a business decision I made due to your tendency to make things difficult."

"What did you do? What was it you did that didn't require my assistance?"

"None of your fucking business."

"And you fucked her."

"I thought we had covered that."

"I bet you'd love for me to leave you on this island with that paranoid, self-righteous bitch."

"And if you stay, don't fuck this one up like you did the last time."

She went into the bathroom, slammed the wooden door.

"You never told me how you lost the target in London. What happened in ten seconds?"

"I didn't fuck it up."

"Like hell you didn't. Just like you fucked up the job down here."

"I did the goddamn job."

"And you fucked it up."

"By myself. I took care of it by myself."

"Like you fuck everything else up."

"I did the goddamn job without any fucking assistance whatso-ever."

"Five for one? I'd suggest you go get a job at Starbucks, but you'd probably fuck up a latte too."

"I did the fucking job."

"Three bullet holes are in you. That's three fuckups you need to remember right there."

The front door opened and slammed.

Now her world was silent.

Her heart raced; her hand trembled as much as her legs.

She sat on the shower floor, warm water raining on anger, nausea rising, come draining.

Twenty-one

the boxer

Vicious pounding on the cheap hotel door woke me up with a start.

"Hello? Hello? Housekeeping. Hello?"

The door opened fast but was stopped by the chain. I had jumped up, was about to charge whoever came inside the room, my fists, knees, and elbows the only weapons I had on me at the moment.

"Housekeeping. You alive or dead? You hear me? You done over-dosed? Hello?"

"I'm asleep." I took a deep breath, collapsed back on the bed, cleared my throat, the room starting to spin because I had jumped up too fast, tried to shake off the meds, and yelled, "Come back later."

The raspy-voiced woman at the door yelled back at me, "What time you checking out, mister?"

I struggled to find my voice. "Not checking out today."

"Then you better go down to the office and tell them that."

I coughed, every word sounding coarse. "Will do in a little while."

"*Are you deaf?* I said you need to go down there *right now.* I'm not going to be cleaning up these *damn* rooms all day. I need you to get up and *go pay for the damn room* so I can make my rounds."

My door slammed hard enough to boom like thunder. Curses sprinkled as her cart rumbled.

This was not the Four Seasons.

I swung around, put my feet on the floor. My movements remained laced with pain.

I don't know how long I was unconscious, just knew it wasn't long enough.

More antibiotics were on the nightstand. Not a lot, enough for a day or so. There was water, Gatorade, fruit, and a few snacks. And there was B.C. Powder. Hawks had left a care package in the chair where she had been sitting. Wounds were starting to itch. That meant I was healing.

Got up. Drank water, looked over my care package. Hawks had left me oxycodone for pain, the antibiotic Flagyl for the infection, and Benadryl that could knock out my stuffiness and kill the itching.

Looked over my stitches again. Hawks had skills. Seemed like she'd been living on a battlefield.

Took my temp again. Down to 99.7. My body told me I needed some more meds.

I popped one of everything Hawks had left, then forced down a banana and an apple. I went to the window, pulled back the curtains. It was my first time looking out on the boulevard. Pawnshops. Chicken houses. Flea markets. Simply 6 Clothing. Laundromats. Package stores. McDonald's. An area that had human trafficking and the prostitution of minors. R. Kelly–ville. Pedophile Alley.

Something told me to get out of there before trouble found me. I sat up, inhaled the staleness in this prison cell, stared at my clothes, listened to the rain, but that was about all I could do.

I used the bathroom again, took a quick shower; didn't want to smell unfresh any longer.

I dried off, then kept that paper-thin towel wrapped around my waist while I changed my dressings. The pus from my infection didn't look any better, but I wasn't feeling as bad. Hands could open and close a little easier. Fighting did a lot of damage to the hands. I felt all of that destruction. Another NexTemp thermometer told me my fever was staying steady. My feet were holding me up and my wobble wasn't as bad; didn't feel like I was riding in a rowboat during a hurricane anymore.

My illness was heavy, had become chains around my torso and legs, weights on my arms.

Hard knocks were at my door again.

"I ain't playing with you. Wake up and get your ass to the office and handle your business."

Then she walked away, not waiting for an answer.

Despite my nose being less stuffy I smelled marijuana, meth, beer, and hard liquor tinting damp air that was filled with the sounds of crunk, hip-hop, R&B, and gospel music, all of those competing and annoying noises used to cover the nonstop moans from paid-for sex. I smelled the fucking, inhaled the stench of cheap perfumes. Another breath revealed odors rising from urine-stained sidewalks.

This stench took me back to the red-lit world I had grown up in.

I dialed Hawks's number. She didn't answer. Didn't expect her to.

When her answering service kicked on I left a message. "Thanks. Take care of yourself."

Then I hung up the phone. Hung up to the sound of pounding at the cheap wooden door.

"Last time. I ain't playing with you, mister. Don't make me knock again."

It took a minute, but I washed my face, rinsed out my mouth, pulled on my clothes, made my way down to the front office to pay my bill, needed to do that so housekeeping wouldn't put a hit out on me.

"Good afternoon, son," the old man said as soon as I opened the door to the main office.

"Good afternoon." I coughed, head still aching. "Nurse Ratched told me to pay my bill."

"Who?"

"Housekeeping. The real nice one working my room on the second floor."

"We don't have any nice people in housekeeping."

"Yeah. I noticed. She's a pit bull on gunpowder."

"Looks like one too, especially around the mouth."

"I didn't see her."

"You didn't miss nothing worth seeing." He nodded. "Your friend called asking about you."

Before I could ask what friend, the old man backtracked and introduced himself, extended his wrinkled, feeble hand and said he was Kagamaster, the manager at this no-star hotel, a place sitting on a road leading to a slow hell. He was an old man who shuffled along with the help of a coal-black cane, the keys on his right hip jingling as he moved. The right side of his face was slack, like he'd suffered a stroke, but his speech was clear. A little slow, but his words were as strong as James Earl Jones's. A brown hearing aid was in his left ear. He'd been sitting down reading over a newspaper until I came in.

I asked, "Was it a woman?"

"Shhh. Lemme hear this part of the news. That twister done tore up everything."

A small television was on in the back room. Heard the newscaster saying that while downtown was being dismantled by the winds, the Englewood Manor apartments in southwest Atlanta had flooded because a storm drain was clogged up with leaves; people had woken up in water up to their knees.

Kagamaster said, "Clogged storm drain. Ain't that some mess?"

The newscaster was Jewell Stewark. I recognized her voice. Had a brief flashback.

I went back to the original conversation. "Was it a woman who called?"

The old man said, "Sure was. She said you were sick and called to check on you. Told me to tell you that. She didn't leave no number or nothing."

That meant Hawks had called since she left.

The room I was in cost thirty a day. I took out cash and paid for another twenty-four hours.

The old man looked down at the money. "What's that, some Monopoly money?"

I looked at the money, adjusting my mind to where I was. I had given him British pounds. If he had known the difference he would have realized I was paying him twice what the room cost. I took the money back, found American money in my other pocket, paid him in the proper currency.

He put a copy of the *AJC* in front of me and said, "You see the paper this morning?"

"I haven't seen anything but the inside of my eyelids."

"Read this mess. Paul McCartney gotta give that heifer he married fifty million dollars. She only had one leg to stand on when she met him. Bet she didn't have a bedpan to piss in when he met her."

"It's big news over in England."

"Damn shame a man work hard for all those years and end up losing a chunk of money like that. Heifer being that greedy. They ain't got but one kid. Don't take that much nothing to raise no chirren."

"And his baby mama deserves every penny." That voice came from the back, beyond a door behind Kagamaster. *"I don't care how many legs she got, she deserves every penny."*

"She don't have *legs*. She got *leg*. One *leg*."

A young woman came out with a book in one hand, her other hand on her hip. Early twenties. She had on a sweater and tight jeans, a bandana on her head, all of her colors in reds and yellows and oranges. She was small up top, heavy on the bottom, with thick arms and a small head.

Kagamaster said, "Bunny, what I done told you about getting in grown men—"

"Where you from?" she asked me. "You talk like you're from another country."

"Bunny, didn't you hear me and this young man having a conversation?"

"You get in a fight or something? You look tore up from the floor up."

"Bunny, leave the man alone."

I turned to Kagamaster and asked, "How far is Walgreens from here?"

"Walgreens? Right up that way toward the highway. By Run N' Shoot, I think."

I covered my mouth and coughed. "Can I walk there from here?"

Kagamaster said, "You not driving in this weather?"

"Walking."

"Well, it's about a thirty-minute walk from here. You gonna catch pneumonia. And if not pneumonia, in this area you might catch a bullet. Both'll kill ya. Just one is faster than the other."

I coughed again. "Can you call a taxi?"

"Let me look one up in the phone book. I got one or two circled already."

"See if they have any bulletproof taxis."

"I doubt it, but I'll ask 'em."

Bunny kept smiling at me while Kagamaster flipped through the yellow pages.

Kagamaster told her, "Ain't you got something to do 'sides stare at this young man?"

Bunny winked at me, then disappeared into the back.

An Escalade pulled up out front. An older black man was behind the wheel.

His eyes met mine, his face made of stone. I tensed, glanced around for something that could serve as a weapon. Then a young girl jumped out on the passenger side, a girl who was no older than twenty, and she rushed through the rain, umbrella high over her reddish-blond and purple hair. She had on a dungaree miniskirt and thigh-high boots. She smiled at me and said hello when she came inside.

Kagamaster gave her a room key and two Trojans. She pocketed the rubbers and hurried back out. She hopped in the SUV with her ancient sponsor. She and the old man vanished in the rain. I'd grown up in a world decorated with red lights, had witnessed scenes like that since birth.

Kagamaster looked at me, shook his head, and said, "Yessir, they all gonna end up in West Hell."

"I heard the tornado had the city shut down."

"What that girl selling never shuts down. Sells in all kinds of weather, day or night."

I thought about the pedophile I had dropped off somewhere between Birmingham and Atlanta. I looked at what was going on around me and thought about some of the things he had said.

Maybe there wasn't a God.

At least not one who gave a shit about the world He had created.

Men who abandoned kids, maybe they were doing the same thing God had done.

I thought about that because Catherine had told me that my old man had abandoned me.

I didn't know him, but in my mind he was still a god.

A god that had died when I was seven.

An orange cab pulled up.

I expected the driver to toot the horn, but he got out and jogged through the rain. He was big and it was like watching a mountain rush at us. He leaned to the side when he came through the door, leaned and ducked, like he was used to doorways being too small.

"Good morning, everybody," he said. "I mean, good afternoon. After twelve now."

Kagamaster spoke and I did the same.

"Ain't you a boxer?" Kagamaster asked.

"Yessir. Name is Alvin White. I used to fight a li'l bit."

"White, White. I know that name from somewhere."

"The White boys. Only we ain't white."

"I remember y'all. Your older brother fought too."

"Yessir. Joe-Joe was in the ring knocking 'em out until he joined the service. Went over to that Gulf War and he ain't been right since. Those chemicals they fighting with messed him up in the head. Came back here and can't get no kinna job. Government ain't doing nothing to get him right."

"Damn shame what our boys go through over there, then come back here to nothing."

"Me, Joe-Joe, Baby Brother, all the White boys fought, just like our daddy."

"Hold up, what did they used to call you?"

"Shotgun."

"You that one? They said every time you hit the bag it sounded like a shotgun blast."

"I busted quite a few bags in my day."

"Alvin 'Shotgun' White. Right here in front of me as I speak."

"That was me. I just go by Alvin now."

Kagamaster motioned toward Alvin's taxi. "You done retired from the ring?"

"Oh, I'll still take a fight if I can get one. Or be a sparring partner."

"Uh-huh."

Alvin went on, "My sister-in-law got me on at BellSouth about five years ago, lost that when they let a buncha us go last year, and my wife lost hers at Kmart when they closed all those stores."

Kagamaster nodded. "Hard times all over."

"Yessir. Hard times all over." He laughed. "But it looks pretty busy around this way."

"The worse it gets out there, seems like the better it is in here."

"If you need any help around here, I can paint, clean, fix just about anything."

"You don't say? A dump like this always needs something fixed."

"Or if any of your customers give you a problem, I can come around and fix that too."

Kagamaster shook Alvin's hand, then looked behind him. "Bunny, come out here. I want you to meet a celebrity. This man is a great fighter. Comes from a family of great fighters."

Bunny was in the back watching television. I made out the sounds of women fighting over a man, emotional screams, profanities being bleeped. An announcer said the show was *Cheaters*.

Bunny lowered the volume and yelled, "Is it Holyfield?"

"Bunny, get out here and meet this man."

"Is it Mike Tyson?"

"Get your butt out here right now."

"Mike Tyson and Holyfield both broke, so I don't need to meet no broke-ass man."

"Bunny. Last time."

Bunny mumbled something, then came out to meet Alvin.

"Bunny, this is my brand-new good friend Shotgun. Alvin 'Shotgun' White."

Bunny saw Alvin's size and her attitude adjusted, that flirty smile came back, and she pushed her chest out and said, "Wasn't you a bouncer at one of those clubs in Buckhead before they all closed up?"

Alvin nodded. "Was. On the weekends."

"You the one who beat my ex-boyfriend up one night."

"I did?"

"You beat him into the ground, did him up real good. He was in the hospital for two months."

"Tell him I said hello."

"I don't talk to him no mo'. Nice meeting you."

"Nice meeting you too, ma'am."

"I don't have a boyfriend no mo'."

"That's a shame. Young woman as pretty as you with no boyfriend."

"Especially this time of the year."

"Gets cold at night."

"Sure does. Gets real cold some nights. Sure could use some heat."

They exchanged lingering smiles until Bunny pulled away and hurried into the back room, running to get back to her television show, the volume going up and revealing a catfight was still going on.

Alvin extended his hand toward me. "Forgot . . . what was your name again?"

I shook his meaty hand, said, "Gideon."

Before we left, *AJC* in hand, the old man leaned forward the best he could and whispered to Alvin, "You hear how much that gold digger got from Paul McCartney? Read right here where the judge says that gold digger wasn't nothing mo' than a . . . what the judge say . . . read it right there."

Alvin shied away from the newspaper, wouldn't touch it, said, "I'll take your word for it."

"Now the judge . . . even *the judge* . . . said that gold digger had a 'warped perception of the world and indulged in make-believe.' . . . That heifer wanted eighty thousand dollars a year to buy wine."

I stood to the side while Kagamaster shook his head and read Alvin the whole story, while he broke down every penny that McCartney's ex-wife had asked for, including money for horseback riding.

Kagamaster said, "She got one leg and asking for horse-riding money. That is some bull."

Alvin whistled. "All that money?"

"They was married, what, about two years?"

From the back room Bunny yelled, *"And his baby mama deserves every penny."*

Twenty-two

taxi driver

The rain slowed down. I jogged out as fast as I could and sat up front in Alvin's taxi. He asked me to. It took that mountain of muscles a moment to get in because he had to maneuver his right leg in first, then bring his body inside, then work his left leg inside. His seat was all the way back, almost against the backseat, and still could have used another foot for comfort. His head was at the roof of the car.

It wasn't until then I noticed how much debris was scattered in the streets. Tree branches and a couple of downed trees were in sight. Lots of trash lined the boulevard, but I didn't know if that was from the storm or if that was just the way it was on this shopworn side of town. If it was Buckhead I'd know.

Alvin laughed. "That Bunny all steaks and chops, ain't she?"

I didn't answer because it didn't sound like a question. My wounds were itching pretty badly now. I was trying not to scratch too much and ride out the pain.

The inside of the taxi smelled like cigarettes and old socks, the black vinyl seats cracked here and there. A Krispy Kreme box was on the floor kissing an empty Starbucks cup. The windshield wipers worked overtime and Alvin never stopped laughing and talking to me like I was his new best friend.

He asked, "Where you from?"

Again I improvised. "Los Angeles."

"Always wanted to get out to California. Bet there some pretty red-bones out in California."

"Pretty women come in all hues."

"Who what?"

"Nothing. Yeah, pretty women out in Cali."

"Yessir, would love to get my hands on one of them California red-bones. If I ever got my hands on a Beyoncé or a Halle Berry . . ." He laughed and shook his head at his fantasy. "Lawd have mercy."

By the time we made it two lights I knew that he'd been married for twelve years, had two kids, was from Brooklyn but had been living in Atlanta for the last ten years.

He asked, "You in trouble with Johnny Law?"

I shifted. I'd lowered my guard and fallen into his friendly trap. If I was stronger or if he wasn't the size of Shaq and built like Luke Cage, I'd have been getting ready for another battle, a battle that I would, in this condition, have lost as soon as Alvin "Shotgun" White landed his first blow. He was a giant among men.

I asked, "You with the police?"

"No, sir."

"Informant?"

"No, sir."

"Associated with any branch of law enforcement?"

"No, sir."

I looked at the meter. It wasn't on. I brought that to Alvin's attention.

He waved like it was no big deal. "Just give me whatever you can when we get done."

"Turn the meter on so we can keep it honest."

"Just give me what you can, that's honest enough for me."

I let it go.

Alvin said, "So you in trouble with the law."

I said, "Not at all."

"It's all right if you don't want to say."

All words evaporated and we rested in a pool of silence for a moment.

I asked, "You done time?"

"Naw. But all my brothers and just about every other man in my family has for one reason or another. If you don't mind me saying so, hard for a black man to stay out of jail down here. Law harder on black people than white people. Jail time longer for a black man. Mostly drinking and fighting, the kind of thangs a man does at the end of the week after he done been talked down to by Mr. Charlie every day and shortchanged at the end of the week. Or he comes home to a nagging woman. Some in for, you know, drugs. Trying to get by by doing a little of this and that. Nothing too crazy. I've been blessed that the law ain't messed me around like that. Boxing kept me in the gym and outta too much trouble."

"Hard times all over."

"Sho 'nuff. People wake up and realize the American dream ain't for all Americans. Like those girls back at that hotel; I can't fault nobody for doing what they gotta do to make a living."

I nodded, then I coughed a little.

He said, "You real sick?"

"Getting there."

"That flu is going around. I got some chicken soup."

"I'm cool."

He was reaching his long arm over to the backseat, taking out a lunch pail, opening that up as he drove with one hand, the car never veering off the road.

Alvin said, "I had that flu real bad last week and my woman made me up some chicken soup."

"Smells good."

"That girl can cook better than the people at Cantrell's and Q-Time. The broth is the best part. You drank some of that, you'll be turning cartwheels in no time. That's why that flu can't stick to me."

The soup he'd given me was in a Styrofoam cup. I opened it up and sipped.

I said, "Your wife makes some good soup."

"My girlfriend made that. My wife does a'ight, but she can't make soup as good. Now, my wife is better with cakes and pies, things like that. People at our church line up to get a piece of her cakes."

"A girlfriend and a wife, huh?"

"You know how it is. Man needs a place he can rest his head and not hear a woman nagging."

We both laughed the laugh of men.

I sipped a little more of the broth, then went back to scratching my itching wounds.

He said, "You don't talk much, do you?"

"Not really."

"A thinking man."

"Sometimes."

"The best kinda man to be."

"Lot on my mind."

"Yeah, you a thinking man." His voice had lowered, almost to a hushed tone, like he was thinking out loud. He sucked his bottom lip, bobbed his head. "Sometimes I think I need to think more and talk less. I woulda done much better fighting if I had learned to listen instead of running my mouth so much."

He stopped at Walgreens. I went in and picked up my prescription.

My mind on Hawks.

Back at the Alamo I paid Alvin a decent fee, plus a hundred dollars. He said that he didn't need that much, that he didn't want to take all of my money. I pushed it back into his huge hands.

"God bless you, Gideon. God bless you and bless you and bless you."

"Just take care of your family. And that good-cooking girlfriend."

"You need to go anywhere, or you need anything, make sure you call me, no matter what time."

"Will do."

"I promise to try not to talk so much next time."

"No, you're cool. On Benadryl and other stuff. World is a haze right now."

"If you don't mind my saying . . ."

"Go right ahead."

He said, "You look like you work out a lot. Maybe next time you here I can take you up to Run N' Shoot. I shoot hoops, push some weights down there. I have a friend who can get us in at the Crunch Gym over in Smyrna. I goes up there and hits the bag and do some work in the ring time to time."

"Another girlfriend at Crunch?"

"Yeah. Slim and pretty. That one can't cook. Most skinny girls can't. But she real nice, though."

"Sounds good."

"One more thing."

"Okay."

"I see you got a few bruises and whatnot. If somebody bothering you and you need me to fix it for you, just let me know. I do that kinda work too. Not too much. But I can make people leave you alone."

I nodded. "I'll keep that in mind."

"Don't matter who or where. Need me to fix it, I can fix it."

"What do you charge for your services?"

"I'm reasonable. You can look at my clothes and see I'm not a rich man, so I won't ever ask for rich man's money. I'll take what you can give me to do what you need to get done. No questions asked."

We shook, his grip strong and sincere, his hand swallowing mine like a whale eating a guppy.

I asked, "Can you get guns?"

"I have a few with me."

"You're riding strapped?"

"Not safe out here, everybody robbing everybody, so I keeps one or two with me most times."

"What do you have?"

He went to the car and came back with a bag. Inside he had two .38s and two .22s.

I asked, "These clean?"

"They clean."

I bought a .38 and a .22 from him. He had ammunition and I bought that too.

Just like that we had become partners in crime.

He asked, "You ain't planning to rob no bank, is you?"

"I'm not a thief."

"Just asking. 'Cause I know a couple of people who are good drivers. And I know a couple of banks that would be easy for you to get in and out of, if you didn't already have that kinda information."

"Not robbing a bank." I coughed a little. "I just have a couple of people after me."

"Need me to fix it?"

"These are the type of people you have to fix with bullets, not fists."

"Drugs?"

"Not drugs."

He nodded. "What kinda work you do?"

"The kind that I don't talk about and you don't need to know about."

Again he nodded.

He asked, "Need me to look out for you? I could watch your door or something."

I motioned to the hardware I had just purchased, told him I'd be okay, would call if I needed him.

He was a big man, but a little bullet could reduce him to dead weight in an instant.

I wouldn't want his death on my conscience.

Then he left, his big body making the walkway outside my door rumble with each one of his steps.

The hotel phone rang after the sun went down. I woke up with a loaded gun on my lap, another nearby. I'd made a pallet on the floor. I was on the floor so if my door was kicked open, the first thing they would see would be an empty bed, not me half-naked and in a daze. The illness and medicine tried to hold me down on the stained sheets and pillows I had on the dirty carpet, but I sat up. In the room next door, a sex therapist and her client were moaning for Jesus and trying to bang a hole in the wall.

I reached up over my head, picked up the phone.

She said, "Gideon."

Hawks was on the line. She said my tag and I could smell lemons and tea tree and eucalyptus and rosemary all mixed with sandalwood and lavender and orange and sage. I saw her haunting eyes.

Hawks asked, "Feeling better?"

"Yeah. I'm healing. You know how people with mesomorphic body types are."

"Somebody's trying to get eighteen points playing Scrabble."

"Looked it up on the Internet. Read about the three somatotypes."

"Endomorphic, mesomorphic, and ectomorphic. Nice Scrabble words too."

"From what I read, I guess you have an ectomorphic body type."

I took easy steps and went to the window and spied out, gun in my right hand, the receiver to the phone in my left hand and up to my left ear, the cord stretching with every step.

I said, "Surprised you called."

"Was up. Konstantin called. I'm picking up a job or two."

"What about your administrative assistant gig?"

"Got fired."

"You serious?"

"I took off that day to come get you from exit 22. Sort of left and didn't tell anybody I was leaving. Got reprimanded. Then I did it again when I drove to Atlanta to make sure you were okay."

"Hawks."

"Hush."

"Okay."

"Needed to tell you something."

"After Dallas you were pregnant and had my baby."

"You wish. I'd send it down the toilet if it was yours."

"That's cold."

"No need to make a kid suffer for my bad judgment. Hell, if you couldn't remember to call me, would hate for you to do the same to the kid. I went through that mess with my old man. Still waiting. Oh, wait. Guess I'm being *cheeky* since I didn't get over that heartbreak and allowed you to let me down too."

"I was joking."

"I don't know what would be worse, me getting stuck with a kid that turned out like you or turned out like me. If that's not an argument for being pro-choice, I don't know what is."

I eased the curtains back and peeped outside. Men wearing baggy pants in cars with shiny rims were doing a drug transaction. Women were half-naked and freezing as they walked back and forth on the stroll. Other cars slowed down, inspected the young girls; some stopped, others sped away.

I was surrounded by the children of the night.

I went back to my pallet and sat down before I asked Hawks, "What do you need to tell me?"

She said, "I should apologize for trying to slap you to the devil."

"You should."

"But I won't. I'm not a very apologetic person."

"Character flaw."

"I don't see the point of apologizing for doing something I meant to do."

"I got what I deserved."

"Well, I think you deserved to get shot."

"Over a phone call?"

"This is not about a phone call. This is about a promise."

"That's a bit over-the-top, don't you think?"

"Well, I only hit you half as hard as I should've hit you. It was open-handed. Would've used my fist but I had just done my nails. All the way to pick you up, you have no idea. Just be glad there weren't any bricks lying around where we were. Be real glad I slapped you and walked away like I did."

"Sorry I didn't call."

"No need to be sorry. I set myself up for that letdown. Me and my impulsive decisions."

I waited. My thoughts in too many places at one time.

Hawks said, "Gideon?"

"I'm here."

"Got something to say. What I have to say might not mean much to you, but it's important to me that I say it, because if I don't say it, then I'll kick myself for not saying it and I don't like kicking myself."

"Okay."

"So you listen and don't say anything back while I talk."

"Okay."

There was a pause.

"You made me feel so pretty when we were in Dallas. The way you dressed me up and took me out, you made me feel so special. I still remember your arms around me. I've missed that the most. Even while I was married I missed that. If you had called while I was married, I would've broken another commandment, would've left my home in the middle of the night to get to you. You never left my mind. Loved the way your arms were around me when we slept in that fancy hotel. The way you were kissing me, stealing my orgasms . . . the way you made me look at you when I was having an orgasm . . . and the next morning . . . the way you were looking at me when you were doing me sideways . . . the way you fed me breakfast in bed . . . the way you kissed me good-bye at the airport . . . hard for a girl to forget all of that."

Silence.

"Okay, I am stopping now. Already said too much and I don't want to get too worked up. I think about you and I get all hot and bothered. Then I get so angry, I mean breaking-and-throwing-things angry. And then I saw you, guess all that heat and anger had to go somewhere and I exploded. No other man has ever made me act stupid like that. Not even the man I married, that worthless piece of nothing."

Silence.

"You didn't even notice."

I waited, tempted to say something, but I didn't.

"The jeans I had on, you bought me those in Dallas. Hadn't put them on in a long time. The day I finally put them on, you called me from Huntsville. Had them on that day and today. And you didn't notice. Didn't matter. Only reason you called was because you needed help. Then you tell me you had been living up in Stone Mountain. Not overseas, just a few hours away. Guess I figured you were living in some faraway land and that was why you didn't call me. You were my neighbor. You promised to call and you never called, and you weren't that far away from me. Yeah, I have said way too much."

Then Hawks hung up.

I sat there, holding the phone, waiting for Hawks to call back.

Hoping she would call back.

Knowing she wouldn't.

I needed sleep, but I didn't want to take the chance of that sleep being my last.

I called Alvin White, asked him if he wanted a job that evening.

He said, "What you need done?"

"You said you could watch my room for me."

"I can do security work if that's what you need."

"I need to take some meds and these meds have codeine in them, and that codeine will pull me into a deep sleep. I need you to hang around as long as you can and watch out for me."

"Want me to sit outside your door until you wake up?"

"Too cold and wet out. Just park down below. Anybody stop by my door start flashing your lights and start blowing your horn. That should make them back away. Should get me up."

"That go for women too?"

"That goes double for women."

"I can do that."

"How does five hundred sound?"

"I'll do it for a hundred."

"Job pays five. Cash money. About fifty an hour. But I don't think I'll need you that long."

"Yessir. I take what the job pays."

"And keep a gun in your lap. Just in case."

With that I ended the call.

A hit man who needed a bodyguard. If I hadn't died in London I would've laughed.

I checked my messages. Had one from my hookup at DNA Solutions.

She got my message. My package had been received. Was put at the front of the line.

A new fear moved through my blood, made bumps rise on my skin.

Thirty minutes later a horn blew and I looked out. Alvin White was there. I waved and he flashed his lights from high to low, then turned them off. Anxiety rose from my body.

I took some more meds, relaxed on the bed, continued down the road to healing.

Seven hours later I looked out my window and Alvin White was still there. I called his cellular, told him I was awake and ready to leave this dump on Ho Stroll. I told him I needed to clean up, then asked him if he could take me from Metropolitan Parkway and drop me off at the airport in a couple of hours. Told him I had his money, if he wanted it right now. He said he could wait until I was ready to leave, that he'd keep watching my room until then. He wanted to work the time he had promised. After that I asked him for another favor, asked if he could manage to get me some more of his girlfriend's chicken soup.

He laughed and said he had a big bowl of it in the car with him, had brought it for me.

He was looking out for me in more ways than one.

That loquacious and gregarious giant was the closest thing I had to a friend.

I tried to remember who my friends had been when I was a child.

Then I struggled to remember a single friend.

No one came to mind. I knew people; they came and went; none were ever true friends.

None knew the darkness that lived inside me. None knew my truth.

Twenty-three

in cold blood

iPhone in hand, I connected to the Internet. Pulled up the cameras at the house in Powder Springs. Something was wrong. Catherine was crying, her shoulders going up and down as she sobbed, shaking her head, rubbing her hands. My first thought was something had happened to the kid. But the kid stepped into the frame, sat next to the woman he knew as his mother, put his hand on hers, tried to calm her down. His efforts didn't work. She was grief-stricken. There wasn't any sound, just the video from the cameras, so I couldn't listen in, had no idea what was being said.

I used the phone in the room, called Powder Springs. Catherine jumped when the phone rang, wiped her eyes, and straightened her knee-length dress before she rushed into the kitchen and answered the cordless phone. I had the hotel phone up to my right ear, my iPhone in my left hand.

I said, "The sound of your voice, what's wrong?"

"Just received bad news."

"What happened?"

"Two of my friends are . . . they were murdered . . . just got word they were both found dead."

"What friends?"

"Friends from my old life. Friends in London."

"You keep in touch with them?"

"They are my friends. They worked . . . the last place I was when I was there."

Blood had been shed on Berwick Street.

An eighteen-year-old model had been found dead, her body badly beaten, her throat cut, her mutilated and battered body left on the floor of the flat where she conducted her business.

I asked, "When were they murdered?"

Catherine told me the day the bodies were found. They were discovered the same day I had been in Central London, discovered later that night. The same day the strawberry blonde and her red-haired male companion had tracked me from the West End and attempted to ambush me on Shaftesbury Avenue.

I asked, "Were they raped?"

"It was not a rape. It was a brutal, senseless murder."

"Who was the other woman?"

Catherine sobbed harder, no longer trying to hide her tears.

Another of the models had been subjected to a fate more tragic than the first one's. The second body they found had been beaten, eyes swollen, teeth knocked out, cut dozens of times in ways that didn't kill her right away, just ensured a slow death.

As if she had been tortured.

The first model, the one who was tortured and killed first, she was Yugoslavian.

The second model was from Africa. Her name was Nusaybah.

Catherine's best friend had been butchered.

She said, "You were in London."

"I went to Berwick Street."

"Why?"

"To ask questions."

"Questions."

"About the kid. About you."

"You went all the way there asking questions regarding my son and me?"

"I did . . . it was before I gave you the DNA test."

She sobbed. "Did you go to London . . . there to hurt my friends?"

"No. When I left they were fine. I only talked to the Yugoslavian."

"I did not know Ivanka that well."

"That is what she told me."

"She came to London . . . started working there right before you came to . . . when you beat me."

I rubbed my eyes, guilt swelling. "I didn't talk to or see Nusaybah."

"My old world is following me. All of my sins will never wash away."

"I saw Nusaybah's son. He could tell you I left, that I was only there a few minutes, no more than five, and the Yugoslavian was not harmed when I left Berwick Street. No one was harmed."

"Steven's friend saw you."

"Where is Nusaybah's son?"

"No one knows."

"Was he hurt?"

"No one knows. All they know is that Nusaybah is dead and her son is missing."

I wondered how they knew where I had gone, but the answer came to me within the next breath. Occam's razor. All other things being equal, the simplest solution was the best.

The CCTV cameras.

They had tapped into the cameras, saw where I had gone; maybe they had lost me after that visit, unable to track me when I had gone to other places, lost me before Myhotel. But they had seen me talking to the Yugoslavian. Had gone after her, questioned her, and tortured her. And to save her own life the Yugoslavian had given up the African woman, the woman who had been Catherine's best friend.

Catherine said, "You have beaten me before."

"I'm not like that anymore. I'm not angry at you in that way."

"You came to Amsterdam to kill me before."

"That was a lifetime ago."

"It was yesterday in my mind."

"I've changed."

"You are still that person."

"I am not that person."

"You are. I saw that in your eyes when you were here. I saw the hate was still there."

"All I'm trying to do is make sure everything is right."

"You come here, you teach my son to fight."

"To protect himself."

"You think I do not know, you think my son does not tell me that you take him and teach him to use a gun. You teach him violence. You teach him to be like you."

"*I teach him the same shit you taught me when I was supposed to be your fucking son.*"

"You are still angry. So angry."

I caught my breath. "I teach him how to protect himself and how to protect you."

"*What do I need protection from, besides you, Jean-Claude? What else do I need protection from?*"

"I am not your enemy."

"You come to my home, *threaten* me, tell me you would take my son away from me."

"*I used to be your son.*"

"Why didn't you leave us in London, leave us where we were? Why bring us here?"

"I wanted you to have a better life."

"A life you can take away whenever you feel like it."

"That's not . . . Catherine . . . I'm . . ."

"You are Margaret's son."

"I don't know Margaret. I only know you."

"And now two more of my friends are gone to be with Margaret."

"I'm back in the area. I'll come over for a while. We can talk face-to-face."

"Please do not come over. I know this home is the home you pay for, and you have the right to come and go as you please, a right I would never interfere with, but this one time, please, do not come."

I took a breath. "Okay."

"I have to go, Jean-Claude. I have to wash my face, have to make my son his dinner."

"Wait, hold on. Look, I think this thing . . . someone is after me."

"You think they did this horrible thing because they are looking for you."

"I can't prove it. But I think so. Some bad people. They were after me in London, probably followed me, saw me talking to the Yugoslavian. I had asked her about you and the kid."

"So . . . someone is following you . . . because of what you do."

"I'm doing what you taught me. This is your nurturing."

She paused. "Someone wants to do harm to you and anyone who knows you."

"Something I did a while ago. It's coming back at me now."

"And because of you and the things you have done they killed Ivanka. You spoke to Ivanka one time and they killed her. They killed Nusaybah. You did not know Nusaybah and they killed her like she was a worthless dog. And they have taken her son, probably have killed him as well. Because of you."

A moment passed, my anxiety growing exponentially. "I'll be there in about thirty minutes."

"*No no no no no.* If they are after you, then you should not come back here."

London. Cayman Islands. Huntsville. She was right.

She asked, "Did you go back to London and murder my friends?"

"I'm not a murderer."

"Did you kill her son?"

"I didn't touch any of them."

"What did you do to her son? Answer me. Tell me. Did you harm him? Did you?"

I snapped, "The boy was in the alley playing soccer when I left."

"I have seen what you do, Jean-Claude. I have seen the person you are."

"The person you made me. I am the person you made me to be."

"You were already that person; when you were born you were that person."

"Is that how you see me?"

She sobbed, cried like her only family had died at the slaughter.

I said, "I killed a man to protect you."

"Because you were like the man you killed."

I fumbled with what to say, no words coming, just said, "Talk to you soon."

"You should not call here, Jean-Claude. Until you have fixed what is wrong, do not call."

"Okay. Keep me posted. Let me know if they find the boy."

"I cannot. I have to protect my son. He is all I have left in this world. All I have."

Catherine hung up the phone, her tone filled with anger, tears, fear, and confusion.

I had been cut off from the kid. It felt as if my heart had been ripped out.

Batman. Golgo 13. A demon. Catherine saw me the same way.

I pulled up the house cameras again, saw her on the sofa crying. The kid rubbed his mother's arm. She moved away from him; her pain put pain and suffering in his face. The kid cried. Didn't know he ever cried. Had to remind myself that he was a kid. He might have kept his feelings deep inside, but he had feelings. I watched that as long as I could stand to watch it, that grief exacerbating my illness.

X. Y. Z.

Detroit was desperate, butchering innocent people to find her way to me.

She had forced me to sell my homes; now she had destroyed what little family I had.

Her evil had infected my personal world. Had spread to what I had considered to be my family.

I had slaughtered a dozen of her bodyguards when I had gone looking for her.

Men who would've done the same to me.

The number I had called in Huntsville, it was still locked in my mind.

I called.

She answered.

I snapped, "Bitch, you killed those women in London."

"Gideon."

"You crazy bitch. I'm coming after you. I'll find you wherever you are."

"You sound upset."

"You think I'm fucking playing with you?"

"What's wrong? Feel me breathing down your neck? You feel me? Are you afraid, Gideon? You should be. I am not to be fucked with. Ask my dead husband about that. You can't escape me, Gideon. Every day I'm a day closer to killing you. Every hour I'm an hour closer. Every minute, a minute closer. I can find you. I know someone who can find anybody. And he will find you. Lowlife piece of shit."

"The women in London had nothing to do with this shit."

"You're dead. Anyone you know is dead. Anyone you talk to is dead. I will kill as many as I have to in order to get to you. I shall see my vengeance. We've come too far to turn back now."

"You're a fucking coward. Why don't you stop hiding, come see me, face-to-face."

"Bet you're losing a lot of sleep. Always running. Always hiding. Bet you're afraid you're going to slip. Knowing it only takes one bullet. You want me to stop chasing you? To not find who you know and kill them? Then do me a favor and kill yourself. Because if you don't, I will get it done."

"Fucking coward."

"Don't sleep, Gideon. Don't sleep."

She hung up.

Three hours later after that tragic news I was heading toward Hartsfield. My hardware had been entrusted to my new friend; I told Alvin I'd get the guns from him whenever I made it back.

He asked, "You okay?"

"Not really."

"Get some more rest."

"Have to keep moving."

"Because of the trouble you're in?"

"I have to keep moving."

I had promised him five hundred American dollars, but I paid him twice that amount.

Alvin whistled and said, "Now that is one good-looking redbone."

A bus was next to us, an advert for the local news, Jewell Stewark's smile looking me right in my angry eyes. Her hair blond and straight, that dyed mane parted on one side, conservative and proper.

Alvin said, "Heard she has some temper though. Folks said she spat in some woman's face."

"Why would she do that?"

"Probably something to do with her husband. My wife gets the same way sometimes."

"She spat in somebody's face."

"At Starbucks on Cascade Road."

The bus passed and so did the memory of Jewell Stewark.

Then came the part with the larger trust. Hawks was gone and I couldn't risk going to Powder Springs, not after the news that had been dropped on me, so I didn't have much of a choice. I handed Alvin my messenger bag, kept my backpack with me.

"Alvin, I have something I can't risk trying to take on the plane with me."

"Drugs?"

"Money."

"Drug money?"

"Not drug money. Need you to keep it for me."

"You sure you want me to do that?"

I nodded, slow and easy, thoughts so heavy nodding was almost an insurmountable task.

He said, "How much money you asking me to watch?"

"Between fifty and sixty thousand."

He whistled. "That's a lot of money."

"I know."

"You done counted it all?"

"Didn't count it."

"How would you know I didn't take some?"

"I'll leave that up to you."

He said, "Sure you want to do this? I mean, this is a lot of money. Like Mr. Kagamaster said, hard times all over. Home Depot is closing a dozen stores, city has a two-hundred-some-million-dollar hole in its budget, and the mayor done laid off people to balance the city budget and whatnot, doing all that while she trying to get taxes raised. She taking away jobs and letting those who left with paychecks pick up the slack. What I mean is, well, this is a lot of money to put in the hands of a man in hard times."

The big man took the money and trembled.

Losing that money was the last thing on my mind, something I didn't care about.

I handed Alvin a sheet of paper. The address in Powder Springs in black ink.

He asked, "What's this?"

"Need you to be an angel in a world where I am a demon."

"Okay."

"It's a woman and a kid. Her son. Watch the house. Look for trouble."

"What you want me to do if I run into some trouble?"

"Whatever you have to do."

"These some bad people after you, huh?"

"Some real bad people."

He nodded.

An hour later I was between fifty and sixty thousand dollars lighter, on the other side of security, uncomfortable because I didn't have a gun on my person, waiting to board a plane to Fort Lauderdale.

The image of two innocent women left butchered on a piss-stained street in my mind.

That had been the work of a monster.

What had happened to those women, that was what would have happened to me in London.

Twenty-four

the terror

Miami, Florida.

I had trailed his chauffeured stretch Hummer from the Tides Hotel in South Beach on Ocean Drive, a place described as a sanctuary of extravagance, had followed that oversized monstrosity as they partied up the MacArthur Causeway, chrome sparkling every time a sliver of light touched its lavishness. I shadowed that gas guzzler until the causeway became I-395 and merged onto I-95 right behind them.

They exited at Miami Gardens Drive, made a right, and less than a mile from that exit was their destination, Tootsie's Cabaret, a playground for men that was the size of a football field, every square foot of it crowded with strippers and international people holding bottles or glasses of mood-altering liquids. Four-hundred-foot main stage, projection screens all over, luxury seating, skyboxes, champagne rooms.

It was like a combination of a meeting at the United Nations and a birthday party at Studio 54. Droves of international men. Hundreds of international women either naked or in thongs, bodies accented by six-inch heels and designer perfumes, some decorated with dollar bills, faces made up like movie starlets, walking around smiling and flirting, more comfortable butt-naked in this cavernous room than they would be fully clothed at a church bake sale. All the girls reminded me of Jennifer Lopez, Paris Hilton, or Eva Longoria. A few were in the Halle Berry category, fewer of the Gabrielle Union type.

Like my target, most of the people in the room were under thirty, but every now and then I passed by an old rich man pawing at the boobs on women the same age as his granddaughters.

A waitress came over. Slender number dressed in black, hair dyed brown, colored with highlights, very Miami Beach in frame and attitude. Tight eyes and a no-nonsense smile. She asked me what I wanted to order and I sent her to get me a Jack and Coke.

When she came back and handed me my drink I asked, "Filipina?"

She shook her head. "Mother is Chinese and my father is Japanese."

"Didn't mean to offend."

"Nothing new, sweetie." She sighed. "Happens all the time."

"You're a pretty woman."

"Would probably be prettier to you if I was Filipina instead of a Japanese China doll."

"Guess I blew my chance with you."

She waggled her hand, showed me an engagement ring. "Dude, you never had a chance."

I paid her and tipped her, and she walked away in a hurry. I went back to monitoring my target, held my drink but didn't sip any. Couldn't do alcohol if I wanted to. Was taking the meds Hawks had given me. Hands were scratched, but no open wounds. I ached, but B.C. had that under control.

Thoughts about women slain on Berwick Street stayed with me. I was worried about Powder Springs. Had checked the cameras all day long, Catherine still devastated by the death of her friends.

I wondered if she had cried that way when Margaret had been killed and left in a Dumpster, wondered if that tragedy had ripped out her heart, compelled her to take me and raise me as her own.

I wondered why she wasn't the type of mother to me that she was to Steven.

But he was her son. She told me I was the stray she had rescued from a life in foster care.

It was too much to think about right now.

My target had been impossible to get to because he had spent most of the night upstairs in Tootsie's Transit Car. That was a scaled replica of a New York subway car that was only in the VIP area.

The waitress came back. She handed me a napkin; on it was her phone number written in ink.

She said, "I hope you don't think I do this all the time."

"Guess I said something right."

"You have this roughness about you. You look like a leading man. The man who is up on the movie screen and women can't take their eyes off him. Charisma, panache, strong sexual energy that surrounds and emanates from you. Intoxicating. It crosses racial lines, what you have. Bet all kinds of women are attracted to you. Cuban, German, Australian, Japanese China dolls . . . all kinds. Am I right?"

"You really want an answer to that?"

"No, I don't."

We laughed.

I said, "Not all women. Not all."

"Somebody you can't get to, huh?"

"Somebody I've never been able to get to."

"Well, whoever she is, she is a fool."

"Can I buy you a drink when you get off?"

"I don't drink. Alcohol is bad for my legs."

"Do they swell?"

"No, they spread."

I smiled. She winked at me.

"I'm getting married in July, so don't wait too long to look me up."

"You live nearby?"

"Miki Morioka. South Miami. Dixie Highway. I'm listed in the phone book."

Then Miki Morioka was gone, her cute little ass doing a nice side-to-side move as she strolled.

Flirting with her had been part real, part cover, helped me look like I wasn't lingering.

I kept my eyes on the doors and sat down at La Colonne, their full-service restaurant, ordered grilled shrimp, and sat at an angle where I could see the target when he left VIP and headed for the front door. Saturday night the place was open until six in the morning, but I lucked out and he left around three. It was still dark enough.

As dark as my thoughts.

Nusaybah had been butchered. So had Ivanka, the eighteen-year-old Yugoslavian.

They had not been soldiers in this war. Now this war had no unwritten rules. No one off-limits.

I had done my best to find where my Detroit problem was hiding out. All I knew was she had left Motown, had taken vacation time in the middle of a political scandal. But because they said she was gone, that didn't mean she was gone. I needed to finish up here and fly into the Midwest, ease into Detroit. Would have to fly in on a Cessna. That way I could load up whatever I needed to do a job, have what I needed when I landed, no need to make contact with some connection at the other end to get me a piece, no one to warn her. I was going to procure a thirteen-pound sniper rifle before I headed north.

She would have to go back to Motown at some point. She loved Detroit too much to stay gone too long. And when she returned, I would be there waiting, eager to put her arrogance in my crosshairs.

Two hours later I was at a safe house on Miami Gardens Drive, between Fifteenth and Sixteenth streets. First Moorings condominiums, across the street at the Shops at Skylake. Publix and L.A. Fitness were across the street. Julio's Natural Foods, Wachovia, T. J. Maxx, Goodwill— there were dozens of eateries and shops in the strip mall. Going east, the boulevard was lined with shops, with Aventura Mall not far away.

I was inside a second-floor unit, one bedroom, the rear windows covered with thick curtains.

I cracked the curtains, the view opening to palm trees and a lake. I made it in just in time to look out and see the ducks mating. Male ducks lined up and chased the female duck. One of the chasers caught her in the pond, had his way, damn near drowned her trying to relieve itself of the need to come.

Again I looked at the cameras in Powder Springs; nothing on but night lights, everyone sleeping.

I was tempted to call Alvin, but I didn't bother him. Didn't know anyone else to chat with.

I turned the television on, changed to the local news, WSVN on channel 7.

A report was on. Two miles away the occupants of a stretch Hummer had been gunned down underneath the overpass at I-95. One of the occupants was an informant, set to testify against a politician in Albuquerque, New Mexico. The rest were bodyguards who were taken by surprise.

My cellular buzzed. I checked the message. FUNDS TRANSFERRED.

I couldn't relax. Turned the television off, began pacing in the dark; I opened the windows and curtains along the back side of the condo, letting a view of the stars and a decent breeze into the rooms. Gun in my hand, I walked from kitchen to sunroom to the opening that came back into the single bedroom, back through the bedroom door that led to the kitchen and living room and back toward the sunroom, did that over and over, plotting, imagining, teeth clenched, jaw tight, a thousand veins in my neck.

Then I was on the landline, having a conversation with a man who supplied the business, a New Yorker who could deliver to me what I needed. I wanted to transport a .223 M4 and a case of Black Hills 77-grain .223 with a scope. I had maps of the city sent to me, downloaded the information on my iPhone. The map had details that weren't printed on a regular city map, information about how to maneuver underneath the city, tunnels that created a maze of exits. Police would be looking aboveground while I was under their feet. Would print that out later, map out my entry and exit plan. I ordered tactical gear, a vest, military shoes, ordered everything but a nuclear bomb. Then I transferred money from my account in the Caymans to his account in Switzerland. My mood was extreme, my angst too deep to handle, emotions high, logic nonexistent. I would've taken the Cessna high over the Manoogian Mansion and dropped a bomb on the mayor's home, would have leveled every house within a mile of 9240 Dwight Street, would have destroyed the Berry Subdivision Historic District, taken out the city's east side up to the Detroit River, would've done that to get that tick off my skin, to get my revenge.

I had to use the bathroom, gun in my hand, heeding the threat from my enemy. There were two bathrooms in the condo, one inside the bedroom and the other by the front door, both toilets situated on the front side of the apartment. The windows faced and opened to the walkway and front side of the building. The window in the bedroom bathroom was open, night sounds creeping inside. First I sensed vibrations, someone coming up the stairs. Someone was easing down the walkway. I reached and turned the bathroom light off. Waited. Listened. The building was populated with Jews and Puerto Ricans older than Jesus, so I doubted any of the geriatrics were up at this hour. And if they were up they wouldn't be outside, not in Miami. They wouldn't tiptoe in the night. More vibrations; a second person came up the stairs, someone lighter, someone whose gait had a different pace. Two people were out there. Neither talking. Both began moving, took slow steps, stopped right outside the front door.

Minutes after I ordered equipment a terrorist would use, someone had come there.

No sound. Not a whisper. In my mind they knew I was in there, they had gone silent, were using hand signals. Pants up, I eased to the bathtub, peeped out the window. If it was the police, if they had tracked me there after the scene I had left down at I-95, then the parking lot would have been full of cops.

There were no police cars in sight. No FBI. No CIA. No Homeland Security.

The parking lot was hushed, just a night breeze blowing through, tickling palm trees.

They were picking the lock. The front door opened in less than five seconds, a mild creak on its hinges. They had entered. They were on the other side of this painted drywall, guns leading the way.

A light came on, lit up the dining and living room; that same light threw luminescence into the bedroom and back toward the sunroom. Three footsteps. Not loud. Someone had stepped inside. Two steps. Different weight, lighter. Two were inside. Front door closed. Imagined them giving hand signals.

My heart was in my throat, breathing shallow, tried to breathe slowly, hardly blinking, gun leading the way as I stepped out of the bathroom, a room that could have me trapped. I took two steps into the bedroom, which was one wall away from the front room. The condo had two doors; both were on the other side of that wall, both facing the boulevard. Windows were along the back side of the building facing the lake. No way to run and break out a window. This wasn't a movie. Running and diving into double-pane glass wouldn't shatter the glass like it did the breakaway they used on television. But I might have to try, put a few shots into the glass to weaken it, then hope for the best. The windows were more horizontal than vertical, crank-out style, and opened inward, each pane about two feet wide.

That idea was a no-go; diving sideways was not going to work, not from two stories up.

The only way out of this condo was through one of the front doors.

I would have to shoot my way out.

Hard-soled shoes moved across tiled floor, took two quick steps, the pace that of a killer in no hurry. I waited where I was, ready to fire, not about to move and give away my position.

Suffocated in London. Attacked in the Cayman Islands. Shoot-out in Huntsville.

Trapped inside a condo in South Miami, time moved like cold molasses.

The assassin took another step. Then another. I waited. The start of a silhouette rounded the corner, inched inside the bedroom. My teeth clenched. I didn't know where his partner was, didn't know if the other half of that team had moved across the living room, from there making a right, and was at the edge of the sunroom, another room that opened into the bedroom, or if they were holding position in the front room, blocking my chance to exit out the front door. As soon as I moved his gun was on me.

My gun pointed at the center of his forehead and his pointed at the center of mine.

Twenty-five

those who walk away

The lead assassin had salt-and-pepper hair and a George Clooney face, could pass for an aging international model but was a clean-shaven Russian, born in the world's largest country, a nation that covered eleven time zones and possessed all climate zones except tropical.

He said, "Son of a bitch. Gideon."

His partner was behind him, a woman who held two guns at her sides, both nine-millimeters.

She wore boot-cut Levi's, a big belt buckle that depicted a knife inside a big red heart, Lucchese crocodile cowboy boots, and her standard black T. The top part of her burgundy hair with the highlights was braided toward the back, those braids stopping at the back of her neck; the rest of her loosened mane hung to her butt.

I lowered my weapon and took my finger off the trigger, my heartbeat at a strong gallop.

He had already moved his .22 from my face.

Some people called him The Man in the White shoes.

I said his name. "Konstantin Pentkovski."

Seeing him with Hawks was the bigger surprise.

Konstantin told me, "Don't scare me like that. Almost gave me a heart attack."

I said, "Didn't know you were using the safe house."

"You always go to a hotel."

"This was closer."

"We tried to come up I-95. Shut down. News said body bags were everywhere."

"Was in a hurry. Had other things on my mind and wanted to wrap it up."

"Next time you change your agenda, you need to let someone know."

"I'll put a sock on the doorknob next time."

"A text message would be better."

He opened his arms, and guns in hand, we hugged like old friends. His heartbeat was twice as fast as mine, his hug telling me he was relieved he hadn't made a mistake, that he had been scared too.

We talked off and on, but we hadn't been face-to-face in over two years.

He looked good. For a man with cancer, he looked damn good.

His homeland, Russia, had over one thousand major cities, over a dozen with a population of more than one million. The rumor was each city would have had a population of more than two million if not for him. He had grown up putting people in the ground in Moscow, St. Petersburg, Nizhniy Novgorod, Novosibirsk, and Yekaterinburg, as well as many other places, before he came to America to do the same. The man in front of me was a chisel-chinned hit man wearing a double-breasted suit, an unlit Belomorkanal cigarette dangling on his lips, frowning like he had just stepped out of an Edward G. Robinson movie.

Konstantin said, "Bad weather up north. Tornadoes in Atlanta and Oklahoma. Airports closed, canceled flights, so we got stuck here after working, decided to leave in the morning."

Tension gone, we laughed the laugh of men who would live to see another day.

Hawks didn't laugh, her angered expression telling me I was the last person she wanted to see.

Hawks said, "You should've shot him anyway. And I'm talking to you, Konstantin. Would've shot him myself but you were standing in the way. But if you could manage to scoot over just a wee wee little bit

I'd be more than happy to engage in some impromptu friendly fire with that worthless jerk."

Konstantin clunked his .22 down on the dining room table. I went back to the bathroom and finished up, then took a long, hot shower before I came back out and sat at the wooden dining table.

Hawks was gone.

I asked Konstantin, "Where did she go?"

"Said she was going to sit by the pool."

"She can't stand being in the same room with me."

"She's a woman first. Don't forget that."

I nodded, then asked, "You have any information for me?"

"The team that was on you in London? Nothing as of yet."

I told him about the women who had been tortured and butchered on Berwick Street.

My frown deep, I said, "They did it. They did it to get to me."

"So one of them uses a knife."

"Like a butcher."

"But they didn't get any closer to you. No problem with your family."

"No. You helped me move things around; so far everything has been untraceable."

"The workers could've been from anywhere. From London, Ukraine, Paris, Utah, South Africa. Nothing solid has come my way. Your Detroit problem, all I can find out is they say she's out of the country. Working on getting her passport information. You can track her if she is out of the country."

"I already found out that much, that she was out of the country."

Konstantin tapped on the table, frustrated. "Sorry I haven't found out more."

"I'm making my own plans. Time to bring this to an end."

"Well, at least tell me what type of war you're planning."

"I need another Cessna to transport a few things."

"When?"

"In a week. Ten days tops."

He nodded, not pushing it.

I let that go, slapped down on the table, smiled, and asked Konstantin, "Hungry?"

"Starving. Fix me a plate of whatever you can find in the cabinets."

"Homestead." I headed toward the kitchen. "You were an hour south of here."

"We canceled a few tickets and the tornado canceled a few flights."

"You called Hawks in, gave her some work."

"As you suggested. I was going to call you when I got here. New job came in."

"Where?"

"Antigua." He took an iPod out of his inside suit coat pocket. It was one of the slim iPods that had Internet access and about thirty-two gigs of memory. "When it came in I downloaded it on here."

I said, "Let's eat first."

"I have a bag of fruit. If nothing is there we'll eat some of my honey-do list."

"Let me check the cabinets first."

The best I could come up with was crackers and some sort of canned chicken meat. I put that on a plate, sat it on the table, and we ate it like it was caviar.

I said, "You haven't mentioned your health."

"I know."

Like me, he was afraid of dying. Not death, but the road we would take to get to that end.

They had just come up from Homestead, had done a job a mile or so from the tropical fruit stand Robert Is Here. The area he had been in was more than an hour south, not too far from a prison. His contract was connected to the job I had done earlier. I didn't ask the details and he didn't offer any more than that. Konstantin had been in the wetwork business for decades; his career had lasted as long as the stylish black suit and dark tie he had on. Konstantin was a man of action, not a man of fashion.

I asked, "How have you been? Don't bullshit me."

"Skip it."

"Not talking about it won't make it better."

"I'm still here." He nodded. "I'm still walking on top of the ground."

"How often you taking chemo?"

"Once a month." He smiled a broad smile. "Still popping pills. Still on top of the ground."

I nodded, then asked, "What's in the bag?"

"My wife made me go shopping. I come to Miami, Svetlana sends me shopping. I tell her I'm going to Homestead to put a man in the ground and she tells me to stop and get fruit when I'm done."

He opened a bag and took out some of the exotic goods he had bought at the tropical fruit stand. He offered me a *Monstera deliciosa* and I took it without hesitating. A *Monstera deliciosa* looks like a giant green ear of corn but tastes like banana and pineapple. He had picked up carambola, mamey, lychee, atemoya, papaya, and jars of honey. His wife had given him an extensive shopping list.

Konstantin said he had been married four times, engaged a fifth time, then fifteen years ago he met the woman of his dreams when she hired him to take care of a little problem—her former spouse. People in the business said he was romantically linked to Marilyn Monroe, Jayne Mansfield, and a few other Hollywood starlets. Who he took to bed, who he put in the ground, he'd never say.

Konstantin asked, "Think you will ever get married?"

He said that and Arizona's face intruded in my mind. Old memories died hard.

I said, "Doubt it."

Something inside me fell when I answered that question.

He said, "Hawks married. It didn't work out for her."

"She told me."

"She married the wrong man. She has to marry the right one."

Then, with a smile, I asked him to power up his iPod and show me what contract had come in.

The West Indies contract was being offered at 20 percent over my normal price, and the job sounded like it was 75 percent easier than most of the jobs I'd had in my career.

Whatever was needed to do the job would be waiting at the airport, inside a rental car that was to be left in the employee lot at V. C. Bird International, a small dirt lot that would be to the right as I exited the airport. It sounded like an easy-in, easy-out deal. I knew my way around most of the island, had done a Jumby Bay contract a few years back, lured him off his private island and captured him as soon as he stepped off the ferry, left that problem swimming in the Atlantic Ocean, the rough and shark-filled waters down at Devil's Bridge. Stayed in Jolly Harbour when it was done. This contract wasn't as complicated.

Still, other things were on my mind.

I had to plan my own mission, had to get ready to fly to Detroit and put that problem six feet under. I told him that. Konstantin wanted me to think it out. Said I could do the Antigua job, then sit it out for a couple of days, let him see what he could find out, let him help me plan my trip back to Detroit.

I passed on the job.

Konstantin nodded, not questioning my decision.

After eating, Konstantin found a DVD on top of the television, popped it in, and took to the chair, started watching *Du Rififi Chez les Hommes*. Jean Servais. Carl Möhner. Robert Manuel. Those actors made it a true noir from the start. A film filled with gangland patois and gangsters who did horrible things, not stopping at necrophilia. Konstantin loved it because it had a brilliant heist sequence, thirty-two minutes without dialogue or a score to fill in the silence. At times noise was the enemy.

I watched the film to its end, took in its ironic wit and watched the main character driving the streets of Paris, his tense face revealing his ever-deepening agony, the pain from being mortally wounded, quarts of blood spilled in a scene that showed cinematic death, his partners dead, and as he died his one last mission was to return the kidnapped son of his dead partner to the boy's mother.

Fin.

That seemed like it had been a message to me. A message to a man who had been kidnapped as a child. No matter who had been slaughtered, that didn't change my issue with the kid.

He said, "I could've been a movie star if it wasn't for that British actor Archibald Alexander Leach."

"Who is that?"

"Cary Grant. His birth name. I did a screen test or two and the problem was I looked too much like him. In Hollywood every actor has to have his own name and own face. And Cary Grant already had my mug. That was my dream. That Brit was a much better actor, so I didn't mind. He had my blessings."

"You look like George Clooney."

"And Clooney looks like Cary Grant."

Konstantin yawned and stretched out on the sofa, his gun at his side.

Hawks still hadn't returned. I was going to make a pallet on the floor, leave the bedroom to her.

Konstantin yawned. "Go check on Hawks."

"That would be a kamikaze mission."

"Take her a piece of fruit."

"Want to walk down that long green mile with me?"

He chuckled. *"Do zavtra."*

"Do zavtra."

He slipped off his pristine white patent leather shoes and closed his eyes.

Gun in one hand and *Monstera deliciosa* in the other, I went to check on Hawks.

Twenty-six

the drowning pool

Hawks was naked, in the heated pool. Her clothes and boots were off to the side, on a chair. Her hair was thick and wet. She looked up and saw me. Stopped swimming laps.

She treaded water and said, "How long you plan on standing there gawking at me?"

"Brought you some fruit."

"Should I tell you in which orifice to shove that phallic-shaped fruit? And it is not in your mouth."

"Konstantin sent it."

"Then bend over and have Konstantin shove it for you."

"Teamwork."

"Nothing like."

"You don't like me, do you?"

"I am way beyond not liking you."

"So, where do I stand with you?"

"Two blocks from the corner of Despise and Hate."

I undressed, walked into the heated pool.

I said, "Those extra fifteen pounds look nice."

"I found those directions to hell. Got 'em on MapQuest. So you can go there now."

Hawks cursed me out.

She said, "And nobody invited you to come down here. This is not a skinny-dipping party."

I got back out of the pool, put my clothes on, turned, and started to walk away.

She called my name.

I turned around.

She asked, "Who's after you?"

"You talking to me now?"

"Just asking."

"Like you give a shit."

"Well, to be honest, I really don't."

She swam a lap, came back, saw I was still there.

She said, "Konstantin was worried. Said you wouldn't say. You and that ego."

I gritted my teeth. "It's a woman."

"Somebody you forgot to call back?"

I rubbed my neck, struggled with my confession. "Job I did."

"Well?"

"Hawks."

"Don't leave me hanging."

"Don't want you involved."

"Well, you had me picking you up looking like the Creature from the Black Lagoon, had me bringing you medicine in a damn tornado, and five minutes ago you almost gunned me down, so I think I am entitled to a little professional courtesy here. Whether I can stand your butt or not. And I can't."

I sat at the edge of the pool, told Hawks about the job I had done on a winter night in Detroit. Told her how that job had almost gone south and how that had angered me. Detroit hadn't told me about a gun her husband had kept hidden. At the time, in that moment while my heart-beat and anger were high, I had upped my price, demanded a penalty be paid. That was where the problem began.

That was back when I was trying to get a million dollars to make another woman mine.

Like many others, in that moment, I had been motivated by selfishness and greed.

I just told Hawks that in the end the penalty money I had demanded had been returned to Detroit, that I had let her live in the end and moved on, hoping that little refund and a threat would end this matter.

Hawks wiped water from her face, said, "Detroit."

"The religious woman who wanted her husband dead."

"That was the contract I handed you when we were in Dallas."

I nodded. "You were busy, passed on the job."

"That was a while back. But I remember her. Can't forget somebody like her. She came across as the kinda person who was addicted to attention and the idea of being famous. A political Superhead. If you asked me I'd say she loved the fame more than the marriage itself. She married a famous man and used his fame to get as much attention as she could. That's my opinion, from what I can remember."

"I got it under control."

"What does that mean?"

"I'm going after her. In about a week it will be history."

"What are you planning?"

"I liked it better when you weren't talking to me anymore."

"Jerk. This is a struggle, trying to be cordial to you. But excuse me for trying."

She splashed water on me, did that over and over, got me wet. I pulled my clothes off and dived in the pool, dived near her. She swam away from me and I went after her. She splashed water at me and I went underwater, she did the same, swimming away, running from me until I cornered her. I pulled Hawks closer, put my lips on hers, then my tongue inside her mouth. She moaned and reciprocated.

Then she pushed me away, slapped my face, a soft slap, went underwater, swam away again, moving like a mermaid. I chased her for a while, went after her until I was tired of chasing her.

Hawks held on to her frown. "I see you're feeling better."

My energy was lower than I had realized. I went toward her. "Not one hundred percent."

"That's good to know, Mr. Mesomorph." She moved away. "Stitches holding up okay?"

"You did a great job. And thanks for the prescription."

We stayed in the deep end, swam for a while. Swam until she wasn't running from me. Then we swam together. Swimming naked evolved into kissing naked. Underwater kisses, underwater touching.

She said, "Stop looking at me like that."

"Like what?"

"Like that."

Stars overhead. Darkness in all the condo windows, at least two buildings facing the pool; I took her to the shallow end of the pool. I sucked on her breasts, sucked her nipples, and she trembled, held the back of my head, kept my mouth on her nipples, and made sounds like she was about to explode.

I trembled too.

She said, "You better stop being all mannish."

"Come here."

"Stop."

I lifted Hawks as I kissed her, a hand on each of her petite buttocks, and she wrapped her long legs around mine. The water made her buoyant, made her so light, her vagina grinding against me as her hand went into the water and found my erection. Hawks kissed me harder as she put me inside her.

I didn't expect her to do that. It caught me off guard. Gave me fire.

Hawks moaned like she had wanted that for the last two years.

I whispered in her ear, "You have wonderful curves."

She moaned.

I told her, "I love your weight."

"Do you?"

"You were too skinny at first."

"I've never been skinny."

"You filled out the most important parts."

"Did I?"

"The curves, like the way you feel."

"Do you?"

"I remember Dallas. When you were on top of me, damn. Loved it."

"Did you?"

"You were one hell of a rider."

"Hush talking to me like that before you get me riled up."

"Bet with that new weight, that ride would be devastating."

"Hush. I'm not playing. Hush."

"You feel like a woman should feel."

We moved around the heated pool and copulated slow and easy, then I let her turn around and hold the edge of the pool as I took her from behind, pushing deep, splashing water with every stroke.

Her moans were sexy, continuous, euphoric, and preorgasmic, all drawn out.

We came separately the first time, held each other, kissed, laughed, and swam for a moment, then touched again, kissed, back to the water sex, and our orgasms came together the next time.

My orgasm was titanic, had momentum, and came with fervor, like it was long overdue.

Orgasm slowed my blood flow. My erection declined, slipped out of her. I held her tight, kept her body next to mine, caught my breath, my sense of hearing returning as I looked around.

The orgasm weakened me. Felt vulnerable, out in the open, naked in more ways than one.

I carried Hawks closer to the edge, where three guns rested underneath our clothing.

I smelled cigarette smoke. In the distance I saw Konstantin heading in the opposite direction, his white shoes fading into the darkness, those white shoes that were the last thing many had seen.

Guess he had come down to make sure Hawks hadn't shot me and caught himself an eyeful.

Either Hawks didn't see him or she didn't care; she put my hand on her sex and she moaned.

She remained on fire, kissing me, moaned while I put my fingers inside her. Hawks bit my shoulder and moved against my hand, her thighs tightening. I was holding fire. After she came she went underwater, took me in her mouth, didn't do it that long, wasn't that good at holding her breath and engaging in oral pleasure at the same time. She came up, wiped water from her face, moved her long hair away from her face, smiled at me.

She said, "Don't think that changed anything. I still don't like you."

We didn't have towels so we pulled our clothes over wet bodies. It took Hawks a while to wring out her long hair. It was like watching somebody wring out a mop. Then she gathered the loose part and made it one long braid. While she did that I spied around, checked the grounds, listened; every little sound made me tense. Detroit had me fucked up. On edge. Hawks held her boots in one hand, the fruit in the other. She hopped on my back. I carried her, a gun in each hand, each held by its grip.

"You might've unloaded my wagon, but I still think you're a bona fide jerk."

"Shut your trap."

"I mean the jerk of all jerks. Don't let this cloying voice make you think otherwise."

I stepped over duck shit and passed by dozens of the waterfowl. I eased Hawks off my back at the lake and threw my gun and silencer out into the darkness. The middle of the lake opened up and swallowed the smoking gun and its companion. Hawks took her gun from me, pulled the other from the small of her back, tossed both of her shooting irons. That told me both had been used down in Homestead. She had teamed up with my favorite Russian, a man only God could put in the ground, and God was having a hard time making Konstantin take his last breath. Homestead was probably soaked with blood, the way most of Florida was soaked with the blood of Seminoles. I would have hated to see the carnage they'd left behind. Now we were naked in a different way. Windows in all the condos were dark. No one outside but us. All of the residents were dead to the world, hoping to wake up to see another day.

Hawks hopped on my back again, kissed my neck as I carried her up the concrete stairs.

I asked, "Sure you gained only fifteen pounds?"

That made her curse, her curses ending in laughter.

She said, "What you want to do, do like the airlines and charge me for being a little overweight?"

"Don't tell me you're pissed at the airlines too."

"Don't get me started on talking about the airlines." Hawks yawned. "Can't believe that they're gonna start charging fifteen dollars to check a bag at the airport. Fifteen for the first bag, twenty-five for the second, and a hundred damn dollars for a third. Then if my bag weighs too much they will want another twenty-five bucks. Now they charge to have a baby in your lap. And to bring a pet that will be under your seat. They might as well charge fat people a little more since they make the plane burn more fuel."

"Yep."

"The way they are itemizing everything, things that used to be included in the ticket price, they might as well post an airline menu at the counter, have a stewardess come out and take your order."

"They don't like being called stewardesses."

"Well, that's much nicer than what I want to call those rude, no-'count heifers."

"Oil prices. Jet fuel. Consumer pays."

"Ridiculous. Soon they will start charging to use the toilet. More for doing number two than doing number one. Trust me, when that air mask thing drops down, you better have a charge card in your hand because I know the oxygen won't be free. Hell, it's worse than riding on a Greyhound bus. To top it off we pay all of that money and still have to buy food on the plane. On top of that, can't take liquids on the plane and damn near have to get naked at the airport. Damn orange alerts every day."

"You know what I think?"

"What do you think?"

"I think you gained more than fifteen pounds."

She cursed me again, this time the swearing not ending in laughter.

Outside the condo we stopped and kissed like teenagers, the kind of kissing that made a minute feel like a second, wet skin under damp clothing. Kissed until the door to the condo opened and there stood Konstantin in his suit pants and a white T-shirt, no socks or shoes on his feet, his gun at his side.

He apologized, yawned, and told me, "Antigua upped the offer."

"Not interested."

"By *fifty* percent."

"Not interested."

"This is a lot of money. Think about it overnight, talk to me before we part ways."

I nodded and he closed the door.

Hawks asked, "You getting offered work like that in Antigua?"

"Yeah."

"Guess I need to branch out. Become international and all. See some new places. Get some culture. Got time on my hands now. Seeing how I'm divorced and managed to lose my job and all."

"Sorry you lost your job because of me."

"That job was worthless."

"Thought you liked the nine-to-five."

"Thought I liked the man I married too. I lost a husband and a job, but I don't want to lose the roof over my head. My boots look too good to end up collecting cans and sleeping under cardboard."

She was a proud woman. She needed the money but never would admit it.

She said, "Konstantin was talking about all the places he'd been. All over the world. The only Athens, Rome, and Dublin I've ever seen are up in Georgia. Maybe I need to get to Manila, Seoul, Zurich, Barcelona. Might be time to take these boots off and see what the rest of the world is about."

More kisses as my tongue remained with her and my mind went on its own journey.

She bit her bottom lip, rocked, had a hard time getting her words to come up, but finally said, "If you're serious about passing on the Antigua thing, mind if I take a look-see?"

"Go right ahead."

"Never been to the West Indies. What else is down that way?"

I told her about Montserrat and Guadeloupe, white sand, azure seas, and coconut trees, about taking a ferry from Antigua to Barbuda, where the sand was pink, a good place to rest and reflect. Nevis, St. Kitts, St. Barts, and St. Martin a short flight away. Told her Dominica was unspoiled and beautiful.

She said, "I definitely need to trade these boots for some sandals and let the sun kiss my skin."

"You should."

"I could. I have a lot of time now. You want to mentor me?"

"I have this problem I have to take care of."

"The Detroit thing."

"Yeah."

"Well, anyway, can I help you out on that?"

I shook my head.

A year ago in London, Arizona had thought that the hit was on me because of a contract she had passed on to me. And Arizona had wanted to be involved, wanted to vindicate herself, that vindication almost getting her killed. She had been beaten while I was on the ground in front of her, captured, helpless. She had been thrown in the Thames. Because of me. She had been shot at as her body went into that frigid and murky water. I hadn't been able to save Arizona. I hadn't been able to save myself.

I didn't want that to happen again.

People romanticized Bonnie and Clyde—Faye Dunaway and Warren Beatty made that film look good—but they failed to see the reality of that union, that if not for Clyde Barrow and his problems, Bonnie Parker would not have died, wouldn't have been gunned down because of her partnership in crime with Clyde.

Everything was romanticized, even the harshest of deaths.

Somehow, as they died, as bullets riddled their bodies, I don't think romance was on their minds.

Detroit was my bête noire, my black beast to deal with, my problem, and the mistake I claimed.

She said, "Well, if my assistance is being rejected, ask Konstantin."

"He has his own problems."

"The cancer."

"Yeah. How is he holding up?"

"He don't really talk about it. Not with me. And I wouldn't know what to say. I'm not good at that kind of stuff. I want to ask him a lot of questions about it, but I don't want to at the same time."

"How was he tonight?"

"That man is the nicest man I ever met, but when he works, talk about vicious."

For a while we stood out in front of the door, two stories up, Hawks in my arms, looking out on Skylake Plaza and Miami Gardens Drive, watching traffic go by, some speeding toward Dixie Highway, others speeding toward I-95, her humming an Elvis Presley song as the sun began to rise.

The women in London. They were dead. That haunted me. Weighed me down.

I said, "You were asking me if the job got to me . . ."

"I know."

"What happened to you? What went wrong?"

She took a breath. "You can't tell anybody."

"I won't."

"I mean, even if Jesus comes back and asks you, you can't say a word."

"Okay."

She took another breath. Struggled. "I had a contract on Big Ed."

"Was that a mafia guy or something?"

"A racehorse."

"You had a contract on a horse?"

"On a Thoroughbred."

"Racehorses and show dogs. Lots of contracts on those."

"Going after a defenseless animal, well, that got to me more than going after people. I mean, people are evil, but an innocent, defenseless animal, that stuck with me like you would not believe."

"A horse."

"People have wanted people put in the ground over parking spaces. That's insane, but this was different. I executed a doggone horse. I went to Kentucky, put Big Ed to bed, and that messed me up."

"What did you do, shoot a horse?"

"Arsenic. Made it so it was untraceable, for the most part."

"Damn. You killed Mister Ed."

"That is not funny."

"Not laughing. No horsing around."

She cursed me, then we laughed, her laughter like sadness as we held each other.

Hawks said, "I never feel that way about people."

"I know."

Hawks took a deep breath. "Can't remember the last time I was that upset."

I faced Hawks, gazed in her bright green eyes.

Hawks whispered, "Why are you looking at me like that?"

I kissed her again. Her arms came up around my neck, her moans growing deeper. Hawks kissed me like she didn't want to be the one to stop first. I kissed her the same way.

Hawks said, "I bet they have real nice beaches down in Antigua, huh?"

"Three hundred and sixty-five."

"And you said you have a few days before taking care of your Detroit problem."

"What are you saying?"

"Wonder what it would be like to have sex on all those beaches."

"You're trying to tempt me."

"With something money can't buy."

"Why don't you show me what money can't buy?"

"Because I don't like you."

"Prove it."

"Ain't that wagon empty yet?"

"Only one way to find out."

"Little less conversation, little more action."

We went inside the darkened condo, the curtains facing the lake closed, Hawks holding my fingertips, yawning, tiptoeing past Konstantin as he slept on the sofa, leading me into the bedroom.

Twenty-seven

psycho

Yacht owners and islanders partied across the road at the Last Lemming, a Falmouth Harbour party that started at sundown, music so thunderous the din echoed like they were jamming in the next room. Pop music, reggae music. Songs by Lionel Richie and the Beatles.

It was midnight and it sounded like the party was just kicking into full swing. Prime time for mosquitoes, twelve bites on her tender legs, bites on her elbows and ankles, between her toes, three little swellings on her forehead. She was vexed. And afraid. Licking her lips as envy rose from within.

Matthew hadn't come back since he had stormed out this morning, disappointment and resentment and chastising anger in his voice, his come seeping from between her legs, her caveman husband.

She had called him; no answer, his calls going straight to voice mail.

She had sent text messages; no response.

She was tempted to drive to Hodges Bay, look for that bitch from Detroit.

The honeymoon was over, had gone from nonstop sex to never-ending anger overnight.

She knew that part of her needed a man like him, a man who could control her, yet she resented him because he gave her what she needed, what no other man had been able to give her. He was younger and yet he was more mature, some sort of a father figure, the first man who didn't bend to her every want, the one who made her do what she should do, what she was unable to do, the one she battled constantly, the man who gave her that high only drama could bring, that drama being another addiction.

She turned the air conditioner to twenty degrees Celsius, whatever that was, laid towels across the bottom of the two French doors that led to the balcony, and put another towel across the front door. The little vampires were already inside. The room needed to get sprayed.

In the Dockyard the music kept calling, begging her to stop worrying and leave for a while.

She sprayed her arm and legs with OFF!, dressed in linen pants and Blahniks, a pair she had never worn, fresh from Nordstrom, Italian shoes designed with camouflage patent leather, gold-tone hardware, buckled strap, open toe, three-and-a-half-inch covered heel. Dressed, she sprayed the bathroom and bedroom and kitchen area with Baygon, sprayed the screens that were on all the windows, sprayed so much Baygon the room looked like she had been inside smoking trees with Bob Marley. Then she changed her mind about her shoes. Took off the camouflage Blahniks. Opened her suitcase, coughed as she inhaled the bug spray, and found another new pair. Leopard-print haircalf, brown patent leather trim. Buckle strap at vamp and ankle. Open toe. With a four-inch heel. She changed Blahniks and hurried out of the room, closed the door to keep the clouds inside, and moved through the warmth of the night. She decided to stop battling mosquitoes and music; better to join the party than fight the celebration that was rocking the harbor. She went down the brick walkway, frogs and birds singing along with the band, waved at the male guard on duty as she exited Antigua Yacht Club, crossed the nameless road, went past a security bar, walked across gravel and dirt, passed by a donkey tied to a tree, walked past two Rastas drinking beers, and went inside the restaurant, a quaint seaside eatery that had low ceilings, a pool table, and a bar, a place filled with islanders and snowy faces. They were dancing, shooting pool, laughing, liming the night away, the quartet sounding as powerful as an orchestra.

She didn't stay long, walked away thinking about the boy she had left dead behind Sandals.

And the men outside the bar were chattering about the sailor and the men who had been killed up the road.

More music came from down Dockside Drive; she headed that way. People were congregated at the Mad Mongoose, the same next door at the Cockpit, all the energy like Las Vegas at night, English Harbour a real live party zone. She walked around the corner, followed a crowd of people walking up the road, cars heading into the Dockyard, droves of islanders and people who looked like AUA students, all heading to another place called Abracadabra, a disco bar, chill-out garden, Mediterranean café, and southern Italian restaurant rolled into one, soca and reggae setting the night on fire.

It looked like every Antiguan was there, each paying twenty E.C. dollars to cross the velvet rope.

Acres of beautiful swarthiness. This was like stumbling across a little corner of heaven.

Then her stomach growled. She craved sauerbraten with red cabbage and bratwurst.

Which was strange.

She'd never eaten sauerbraten with red cabbage and bratwurst.

She danced alone. Reggae by Dennis Brown. Third World. Garnett Silk. Aswad. Maxi Priest. Dancehall music kicked in, kicked in strong, like hip-hop with a Jamaican patois, the crowd chanting along with Vybez Kartel, Aidonia, Busy Signal, Serani, Munga Honourable, Mr. Vegas, Beenie Man, Bounty Killer, the rhymes as strong as the electronic drums, everyone in the room, every nationality, united underneath the same umbrella and chanting at the speed of thought, every dancer getting raunchy, infected with a different kind of holy spirit. Abracadabra was transformed into the Church of Shabba Ranks. When a young man came up on her smiling, his hips gyrating, she returned the smile. Her hips gyrated to the same rhythm, in the same motion, and she danced with him, wining up on a foreign man who danced the dance of sex, lost herself in the music and the madness, moved like the island girls, pushed her ass back into the man, who was grinding on her backside, his genitals practically resting in the crack of her ass. She glanced over her shoulder, gave him a look that dared him to keep up with her, moved her hips and butt like the Jamaican Patra, wukking up like the Bajan Rihanna, moving like the Wadadli songbird Shermain Jeremy. Surrounded by island girls, African girls, Spanish girls, European girls from London and the Netherlands. Every woman danced the same way, lost in the music, uninhibited and free, grinding against the men. They stood against the walls and leaned against wooden railings, some men holding on, some women grinding and wining so hard the men could barely keep their balance. Some men held the girls' waists and gave it as good as they were getting it, following the sweet moves of the asses as they dropped down to the floor. Beat thumping. Hundreds of people on the grounds of the restaurant. All doing the mating dance. Sweat rising like heated desire being fueled by movements of the body. Facial expressions a combination of sexual and spiritual intoxication.

She danced.

With every wine of her hips, every movement by her dance partner reciprocated, the thickness of his dick grew up against her ass like he had had his Irish Moss. Her partner danced, massaged her ass with a growing thickness, her every movement in sync with his as his grinding fired up her mons, created a wonderful tingling, made her wet, made her close her eyes and swallow little moan after little moan, his arousal sliding against her and creating erotic flashes. The music thumped, sent an echo of the beat through her body. The beat was strong and steady, felt like a Caribbean vibrator.

The dancing, the grinding, the sweating, and the freedom made her miss being a single woman. Her only wish was for this life, this seductive moment, to never end.

Dancing in fine linen and Blahniks, the primal smell of sweat, the scent of testosterone filling the night air, the intense dancing, the reggae, the way she joined the women who gave men rhythmic access to their bodies, the dancing a promise of carnal knowledge yet to come, she didn't want this to end.

As she wiped the sweat from her eyes she looked up, startled.

She saw him. It was the boy from the beach. The young boy she had been with at Siboney. Her dead lover was looking at her. His photo was large, his grin wide. She gazed around the room. Saw his youthful photos were all around. It took her a moment to realize what was going on.

This outpouring, this party, was a benefit for the murdered boy from the village named Swetes.

The boy had lived on Matthews Road. Matthews Road. Another Matthew.

She closed her eyes, lost in the music, grinding against a stranger's erection.

In her mind she wasn't dancing with her virile partner, she was riding him. Fucking him on the beach. The salty waves moving back and forth with the flow of their bodies, sand sticking to their sweaty skin, her body wining like she was sitting on top of him, a gentle breeze struggling to blow across her heated body, wanting to feel his strong hands cup her soft breasts, her pussy so hot and so wet.

Her dance-floor lover held her waist, his grind as strong and as stimulating as his grip.

Her stomach growled again, that craving for sauerbraten with red cabbage and bratwurst.

She opened her eyes, saw a group of girls on a raised stage, dancing in the spotlight.

Standing in the dense crowd, beer in hand, underneath one of the photos of the boy from Swetes, she caught a glimpse of a man with red hair. Then as the crowd moved she saw his face. His jaw tight. Her husband was there. Matthew was inside the club watching her. El Matador had resurfaced.

Hat-wearing men were at his side, men she recognized, gum-chewing Americans, mouths opening and closing like grazing cows, some of the men who had come to the island with the Lady from Detroit, a few of the survivors. If Matthew hadn't been with them, if they hadn't been chewing gum like it was cud, the stylish summer hats would have been a tell. Selentino. Panizza. Henschel. Borsalino. Dobbs. Angelo. Maybe a Steve Harvey. She saw that she had had an audience. Her mouth opened in surprise, her eyes locked on her husband's glare, his frown deep and unsettling, a frown that let her know he had been watching her for a while, had seen her dance of ecstasy, the look of until-death-do-we-part in his eyes.

She broke away from her mating dance, the generous erection that had rested in the crack of her ass left on its own, and moved through the dense crowd, searched for her husband, unable to find him.

El Matador was gone.

Back at the Antigua Yacht Club.

Matthew grabbed her arm as soon as she stepped in the door, grabbed her and threw her on the bed. She looked up at him, frowned, mouth tight, ready to curse him as he stood over her, a long-bladed knife in his hand. That blade found its way across her angry face, not cutting her, but the look in his jealous eyes made it clear that he was threatening to destroy what he loved. She fought to get up and he shoved her back on the bed, held her down as she squirmed, cut away most of her fine linen pants, cut away her top, cut her blouse, took the knife to what he knew she took pride in, destroyed what she loved, shredded all the expensive clothing she had bought in Beverly Hills and on South Beach, everything she wore being surgically removed. She cursed him, kicked at him, kicked and hit him until he grabbed her legs and jerked her hard, spread her legs. What he was doing repulsed her. And excited her. She grunted in both pain and fear, in anticipation, her body covered in sweat; her skin smelled of swarthy men, her lips pulled in, refusing to protest, refusing to give him anger or give him her moans, staccato breathing caught in her throat as he went inside her, slid inside her with no effort.

He frowned down on her, shivered, moaned, "Why is your pussy so wet?"

She sucked her lips in, struggled to subdue her own moan.

"Why is your pussy so motherfucking wet and wide open?"

He stopped, rolled away.

She heard him take a breath, heard him swallow.

She glanced his way, saw him staring at the ceiling, his jaw still tight, that long-bladed knife in his hand, gritting his teeth like he was struggling to decide whether to fuck her or kill her, held the knife like he still hadn't decided how to end this night.

She cleared her throat and asked, "Where were you?"

A moment passed.

She repeated, "Where were you? Where did you vanish to?"

He cleared his throat. "Barbados."

She paused. "Barbados."

"Did a quick little job."

"Without me."

"It was quick."

"We're partners."

"It was little."

"We're married and we're partners."

"Didn't need your assistance."

"Didn't need me tagging along and messing it up."

Silence.

She asked, "Where was the job?"

"Just told you."

"Well, tell me what happened."

He had left her and flown Liat, had to hurry and get to the Sheraton Centre. Food court. At a table at the restaurant Café Jungles. Contract on a bank worker who always ate lunch in the Centre, was having an affair with a FedEx worker. Café Jungles was their favorite place to eat, their love spot.

"I popped him after he had his mahimahi and pasta."

"You used a gun."

"I was in a hurry."

"In a public place."

"Parking lot. It's covered. Let them get in their car first. Walked over with a map, pretended I was a lost tourist. He let the window down, smiled, gave me directions. Had a silencer. Pop, pop."

"The girl who worked at FedEx?"

"Pop, pop."

"Where you lose the gun?"

"Atlantic Ocean. Outside the Crane."

"So it was about him having an affair."

"Don't think so. He was in *The Barbados Advocate* and *Daily Nation*. Saw those articles when I was leaving. Protesting the government and the price of chickens and dairy products going up."

"So you just up and left the island and flew to Barbados."

"Doesn't look like you were too lonely."

Silence.

He asked, "You fuck him?"

"I fucked him, sucked him, and swallowed the evidence."

"It wouldn't surprise me."

"I don't even know who he was. We were just dancing."

"You were practically fucking him on the dance floor."

"That's the way people dance down here."

"I could go back and kill him right now."

"Don't."

"Why are you protecting him?"

"That's the way they dance down here, means nothing."

"Well, you're not from down here."

Silence.

She said, "You have me here working for a bitch you used to fuck. Not cool. Not cool at all."

A frown covered her face. She wondered which was harder, raising a husband or raising a baby.

A moment passed before he said, "You're deceptive."

Her heart raced. She swallowed, then asked, "What have I done that's deceptive?"

"What haven't you done?"

"Over a dance? Get over it."

"That wasn't a dance."

"Did you not see everyone dancing the same way?"

"I was married to only one woman in that room."

Silence.

He said, "Gideon should be here in the next day or so."

"So the Gideon thing is back on."

"He took the bait."

"Thanks for telling me."

"While you were fucking around I was setting things up."

"From Barbados."

"Everything is moving as planned."

"So you're buddy-buddy with the hat-wearing, dapper fellows from Detroit."

Her husband coughed a little. "Most of them aren't from Detroit."

"Where are they from?"

"All over. She would be stupid to use people from her own city. Too traceable."

"Where did she find her crew?"

"Probably on the Internet."

"Wouldn't doubt it. Craigslist is one-stop shopping."

Matthew said, "Was joking."

"I know. Wherever they are from, you're their new best friend."

"Let's just say I have their attention."

"You killed two of their friends."

"Coworkers."

"Same difference."

"Fear works when respect won't do."

"Where are they now?"

"Wendy's."

"I see. They went up on Popeshead to hook up with some exotic and reasonably priced whores."

"I didn't ask."

"They are gone to get fucked."

"Looks like you were trying to do the same."

She licked around the inside of her mouth. "I don't like it when you are rough with me like that."

"The guy you were dry-fucking in front of the whole island was a lot rougher than that."

"That sure got your dick hard."

"You just don't know how lucky you are."

"And you can't keep cutting up my clothes."

"Clothes I paid for."

"You were too rough with me."

"And you were just as rough with that motherfucker who was all up inside your ass."

"He wasn't in my ass."

"Like it was a parking space."

"This outfit is—was Ralph Lauren."

"I don't care if it was Ralph Cramden."

"And you can't keep choking me while you're fucking me."

"You like that."

"Not the rough way you do it."

"It turns you on."

"Not when you are angry."

"Makes you come real good."

"I want to come hard, not die coming."

"You think I give a shit?"

"I don't like it when you do that, just grab me and stick your dick inside me."

"Since that is the only pussy I get and I'm married to it, I will be allowed to get this pussy anytime I want it and any way I want to have it. You can feel the same way about this cock over here."

"I still don't like it."

"We're married. I don't have to give a fuck what you like."

Silence.

"Am I in on this Gideon contract or have I been sidelined?"

"You never explained what happened in London."

"I did."

"Not to my satisfaction."

"The bitch from Detroit doesn't want me on the job."

"She's wondering if you have some connection to Gideon, maybe a double-cross."

"That bitch is delusional."

"You're needed. She set something up that she needs you to facilitate."

"I'm *needed*. *Facilitate*. What the hell does that mean?"

"Means I need you to go to Rituals and meet somebody."

"What is Rituals? Is that a church or something?"

"I have no idea. Find out and be there at noon."

"Who am I meeting at Rituals?"

"They will know you."

"What am I meeting them for?"

"They know that too."

Silence.

She asked, "Are you setting me up, Matthew?"

"What, you don't trust me? If you don't trust me, that means I shouldn't trust you."

Silence.

She whispered, "Why did you stop?"

He didn't answer.

She said, "I didn't want you to stop. I never want you to stop."

He didn't answer.

"Am I not attractive to you anymore?"

No answer.

"Make love to me."

No answer.

"Since that is the only pussy you're going to get and you're married to it, come get it."

No response.

She crawled to him, kissed him, kissed him until he kissed her back, moved his knife, took him inside her mouth, made him hard, pulled him on top of her. He tried to pull away, but she didn't let him.

"Since that is the only cock I get and I'm married to it, I will be allowed to get that cock anytime I want it and any way I want to have it. And I want it right now. Stop pretending. Your cock is so damn hard. Look at it. You want me. You want to get up inside of me. Come on, be mad inside me. Fuck me."

He gave in, kissed her, came to his wife.

She whispered, "You know you want this."

He filled her up, fucked her hard.

She said, "Slow down, Matthew."

He moaned.

She ran her hands across his face. "This what you want?"

He moaned louder.

She whispered, "What do you want me to do to make it right, baby?"

He moaned, her ragged and ripped clothing hanging from her body, his pants at his ankles.

Her husband told her to move her ass for him the way she had moved her ass for that island man, slapped her ass until she started to wine. He grunted, repeated for her to move her ass like she was doing another fuck dance, if she could fuck dance for a so-called stranger in a crowded room she could fuck dance for the man she married when they were alone. Her ass dipped and rotated as he spanked her, corporal punishment for a naughty and disrespectful wife, for a frustrating wife, spanked and fucked her, her orgasm rising, making her pant, moving her toward a summer solstice.

Matthew came, his volume lacking, but his load feeling heavy and deep as it flowed inside her.

She held him, shivered, moaned for him to keep moving until her orgasm arrived.

The rapture consumed her. The summer solstice so beautiful.

She held him for a while. Held him until the heat was too much to stand.

She rolled away from him, caught her breath, her head on his stomach, looked at his sweaty face.

This energy. It was the energy she had grown up under. The powerful energy of conflict.

She didn't know how to get away from that type of energy.

And if she did, she didn't know if she could survive without it.

It was hard being a wife when you knew you were cut from the cloth of a mistress. She would be more comfortable being a mistress. Marriage was a full-time gig. She didn't like working that hard. But she would try. She would do her best.

She cleared her throat, asked, "How do I know who to meet?"

"Meet?"

"At Rituals."

He pulled her face up to his, kissed her, put his tongue deep inside her mouth. She loved it, the kiss, her body expecting him to take her again. Wanted him to take her, show her passion, show her he loved her in that primitive way. Then he pulled away. Stared in her eyes, his stare unreadable, disturbing.

That knife still at his side.

He took a breath. A harsh breath that brought the negativity back in a rush.

Defensiveness rose. The good-feeling moment over.

She asked, "What was that?"

"You're not the most discreet person on the island."

"What does that mean?"

"They will know you."

He pulled up his pants, penis still swollen, damp with sex.

He said, "You drive me crazy."

"You do the same."

He paused, looked at her, his expression telling her he was frustrated, disappointed, unhappy.

She asked, "What's the problem?"

"You barely made it up the hill."

"What hill?"

"When we walked up the hill to get to Pigeon Point. You barely made it."

"I had been up all night. I was tired."

"You're getting fat."

"I'm not."

"That's why you're so slow."

"I'm not slow."

"Your center of gravity is off."

"Fuck you."

"Ass gets any bigger you'll qualify for handicapped parking."

She snapped. "Black men like it. Black men *love* it."

"Well, you're not married to a black man, are you?"

"Not this marriage."

"What does that mean?"

"Means what it means."

"Death do us part."

"Is that a threat?"

"That shit you did tonight, do it again and find out."

He picked up his blade and walked toward the door, his pace urgent.

She asked, "Where are you going?"

"Where were you when I got to Antigua? Where were you all night?"

"I was high. I got a room so I wouldn't have to drive. Then you called."

"How many lies can you tell?"

"I did."

"Where?"

"Siboney."

"What charge card did you put it on?"

"Paid cash."

"That's convenient."

"I dumped the weapons. Bought some E. Smoked a joint. Was stressed. Got a room on the beach. Would've come back here after all that work, but it's a long drive from one side of the island to the other. Woke up in the middle of the night. Woke up when you started calling me and came back here."

"If you were loaded, had a room, why didn't you wait until morning?"

She blew air, didn't answer.

"Who were you with?"

"Nobody."

He walked to the door.

She said, "Show me your ticket."

"What ticket?"

"Your plane ticket to Barbados."

"You know I don't keep a paper trail."

"Why should I?"

She felt him glaring down on her, knife in hand.

He walked out of the room.

She stared at the ceiling. Nervous. Clothes shredded. Tattered like they used to be when she was a child. No matter how she dressed herself, no matter how nice she looked, that feeling never left.

She was afraid.

Afraid of her lies being revealed. Afraid of her unhappiness being revealed.

Afraid of having to go back to being who she used to be.

Afraid of growing old, knowing how unkind the world was to the poor, the ugly, and the aged.

She shifted, felt pain. Breasts were tender. Maybe Matthew had been too rough with them.

Tears in her eyes. Sex no longer calmed the savage beast inside her husband.

Didn't calm the beast that lived inside her.

Hormones on fire.

She closed her eyes, searched for peace, craved food.

Twenty-eight

power, passion, murder

She screamed.

Panted hard. Her feet in stirrups. The doctor told her to breathe, to push, her contractions intense. Matthew was at her side. Her belly swollen, the end of nine months of pregnancy. Pushing and begging for an epidural. Pain so intense. She pushed and pushed. Until the baby came out.

Matthew was smiling. His smile disintegrated. Became a look of horror as he looked at her.

The baby was beautiful.

But the baby was blacker than asphalt.

Matthew pulled out his blade. El Matador cut everyone who got in his way, cut doctors and nurses, pushed everything aside, came after her, tears in his eyes, teeth clenched, blade held high.

She jerked awake from her nightmare, woke up reaching for her gun, woke with the sheets tangled around her legs, woke up blocking her neck from an imaginary knife, woke up falling off the bed, woke up trying to run away.

She woke up from her stream of nightmares, woke up alone.

In a fit, terrified, she called out for her husband, made it to her feet, and searched for Matthew, the room freezing, twenty degrees Celsius, yet she sweated like she was in a sauna.

It was nine in the morning.

Matthew had walked out, hadn't come back.

She looked down, still had on the ripped clothes she had worn last night. The nightmare had been too real, sent her to the mirror to check herself. She washed her face, pulled off her ripped clothing, pulled on a colorful robe, then she stepped out onto the balcony, the sun bright, island heat already unbearable. She caught her breath and looked out toward the yachts, the lush hills and rolling tropical mountains, nervous, the nightmares forcing her to think about the young lover who would never make love again.

She swallowed and thought about how her husband had come inside her, counting the days since her last cycle.

Remembering her trip to Barbados as well.

And the condom her lover had used when she was at Siboney.

She was sure it had been compromised, that it had leaked.

Her hand covered her stomach. That nightmare. Blacker than asphalt.

She called the front desk, asked where there was a pharmacy. When the woman at the front desk tried to be helpful and asked what she needed, the words hung in her throat; she couldn't say it.

It was easy to ask for a .38 or a .357 or a .22.

Not this.

She showered, dressed in linen and Blahniks, then headed to the Seabreeze Café. Metal bistro tables on wooden floors, baseball caps hanging high on the wall, maybe from some of the ships that had come into the harbor. Eighteen-inch television over in the corner, nobody watching, not an American CNN world. At the counter, croissants— roast beef, vegetarian, salmon—and muffins for sale.

She had a salmon croissant, green tea, and a muffin.

The nightmare still with her.

She looked around, leg bouncing, searching for a face she could trust.

All around people were on computers enjoying the free Internet; over in the corner British newspapers were available, *Daily Mail* and *The Daily Telegraph*. Someone had left a copy of *The Daily Observer* behind, one of the local newspapers. Front page. Bold letters. POLICE HUNT FOR GUNMEN WHO SHOT MEN ON YACHT IN FALMOUTH HARBOUR. They were hunting for *gunmen*, not *gunwoman*.

She searched for news about the young boy who had made her moan so deeply.

Articles about a brawl in the magistrate's court, an infant ingesting kerosene, a *youngest* mom award, a serial rapist on the loose, the rising cost of bread, fuel shortages, beginner karate classes on Nevis Street and Cross Street, a fete at Christ the King High and Saint John's Catholic Primary. Finally there was an article about a young man from Swetes being found dead on the beach, robbed of all his wares. Anthony Johnson. A simple name. A beautiful name. Eighteen years old. He was married and lived on Matthews Road with his grandmother. A black-and-white photo was in the paper. They actually showed the boy's dead body as it lay on the beach, his grandmother, Volda, and the boy's young Guyanese wife, Sharon, both standing around the corpse, holding each other and crying over the body.

The boy's grieving grandmother was quoted in the papers.

"Me go fin' out who e be an' me ga tek ma cutlass an' chop dem up!"

She read the words over and over, deciphered what was written as if it was a foreign language.

I'm going to find out who killed my grandson and take my machete and chop them up.

The threats and explicit vengeance of the grieving had been posted in the papers.

Anthony Johnson. She still felt him; his rhythms stirred her, his scent rose from her skin.

This was a nightmare.

There had to be somewhere she could go. Had to be somewhere on this island she could go.

She looked around. Glanced down the way at the Skullduggery. Saw a woman sitting out there with two kids. European woman with mixed-race babies. Then she saw another woman, darker hair, her children of mixed heritage. Not many, a few, crowd of thirty, maybe more. A white British man with his hair twisted into locks was there with his beautiful little girl, smiling, laughing, smoking, suntanned, and wonderfully happy, as if he had run away, reinvented himself, found a place that was Kumbaya. She looked around and saw another white man, sipping tea, a beautiful dark-skinned island girl at his side.

It terrified her. The thought of having a beautiful mixed baby, a baby whose hair she wouldn't know how to comb in the beautiful styles that little girls with curly and strong manes wore their hair in. Looking at the white Rasta with the pretty little girl and assuming, imagining herself in that man's place, her skin tanned and her locks long, eating a muffin with a beautiful daughter at her side.

She hurried away, that desperate sensation swelling inside her, crossed the nameless road at Falmouth Harbour, headed back to the yacht club, made her way to the security hut, the female workers there now, men working only at night. The daytime workers working twelve-hour shifts. She approached one of the young women, one who looked like she was in college, asked her if she could have a word.

The girl said, "I know what you want to know."

"Do you?"

"You want to know how to get to Hawksbill Bay, no?"

"What is that?"

"The nude beach on the other side of Five Islands."

"Uh, no. Not looking for that."

She took a breath and lowered her voice, whispered her problem to the security guard.

The security guard nodded, not as a security guard, but as a young woman who understood.

"There is a certain pharmacy in town where anyone will send you if you have a problem like that."

"Is it legal to buy that?"

"They sell it."

"Where do I go to buy it?"

"Redcliffe Street. There is a clear guy who sells it."

"I'd rather buy it from a woman."

"Only this guy who sells it."

She took a frustrated breath. She didn't have the luxury of time.

She asked, "Where on Redcliffe?"

"The block between Market Street and Corn Alley."

The girl told her where to find the mysterious clear guy, reminded her to be discreet.

The girl asked, "You ever use that before?"

"No."

"Two pills. And one for inside you."

"Inside me?"

"Yeah. One dissolves up there. Then you swallow two when that's put up there, and one more later on in the day. Then I think you take another pill, have to take one a day for a little while, maybe a week. This pill you need, it can be taken up to eight weeks into the pregnancy. I was at six."

"Were you?"

"Yes. Unfortunately. You cannot go back to school when you are pregnant."

"You can't go and get an education if you are pregnant?"

"No, they kick you out."

"Really?"

"If you get pregnant at thirteen, your education is over."

"Wow."

"I was six weeks."

"How are you supposed to make a living with no education and a baby?"

"That's the way it is."

"But the boys who get the girls pregnant, are they kicked out of school too?"

"Nobody cares about boys getting girls pregnant. They have babies with three or four different girls and nobody cares."

She nodded, understanding, feeling the girl's pain.

She remembered what she hadn't paid attention to, all the young girls working at full-service gas stations, up early walking the roads to go to work, selling wares on the beaches all day long, working at the market in town, never wondering why all the young girls were at work from twelve to fourteen hours a day, not questioning any child-labor laws in this land, not understanding what she had seen.

She had a lot in common with those girls. It didn't show. But she did.

That commonality: her fear.

She handed the girl one hundred dollars, Eastern Caribbean, price paid to forget a conversation.

The sun beat down, left boiling sweat on her brow, on her neck, and she'd been outside only ten minutes. She returned her scooter, exchanged it for a car. Wouldn't have to chance being run off the road, or have to inhale carbon monoxide, or have loose debris and pebbles thrown in her face. She parked in the West Indies gas station lot on Dockyard Drive and bought breakfast from a food vendor who set up a tent across from Sam and Dave's Laundry, a vendor who offered home-cooked breakfasts from the back of her truck. Salt fish, bread, plantain, eggplant mixed with spinach, okra, fried plantain, boiled eggs, cucumber and tomatoes, lettuce, chicken sausage, egg omelets filled with corned beef. She asked for it all. Then she stepped inside the gas station and bought two bottles of water.

She had eaten at Seabreeze, and now, less than a mile later, she was eating again.

Nervous. Famished. Terrified.

"To the left . . . to the left . . ."

Then she drove away, struggled to adjust to driving on the opposite side of the road as she sat on the opposite side of the car, the rearview mirror to her left instead of to her right. Felt like she was going to destroy the left side of the car at any second. Thought about her young lover as she hit a patch of rugged road. Thought about her husband as she tried to make turns without swinging out too far. She headed up the snaking curves, up All Saints Road, fear in her gut.

She shuddered as she remembered her dream.

Without warning cars stopped moving. No room to go around. Trapped in traffic that curved through Liberta. People were in the road, like they were marching in a parade. Up ahead she saw what they were waiting for, saw the party machine coming toward her. A gigantic truck that had been converted into a rolling boom box, people on board dancing, jumping up and down, women bent over and grinding against the men who were behind them. Abracadabra in the daylight hours. Men dressed in hip-hop gear, baggy pants, shirts off, girls and women in short shorts. Locals surrounded the truck and jammed. She was trapped in her car, an urgent errand on her mind, not able to move. The eighteen-wheeler took forever to move ten feet, then stopped for another thirty minutes before it inched her way. People moved between her car and the one in front of her, moved around her car, then the crowd doubled again. People were too close. The smell of weed and alcohol perfumed the island air as people leaned against her car, pushed up against it, the car rocking as she blew her horn and panicked and yelled, yells that were ignored, lost in the music and celebration.

The crowd surged and pushed a big man against her side mirror. She blew her horn over and over. Screamed as she watched the mirror being bent. Yelled for them to get off her car as the mirror snapped off. She reached out and grabbed the mirror before it dropped into the parade. People moved on. No apology. Left her screaming and holding a mirror that had been left hanging by its wires. She screamed until she couldn't scream anymore. She screamed in vain. The music dwarfed her scream.

The dancing and jumping continued; no room to move forward, but still she laid on her horn, blew it with urgency, blared it over and over as she held the mirror with her other hand. People looked at her like she was a stupid tourist, but she blew the horn anyway. Time was of the essence.

The moving boom box stopped in the middle of the road, left her surrounded by the celebration.

Left her screaming, blowing her horn like a madwoman, broken side-view mirror dangling.

Rituals was located on the other side of Woods Mall, west of an area called Gambles, across from AUA, in Jasmine Court on Friars Hill

Road. She had all of that written down and still ended up lost, drove back and forth for more than two hours, ended up at Blue Waters Hotel the first time, then at Jabberwock Beach, finally found her way back to Friars Hill Road, again driving past Woods Mall and Friars Hill Power Station, the landmarks she had been given, over and over for the better part of another hour, past the sign that said JASMINE COURT a dozen times. Not many had heard of Rituals, which was a coffee shop, a Trinidadian business new to the island of Antigua.

When she made it to the coffee shop she looked around the courtyard, saw no one who caught her eye, then ordered a chicken salad panini. Mango guava smoothie. She looked down at her legs, saw mosquito bites, and cursed, didn't want to have the legs of a woman marked by mosquito bites.

She was across from American University of Antigua College of Medicine, tucked in the mouth of a U-shaped two-story business plaza. Lots of trees, lots of shade. Exposed wood ceiling, one wooden ceiling fan, not needed because the breeze was nice. Spanish-style ceramic tile. Maybe clay tiles. Wrought iron chairs, same for the tables. A dozen tables, four wrought iron chairs at each.

Spanish, Trinidadian, East Indian, Portuguese, and Guyanese people came and went.

She looked around, tried to pick out the contact, no idea what nationality the contact would be.

Matthew was testing her. Fucking with her. Sending her on a damn errand run.

Like he was her goddamn daddy.

Young Arabs. Americans with East Coast accents. Spanish-speaking people about the same age, the age of college. Lots of Indian girls, a couple wearing T-shirts with AUA across the front.

She checked her watch, nervous, knowing she was late, knowing she had fucked up again.

A student walked up to the counter, ordered a smoothie, beautiful Punjabi girl, her long black hair parted down the middle. The girl looked back at her, her eyes going to her shoes, and the girl smiled.

The girl said, "Those are *killer* shoes."

"Yes, they are." She wanted to curse the girl, that line so lame, immature. "Killer shoes."

And the girl smiled.

She followed the girl out to the parking lot, where another man was waiting, a tall and lanky young man who had feet the size of boats but looked like he was barely old enough to be enrolled in college.

The girl said, "Was about to give up waiting on you."

"Got lost. Somebody should put up some street signs."

"The only street signs are in town."

"Lack of signs. Not exactly tourist friendly."

"How are you enjoying the island?"

She told the Punjabi girl that she hated the roads, so narrow, so many deep potholes, some roads unpaved, some made of gravel, some streets with no names, so it was easy to get lost, especially since they weren't hooked up for GPS. And they drove on the British side of the road.

The Punjabi girl shrugged like she had heard that complaint so many times that the conversation was pointless and cliché. She said, "Open the boot."

"Boot? I'm not wearing boots."

"Oh, you're American."

She hesitated. "I'm American."

"Assumed you would be British."

"What were you saying about a boot?"

"*Boot* means 'trunk' in Britain. Open your trunk."

The young man with her loaded two heavy boxes inside, never speaking a word.

The Punjabi girl said, "These are brand-new SR9s. Seventeen plus one."

That meant nine-millimeters, seventeen in the magazine, one in the tube. Eighteen shots. Manufactured by Ruger, one of the premium gun manufacturers in the history of violence.

She told the Punjabi girl, "Haven't used an SR9."

"Feels good in the hand. Reliable. You have small hands, so you will love it. Ambidextrous magazine latch. Low-profile slide stop. Reversible rubber back strap."

"What's the weight?"

"Under two, empty."

"Trigger pull?"

"Six and a half."

"I can deal with the two-pound weight, but six and a half on trigger pull—"

"Actually, it weighs less than two. Empty."

"That's fine, but considering what I'm going to need it for, I'd like it a bit lighter on the trigger pull."

"After you go through a few magazines you'll get used to it."

"Don't have that kind of time."

"This was all I had available. Last-minute order. The request was for something reliable, easy to conceal. These SR9s fit the order. They sell for five but I'm letting them go for half that. Need the cash. Fees at the university are kicking my butt. And the gas prices, that's cutting into my war chest. Caught me on a good day, so be thankful. Need the fast cash. Trust me, it's a good pistol."

"Suppressors?"

"In the box. I made them myself."

"Bootleg silencers."

"Nothing I do is ever bootleg. Been in this business for five years. My shit works."

"You use plastic?"

"Steel. Fits half the barrel, doesn't interfere with aiming. I do my own drilling. Test each one myself. No sharp edges left to cause inaccuracy. Feel free to test the suppressors."

She nodded.

The Punjabi girl asked, "What happened to your driver-side mirror?"

She told her about the crowd, the music, the jumping, the street party, the madness.

The girl laughed. "That was a *J'ouvert*."

"I thought they were about to destroy the car."

"You have to keep away from those celebrations in your car."

"I noticed."

"That's going to cost you big time."

"I know."

The Punjabi girl got in the passenger side of the car; her male friend backed out of their parking space and drove away, the sun high over their heads, speeding down Friars Hill Road, sipping smoothies.

Two hours later she was on Redcliffe at the Big Banana, a restaurant that stood out and caught her eye because of its non-Caribbean design and gray and blue colors, subdued colors compared to the rest of the other island businesses, seven silver ceiling fans spinning over her head, stylish, as if this eatery had been plucked up from the center of Times Square and dropped on Redcliffe and Thames.

She had a car filled with weapons. Soon this Gideon thing would be done.

Whenever the target made it to Antigua he would be a goat entering a wolf's cave.

Lots of chatter blended in with the sounds coming from the cricket game on the plasmas anchored overhead. She sat outside on the patio, saw girls walking down the road, baby powder on their chests and neck. She looked around. Andy Warhol–style images of Brando, Gandhi, Marilyn Monroe, John Lennon, Che Guevara, Miles Davis, Mona Lisa, and a couple of faces she didn't recognize were on the light gray walls. But there were enough oranges and blues and other colors that said this was a Caribbean spot, just not as flashy as most of the other businesses and restaurants.

Angst rose as she ate a fish burger and plantain, pineapple juice at her side.

She didn't know what to do. The *J'ouvert* had destroyed half the fucking car, the driver's-side mirror still hanging by the wires, a mirror she had to hold as she drove the narrow roads. The good thing was the island was single-lane traffic in two directions, downtown having one-way streets, so she didn't have to worry about changing lanes, just staying in her lane and not panicking when drivers zoomed by.

Fucking mirror hanging and the fucking rental car scratched the fuck up.

That would cost her a grip, just knew she was going to get screwed on the price.

She cursed.

She looked up; the television was on CNN. Myanmar. Children dead. Bodies floating in rivers. The aftermath of a cyclone. The graphic images shown had caught her off guard and disturbed her, made tears come. She watched those horrific images and wiped tears from her eyes.

Dead children. Dead babies.

Not what she needed to see right now.

Everything felt magnified, all of her senses, all of her emotions.

Pills were in her hand. Pills she had bought to fix her little problem.

She had stared at the pills for over an hour now.

She whispered, "I'm sorry. Mommy is so sorry. Please forgive me."

She took the pills. Washed them down with the last of her pineapple juice.

Wanted to cry.

Wanted to put her fingers down her throat and throw the pills back up.

Her cellular rang. It was Matthew. He was in town, at Planet Hollywood Barbers on High Street, next to Gentle Dental, across from Francis Trading, told her to pick him up some fresh clothing to wear.

Being the good wife, she had already picked up enough guns to take over this island; now she kept being his flunky and headed to Sunseakers, bought her husband shorts, shirts, Crocs, and sandals. Then she went to the Source Denim Company, bought Matthew two T-shirts, one from French Connection, black with white lettering, FCUK ME. Nothing for herself. Except the morning-after pills.

She gazed down Redcliffe, looked where the road sloped downhill toward Heritage Quay.

She looked down at the road and shivered. The aftereffects of the nightmare.

A baby as dark as asphalt coming out of her womb as Matthew looked on in horror.

That nightmare had been too real, *scared* her and *scarred* her; she knew that if that happened, as soon as the baby was born, Matthew would murder her on the spot, that baby an orphan before its first breath.

The rental car's mirror destroyed, the right side scratched to the primer.

And now the pills were in her body, pills that had a 90 percent chance of working.

That meant a 10 percent chance of the pills not working.

They had to work, put to sleep what might be inside her. For the first time she felt like a murderer.

The morning after a wonderful night was a motherfucker.

Two days had gone by since she was with the boy on the beach.

She took the car and drove to the area where Matthew was, on High Street.

More girls and boys in school uniforms, bank workers, taxi drivers, bootleggers, and vendors. Groups of overweight tourists appeared; shorts, pale legs and arms, most in sandals, carrying cameras and back-packs. Pale skin and expensive cameras. At least one cruise ship had docked. The world was busy.

In the distance she saw a large church. She stopped and stared, her throat tight.

A knot was in her heart. A guilt that might never end.

She walked toward the church. St. John's Cathedral. A few blocks over on Newgate Street. It was a magnificent stone building with twin silvery towers, standing high above the heart of the town.

She went inside, faced the altar, the cross and what it symbolized. She took her grieving and fears, went to the pews, got on her knees, hand on stomach, begging for forgiveness.

She found the barbershop, easy to find actually, a guy set up outside selling bootleg gospel music and DVDs, the same movies that played a block away at the cinema. She stepped inside. Shotgun room with square fans anchored to the ceiling, air conditioners high up on the back wall, four barber chairs. Matthew was in the back chair, a Dominican giving him a razor shave while island girls sat on benches and braided customers' hair, their workspace small, their work phenomenal, like art, like Blahniks. She asked how much to get her hair braided and one of the girls said the price was twenty E.C.

That was less than ten dollars U.S. One-fifth the price they charged in the States.

She got her hair braided. Then she had her eyebrows done by one of the barbers.

As she was getting her eyebrows done she listened to the men talk, their dialect thick and fast, filled with passion as they gossiped and ranted about some incident. She focused on their words and tried to decipher them. The word *Abracadabra* stood out. So did the words *murdered, butchered, killed.*

"Dem fine he dead, chop up lakka meat."

They found him dead, all cut up.

"A so somebody butcher he?"

Somebody butchered the man?

She looked at her husband. Matthew stared at her, coldness in his green eyes.

She noticed his shirt was light blue. Red specks on its front. The color of blood.

The girl who had braided her hair walked to her and asked, "You buy those shoes on Redcliffe?"

"In New York."

"What kind of shoes are those?"

"Blahniks."

The girl came over and looked at her Blahniks. Burgundy and topaz patent leather. Crisscross vamp. Slingback with adjustable buckle. Covered stiletto heel.

The girl was excited. "May I take a picture of your beautiful shoes with my camera phone?"

"Go right ahead."

Her husband watched the woman photographing her shoes, displeased with the attention she was getting, not understanding how important the moment was to the woman who braided hair, as important as it was for her when she had touched her first pair of shoes by Manolo, the same reaction people had as they walked through the Louvre and stared at masterpieces they'd seen only in books.

The camera flashed six times in a row, all shoe shots, flashed as if a celebrity was in the room.

After her hair was braided, she left with her husband, held his hand as he carried the bags, strolled on the street's mild incline, headed back toward the island's lone cinema and the sounds that came from the construction of a new parking garage. She passed another group of girls, tight jean shorts and sandals, all with baby powder on their necks and chests, smiled at them and walked the incline, tried not to show how low her energy was, didn't want any criticism from Matthew. She weaved around droves of people, schools out in the early afternoon. Hundreds of kids walked the roads, some in gray uniforms. She did her best to keep to the inside so she could avoid the sewage grates, grates wide enough for her foot to slip inside, with the man she married, not feeling comfortable with him, not at all, knew she was slowing him down.

She said, "You went back and had words with the man I was dancing with."

Her husband didn't confirm, didn't deny. "The focus is on Gideon. Get focused."

She said, "That's the way they dance down here, Matthew."

No response.

The sun kissed her skin; the heat created a river of sweat.

He asked, "Any problem with the pickup?"

"No problem."

"I heard you were late and the pickup almost didn't happen."

"Detroit called you."

"The girl called Detroit and Detroit called me."

She took a sharp breath. Didn't want to tell him that she had been lost.

She said, "Sort of had an accident in the rental car."

"An accident?"

"I didn't cause it."

"You've had the goddamn rental car what, three hours?"

As they headed up High Street, her husband saw the damage to the rental car and once again his jaw tightened.

Didn't ask her if she was okay, just saw the damage and shook his head.

She tried to explain what had happened, how it wasn't her fault, but he didn't give a shit.

He snapped, told her to hand him the keys, his voice rough, islanders looking at them, her embarrassment high.

He took the hanging mirror, yanked the wiring loose, and threw it in the backseat.

That was when he saw the long, deep scratch running down the driver's side.

She said, "It was a hit-and-run. This truck. Asshole kept going."

Her husband cursed, climbed in, and started the car as she got in, took off before she had her seat belt on, never said a word. He zoomed up Independence Avenue, took a different route, and turned up the narrow Vivian Richards Street, connected with All Saints Road, then drove too fast for her to feel safe, zipped in and out of traffic, passed cars, trucks, vans, kicked up debris, drove like he was reenacting a chase scene in *The French Connection*.

"*Slow down Matthew slow down slow the hell down.*"

"Answer my questions."

"Matthew. That was not necessary."

"Was what you did necessary?"

"What the fuck did I do?"

"I'm not stupid. You fucked him."

"I did not have sex with the man."

"You said you *fucked* him, *sucked* him, and *swallowed* the evidence."

"I'd just met him."

"You think I'm an idiot?"

She looked away. "We were dancing, that's all. Dancing just like everybody else."

She closed her eyes; the rental car bounced over speed bumps; they were in a school zone.

He asked, "Is that who you were with when I made it to Antigua?"

"Of course not."

"You still haven't made it clear to me where you were the night I arrived."

"Matthew, please. You disappeared for two goddamn days."

"What if you hadn't seen me at Abracadabra? I walk in with the men I'm working with, men I've got in my pocket so far as respect is concerned, then one of them taps my shoulder and points, 'Hey, ain't that your wife over there?' You know how the fuck that made me look? Do you have any idea?"

Silence.

"You see all the big red lettering on the big white billboards talking about rapists? Even if you didn't plan on fucking him, what if he didn't see it the same way after you dry-fucked him like that?"

"Slow down, Matthew. Slow the damn car down."

"But he wouldn't need to drag you down to Burma Road and rape you."

"Watch out for the—" Another speed bump jarred her. *"Slow down slow down slow down."*

"He had your pussy so wide open I almost fell in and went to the other side."

"There is a blind curve . . . why are you speeding up?"

"Answer my fucking questions if you want me to slow the fuck down."

The world whizzed by, Caribbean homes and lush mountains, billboard for Romantic Rhythms music festival, more speed bumps, Matthew switching lanes to pass drivers going forty kilometers per hour, more zooming to the right lane and into oncoming traffic to pass other slow-moving cars and trucks and machines used on construction sites, zooming at drivers in the opposite lane, her heart about to explode, then swerving back into the left lane seconds before a head-on collision, moving at warp speed, the back end of the car hitting the curb in a section of a town that had sidewalks, the car swerving, Matthew almost losing control as she screamed for him to slow down, screams that made him accelerate.

"I'm sorry I'm sorry I'm sorry."

"Are you?"

"Sorry I danced with that man like that."

"You're sorry you got caught."

She lowered her head, put her hands over her eyes, waited to crash, waited to die.

Then the car slowed, was forced to when Matthew hit the curves in Liberta, droves of people, maybe the entire village was still out, liming on the sides of the roads, street vendors selling food.

She whispered, "You're crazy."

"Dancing like you make your money a dollar at a time."

"You are fucking insane."

"Would you have fucked him?"

"No, Matthew." Her voice trembled. "This pussy is your pussy. Nobody's pussy but yours."

A moment passed. Matthew nodded. Argument over. For now.

Matthew said, "We have a couple of other issues that have to be addressed."

"Not now, Matthew."

"In due time."

"Slow down before you kill somebody."

"I'm not a fucking idiot."

She looked at her hand, the way it trembled.

Fear abating, she swallowed, took a deep breath, and said, "I'm hungry."

Back in Falmouth, as they sat seaside at Zanzibar eating rotisserie chicken and rice and peas, her hunger never-ending, she pondered all of her bad luck, how it followed her.

And it had followed her here, sat in the next booth as she ate, two people reading the paper, a man and a woman, talking about the young boy who had been found dead on the beach.

"He grandmudda say she a go fine out who kill she grandpickney."

His grandmother says she will find out who killed her grandson.

Those people left, but their words remained in the air, the newspaper left behind as well.

She thought about the days in foster care, the abuse, how she had only one pair of shoes, how she had only a handful of clothing, how she had only one decent dress, how she was forced to wear the same tattered clothing over and over, how she had told herself she would do whatever it took to get away from that abusive lifestyle. The abuse. The last foster parent. The old man who had come inside her room in the middle of the night, told her he needed her to do something special for him.

That type of input, the high drama, the screaming, the cursing, the pain—she wondered if she had gotten used to that over the years, if she was unable to function without conflict in her world.

The idea of opening up to a therapist, talking to a stranger about that, being open and honest, that terrified her more than the insane ride with Matthew. She wasn't built to face things like that head-on. She had searched for what made her feel good. The shopping. Having things when she had grown up with nothing. The high she got when she was in that mode, it was indescribable.

The Blahniks. Those were a symbol, a statement, not just something to cover her feet.

It told the world she wasn't a foster-care kid anymore, that she was living better than the ones who had abused her. Things had been going great for her, the best days of her life before the marriage.

Going to New York, meeting the women from *Sex and the City*, it was more than a crazed fan spending twenty-four thousand dollars to see the celebrities. She wanted to see them, thank them.

She had come from nothing, risen from the ashes of abuse and poverty like a phoenix. And she wanted the world to notice her, see her victory, wanted to be part of that upper class that had pissed on her world from the day she was born. She wanted to be special. She needed to feel special. Success was always the best revenge.

Matthew asked, "You okay over there?"

"I'm fine."

"What's on your mind?"

"Nothing."

"Nothing or nothing you want to talk about?"

"Either or."

The black men. Men the opposite color of the ones who had abused her.

Men who had made her feel good. Men she knew she'd never get too attached to.

With attachment came pain.

Then she met Matthew.

She had an epiphany. Matthew had been her bad luck, the start of her downward spiral.

Matthew reached over, took her hand. "You mad at me?"

"Should I be?"

She pulled her hand away.

He said, "I love you."

"You love me so much you have me running errands for a bitch you used to fuck."

He leaned over, kissed her, gave her his tongue.

Her mind was in another place.

She had never missed a shot before meeting him.

She had never had a man follow her down a rugged road shooting at her.

She had never had her car attacked by a mob during a J'ouvert celebration before.

He had been the black cat that crossed her path, the broken mirror in her life.

That stayed on her mind as they headed back to Antigua Yacht Club, as Matthew carried two boxes that had been in the trunk and she carried the bright orange Sunseakers bag, as they walked past security and waved, as the girl who held her secret made eye contact but said nothing, as she and her husband climbed the concrete driveway and went inside the room, as they opened the boxes and took out a dozen nine-millimeters, as they inspected the SR9s, as they inspected the ammunition, as she showered, as she slathered Anthisan cream on two dozen mosquito bites, as she listened to Matthew shower, as he came out naked and wet. She didn't raise her head, kept putting lotion on her skin.

He said, "I love you."

"I know."

"If this is going to work, we have to make it work."

"I love you, too."

He stopped her from lotioning her skin. Kissed her like he couldn't live without her.

He said, "You drive me crazy."

"I know."

He sucked her breasts, put fingers inside her, ate her out while she was on a bed surrounded by guns. That used to turn her on, used to get her so hot, the sex surrounded by the danger. She gripped the covers and arched her back, understood this was his way of apologizing. She felt so much love for him, allowed him to lead, knew he wanted to have sex again, knew that if she didn't have sex again it would become an issue, and she couldn't handle another issue right now. She mounted him and rode him with her eyes on the nine-millimeters, gave him the erotic asphyxiation he asked for, gritted her teeth and choked him, wished she was a lot stronger.

He moaned.

She felt him. Felt him moving inside her, changing her mood. Felt him making her want this.

She struggled, an intense control struggle, before she moaned. "*Sssshit.*"

He had her swimming in fire, about to come, confused.

She thought about the morning-after pills she had taken. About what she had done.

The life she lived, not the lifestyle meant to bring a kid into this world.

No matter how badly she wanted a kid.

She trembled and tears fell, mixed with the sweat that dripped from her face.

Matthew touched her face. "You okay?"

"It feels so good. You're making me emotional, that's all."

"Want me to stop?"

"Keep going, baby. Keep going."

She closed her eyes and moved, felt her husband swelling, knew he was about to come.

She was about to come again. She was about to come with him.

Coming and crying, thinking her husband didn't need to kill that man, that she wished she hadn't been so taken with the boy she had met at Sandals, so taken with his youth, his innocence, his smile.

A rough hand grabbed her, its grip firm, began shaking her, shook her hard.

She opened her eyes and faced an old woman. Tall with dark skin, her hair short and curly, sandals on her work-callused feet. The old woman shook her and shook her until she sat up.

Matthew wasn't in the bed anymore. He was gone. Had left her on the bed naked.

She looked at the old woman. A woman dressed in a black skirt and yellow polo shirt.

It was one of the workers at the hotel, one of the women who serviced the rooms.

She tried to stand and when she did the old woman shoved her back down on the bed.

Pushed her down hard with her right hand, never let her go, her grip firm.

The old woman, strong, years of labor, hands callused, harder than concrete.

The old woman gritted her teeth as tears fell from her eyes, as saliva drained from her mouth.

Through gritted teeth the old woman growled, "Mrs. Robinson."

The name she had given the boy when she met him on the beach.

Those two words put panic in her eyes and fear in her heart.

The old woman held her as she struggled to get free, as she fought pain and grabbed the old woman's hand, a hand she couldn't move. The door opened and more hotel workers came inside the room, women in black skirts and yellow polo tops, women who closed the door and glared at her.

They all frowned and said, "Mrs. Robinson."

The old woman. The resemblance was in her face, in her eyes.

It was the dead boy's grandmother. She had found her.

One of the women walked over, a young woman. She had seen her face in the newspaper. It was her dead lover's beautiful wife. The young girl nodded and handed the old woman a cutlass.

The cutlass was a beautiful, thick saber, a marvelous slashing sword, its blade slightly curved; its edges looked freshly sharpened. A tool that had been used as the sailor's weapon of choice, had been used in the sugarcane fields, a tool used in the act of robbery, a weapon used in dismemberment and murder. A cutlass. Cousin to the machete. Its blade as long as a madman's sword. A blade the old woman drew high over her head of salt-and-pepper hair as the women frowned and moaned that she was a murderer. She fought in vain, fought and looked up in shock, eyes wide and fixed on a blade aimed at her throat, a blade that an old, grieving woman brought down with an indescribable vengeance.

She jerked awake. Heart racing.

Matthew was in the bed next to her, naked, asleep, and unaware of her nightmare.

She went to the kitchen, caught her breath, took out a bottle of water, drank most of it.

Stood there naked, trembling, glad her husband couldn't see her now.

The guilt subsided.

She watched Matthew. His chest rising and falling. Asleep on a bed surrounded by guns.

The things he had said to her. The way he had driven and terrified her on the roads.

She picked up a nine-millimeter, loaded it, pointed the business end at her husband's head.

So close to pulling the trigger on the gun.

She dressed and left the room, a loaded SR9 in her bag, seventeen plus one, less than two pounds of weight making her feel comfortable and confident. She took her damaged rental car, drove to town, went to eat at Papa Zouk; stuffed clams baked with cheese, bouillabaisse, pan-fried red snapper.

She wasn't old. She wasn't incompetent.

Her hormones had been going crazy, messing with her equilibrium, her balance, her timing. The pills would map her back to being normal. Everything should go back to the way it was.

Her body felt strange.

Felt like Suicide Tuesday was tapping her on her shoulder. The backlash from using E. Body suffered from the depletion of serotonin. Wished she had taken 5-HTP, L-tryptophan, vitamins, and magnesium supplements. Instead of the morning-after pills. But she didn't have the luxury of time.

Was too late to reduce the depression effect by replenishing serotonin levels.

She'd deal with it.

She had a day. Maybe two. Would be in perfect condition before Gideon arrived.

She had to get her swagger back, a swagger she was losing with every breath.

Gideon. In London she had stared into his eyes. Eyes that were cold, bottomless, the doorway to death. Eyes as powerful as Matthew's. Eyes that had, for the first time, caused her to hesitate.

Her eyes would be the last eyes he saw. She would kill him. Get her mojo back.

Twenty-nine

a masterpiece of revenge

V. C. Bird International Airport.

Matthew glanced at her as he drove. "You okay over there?"

"I'm okay."

"You're looking extremely flushed."

"Turn the A.C. up."

"I have the A.C. on high."

"You sure?"

"You on drugs? You on E?"

"No."

"Why are you sweating like that?"

"Because I am hot."

There was only one way inside V. C. Bird, from Airport Road, no multiple entrances like LAX, no multiple levels like Atlanta, not complicated like Chicago's O'Hare, not convoluted like Heathrow and Gatwick. A simple turn inside, one lane of driving past the cricket stadium and a printing company. The check-in area was outside, different carriers elbow to elbow. Could walk end to end in under two minutes. She took it all in as Matthew circled the front of the airport, a wishful scene in her mind, a scene where Gideon walked out of the terminal unaware, one shot to his head, and screeching out of the airport, ripping Airport Road back to Old Parham Road, getting lost in the web of communities, no helicopters to chase them like LAPD, no CCTV cameras to track them like in Central London, a clean getaway.

In her mind. In reality it wasn't that easy. Sometimes less was more. Sometimes less was less.

Traffic could prove tricky if the target arrived when the terminal was this busy, when droves of tourists and locals were hustling up and down the brown and gray tiled walkway, others leaning and waiting against the stucco walls, salmon and green the most dominant colors. Matthew pulled over in the car park by the Sticky Wicket. They headed down the walkway, sweaty people passing them carrying tons of overpacked luggage, making their way to cars and vans that served as taxis. They blended in, just another snowy-faced couple at the airport. Snowy faces with mild tans. She slowed down when Matthew did the same, looking out at the grounds between the terminal and the Sticky Wicket, a striking landscaped area that, if there was a way for it to be done, could be used to pop the target from a distance.

She spied around, not seeing a clear getaway, no exit route that would make the job easier. She looked to her right, looked at her husband; Matthew driving, studying the ingress and egress, nodding.

She said, "Only one way out."

"Looks that way."

"It's that way."

She looked across the tropical grounds at the Sticky Wicket; grass the greenest of greens, palm trees, probably the most beautiful part of the island, maybe the most beautiful part of the world.

She asked, "Any idea what *sticky wicket* means?"

"Cricket term. Means a difficult circumstance."

"Place looks amazing."

"Probably the best-looking area on the island. Rich guy owns all that."

She asked, "Who?"

"The guy who owns the Stanford Twenty/Twenty."

"His name?"

"Sir Allen Stanford. Billionaire financier. Fifth-generation Texan."

She said, "Wealthy guy."

"He owns the restaurant, the cricket stadium, the bank we passed coming into the airport, the best gym on the island, that printing company across the lot, and God knows what else."

"Ridiculously wealthy."

"This section of the island is pretty much his."

She motioned at the airport. "He flies in here and mingles with the locals?"

"Private plane. Has his own airstrip, gets out and rides his private boat over to Jumby Bay."

"Jumby Bay. Is that where Britney Spears was?"

"No, she was at Crossroads Centre."

"What's that?"

"Rehab place. Eric Clapton built it. Whitney Houston was there too."

"Go to rehab on a tropical island, hang out with all of the celebrities. Must be nice."

"Glad you brought that up."

"What are you talking about?"

"I went to Crossroads. Checked the place out."

"Another job?"

"The facility is at the bottom of the island, southeast, overlooks Willoughby Bay, largest bay here. Has its own beach on the shoreline. Beautiful and serene, tropical, like Stanford's property up here."

"Who is the contract on?"

"They have thirty-eight or thirty-nine beds."

"Not too many people. Nice. Sounds like an easy in and out."

"Place stays full. They have one empty bed. Wanted to take you down there."

She chuckled. "You plan on taking us down there for a second honeymoon?"

"No. Not us. You. Just you. You're going."

Her laughter ended. "You're joking, right?"

"They help people with compulsive behaviors."

"I'm not going to a place filled with alcoholics and crackheads."

"That problem of yours. That problem of *ours*. You're getting some help."

"You're joking, right? I mean, this is a joke and you're getting to the part where we laugh, right?"

"We get this contract done, you check into Crossroads. You don't leave this island. You don't go to Miami or New York or Los Angeles or Paris or London or anywhere you might step off the plane and lose control. We get you help right here, right now."

She didn't say anything.

He said, "Shoes are your crack."

"Blahniks are not shoes."

"And crack is not cocaine."

"Blahniks are Blahniks."

Matthew went back to staring at an observation tower in the distance, studying the grounds.

She asked, "Are we sure we want to pop Gideon here in the middle of paradise?"

"If we could spot him in the crowd, we'd need a sharpshooter to hit him from that distance."

"So you're thinking about doing a Lee Harvey Oswald."

Matthew studied the area. "And post him up on the other side of the grassy knoll."

"And create mass panic. Not a good idea."

"We could vanish in that mass panic."

"If for some reason they managed to block the one and only exit—"

"I know. We let him get out. Away from the crowd. Find a way to box him in."

"Gun him down."

He nodded. "Plain and simple. Keep it simple. Old-school simple."

She said, "We need to be out front, waiting and watching the flights."

She watched the people, the crowd out front. Every face potential collateral damage.

She said, "Another problem is Gideon has seen us."

"Well, whose fault was that?"

She didn't reply. The fuckup in London would always be thrown in her face.

She asked, "Any more options?"

"I wish I could see inside. Need to see where else he could come from."

"Didn't you look when you came in from Barbados?"

"Want to double-check. And let you look at it, see if you see something I missed."

She almost smiled. Almost. Didn't. Just said, "Follow me."

"What are you going to do, just walk past security and stroll inside the secured area?"

She told him, "Follow me."

She went to the Liat counter, asked where she would go to see about lost luggage. They directed her to the opposite end of the terminal, pointed toward a guarded door, said lost luggage would be in that area. A guard was situated outside the glass door that led inside the terminal. She walked up to the guard, said she had flown in from Barbados last night and her luggage had been lost, that she wanted to check and see if her bag had shown up yet. The guard asked for the proper paperwork, the claim she should have filed with Liat. She told him she had left it all back in her room, said she had taken another taxi all the way from the other side of the island to check on her luggage. The guard made an unfriendly, irritated face, one that looked as if he was silently speaking of his disdain for tourists and their sense of entitlement, folded his arms in front of his drab and colorless uniform as he looked her up and down, saw white Cavalli jeans, the Blahniks, the low V-neck white blouse with vertical black stripes, a blouse bought in Paris on the Champs-Elysées and accented with a broad leather belt, the wide lenses on her Tom Ford Whitney sunglasses, inspected her haute couture from head to toe, the mechanisms inside his mind at work, came to some conclusion, then took a shallow breath that released a corner of his irritation, made a dismissive motion toward the doors, not saying a word, and let her inside.

She took the lead, let Matthew follow her inside, where she grinned and waved at customs, men who were busy screening passengers, men who stopped to address her. She told them she was looking for lost luggage. One of the customs agents was busy with an older woman, a small woman in a flowered dress with gray hair who spoke in patois, asking the old woman to step to the side, ignoring the old woman telling them she was in a hurry to get to a family gathering in Parham, opening the woman's suitcases, old suitcases that had seen years of travel. The customs agent paused searching the old woman's bags, pointed toward a single door between immigration and baggage claim, the door for Liat.

She headed toward that door. Inside a small room a girl was working alone, two people in her office, in search of lost luggage. When it was their turn, sunglasses off, she repeated the lost luggage story, had Matthew give her the information on the flight from Barbados. The girl pointed at a section near baggage claim that had at least one hundred pieces of luggage, all lost. Told her all lost luggage from Liat ended up in Antigua, invited the Assassin with Ass to look at the stacks of unclaimed and lost luggage, said there was more unclaimed and lost luggage in the back storage room. Then the svelte young girl went back inside her modest office and closed the door.

She told Matthew, "See what you need to see so we can go."

"You do the same."

"Already on it."

While she pretended to look for her lost luggage she let Matthew inspect the layout, let him drift over to baggage claim, blend with the rest of the people who had come through immigration. The svelte girl from Liat came over, professional and concerned, doing her best to be of assistance, asked for a description of the lost bag, and she told the Caribbean girl that the lost bag was a Louis Vuitton on wheels, which should be easy to spot, then the Liat employee escorted her to another room that had hundreds of pieces of unclaimed luggage, luggage from all around the world. Again she was left alone. Alone thinking about too many things. The dead boy named Anthony Johnson. The faceless man she had danced with at Abracadabra. The morning-after pill.

Five minutes later she came back out of the dusty room, stifling a sneeze, and the more-than-helpful Liat employee asked her if she had filled out a form, then handed her one and walked away.

Matthew nodded, signifying he was done. They exited the same way they had come in.

She walked out first, sticking the useless form in her purse. Matthew led and she followed him, and she took in the area outside the exit, moved through the sweaty madness, taxis loading passengers, pickups and drop-offs at curbside, tourists getting rental cars, representatives from Sandals and from practically every resort and hotel on the island situated right outside the door, holding up signs; that activity would be massive when several flights arrived at once, making it easy for whoever came through to vanish in the crowd. A Big Banana restaurant was upstairs, and so was a lounge, but that lounge was for departures only. She saw something other than the taxi dispatchers, a post office, and a bank.

A police post was right in front of her face, right outside the exit, its façade blending in with the bank, snack shop, and everything else, its front door and POLICE sign being blocked by the growing crowd. The only reason she noticed it was because the door to the police station opened and officers rushed, came right at her, intense faces that made her want to run. The police officers bumped her out of the way, moved by her, damn near knocked her over as they rushed toward customs. She pointed that out to Matthew. He had missed the indiscreet outpost.

He nodded and walked on, went to Charles Snack Shop and bought two bottles of water, gave her one. By then the police were coming out of the terminal, the old woman handcuffed, the wig taken off her head and in a police officer's hand, her dialect thick, first claiming she didn't know how her bag and wig magically became filled with pounds of marijuana, then as they took her away shouting, "A little bush weed for me to smoke, just a little for me to smoke."

Matthew took her hand and walked through the rumbling crowd. She held his hand in return and headed back toward the end of the terminal, stopping in the shade in front of the Virgin Atlantic counter, no one there at the moment. When Matthew stopped walking she did the same and looked back.

She sipped her water. "One way out. The target has to come through customs, out that door."

She told Matthew he should post somebody at the door that led from customs into the country.

Matthew said, "I could post a guy, have him on a bench in front of the snack shop."

"More than one. Just in case one of the boys needs Lasik surgery."

Matthew nodded. "Any other suggestions?"

Now he needed her. Now she was the one in charge. The Cheney to his Bush.

She said, "Since you have a football team on your roster, post some of the steroid eaters outside the door. Put point men in both directions, opposite ends of the terminal, one toward the walkway that leads to the parking lot near the Sticky Wicket, another to the right, in the direction of the employee parking lot. One way in, one way out. Post somebody in a car down at Airport Road, that dirt lot that was right across the street as we turned into the airport, he sits there and if the target slips by he can establish a tail before he vanishes. Everybody armed, but nobody is to shoot, not without your order."

Again Matthew nodded as he picked up his cellular and dialed.

He was a great assassin. Younger and agile.

She was older and cunning, skilled, smarter than her husband; she knew that.

He finished his call and hung up.

She asked, "We done?"

"Not quite. One more issue to resolve before we move forward."

"I'm not going to Crossroads."

"Crossroads is not the second issue."

"What then?"

"You've been deceptive. You thought I wouldn't find out. But I did."

She paused, waited to hear him say something about the boy on the beach at Sandals.

He frowned, his intense stare focused on her eyes. "*Sex and the City.*"

He knew.

He said, "You want to tell me about it or should I tell you about it?"

She took a breath. Not much got past Matthew. Not much.

He said, "Cancel it or I will cancel it for you, and if I cancel it, it will not be pretty. You are planning to spend *twenty-four thousand dollars* to go to a movie about four dumb and desperate women, a movie that you can get at Blockbuster for twenty dollars? You've fallen off the deep end and lost your mind."

"They are not dumb."

"You're right. They're smart enough to get you to pay twenty-four thousand to see them. How much do you think they would pay to see you? This bullshit ends here. This bullshit ends now."

She nodded, not in agreement, but in compressed anger, in confirmation of what she had to do, acknowledging that her husband had pushed and pushed, and now she was cornered.

He said, "Crossroads. That empty bed has your name on it."

Her jaw tightened.

"So you want to send me to a place filled with drug addicts and washed-up celebrities."

"For your own good. For the good of this marriage."

They were at a crossroads.

Her marriage was a sticky wicket, a difficult circumstance that had to be resolved.

She looked from the terminal to the restaurant, her eyes staying on the eatery.

Sweat trickling down her back, she fanned herself and said, "I'm hungry."

Thirty

crime boss

The Sticky Wicket.

She walked up the stairs and Matthew opened the door for her, the perfect gentleman, and he pulled on silver door handles shaped like cricket bats, both set at an inward angle. The hostess led them to the left, toward the sports lounge. Matthew walked behind her, unable to see her frown; the echoes from his stride didn't hide his frustration and disappointment. Her stride didn't hide her anger. Sweat dripped down her neck, her flesh being cooked, the Caribbean sun strong and unkind. Jeans and a linen top were too much to wear in this heat, heat made for beaches and bikinis and drinks with sexy names.

Flagstone columns. Classy sports bar. Posh lounge. Cricket memorabilia all over.

She ordered food. Conch fritters. Ribs. Beef brisket. Passion-fruit juice.

Matthew ordered. Mahimahi with a passion-fruit, mango, and lime salsa. Ginger ale.

Four televisions above the bar, one over her head, cricket match on, information about BOWLING SPEED, ALL DELIVERIES BOWLED, the game in progress, the world of cricket not interesting her.

He mumbled, "Twenty-four thousand dollars to see a fucking movie that will play the next day at the same movie theater for ten bucks. You really need some help. And you need it bad."

She didn't respond. Didn't argue. Only a fool would argue with a fool.

She was eating barbecued ribs when the team showed up; jeans and T-shirts that made them look like walking billboards, all wearing shades, all wearing hats, shades and hats that Matthew asked them to remove, shades they all took off without hesitation, hats they did the same with, all deferring to Matthew, following the words of El Matador as if he was a god.

Matthew sat at the middle of the table, made sure all could hear his voice. They sat around him like he was their Jesus and ordered more barbecue, roasted half chickens, crab cakes, whole snapper, pretty much everything off the "Sticky Starters," "Wicket Greens," "Wicket Mains," and "Cricket Sandwiches" sections of the menu, food that came not with the casualness of most Caribbean eateries, but with the quickness of an American restaurant, places that had substituted real cooks with frozen foods and microwave ovens. She preferred a skilled chef over a microwave technician.

But the food tasted fresh, as most island food did, tasted better, fresh, no preservatives.

The men, the bodyguards, the soldiers from Detroit, didn't look at her the way they had done at Pigeon Point Beach, never let their eyes drift her way, no comments about her ass, no lingering looks, not a single glance at her, knowing that a glance at Matthew's wife, at El Matador's woman, would leave blood in the sand. And she didn't make eye contact with any of the men, the drama that had happened at Abracadabra still on her mind. She listened as Matthew regurgitated her strategy as if it was his own. He was the quarterback and she was being treated like a cheerleader. Fuck that. She left the table, gave up staring out at landscaping more impressive than the grounds in Beverly Hills, went to another section of the restaurant, left the testosterone and steroids and ordered dessert from the "Sweet Tail Enders" part of the menu, took in the five-star sports bar and air-conditioning, tapping her fingers without pause, her resting place overlooking the cricket stadium, cricket on all of the monitors throughout the restaurant.

Cricket. The only sport more boring than baseball. Badminton was more exciting.

She ate cheesecake, glowered at her husband.

Then something went wrong.

Nausea.

Sickness hit her, her insides hot, guilt bubbling in acid. She moved past the bar, found the bathroom to the left in an alcove, went inside a stall, the wave hitting her hard, regurgitating all she had eaten. Sweat came as cramps followed. The side effects from taking the MAP had come with quickness.

She didn't know how it would work with her, if it would work.

Didn't know if she would bleed for a week, like a normal period, slight cramping, then her world would go back to normal. Or if she would bleed like a hemophiliac. She threw up like crazy, retched and felt severe cramps for a moment, couldn't walk, couldn't stand, cried and wished she had painkillers, heating pads, hot tea. She cleaned herself up, pulled it together, leaned against the counter.

It felt like it was more than the MAP.

It felt like she had been attacked by demons of the dead and the dying.

The ecstasy. The marijuana. The alcohol. Inside her body like a cocktail.

She needed fresh air. She felt dizzy, had difficulty breathing, sharp pains in her joints, sharp pains in her abdomen. Five minutes passed. Then ten. She left the bathroom trying not to panic.

What she saw, who she saw, paused her.

The Lady from Detroit was there, legs crossed, Christian Louboutin pumps on her feet, now clothed in a colorful dress in blues, reds, and oranges, very chic and expensive, her exotic jewelry just as colorful, her expensive perfume, her presence, her posture, everything about her looking like springtime in Paris, everything about her dominating the sports bar, dominating the building, dominating the island. The dress wasn't tight, but the way it flowed made it appear more form-fitting than what she had worn before at Pigeon Point Beach, more casual, more sexy;

it was sleeveless, with a V that showed off her jewelry and cleavage, her breasts round and looking brand-new. She was sitting next to Matthew, chairs touching, sitting next to him like they were the team leaders.

The politician's colorful dress was pulled up to her thighs, as if she was trying to cool off, escape the heat.

Or pulled up as if she were showing flesh up to the middle of her thigh, trying to create some heat. Matthew and his ex-lover, the woman he had fucked, were side by side; he and the woman he had probably fucked in pussy, mouth, and ass were practically shoulder to shoulder, brainstorming.

She went to Matthew, her eyes locking with the Lady from Detroit's. There was no greeting between her and the politician. She reached beyond the politician and tapped on Matthew's shoulder, smiling a rugged, painful smile as she called her husband to the side, fought with the nausea inside her body as she took a few steps and waited for him to get up, now everyone turning to look at her as if she had a problem, as if she were a problem, as if it were her fault this wasn't taken care of across the pond, her eyes saying fuck all of you, the ills and the poison inside her as Matthew came her way, taking deep breaths as she led him away from the group, as she took another breath and paused between the sports bar and the hostess stand, stopped where she could see the Lady from Detroit and her imported thugs.

"I'm bowing out, Matthew."

"Bowing out?"

"You have a solid plan. You have guns. You have a crew."

"Those are *her* men. You are the other half of *my* team."

"Doesn't take that many people to get one man."

"Well, apparently Detroit thinks it will take that many people. Plus some. In her mind Gideon is some kind of a beast. She talks about him like he's a creature from Greek mythology."

"It's one fucking man, Matthew. He will be unarmed. You have a dozen people. That's overkill."

"How are you going to bow out of a commitment? Half the money has been given, and that half has been spent. We have bills to pay, your debt, mind you. You have to see this thing to the end."

"Don't feel like it."

"Don't feel like it."

"Might go to Touch Therapies, get a massage and a facial."

"You're joking, right?"

"Do I look like a stand-up comedian?"

"*Me me me me me.* That is what you always sound like. *Me me me me me.* This is about teamwork, not about what you feel like. Not *you*, not *me*, about the *team*. She hired us to do a job."

"Are you still sleeping with her?"

"Is that what this unnecessary and unprofessional attitude is about?"

"Are you?"

"If I didn't know any better I'd swear you were projecting your own guilt on me."

"Just answer the question and I'll turn my projector off."

He said, "You worry about where you were the night I got here; you worry about that."

"You pop up unexpectedly, God knows when you got here, she happens to pop up at the same time you get here, now you keep leaving the room, gone for hours, coming back, being an asshole, chastising everything I do. She shows up and sits all up under you like you're at a damn drive-in movie."

"Everybody is sitting close."

"Not with their breasts damn near in your mouth."

"Take it down, take it down."

"Are you fucking her?"

"Don't be so repetitious. Can you at least find a fresh accusation to amplify your insecurities?"

She smiled. "I'll leave a present between her eyes if you are."

He stared at her. "You're flushed and sweating."

"I'm hot. This heat is getting to me."

"The heat or the lies?"

"Don't be repetitious. Find a fresh accusation to amplify your insecurities."

He nodded at her. "It's cold in here."

"Your bitch's nipples told me that."

"No one in the room is hot."

"Well, she's hot for you. She looks at you like she's on the verge of spontaneous combustion."

Behind her, from the sports bar, as cricket matches played on at least a half dozen mounted televisions, the Lady from Detroit and the crew from Motown were watching; she felt the stares on her neck.

In front of her Matthew had drawn a line in the sand, was daring her to cross it in front of them.

In front of his former lover, in front of Detroit, in front of the woman he had her working for.

She felt it; this confrontation wasn't a husband facing his wife.

She was facing El Matador, a man who had forgotten what she did for a living.

He said, "Humor me."

"What?"

"I take it you're pissed about this *Sex and the City* thing."

"What difference does it make?"

"Which one do you think you're like? Humor me. Which one do you think you are?"

"Carrie."

"That's funny."

"What's so funny about that?"

"From what I've seen, I think you're more like that one called Charlotte."

"I'm nothing like Charlotte."

"She thinks she's sophisticated, intelligent, and classy, always dressed up . . ."

"What's wrong with that?"

"And she's nothing more than a naïve *idiot*."

"Charlotte was not an idiot."

"A five-star idiot in expensive clothing."

"She never thought of herself as an idiot."

"Idiots never think they are idiots. The Three Stooges didn't think they were idiots. At least three of them are anyway. I've seen a few episodes, forced to watch that idiotic bullshit night after night because you had the remote control in your goddamn hand, damn near every episode TiVo'd so you could watch it on demand. Charlotte is so damn annoying, naïve, and a prude. Carrie's slut-with-a-heart-of-gold act is nothing to look up to. And Samantha's just an old-ass worn-out slut without a heart at all. Miranda is as bland as tofu out of the bag. Why would any woman look up to those women? I watched the damn show and couldn't figure out for the life of me why those four women would be friends. They don't like each other and it shows. Then I understood why they were friends. Because they are all idiots. Those lost women on that pointless show make the old hags on *The Golden Girls* seem like Einstein, Ben Franklin, Madame Curie, and Oppenheimer. The men on the show are not men. Not *real* men. Those pitiful, pussy-whipped, low-self-esteem bastards have been injected with estrogen and castrated. Pussies. I have yet to see a real man on that show. Not one has any balls. Pussies and idiots."

He had become an angry atheist ridiculing what she believed, ridiculing the core of her being.

She was about to lose it, his every word making her want to snap.

But she gave him a hard stare and silence.

She pushed her lips up into an angry smile and asked, "You done playing Siskel and Ebert?"

He tightened his jaw.

The stare of El Matador. The man who took contracts on anything breathing.

She said, "Your bitch is waiting on you."

"I'm looking at my bitch."

"No, you're looking at your idiot. I'm not smart enough to be a *conniving bitch*."

"And I was a bigger idiot to marry somebody as self-centered and financially destructive as you."

He didn't take his eyes away from her, didn't move.

Sweat pouring down her face. Down her back. Her body a heat lamp.

He nodded. "Your lies are like a silent fart. Can't see 'em, but I can smell 'em."

"What lies, Matthew? Either show your hand or shut up with it."

"I can do that." He nodded. "That night you dumped your goods, where did you say you were?"

"Why?"

"You said you were riding that scooter from the northwest part of the island."

"What's your point?"

"They found a guy dead up that way. Was shot up close. Same caliber as your backup."

"Why are we having this chat about a dead gangbanger?"

"Guys at the table were talking about it just now. Last night when they were at Wendy's the working girls and the locals and tourists who came to see them dance were talking about it."

"They were having conversations with whores and taking advantage of their poverty; so what?"

"Word on the street is that the dead guy was a rent-a-dred."

"What's a rent-a-dred?"

"Make sure you don't find out."

"Fuck you."

"That's your last time."

"Or what?"

"Try me. Go ahead." He spoke in a deep, commanding voice. "Try me right here, right now."

Revenge. She thought about revenge. That overpowering sensation, a need that destroyed logic, made the wise foolish, the need for revenge being a demand that was satisfied only by action, an action that was greater than the offense itself. Revenge was more compelling than calculating, a passion that was not a thought, a desire that was not an idea but an ideal. She felt the need for revenge.

Revenge was not about punishment. It was about equity. The equity of suffering.

And she was suffering.

Suffering and angry, her mind on its own, in killer mode, focused on the type of vengeance that would generate equal and appropriate levels of suffering for the man in front of her. None would be good enough. Her hand was inside her purse, on her weapon, Matthew's gut in the line of fire, point-blank range. He could out-argue her, but one bullet would widen his eyes and change his disposition.

If she shot him she would have to kill him, give herself a nine-millimeter divorce.

He was trying to force her to be the woman he needed her to be while she was fighting to get him to be the type of husband she needed him to be. The epic battle between man and woman.

Her stomach; twinges of pain came and went, mild throbbing that she kept well-hidden.

Unyielding, Mathew said, "I expect you to see this job through until its completion."

She nodded, her agreement not hiding her reluctance, then she said, "One more thing."

"What?"

"Be glad that I love you. Right now you should be very fucking glad that I love you."

She turned around, fighting cramps, heels clicking across the tiled floor, queasiness rising.

Matthew rushed out behind her, followed by the rest of the team, men who had put their shades back on before they were greeted by the brightness of the sun; some had their hats on before they exited the restaurant, others had hats in hands. The Lady from Detroit came out in the middle of that pack. They all had tense expressions. They moved down the stairs at top speed.

The Lady from Detroit made eye contact with her, sneered as she passed, surrounded by bodyguards, secret service guarding the first female president. So much disdain was in her eyes.

Matthew came to her. "Gideon is on the way."

"When does he get here?"

"His plane is about to land."

"You're shitting me."

"Showtime. Get your shit together. Time to pay some bills."

Thirty-one

judgment in stone

Antigua was less than one hundred miles up ahead. From San Juan it was a short flight to V. C. Bird International, a little over an hour, the layover at gate seven longer than the flight itself.

Hawks had my binoculars in her hands, looking out the window as she said, "Skies are so blue."

"We're coming up on the island."

"I was in Puerto Rico and now I'm in the West Indies."

"Puerto Rico was a layover."

"I was in Puerto Rico. I don't care if it was just the airport, it was Puerto Rico."

"If you say so."

Hawks was excited, but my mind was somewhere else. My mind was on a woman who lived in Detroit. When I got my hands on her I was going to do more damage to her than heroin and crack cocaine had done to Motown, was going to do more damage to her than Butch Jones, Maserati Rick, and the Chambers Brothers had done to that shopworn city. I would be her Twelfth Street Riot, would leave the bodies of anyone who came between me and getting my hands around her neck slaughtered.

Hawks said, "Well, this spectacular moment will definitely make it in my diary."

I shifted, created a smile. "You have a diary?"

"I sure do. And you're in it. Some really nice things followed by a lot of not-so-nice things."

Jolly Harbour and its north and south fingers came into view first, mostly villas and timeshares. Hawks focused on that area as the plane passed over, saw the casino, Epicurean, other shops. She had the window seat, seeing the stunning island for the first time, smiling like a little girl.

"Good Lord, all those palm trees."

"The tall ones are coconut trees. The short ones are palm trees."

Hawks smiled. "I can't wait."

"To get this contract over with?"

"Not that. Not even thinking about that. Sounds like a five-minute job, if that."

"Then what?"

"Can't wait to put on a bikini and unload my wagon in another country."

I laughed.

She smiled. "Where did you say the snorkeling place was?"

"Snorkeling at Long Bay."

"Never seen a steel band before. I want to see that and listen to calypso and reggae music while I wriggle my toes in the sand of one of the beaches. I want to see that Sandals place. See billboards for that place all over America. And I want to see historic sites in English Harbour. And see Barbuda."

"You're excited."

"A little." She laughed. "On the way back we should stay in Puerto Rico a night."

"Your wagon must have a mighty heavy load."

"I want to do some of those things you were telling me about. Always wanted to see a rain forest. Hike to the La Mina waterfalls. Parasail and kayak. Sit on a beach and read until I get sunburned."

Other things came to my mind.

I said, "I can't do it after we leave here."

"Your little problem."

I nodded. "After that is done, when it's safe for me, we can come back to Puerto Rico."

"There you go promising stuff."

"I'm serious."

"From a man who can't remember to make a phone call."

"You're never going to let me live that down?"

"Not in my nature. Forgiving people, that's just not in my nature."

First the American Airlines flight passed over Jolly Harbour and the villas on its north and south fingers, then out in the distance was the snaking All Saints Road; seconds later we were over Factory Road, then passing an area where they were building a new soccer field. All of that passed by on the plane's rapid descent. As soon as the packed plane touched down everyone started turning their cellular phones back on.

Hawks said, "Small airport."

"This airport was an American military air base back in World War Two."

"Baggage claim at Miami International was bigger than that."

She handed me the binoculars, Bushnell Digital Stealth. I slipped them inside my backpack next to another pair of binoculars, that second pair capable of night vision as well.

Our flight landed and I took out my iPhone to check on Catherine and the kid, was about to look at the cameras in Powder Springs, stressed and worried, but I had problems getting online. I needed to call Alvin White and make sure he was watching over them, but I felt safe with him on the job. First thing I did was call my message center. I had an urgent message. I cursed. Had to be a delay on the Cessna or the other hardware I had ordered to take my anger to the Midwest. I was wrong. The message was from Konstantin, a message I wished I had gotten before I had boarded this flight in Puerto Rico.

"It's a setup, Gideon. It's a goddamn setup. Don't get on the plane to Antigua."

Everything stopped as I listened to the message from Konstantin.

"Son of a bitch used me to get to you. It's your Detroit problem setting you up. Handler I trusted, handler who called me for this contract and asked for

you specifically, rest assured, he'll be in the ground by the time you get this message. Whatever you do, do not get on that fucking plane to Antigua."

Hawks was trying to check her voice mail but couldn't. Verizon's signal didn't reach this far.

"It's a setup. It's a goddamn setup. Detroit is paying top dollar to have you come to your own funeral. She took a team down there. A fucking setup. I don't know what to say . . . do not go to Antigua."

This flight had already touched down. There was no going back, no going anywhere, not without getting off the plane, not without going through customs, not without leaving the airport to buy a ticket. The only way off the island was by plane or boat. I didn't have access to a boat. I'd have to go to the ticket counter to book another flight, would have to step into an open area, an area that would have security watching, making sure everyone went in the same direction, no chance of slipping in another direction and making my own exit. In the blink of an eye I went over my options. There were none.

I had to get off the plane.

I said, "I have a problem, Hawks."

She looked at me, wondering, her long ponytail hanging over her shoulder, that girlish smile slipping from her face. The face of a strong woman returned, one who did harsh things for a price.

My expression was dark, intense, a powder keg, and my thoughts gave off sparks.

I whispered, "There is no job."

She whispered in return, "It was canceled? The Stanford contract was recalled?"

My jaw was tight, anger suppressed. "Never was one."

I leaned over, got closer to Hawks's ear, told her as much as I could in a few seconds.

She said, "Detroit?"

I nodded.

"No way. You're telling me that woman paid that much to set you up?"

Again I nodded.

Hawks said, "Contract was offered at a half a million dollars Eastern Caribbean."

Again I nodded.

"And half was paid up front. They dug deep to get you to come down here."

"They dug deeper than a brand-new grave."

Hawks paused, moved braided hair to the back. "What do we do?"

"Separate."

"My cellular doesn't work here."

I nodded, knew what she meant. If her cellular worked we could have separated and remained on the phones, pretended we were chatting with other people while we communicated and planned our moves.

Hawks said, "Stay mixed in with the people. Get in the middle of a group."

I almost smiled. She told me what I already knew, just wasn't sure if that would matter.

Death was out there waiting for me and I thought about the kid. Thought about Catherine.

X. Y. Z.

It didn't look like I would live long enough to know.

I leaned and looked out the window. Looked like several flights had come in at the same time; the line going to customs was going to be long. Other flights were boarding. Pandemonium in a small space. The flight attendant announced they were deplaning from two doors, one at the rear of the plane and the other at row nine. Our seats were about halfway between both. I spied the aisle to see if anyone on this flight was on my tail, if anyone here had followed me from Atlanta to Puerto Rico to the place Detroit was about to make my final destination. Again I leaned and looked out at the blacktop.

Security. Customs. The police. Anyone who took dollars over a badge could be on her team.

I had gone through airport security in America so I had no real weapons. And neither did Hawks. I was naked. It was a perfect setup, money being the cheese in this trap.

Hawks asked, "Do they park the plane at a gate and we walk into a breezeway?"

I shook my head. "There are no gates here, not like in the States. No walking inside an airport directly from the plane. Everybody lands and walks across the tarmac until they get to the terminal."

"Wide open. James Earl Ray didn't have that much room to play with."

"Thanks for pointing that out."

Hawks opened her purse, took out two charge cards, handed me one. She gave me a Bic pen too. Blue ink. I opened my backpack, took out four pencils that had been sharpened, taped two together with masking tape that I had brought along, handed those to Hawks, then I taped two more pencils together, slipped those inside my back pocket.

Across the aisle one of the passengers was finishing a can of ginger ale.

Hawks leaned over, asked the woman if she could have the can, said she was a collector.

I put the can inside my backpack.

Hawks asked, "Anyplace to shop between here and customs?"

"Nothing you can get to. Outside, soon as you leave the building there is a little spot called Clarkie's Snacks and Liquors, right on the other side of the door; they sell liquor."

Hawks nodded, then unzipped her carry-on, pulled out a small, empty backpack.

I had Hawks mix with the crowd and move toward the rear exit, the section that would get off the plane and make it to the gate first. She did that while I moved to my right, blended with the rest of the travelers, and headed toward the exit near row nine. I pulled my belt out of my jeans. Grabbed a few airline magazines, rolled them up until they were tight, hard enough to strike with, and held them in my hand. Inside my backpack I had two ink pens. I took those out too.

The empty can I had confiscated, I worked it as I stood there, bent it until I could tear it in half, then dropped those halves inside my backpack, made sure those ragged pieces of aluminum stayed near the top. People saw me doing that, but no one questioned what I was doing in the name of recycling.

Everyone moved slowly, dragged overpacked luggage and back-packs, carried babies to the stairway so they could hike down that narrow roll-up to the heated blacktop, a steep walk that would leave everyone two or three steps apart for safety, the angle perfect for separating targets, that two or three steps between passengers enough room for a sniper to find his target. And if I made it to the bottom I had to move across the open lot to the terminal, again out in the open, easily seen and a closer, surer shot.

Man, woman, young, old—I had no idea who the trouble would be this time.

Hawks peeped back at me as she moved with the crowd, pulled her carry-on luggage, on her own as she headed in the opposite direction. She looked back as if it might be the last time she saw me alive.

In the blink of an eye the back door to heaven had become the front door to hell.

I moved with the crowd, headed down the roll-up stairs to the tarmac, on full alert as I moved through the heat and humidity. To my left was an area separated by two layers of barbed wire and fencing, a perfect place for a sniper to lie in wait. Or the bullet could come from above.

I looked up and there was a row of floor-to-ceiling windows, the departure lounge, and the area that had a masseuse on duty. That area was well-secured. She was there. Standing in one of the windows. Watching me walk the green mile she had created. Her brilliant colors caught my eye, her wardrobe that of an arrogant movie star, her stance like she was more important than any man's deity.

Detroit. The woman who wanted me dead, the ultimate return on her investment.

She had been watching me the whole time. I paused in the heat, sweat draining down my face and back, this moment prayed for and unreal, as if the heat had created some sort of mirage.

Detroit was here in Antigua.

I stopped walking.

She smiled. She smiled at her living nightmare. I frowned at mine.

She was on the second floor of the building, behind glass. No way to get to her.

We had created widows, orphans, grieving parents and family members, had created work for morticians and members of law enforcement who had been assigned to unsolvable cases.

Three men came up, stood at her side. Men in dark shades and hats. Her killers for hire.

My enemy took out her cellular, no doubt making a phone call to the harbinger of Death, sending out an alert, never taking her eyes off me, front row and center for whatever was about to happen.

Then my cellular rang. I answered. It was Konstantin.

He said, "Tell me you're not in Antigua."

"Just got off the plane."

"Well, I'm with the handler who helped set you up."

"How is he?"

"He's dead."

"Good."

"Where are you?"

"Walking the green mile."

I told him where I was, that Detroit was in the window watching, that I had nowhere to hide.

He said, "Let me get a flight down there."

"It will be too late. You know that."

"Fuck."

"I have to go."

"*Fuck fuck fuck fuck fuck.*" His curses were powerful, rapid as gunfire. "This is *fucked*-up."

"My feelings exactly."

"I'm coming down."

"No. You know the rules, Konstantin. You taught me the rules."

"Fuck."

"Stick to the rules."

"Hawks?"

"She knows the rules too."

I hung up the phone and got ready to face my malignancy from the Midwest.

Sweat crowded my brow as my heart throbbed inside my chest.

Detroit was still talking, her eyes on me, her frown stalking me.

My expression deepened. She saw my anger. Saw the man who should've killed her a year ago.

She had killed innocent people to get to me. I had put many in the ground because of her.

In a crowd of at least five hundred, a crowd that was growing because more flights had landed, hundreds of people behind me; Hawks was at least thirty people ahead of me, the way I wanted it.

If anything broke out, if anyone was here for me, Hawks was far enough away to be safe.

Again I looked around, searching for a way out. People hurried toward a multicolored Liat plane, rushed through humidity, rolling hills, lushness, and coconut trees, the background to our silent madness.

When I glanced up at the window again, Detroit was gone, same for her henchmen.

My enemy had run away to hide until this act of vengeance was done.

The line moved at a slow pace. Security watched everyone as if 9/11 had them just as paranoid as it had the U.S., as if they refused to have their own version of London's 7/7.

An airport employee came down the line, one of the crew members, moving slowly, staring at faces until she made it to me, my mind busy looking for a way to escape this prison, calculating how long it would take to jump the fence, how many innocent people I would have to hurt to get out of the airport.

The airport employee stopped in front of me, then she moved closer to me.

I watched her, her eyes on mine, her hand slipping inside her pocket.

It had started. I was about to explode, was about to put the pencils I had deep in her throat.

The girl handed me a slip of paper and paused in front of the adverts for Romantic Rhythms, yielding a brief smile at photos of Brian McKnight and Shaggy before she licked her lips and moved on.

She was no one. Just a messenger. A messenger who had no idea she'd almost lost her life.

On the folded slip of paper, seven words:

POWDER SPRINGS. Catherine. Steven. They will die.

Thirty-two

trapped

Stress sweating, trapped in a sluggish line snaking toward immigration, caged in by barbed-wire fences and too much security to count, I called Catherine and the kid. No damn answer.

Couldn't get online. No wireless signal out on the tarmac.

Images of them butchered, blood flowing like a great river, those images stuck in my mind.

I called Alvin White. His answering service kicked on, I was forced to leave a message.

Outside a sudden storm had come, as they did in the islands, rain coming down hard.

The line zigzagged, moved straight in from the outdoor upside-down-L-shaped pathway, connected to a pathway shaped like an L in reverse, its horizontal leg to the left of the letter, moved inside the building, and my travel changed to a series of right-left-right turns, all leading toward the inevitable.

My heartbeat was fast, breathing brusque, movements calm, thoughts many.

It had taken forever but I had made it inside the heart of the building, the air-conditioning having no effect on my warmth and perspiration. This was my purgatory, my waiting room in hell.

I looked around. A hit inside here would leave the assassin with no way out.

They wouldn't try it inside here, not unless they had government help, not without this being choreographed the same way the U.S. had choreographed Jack Ruby's killing Lee Harvey Oswald.

There were too many people. Anyone who tried it here would be a damned fool.

But vengeance owned no logic.

I looked around, memorized many faces, searched for anything that was a threat.

At least 25 percent of the people were heading toward stations one through six, Antiguans and CARI COM, the Caribbean Community; desks seven through fifteen had the longest lines, held the congestion marked for visitors to their paradise, people who had been lured there by the white sands and 365 beaches, and it also held at least two people who did wetwork and had been lured there under false pretenses. It felt like I was taking step after step toward a warm, welcoming light known as my own death.

Hawks made it to the front of the line, was sent to the customs officer at desk fifteen, the desk for the supervisor. Hawks never glanced back, gave no hint that we were together. Her long hair in a braid hanging down over her black tank top, that braid stopping at her belt buckle, a heart with a knife in its center. If nothing else, her boots announced that she was North American. Just another tourist in search of sunshine. Questions were asked, questions I had told her to anticipate, and answers were given, answers I'd told her to regurgitate in order to make it flow. She was on holiday. Staying in St. John's at the City View Hotel on Newgate. Would be there a week. Was flying out on American.

Her passport was inspected, the inspector looking at Hawks's photo, comparing it to her, turning pages. Satisfied, paperwork was stamped. The officer pointed to his right, her left. Hawks nodded. Grabbed her carry-on. Then she was gone, moving into the heat of the West Indies, making a right past baggage claim, concerned, no doubt heading toward the sign that said NOTHING TO DECLARE. Again answering questions, telling them she had brought no gifts, nothing for sale, feel free to search her bags.

I'd made it from the tarmac inside the building without sniper fire ending my controlled anxiety.

That thirty-minute walk seemed like it had taken thirty months.

The Lady from Detroit had outsmarted me, had pulled me into a dark situation.

She'd paid six figures to get me to step in this rattrap. That meant her team had to be well-paid. When you had enough money, when you were determined, you could find anything, anyone.

I smiled what could've been my last smile.

That meant whatever was planned, whatever was in motion, could start when they saw my fake passport, maybe with the police taking me away. But I didn't think my enemy was interested in my imprisonment, not when I held secrets that could ruin her and have her incarcerated for the rest of her life.

I was the villain in her story. The demon that had to be destroyed.

I made it to the front, was called over to desk eight, answered the few questions, same answers as Hawks, then moved into the baggage claim area, still looking around. No other exit available. Security posted all over. A few minutes later I was on the other side of NOTHING TO DECLARE.

The only thing between me and whatever was outside was a glass door, a door that opened automatically as others pushed tons of luggage and hurried to the outside of the international airport. The doors opened and I saw a man out there waiting. He was in the crowd, but his look called attention. Wide-legged pants, white tennis shoes, chewing gum fast and hard, things that told me he was American. And the hat. Only tourists wore wide-brimmed hats like that. He was just as anxious as I was, eyes on the door, watched everyone as they exited. He saw me and paused, lifted his dark shades, squinted his eyes, lips moved like he was talking into a jawbone earpiece, then he moved away fast, moved out of the line of sight into the multitude of people who waited on taxis, mixed into the rambunctious crowd.

But there was another soldier not too far behind him.

Baggy pants, dark shades, chewing gum like he was nervous. He held his hat at his side.

They were already in position. Ready for me no matter what direction I took.

When I made it to the door, I moved through the crowd, hurried toward the far end, took the problem away from the people, away from innocent children, took it out in the rain, to the parking lot.

They were on my heels, followed me, caught me there, ready to make that my grave.

I turned just in time to see the one closest to me pulling out his gun.

My heart raced and I ran.

Not away from Death.

Toward its messenger.

I ran.

Rain fell like a tropical orgasm, sunlight no more, clouds a blanket over the terminal.

Going at a man holding a gun, sprinting straight at the gunman, meant you were running right into the bullet because all he had to do was pull the trigger and get a center-mass hit. Life would abandon your body midstride and what was left would be as useful as a paperweight. I didn't rush at him in a suicide move, didn't do a zigzag and become a moving target, but I moved with a quickness and did a half-moon maneuver, a move Konstantin had taught me years ago, a move that was in the pattern of a crescent and made my attacker think I was running away, but in reality I was rushing toward him, had arced and closed the gap just as he realized what was going on, but not before he got a shot off, a shot that hit my shoulder as I pushed the muzzle away from my body, a shot that created instant agony, pain that I grimaced against and embraced and allowed to turn my whole body into a weapon. Pain became power, agility, and determination. Avoid the weapon, stay clear of the business end of the gun, and become a velociraptor, embrace the violence, attack to kill, or hesitate and be killed. I threw spearing elbows and knees at a relentless pace. I shut off his takedown attempt with a bone-jarring fist to the jaw, a blow that stunned him but didn't take him out, then pulled him down for a nose-shattering knee to the face.

Rain fell hard as I looked back, saw I wasn't alone, in pain and outnumbered.

Another was coming but was cut off. Hawks ran at him, a man who had no idea what was going on as Hawks swung her backpack, a backpack that was now full and heavy, a backpack that caught the man in his face, the sound of bottles shattering on impact, then Hawks losing her grip on the backpack, letting gravity and lack of friction steal it away. The second man staggered backward two steps, then in a blind rage went after Hawks. She didn't back down, moved toward the fight, not away from the man who was more than twice her size. She had her belt in her hand, its end wrapped around her right hand, snapped it out, the huge belt buckle that had the shape of a heart being stabbed with a knife striking the man in his eye, the bite of a cobra. He backed away from the pain. She beat him with that buckle over and over, battered his head, hands, and face, beat all she could until he managed to grab the buckle and stagger away. She let him have the belt, went after him, running through rain as she went airborne, moved with the quickness of Kyra Gracie, taking her knee straight to the man's wounded face. Hawks hit him hard, then went down hard too, size being on the man's side, but the force from her mass and acceleration being in her favor. She crashed hard, landed on unforgiving rocks and concrete.

But she made it to her feet before the man did, ran at him, attacked him with her charge card.

A charge card that had been sharpened on the edges, that plastic sharp enough to cut like a blade. A charge card that was inside her purse and always made it through security undetected. Like in prison, anything that could become an improvised weapon became a weapon, anything with an edge or a point turning from a harmless household item into a deadly shank.

Hawks. A creative and mean son of a bitch. A pit bull on gunpowder.

Trained by a Russian named Konstantin, the meanest of us all.

Another came up on the scene, moved between the parked cars in search of his friends, not knowing they were down, and I went to him, saw he didn't have a gun drawn as I reached inside my pocket, pulled out the taped pencils I had put there when I was leaving the plane, attacked him before he realized what was going on, becoming a velociraptor once again, sending the sharpened end of those pencils deep inside his sternum, sent both in at an abrupt and upward angle, an unforgiving angle that wouldn't allow him to pull them from his punctured lungs, a different kind of lead poisoning.

As he fought with the pencils, I pulled out the cans I had torn in half, cut the arteries in his neck.

Heard footsteps running toward me.

Then his friend was on me; first his gun pointed in my face and I raised my hands in surrender, rain falling, my left hand not going up because of the bullet wound to my shoulder, and he came closer, pointed the business end underneath my neck, stuck it against my skin as if his plan was to send a bullet from my chin up through the roof of my head. He looked into my eyes. The eyes of a killer. In that moment I saw his fear. Felt that fear making his finger tighten on the trigger. Knowing exactly where I was, a half second from an unrecoverable death. The hand I had up, my right hand, without hesitation I swept it across the gun, moving my head in the opposite direction at the same instant, the gun's muffled discharge going into the sky as I struggled to rip the gun out of the man's hand, the gun firing over and over as I threw blow after blow to his face, blows that slowed him down but didn't stop him, then I took the Bic ink pen from my pocket and tried to gouge his eyes; he turned his face after the first stab, but I kept on giving him the pen, tried to stab his eyes out of their motherfucking sockets, but settled for doing damage to his neck, face, and ear, tried to impale his head so hard he had ink in his brain. That rapid and rabid stabbing gave him severe pain, the kind that made him have to make the choice of flight or fight; his choice was to flee, and that retreat put some distance between us, made him stumble away in panic, the gun leaving his hand and not staying with mine. His blood was all over my hand, being washed away by the rain. He had been stabbed two dozen times and he was ready to come back at me. He was desperate. He was afraid. He was a wild animal that had been wounded and was returning to attack.

Before I could take my pain to the ground and retrieve the gun, there was the sound of muted gunfire. A hole had been put in his head. He crumpled to the ground, rain making his face look like he was crying water and blood. I looked up and saw Hawks in charge of the silenced gun. Behind her was the man she had tackled. He was facedown in the mud and gravel, the Caribbean storm soaking his battered body, still moving but injured, face broken by a backpack filled with bottles of E&J, J&B, and whatever Hawks had bought when she had stepped through customs and hurried to Clarkie's, the man's eyes cut and blooded by a modified MasterCard, his leg broken, the brick that had been used in Hawks's other hand. The wounded man reached out like he was trying to pull himself away from this battlefield, probably wishing he could redo the last twenty seconds of his life. The man whose nose I had broken, he was on the ground, two feet away from his slashed and crippled friend, still disoriented, trying to get to his feet, slipping in mud, making it up on one knee, unsure of which way to go for help.

Hawks limped toward the one crawling on the ground, her cowboy boots kicking grit and gravel. He tried to move away from us, mud taking to his battered body. The man moved like he was a horse with a broken leg, looked up in surrender, unable to see because the rain was blinding him, his expression begging for mercy, saying he quit, that he gave up.

This wasn't a game. There was no surrender.

Without blinking, Hawks eased his pain and suffering, left a bullet in the back of his head. She did the same to the man who had made it up to one knee, a man who saw what had happened to his coworker and did his best to get to his feet, that *pop* erasing life and sending him down on his broken nose. Another man with a broken nose. Hawks's carry-on was on the other side of the men. She stepped over both men like they were the roadkill of the day, the anger in her wet face telling me she was tempted to spit on them. She picked up her backpack, the sound of broken glass singing, and alcohol leaked to the ground, then she struggled to bend over and grab the handle on her luggage. The way her face contorted told me she was injured, but she tightened her lips, pulled her ponytail away from her face, threw it over her shoulder, and took a few breaths like she was shaking off the pain.

The storm was strong; rain fell hard enough to keep people from coming this way.

We went deeper inside the parking lot, anticipating more men from Detroit out there, now knowing they had silenced weapons, on full alert and at the same time searching for a car or truck to steal, that being Hawks's area of expertise, knowing we had to leave this mess as it was. Hawks limped, her leg hurt real bad. My walk was motivated by pain; blood trickled down my shoulder to my hand.

The cars in the lot were modest; most didn't have car alarms. Two rows back was where taxis congregated in the far reaches of the rugged lot, taxi drivers inside their vans, radios on and unaware of what was going on thirty yards away. Next door was the *Antigua Sun*. No one was in that lot.

A minute later we were inside a soft-top, two-door Jeep Wrangler, Hawks in the passenger seat. Not the type of vehicle I wanted to find, but I doubted there were any with bulletproof glass and a machine gun that popped out of the roof. I had helped Hawks get inside, us doing that as fast as we could, her leg hurting her pretty bad, her breathing and grimacing revealing the depths of her pain.

My gunshot wound had me doing the same, grimacing and breathing, my hurting intense.

We sat there a moment, adjusting to our pains, the storm easing up, now a drizzle.

A few seconds later I wished I had left Hawks behind.

The pathway leading from Airport Road to the terminal was teardrop-shaped, with the terminal at the bottom of that teardrop. We were in the lot right before the terminal, meaning we had to pass British Airways, ASA, American, Air Canada, Carib Aviation, and another half dozen carriers, each providing a spot for the enemy to hide and send a shot from a silenced weapon. I pulled out into the pandemonium. Going with the flow of traffic, I passed the front of the terminal, moved at the pace of traffic, and circled to my right, passed people being loaded into cars and vans, headed toward Pavilion Drive, the route that led to the top of the teardrop, then headed toward a roundabout and came up on Stanford International Bank, mind racing as blood ran down my arm, searching but unable to see the gigantic fountains, incredible plants, and flowers that surrounded me. I doubted if Hawks saw them either.

Detroit had left the departure lounge at the main terminal, was waiting, bodyguards surrounding her, one holding an umbrella high over her head, deep anger etched in her face.

A familiar face stood next to her too. Her lieutenant. The man with the red hair.

The man who had brandished his gun on Shaftesbury Avenue in London.

He had been waiting for me to exit customs and go in the other direction, toward where the contract had said a car would be waiting. He wasn't alone. His strawberry blonde partner wasn't at his side, not this time. All men. At least half a dozen hurried toward cars. Before I made it to the end of Pavilion Drive, they were zooming toward Airport Road, growing larger in my rearview mirror.

They were behind me, but where Pavilion Drive met Airport Road, someone was there too.

A left turn would have taken me toward Old Parham Road and the dense population of the island, but the pain in my left shoulder made it easier for me to mash the gas pedal and make a screeching right turn, shooting out in traffic and almost speeding off the road until Hawks reached over and yanked the steering wheel and got me back on track. I accelerated and zoomed by a few cars coming in my direction; seemed like I was about to sideswipe them all. Half a dozen houses went by in a blur. Hawks kept her hand on the steering wheel as I sped up over a small incline and did my best to make the Jeep accelerate like it was a race car, the vehicles following us having a hard time adjusting to the narrow roads, and I gained some ground and moved through an area I thought was called Coolidge, trying to remember the lay of the land. Hawks let the steering wheel go, her pain pulling her back to her side of the car.

Gun in her right hand, Hawks was grimacing, down low in her seat, using the side-view mirror on the left side of the Jeep to look back when she could. I drove fast across the narrow roads, not concerned with being on the right side of the road unless I saw a car coming at me, then hoping that vehicle wasn't part of their team. The island went by in a blur, the sea to the right, homes displaying Antiguan flags on the left, and bullets flying from behind as the smell of liquor filled the cab, the scent from Hawks's backpack; the liquid leaked and moved across the floor, that broken glass crunching and clicking as the Jeep rumbled like a terrified tiger. I knew this land, had driven roads all over the world. The narrowness of the single-lane road was in my favor, making it impossible for them to pull up next to me without risking going head-on into oncoming traffic, impossible for them to zoom past me and cut me off for the same reason. This would have to work for me, for us, the road's ups and downs; the road became wider, smoother, not working in my favor, needed to get to the part with curves and unevenness that would make it impossible for whoever was shooting at us to get a clear shot, because once I made it to that section, the road would be on my side, would be the weapon I would use, because there was no way for a car with even the best suspension and shocks to have a ride smooth enough to allow the best shooter to get a straight shot. But even the worst shooter could have a little luck.

If I lived to see that section of the island.

My death meant Hawks's death. It meant the kid and Catherine would die, if that bitch from Detroit hadn't already gotten to them. My dying would kill too many others.

Death wasn't an option.

I sped toward the end of the road, had to brake and decide if I was going to take this to the left or right. Straight ahead across the intersection was Camp Blizzard, and that was not an option.

Turning left led toward Hodges Bay, Cedar Grove, Mount Pleasant, Blue Waters, and Crosbies. To the right was Shell Beach and Dutchman's Bay. A United States Air Force station was there too. Somewhere after that was a landing strip that was still part of the airport, where the celebrities and rich came in on private jets, an area away from the rest of the common people.

All of that was to the right.

It was easier for me to turn to the right, so pain and lack of time made that decision for me. I turned hard, sent Hawks into her door, almost lost control, then was back on track, speeding toward the U.S. Air Force installation. Those grounds were fenced in, probably unmanned; stopping there was not an option. Stopping now would give them a chance to make my heart stop.

To the left was the Hospitality Training Institute and Lord Nelson Beach Hotel; that left would lead to another dead end, would box me in, so I had to make another hard right, and the gravel made the Jeep slide toward an old Texaco gas storage station that looked abandoned, then I passed the Beachcomber Hotel, fishtailing and seeing they were behind me, not giving up, taking wild shots at us, shots that hit livestock up ahead, a cow falling as we passed.

They were close enough to start shooting and make those shots count. Close enough to tap the rear end, do a police maneuver, and force us to spin, a spin that, at this speed, would be devastating and force me to lose control, a bumper tap that could make us take to the air and flip a dozen times.

Hawks held on, her knuckles the whitest of whites.

Up ahead the road gave me two choices: to go straight or cut and go right toward Liat's cargo hangar, a rugged field in between that straightaway and right turn, livestock in that area, grazing in the grass. I cut to the right, Hawks's body coming toward mine. I turned at the last second and they followed, then about thirty yards later I cut to the left, cut hard without warning, a move that sent Hawks flying in the opposite direction, slamming against her door again, this time the impact causing her to drop her gun, a move that threw my pursuers off, forced them to screech to a halt as I rode over bumpy terrain, the type of terrain a Jeep was made to handle at a much slower pace, my body bouncing up and down and Hawks's body doing the same, like we were on a flight that had severe turbulence, never slowing down, speeding by unimpressed livestock until I made it to the left section of the other road, again speeding and swerving and fighting for control, kicking gravel and dirt, the beauty of the Caribbean Sea at my side.

They were coming. They were a good distance back, but they were coming.

I sped into an area that had no streetlights, a seaside area with plenty of bushes that were indented and had vehicle-sized cubbyholes, spaces that would be occupied by late-night lovers. Winding, snaking, narrow, curving road leading to a shipyard. Patched asphalt. Caribbean Star Airlines hangar; it looked abandoned, its fence locked and covered with barbed wire; was forced to keep going, nowhere to stop and hide, no shelter, then came up on an area that had damaged, maybe abandoned boats, like a boating repair shop junkyard. A strip of ship-repairing businesses and seaside buildings. Not a person in sight. A ship was in my path, *Lola Antigua West Indies*, hitched to a trailer at the side of the road.

The road smoothed out and a lush area appeared, an oasis that was a private landing strip owned by a billionaire. A hangar for his private jet. But that smoothness didn't last for long; as soon as that property whisked by, the new road vanished and eroded terrain reappeared, as if the billionaire never went in that direction so the condition of the road was inconsequential.

The eroded terrain went to the right, back inland, the beauty of the sea becoming a shadow in the dust and debris I left behind, dust that was enough to show my enemies my trail, but not enough to create a usable smoke screen. There were no edges to the road. Then more than 50 percent of the paved section of the road vanished and what was left was more pothole than asphalt, the ride rougher and faster.

Hawks held on, bounced, a helpless passenger as we passed another section of the USAF property, then the amount of road down to 25 percent, maybe less in some spots, signs declaring that to the left side was the U.S. Air Force's property, acres of acacia trees, junkyards, trucks, boats, buses, bushes, goats, a rock quarry, acres of construction equipment, places to execute the living and hide dead bodies, an area that, if it was nighttime, would look like a pool of endless darkness.

I maintained my speed, the Jeep bumping and speeding across dirt, sand, rocks, and tar, the airport now on my right, this route having left V. C. Bird International and backtracking up a different road, taking the shape of the letter U; I struggled to stay on the road as I first saw Liat's hangar, then Geotech's, no place to run and hide without this ground turning into my own burial spot, excavators and backhoes on the sides of the road, side roads no good to take because they were blocked with mountains of debris. Another sugar mill appeared on the left, the road littered with school desks, car seats, a dead dog, bottles, plastic bags, tires, anything people could leave behind.

A construction pit, rocks, boulders, and sand off to the left, nothing but trees and other bushes to the right, nowhere to escape to, forced to keep going, my fight with potholes a never-ending battle, knowing they were still back there. I took us down an incline, past the remnants of a sugar mill and beautiful areas that had been turned into dumping grounds, and came to another intersection, hit the brakes, and skidded to a bumpy stop, a stop that made the Jeep stall out.

They were coming.

I had to shift the Jeep back to Park to get the damn thing to start. To the right was more dirt and gravel, a road that led back to Old Parham Road and Airport Road. I didn't go that way.

They were rampaging down the bumpy hill, maybe thirty yards behind me, behind us.

I took off to the left, sped over unforgiving road, fishtailed in the direction of St. George's Anglican Church. Gunshots came at us, tore through the plastic soft top, hit the windshield. My foot stomped down on the accelerator. Another shot hit the side-view mirror. My foot pressed the accelerator through the floor. Another shot hit the backseats. I sped in desperation toward Fitches Creek.

They were on me, breathing fire down my neck.

At the church, another V-shaped intersection; I faked a left, then made a hard turn in the opposite direction, a hard right that threw the determined driver off. The Jeep turned, skidded, and dropped into one of the deepest potholes I'd ever seen, bounced like it wanted to turn on its side. My injury screamed as I struggled to recover, lost control of the wheel. The back end of the Jeep hit part of the two-foot wall that circled the church, the impact knocking us back upright, jarring me against the door, that jarring like a mean blow, bringing new pain to my gunshot wound. I gritted my teeth, hit the accelerator again, kicked up grass and dirt, stomped down on the accelerator, and bumped up a narrow road that was covered by trees, again making another hard left, a left turn around a dense forest hanging over a blind curve.

As soon as I made it inside the curve, I hit the brakes, skidded to a stop that threw me and Hawks forward, and turned off the Jeep. I had stopped in the most unseen part of a blind curve, an area covered by dense foliage that reached high and hung over the edges of the road. This Jeep was no longer my ride. It was now my two-ton weapon. Hawks reached for her door, pushed it open.

I grimaced. My pain begged for a case of B.C. Powder. I hurried around to Hawks's side.

She had the gun in hand, limped toward me before I made it to her.

I was panting, exhausted, and beaten, throbbing like I had run the entire route.

Hawks's grimace told me she was frustrated, mean as hell, and battle-worn all at once.

She had been in Antigua less than thirty minutes, and this was not what she'd had in mind.

Heartbeats strong, breathing rugged and out of sync, sweat pouring like a river, we waited.

My heart raced, not knowing if they were following or if they had taken that road to the left, had gone around the church; that circular route would bring them up behind us instead, meant we wouldn't have time to get back inside the Jeep and turn it around, meant I'd trapped us.

Just like Bonnie and Clyde had been trapped.

Then I heard gears shifting. From in front of us, the direction we had come.

Heard them in the distance. Gunning their ride. Coming for me. Coming for us.

My guess was they had turned too hard, had run off the road, had to get back on the road; the same route that had tossed and thrown me and Hawks had tossed and thrown them as well.

The roar of an engine was growing louder, like an animal in the wild, an animal that was determined to get its prey. Blood. I smelled my own blood. Felt it mixing with my sweat.

I reached for the gun. Hawks didn't want to give it to me. All communication was with our eyes and anger. Her arm wasn't injured, but I could move better than she could. She wasn't agile, not now.

Two assassins sharing one gun.

A hard call on who got to be quarterback, both of us on the injured list.

Hawks gave me the gun, handed me more than her trust; she handed me her life.

I checked the gun, made sure it was loaded, made sure it was ready.

While I did that Hawks was back at the Jeep, pulling out her backpack, then dumping the broken glass that was the remainder of two of the three fifths of whiskey she had rushed to purchase.

Hawks pulled her tank top off, did that as fast as she could, used her clothing to pick up the neck of one of the broken whiskey bottles, its end long and ready to perform surgery.

The skies opened up again; rain fell and muted the world.

They were relentless, motivated by good money.

With a deep frown Hawks limped to the right side of the road, moved as fast as she could.

The roar grew louder, urgent, the engine screaming as it charged uphill over rugged terrain.

Death's diplomats roared around the blind corner with ambitious speed, chasing what was no longer on the run. The front end of their vehicle crashed into the Jeep so hard the back end of the Wrangler lifted off the ground, rose up like a mule kicking, and the Jeep was knocked sideways. That high-speed collision activated air bags, those air bags working in my favor, exploding and smacking faces, blocking their vision, pinning the occupants where they were, became my improvised weapons, knocked guns away, did to them what had been done to me on a rainy day in Huntsville, Alabama.

The moment their vehicle crashed and the air bags popped, before the noise from that collision faded, gun in hand, I was moving in an arc, shooting, windows cracking and air bags exploding.

The rain came down hard enough to steal the noise from their yells and screams.

I sent them the bullets from the gun that had been shoved underneath my chin, the same gun that was going to be used to end my days, the gun that had caused suffering in my left arm. Unable to use my injured left hand to keep the gun steady, I still managed smooth pulls, didn't jerk. Rapid shots without a pause in between. My jaw tight, breathing smooth, focused. I fired on them, this my only weapon, fired on a vehicle filled with men who no doubt had an arsenal of weapons, because only a fool would come to this party unprepared.

Their vehicle had them trapped, boxed in, had become a coffin on four wheels.

The right-side back door opened fast and hard and one of the passengers ran from his end.

That man pulled the trigger on his gun, his gun clicked, its load shot during the chase.

He wasn't in my line of fire. I didn't shoot at him. Didn't waste my energy, didn't waste a bullet.

Hawks, like the bird that shared her name, had keen sight. Her haunting eyes were capable of making her prey stop in its tracks. In her hand, that broken bottle was more deadly than a true hawk's sharply hooked bill, more powerful and destructive than feet with curved talons. The bird was strong and graceful in flight. On the ground, even when she was wounded, Hawks possessed the same quality.

The would-be assassin raced out of the rear; the dense and impenetrable acacia bushes trapped him, gripped him, ripped at his flesh and clothing as he stumbled and fell into the foliage. Maybe he thought he could run through the bushes to escape; those bushes tore away skin as he tried to pull himself free, clung to him and cut him like he was dancing with barbed wire. He changed directions, only to run into another family of acacia bushes. The thick bushes were in every direction he turned. Those bushes covered the island the way kudzu covered Atlanta. A strong rain came down on his bloodied hands and face while he discovered the power of a prickly bush made of sharp thorns, each prick deep and as painful as shaking hands with a cactus.

Face, legs, and arms punctured and scratched like he had been in a fight with a hundred wolverines, he struggled to get free from the hostile bushes, fled from me.

That was when he stumbled into the rain and met Hawks.

Hawks was waiting, a broken bottle in her hand, the business end sharper than a knife.

Her haunting green eyes, her aggravation, and her fury were the last things he saw in this world.

Up ahead, in front of a single-level home, was a silver Hyundai Santa Fe, a crossover SUV that had the steering wheel on the left, a ride with American-side drive. Two minutes later Hawks was sweating and hot-wiring the car as I stood guard, my arm in too much pain for me to hot-wire the car myself.

In the distance I heard cars speeding toward us.

Hawks was rushing. I looked in on her, looked to see what the problem was.

Besides the one on the ground, there were four cooling bodies inside the vehicle that had trailed us. The man with the red hair wasn't one of them. Then the rear window of the Hyundai Santa Fe shattered. The sounds of zips, more silenced gunshots. The second chase car had caught up with the first. The curved road was only as wide as a man's arm span, blocked by two wrecked vehicles and one dead body, the thick and tall bushes on both sides of the road impossible to drive through.

Hawks kept hot-wiring the car, her effort peppered with hot lead in search of moving targets.

I returned fire, hit their windshield, enough to make them take cover.

Another car pulled in behind them, and just like the one that had arrived a second before, it became trapped by the wrecked vehicles and the stopped one. It was a smaller car, one that would have had a hard time flying over the rough and rugged terrain at the speed needed to keep up with a Jeep.

The man with the red hair had caught up with the chase; the leader had arrived.

Detroit was there, in that car, impatient, wanting to see my lifeless body.

Hawks got the car started. I shoved her inside, pushed her over to the passenger side.

The red-haired man left the car with quickness, ran up the road, shooting as he ran, missing, his coworkers doing the same. I caught only a glimpse of the third car's driver before my adrenaline gave me a new high. It was the strawberry blonde. The woman who had followed me in London.

She wore the clothes of a runway model, had a gun drawn, her stance that of a professional policewoman as she aimed my way, too many of her frantic people in front of her to get a clear shot.

It was only a glimpse, less than a half second, but my mind recorded what it had seen.

Something about the strawberry blonde seemed wrong, unsure, and unsteady.

Something about her had seemed sluggish.

In all the pandemonium, during that brief portion of a second when our eyes met, an abrupt chill had come toward me, hugged and cooled my heated body. She had a severe coldness, one I had never witnessed before, one I had never seen, not without looking in the mirror.

They were blocked in by the crashed vehicles, no way they could chase us in their rides.

I screeched away, expecting another chase vehicle to appear in front of us and box us in, but I made it out of the area, made a hard right, expecting them to pop up in my rearview at any moment, but nothing appeared. I kept my speed as I went through the villages, passed stray dogs and playing children, knowing this was a pause, not a conclusion, a pause liable to end at any moment.

A safe house was supposed to be off Old Parham Road, across from KFC, an empty two-story Caribbean home behind an eatery called Vigi's. An Antiguan who ran a *tyre* shop right across from Vigi's was the contact; he lived somewhere over in Upper Gambles. Knowing at least one more vehicle was out there searching for me, I'd taken the back way out of Fitches Creek, a hilly and rugged drive, the houses beautiful but the eroded and uneven roads not meant for rushed travel, had come out by Antigua Sugar Factory, driving and thinking, taking Sir Sydney Walling Highway, the ride a lot smoother, like being on a one-lane interstate, hit the roundabout near Sir Vivian Richards Stadium, making sure no one was following us, then doubled back toward Old Parham Road, passing by Vigi's, looking, not trusting, pausing at the Tunnel Bar before turning around in the parking lot at Christ the King High School, passing Vigi's again, the traffic congested, moving slow enough for me to peep toward the safe house, that spot looking too dark, not a light on, the perfect setup, that safe house not appearing too safe. I parked in a lot at Lighting Expo, sat there in silence, Hawks doing the same.

The kid and Catherine were on my mind.

I was trapped on an island.

Had to keep moving. I drove on and rode around, took Factory Road, took American Road, drove All Saints Road back to Independence Avenue, then I turned around, drove until I found my way to Valley Road and the southwest side of the island, passing by Jennings and Jolly Harbour, the sea on my right side as I negotiated narrow roads and kept my eyes on the rearview mirror the entire way.

When I made it to Fig Tree Drive I took a chance and parked. Hawks held the gun, didn't ask any questions. This area was lush, a rain forest bordered by the Sherkerley Mountains, some livestock grazing in the distance, an area that had the smoothest roads on the island and very little traffic.

I went to a manchineel tree, the vegetation still dry, the abrupt rains not having showered this strip of the island. The trees were dry. No sap dripping. That was good. I found an empty plastic bag and another strip of plastic on the side of the road, used that plastic to handle and pick as many berries from the manchineel tree as my plastic bag could hold. *Hippomane mancinella*, its fruit extremely poisonous, the plant irritating to the skin, causing blisters and severe itching, like a thousand mosquito bites, and an ache like a deep sunburn. Outside of that it was deadly when ingested. I wouldn't have touched this venomous tree if the rain had come this way; the venom would be dripping to the ground. Either way I made sure I didn't come in contact with any of the milky sap. I rushed, looking back when I heard a car approaching, clothes dank with sweat and rain, left arm aching, an entry and exit mark where the bullet had hit.

I downed a B.C. Powder. Did that more for the caffeine than the analgesic properties.

Hawks looked dehydrated. But she didn't complain.

I handed her the last B.C. Powder. She took it, downed it dry, made a nasty face.

Then we were on the move again, passing by colorful snackettes and vendors set up on the side of the road selling fruit, grilled corn on the cob, some cooking fish and chicken; our stomachs growled as if they were in a battle with hunger. Darkness began covering the island at a rapid pace. I headed northeast, was going back inland. Needed to let some time go by, enough for the rest of that team to have vacated the area by the airport, but knowing they wouldn't leave V. C. Bird International unattended because there was only one airport on the island. The only other way to leave was by boat, either catching a water taxi down in English Harbour or risking catching the Barbuda Express when it left at six in the morning and going to the sister island, an island that was smaller, a place where I'd be easier to spot. None of those options worked, not when I had no idea how many were in that hunting party.

Going to the airport or the dockyards wouldn't work.

Driving around in a car someone might recognize wouldn't work either.

I took Jonas Road, considered my options as I made my way north, blended with traffic heading toward Airport Road. Hawks was on alert as I drove us through the same area we had been chased through a handful of hours before. I headed to where the ferry docked to go to Long Island.

Ten thousand dollars a night. That was how much it cost to lease a villa over in the Jumby Bay section of Long Island. Clients had congregated in the parking lot behind the Beachcomber Hotel. That was where they waited for their ferry. The ferry was prompt, ran every hour, on the hour, during the day. Probably was available all night long. For ten thousand a night, I wouldn't expect anything less.

It was a twin-hull, high-speed ferry, big enough for maybe thirty. We stayed parked until it took off for Long Island, only three passengers taken on this hourly trip. Boat crews wore all white, so they were easy to distinguish. As soon as the ferry was on its way, Hawks and I left the Hyundai Santa Fe. She had taken an Elvis T-shirt from her bag and pulled it on. We headed toward the jetty that was behind the Beachcomber Hotel, a small hotel with darkened lights, one that looked like it had little to no occupancy.

There were rubber dinghies docked behind Beachcomber.

Two were thirteen-foot Saturn dinghies, inflatable boats big enough for four or five people. The closest one was black, and it had an engine, its engine starting like a lawn mower, running loud, like it was its own burglar alarm. A rough-sounding motor. Too late to change dinghies. No lights came on. But that didn't mean nobody had been alerted by the piercing sound.

We were looking back toward the lot, anticipating, focused. Then we were gone, taking to the Caribbean Sea, moving away from the main island, riding the mild waves into the darkness.

The dinghy had a fifteen-horsepower outboard motor, made us move like we were on a jet, our speed around twenty miles per hour. The wind picked up, felt like it was blowing in my face at about twenty-five knots, close to thirty miles per hour. The dinghy wasn't going fast enough for me, but right then the space shuttle would have seemed to move too slow.

I navigated us to the right, didn't follow the route the ferry took to dump people at the jetty at the mouth of Jumby Bay Resort, that area monitored by a Scotland Yard–trained security team. The stolen dinghy hummed, rocked, the waters not too rough but the ride not smooth, still not as devastating as it would have been if we were trying to take this inflatable ride to Barbuda, that current mean and strong.

I was trying to get us to the safest place I could think of.

Long Island was where Jumby Bay Resort and almost three dozen homes were located. There wasn't a hospital over there, but there had to be water and a few medical supplies. Had to be.

I looked back, shoulder throbbing, thought I saw two sets of vehicle lights back at the dock.

Those lights went dark.

My heartbeat accelerated some, not much, had to remain calm.

I went toward the right, along the shore, until we were almost out of sight of the mainland.

Water spraying, riding turbulence, I looked back, saw no one in pursuit.

But they were there.

Detroit was not done.

The security post was at the base of the resort, the majority of the sprawling compounds to the right; the properties circled the island, each with its own pool and private beach. That meant the owners could dock their boats and dinghies and walk across thirty yards of white sand to their own slice of heaven. Victoria's Secret had a property on the island, a corporate-owned property that was more than likely empty, but I didn't try to find that one. I had to go for the first available, and most of them were.

I pulled up on the private beach behind one of the compounds, killing the motor, the sounds of the sea and its rhythm now loud and apparent. Hawks stayed in the dinghy while I took to the sand. I handed her the gun. Hawks extended her belt to me. I shook my head, didn't want to take her weapon. I left her, trekked across the white sands, crept beyond an infinity pool resting at the edge of the sea. I moved through darkness, moved through and over the better part of a half-million dollars spent on landscaping. Bougainvillea. Alamanda. Date palms. Foxtail palms. Bromeliads that grew like parasites on the trunks of the palm trees. Red and white fountain grass. Coconut palms on the beachfront. Crotons. Warm air scented with the aromatherapeutic scent of lippia.

There were no cars on the island, just golf carts. No litter. No homeless. No crime.

This was where a home cost two million dollars U.S. and the cost spent on landscaping was more than the price of a three-level home in the suburbs of Atlanta, Georgia. These vacation compounds were all cash deals. Either you could afford it or you couldn't, because there was no thirty-year layaway plan.

I tiptoed by all the villas. All were empty, sheets pulled over furniture. That was what I had expected. This island had one resort and thirty-three vacation homes, each resting on a two-acre lot.

The houses were so far apart it was like neighbors were in different cities.

So far no one could have heard a gunshot. No one would hear you scream.

I stepped over a walkway, a bridge; below that bridge was a backyard pond populated with at least forty Japanese koi, golden and exotic fish that could cost as much as ten thousand each.

Somebody had to feed them. More than likely someone would come in the morning.

Dehydration tried to slow me down. So did hunger. Both failed.

A minute later I was satisfied the ten-thousand-square-foot property was vacant.

There was no pit bull, no Rottweiler, no Doberman, no German shepherd.

I doubted there was a dog on the entire island.

Off in the distance I saw lights, another ferry heading our way. I tensed, thinking they had found us. It wasn't them. The ferry was *leav-*

ing the island, not *coming toward* the island. Its angle of departure was what threw me. It had to be the employee ferry that went back and forth from Jumby Bay to Parham.

At night the staff went home, left empty homes, hotel guests, and a handful of people, an emergency crew on an ancillary island that probably never had an emergency, not like the ones we had created within the last hour. Not like the one the man with the red hair and his friends wanted to cause.

I took my binoculars out of my backpack, stood waiting, watching the waters, searching the seas.

Unless they were underwater in a yellow submarine, nothing was out there. Not yet.

I helped Hawks out of the dinghy and I got her inside the main house. Vaulted ceilings made from andiroba wood from South America, polished with andiroba oil. Shellstone tile. Travertine. Marble. She hobbled to the bathroom while I held the gun, limped back with a first aid kit she had found, that and a needle and thread. We moved into the kitchen, a large space that faced an outside dining area that looked out over the infinity pool, facing the sea, a good place to stand and be on lookout. Hawks dropped her goods on the marble island. Hydrogen peroxide, iodine, rubbing alcohol, Mercurochrome. She pulled my shirt back, looked at my open wound, saw it had an entry and exit, no surgery required, then she poured hydrogen peroxide on it. Pain came in an exponential way, but I didn't let it show. Then she did the same with alcohol. More pain. She looked me in my eyes. I nodded. Hawks wrapped gauze around my wound, taped it down.

Hawks sat on a bar stool and I pulled her right boot off. She clenched her teeth and swallowed the sounds of pain. Her ankle was swollen, twisted in the parking lot fight. Her left knee was tender too. I went to the Sub-Zero and took out ice, put it in a bowl, but she wasn't ready to ice her wounds. Hawks had moved on, limped around the kitchen with one boot on, opened drawers, pulled out steak knives, butcher knives, forks, anything with sharp edges. I went inside the pantry, found very little canned food and bottled water, but enough Hennessy, Baileys, Midori, Bacardi, Jose Cuervo, J&B, Mount Gay rum, and Russian vodka to fill up their twelve-foot-deep pool. More bottled water was inside the Sub-Zero refrigerator, cold water that was hiding behind bottles of Wadadli, Red Stripe, Heineken, and Carib lagers. Those lagers barely outnumbered the cans of Red Bull they had stocked in this holiday retreat. My throbbing wasn't subsiding, the best of it masked by adrenaline. I sipped a Red Bull as I rolled a cold bottle of water against my skin, then when I finished the energy drink, I opened the bottled water and sipped. Hawks did the same, downed about half a can of Red Bull before sipping water, drinking only a little, not enough to have her slow and waterlogged.

I put four pots of tap water on the stove, set the fire underneath them to high. At least a dozen bottles of Susie's Hot Sauce were on the counter. That red liquid was poured into the boiling water, the clear water turning a deep pink. Hawks found jars of honey, spooned it all into the water. She opened her backpack, dumped shards of broken glass into the pots, added that to the thick, bubbling soup.

Hawks found two towels, cut them into long strips, tied them together, made me a makeshift sling, tied it around my neck, pain rising as she slid my arm through. I took a few deep breaths, kept moving.

Then I searched the cabinets, found a blender, plugged it into an outlet.

I opened my backpack, dumped the fruit from the manchineel tree inside the blender, set it on puree, made the poison start to liquefy. We did all of that with the lights off, moving around each other, trying not to make too much noise, bumping into each other in whatever light came in from the stars above, most of the brilliance reflecting off of the sea itself.

I spied outside. The stolen dinghy was highlighted by stars. I gritted my teeth. Pissed off. If I saw it, everyone else could too. I hurried back to the dinghy, moved it two properties over, anchored it to a jetty, wiped sweat from my eyes, and headed back to our hideaway. Pain stayed on me as I hiked over sand and rock, my night-vision binoculars up to my eyes, searching the seas for trouble. I walked as close to the waters as I could, counted on the waves to erase most of my trail.

I waited.

Trade winds blew like a storm was coming; waves crashed to the shore the same way.

Lizards moved over rocks, darting into hiding places. Mosquitoes buzzed by my head.

I listened.

Peace lived inside silence.

So did terror.

They will die.

Thoughts of the kid and Catherine clung to me, that note the ultimate horror.

There was no answer on their phone. The cameras were dark, all twelve of them.

X. Y. Z.

Had to remain focused. Had to get through this moment in order to deal with the next.

Despite all that had happened, those letters clung to my mind.

They had to be okay. Nothing could happen to them.

If something did happen to them I would disintegrate where I stood.

Images of them dead came to me. I rubbed my eyes, shook those thoughts away.

I focused. I listened. I waited.

We'd be safe here. We'd have to leave before sunrise. Get to St. John's. Find clothing. Get in contact with Konstantin, find a safe house, doctor my wounds, and get off the island.

Alvin White could be watching over the kid and Catherine by then.

Needed to try to reach him again. Needed to dig in my pocket and take out my iPhone.

That was what I was thinking when I heard grunts and yells coming from the compound.

Silence had been shattered.

I took off running, angry because I had been looking out at the sea, anticipating my enemy.

But my enemy was there, had probably crossed the waters when we were in the kitchen.

Their second attack was under way.

The back doors flew open so hard the heavy wood almost left the hinges.

I saw one coming after me. He came out of the kitchen at top speed, his hat leaving his head.

He charged at me like an attack dog.

Without hesitating, I pulled out a knife I had taken from the kitchen and charged at him, dropped my backpack from my wounded shoulder and moved toward my aggressor. What I saw when he was right up on me startled me. His face was melting. Hawks had gotten to him. His hands were trying to pull away what Hawks had thrown in his face, the soup made of broken glass, poisonous fruit, boiling water, and Susie's Hot Sauce. And honey. He wasn't running at me. He was fleeing, trying to get away from the woman who had flipped the script on his attack. He ran toward me pulling goo from his face, but boiled honey took away the skin, made skin peel away like the jacket on an overcooked potato. The hot sauce had soaked into his raw wounds, exacerbating the pain. Whatever damage the honey didn't do, the hot sauce and shards of glass picked up the slack. He ran blind, tried to run faster than the speed of his agony, that goo seeping inside his mouth. When he tried to scream, it scorched and peeled his tongue the same way his flesh had been scorched and peeled, silenced his muffled yell.

The big man's frantic run ended when his panic took him into the deep end of the infinity pool, water splashing high and wide as the sting from the chlorine added torment to his open wounds. Unless he could drink a lot of water, that pool would be his final resting place.

I had to get inside, had to get to Hawks.

But I looked up and there he was, blocking my path.

The man with the red hair. A knife in his hand.

He came at me hard and fast, with fury and a vengeance.

In the blink of an eye Konstantin's teaching played in my mind.

Always avoid the business end of a weapon.

Don't get shot. Don't get stabbed.

Attack the son of a motherfucking bitch like a velociraptor.

The man with the red hair tried to stab me at short range and I twisted, tried a scissor strike, used my footwork to get out of the way, barely made it out of stabbing range. I tried to slap his wrists and force him to drop his weapon. The scissor strike didn't work. He danced, bobbed, and weaved, feinted like he was about to charge at me in order to throw me off, became Muhammad Ali with a blade, floated like a butterfly, keeping me on the defensive until the business end of his knife could become a killer bee.

I couldn't run. Never turn your back on a knife.

The best I could do was control how I got cut. Or where I would be stabbed.

I tried to get in a better position but the agile son of a bitch moved around me like he was at a motherfucking bullfight, made it hard for me to figure out his style, his feints swift and unbalancing, his movements making me think he had learned to knife-fight in the favelas above Rio de Janeiro.

He danced.

I danced.

He tried to throw sand in my face, blind me before he charged, or get me to blind myself to his charge by raising my arm. It worked, but when he bolted at me like he was an American football player, the sand wasn't like Astroturf and he lost his footing, my own footing not good enough to take advantage of the moment. My breathing accelerated. My heartbeat did the same. If he hadn't slipped, if the ground hadn't been in my favor, I would've been writhing in the sand, a knife in my gut or chest, staring up at the constellations as I created a sea of blood.

He moved with arrogance and patience.

I moved like Death was near and time wasn't on my side.

The crashing was the final music one of us would hear, a beautiful death knell.

He came at me, stuck his hand out, and I brought up the steak knife I had, a blade he hadn't seen, caught him off guard, made contact with his right forearm, opened his skin up, tried to cut him down to the bone. He backed away, shocked by my speed, shocked to see I had a weapon, stunned by the pain.

I nodded at the red-haired son of a bitch.

That slowed him down but didn't stop him.

He danced a brand-new dance, one with less arrogance and swagger.

Blood dripped down his knife hand, moistened his palm, and compromised the grip he had on his blade. His deep frown told me he wasn't used to being the one on the business end of a sharp blade.

Again he stabbed at me, threw a series of jabs with his knife leading the way. I stumbled; the sand caused my foot to slide. I tried to recover my balance. The pain in my left arm forced me to use my right hand to get back on my feet. And when I did, I lost my grip on my blade, lost it in the sand. He saw that I was at a disadvantage and seized the moment, came at me like he was ready to put this contract to bed, sand flying with his every step.

He lunged at my heart.

I stepped to the outside of the blade, moved outside the line of fire, grabbed his bloodied wrist with my left hand, my weak hand, and threw a blow to his face with my right fist. I didn't have the pivot I needed, didn't have the footing I desired to throw a knockout blow, but I connected with his chin just the same. Made him stumble in the sand. I went with him as he stumbled, threw blow after blow. He wouldn't let go of his blade. I twisted and kicked him in his gut. Not a deep kick, but I hit my target.

That forced him to drop his knife, a knife covered with his blood, and stagger away.

My blade was a few steps away.

Hawks was forever away from where I was.

Before I could get to my weapon he had charged me, grabbed me as he hit me hard, lifted me up, both of us airborne, crashing where the sea licked the sand. We hit the ground swinging, fighting, his right arm bleeding all over me, my left arm wounded, traded blow after blow after motherfucking blow as the sea crashed down on our fight. We battled in the waves, seawater burning my eyes, salty water burning my wounds, battled from the sea back to shore, the battle taking us away from the knives we'd had, moving us closer to a jetty made of huge rocks, our rage being upstaged by the roar of the sea.

He had a grip on my weakened shoulder, flipped me. From the ground I managed to gut-kick him. He staggered away. By the time he had found his footing, I was up on one knee.

We faced each other, my left arm numb with pain.

That was when I saw something in his eyes, something I didn't expect to see.

Respect.

In between a frown and a grimace, I offered him the same professional admiration. He had tenacity, if nothing else. Then the moment of praise was over and we were back at war. A war that would not end in a peace agreement because he was just a soldier, a soldier sent on someone else's mission of hate, a man who was given a paycheck and sent to do someone else's bidding. He was a good soldier, but in the end he was just a man following somebody else's orders, not understanding that this fight was one that never should've happened, that I was no threat to the woman who had sent him.

This war was unnecessary. But this war was a war.

I wasn't ready. But I had to fight for my life or get buried in the sand.

I went after him full tilt, turned the one attacking me into the one being attacked, his offense switching to defense when the prey became predator, my relentless strikes nonstop and ruthless.

There was no referee. No corner man to throw in the towel.

All about the last man standing. There was only one way for this battle to end.

The last man breathing would be the winner.

My fighting had no one style, but had all styles mixed in the blow: Brazilian jujitsu, tae kwon do, Israeli martial arts, boxing, fight skills accumulated traveling the world; I switched styles whenever he caught on, making it hard for him to defend himself, making it hard for him to counter a fighting style he didn't know or wasn't ready for. But he was good, kept me from getting a clear shot, kept me from disabling him, forced me to use more energy than I had to spare. I got in close, grabbed his head, tried to get a knee deep inside his groin, but he twisted, my knee not finding its target. We wrestled, grappled, went down into the sand. His hand dug into the sand. My eyes closed as he threw a fistful of it across my face. A blow followed, hit my chin, dazed me, but I didn't stop fighting and threw blows to keep him away from me, had to fight him off me, hit him until I felt my hand going numb, until the wound in my left shoulder became crippling, until a sharp pain caused me to slow down. His foot found my inner thigh, an attempted groin shot that missed its bull's-eye by at least four inches, its impact good enough to make me experience a brand-new misery, one that almost matched the one in my shoulder.

His knee found my ribs. I bent with the weight from the pain.

He tried to pull me down into the sand, yanked me like he wanted to shove me facedown, use those granules to fill my mouth and lungs and suffocate me, but I struggled, now on the defense, the last place I wanted to be. He managed to get his arm around my head, his grip powerful as he tried to claw out my eye sockets with his other hand, but I gave him blows that went deep into his ribs and lungs as I struggled and slipped away, his fingernails raking across my face, burning my skin with a new injury. I went after that redheaded son of a bitch, my foot finding the edges of his gut, not a solid kick, not as deep a kick as I had wanted it to be, but enough to make him lose his footing and stagger in the white sands.

He went down on one knee, then struggled back to his feet, didn't come right at me. He was winded. Before he could regroup and chamber his blows, I was on him, in pain, grimacing, throwing punch after punch, each blow hurting me as much as it hurt him, didn't want him to be able to catch half a breath. He was off balance, stunned, desperate, panting, trying to find his footing, the grimace on his face, the fear in his eyes, telling me he was weakening, the pain slowing him down.

That didn't stop that motherfucker. The pain enhanced him if anything.

Just like that he came back at me, hooks and jabs so fast each blow was a blur.

He was a good fighter. Not intelligent, but strong and deadly. More Tyson than De La Hoya. But unlike Tyson, the fighter in front of me was a man who refused to quit no matter what.

The pains I felt were worse than death.

There was a pause. Like we were between rounds.

My chest ached. Needed to catch my breath. Didn't have the luxury of time.

In my mind I was back in London. This was the battle I had been denied.

The face of the red-haired man vanished, became the face of a man with a broken nose.

I was getting my revenge against the man who had killed me.

I went after him again, each blow I delivered closer to demolishing him.

He tried to eclipse my ferociousness but stayed in close, my turn to gouge his motherfucking eyes. Struck with the palm of my hand, hit him hard enough to slam his head back, followed up with ax hand blows, and when he tried to come back at me I delivered a shin kick, articulated my hips the best I could, fought to overcome my own pain and aches to get the angle and power I needed to strike the nerve in his thigh. He did his best to slow my attack, but my aggressiveness couldn't be overpowered.

Neither could his.

He had gotten his second wind; his speed and energy moved back into the red zone. He had me on the defensive; I tried to bob and weave, did my best to block an onslaught of blows, the sand not made for quick movements, making me feel stuck where I was; my foot slid when I tried to get firm footing, left me with the choice of going down or catching myself.

While I struggled for balance he put a blow in my wounded shoulder, a blow that made me want to collapse and howl out in pain. The blows kept landing on that one spot, on my weakness. He beat my bloodied shoulder until I went down on one knee, my other hand gripping the sand like I was trying to hold on to the earth. It was my turn to growl and throw sand. My turn to make him look away. And in that moment I staggered after him, my pain great, but not as great as my fury. With my good hand I threw a punch that pounded his face and bloodied his nose. He staggered away, blinded by my blow.

I was hurting too much to chase him, hurting too much to back away and regroup.

He had staggered to the waters and grabbed a rock. Jagged and the size of a cinder block, solid to the core, had to weigh thirty pounds, more than enough to bludgeon and crush a man's skull. Water rained down from that chunk of the earth as he fought the waters to get back to me with his weapon.

I ran at him, caught his hands before the rock made it to its apex.

I had to battle him with one good hand.

Gave him a head butt, tried to take him to the ground.

The rock fell when he backed away, tumbled down between us, hit my shin, landed on my foot.

Birds and frogs cried as I stumbled with my new pains, did the same as he staggered with his.

The angered look on his bloodied and swollen face, the way blood dripped from his nose across his terse lips, and the murderous look in his eyes told me he wasn't going to stop coming at me.

He was a demon. He would keep coming until I regretted this moment.

I was tired, lungs burning, every part my body heavy and on fire, barely able to stand.

Wounds from Birmingham began to sing. Edges of my illness in Atlanta remained.

And I had lost blood when I had been shot. And hadn't recovered from dehydration.

He had the upper hand. He knew he had the upper hand.

He tried to stand tall, took a deep breath, wiped sweat and sand and water from his wounded face, gritted his teeth, and came at me, dug in deep and raced across the sand like a charging bull.

I did the same, raced at that red-haired son of a bitch like I was a juggernaut.

Two wounded velociraptors collided.

The collision took me to the ground, left me rolling; had to get back to my feet. I looked for him, saw he was down too, putting one knee into the ground, getting up while my pain had become an unbearable weight, the world on the shoulders of Atlas. He kicked my face, stunned me. As I fought I felt his hands on me, dragging me toward the sea, that ocean the weapon he was ready to use. I struggled with him, swinging with one arm, my left arm numb, dead, useless. He put blows in my ribs, struck my kidneys. Then I felt the rush of the sea, its water chilling, its salt stinging, cauterizing wounds old and new. I struggled to get a lungful of air, held my breath while he pushed me down, held me down, the world vanishing as I was forced into a liquid darkness that had no air. A watery grave that had claimed many. The wave pulled away and I found some air only to have the sea rush back and cover me once again. That motherfucker held me down, put his body on top of mine, choked me.

A wave pulled us toward the sea, sucked us away from the shore.

Then another wave came in hard, crashed over us; the sea swallowed and tugged as if a hundred octopi wanted to drag us out to sea. The undertow yanked the fight into deeper waters, closer to Davy Jones's locker. The red-haired man stayed on top of me, weighed me down, hit me where he could as I battled his fury and the power of the sea. He stayed with me, tried to force me to exhale so I could gasp for air and take my final breath.

I wrestled until my face broke the surface, until I stole a lungful of air.

The red-haired man jerked, lost his grip on my neck, moved away from me, did that with urgency. Moved like he was trying to fight something off him. Then I felt the sting of one hundred mosquito bites. Something was in the water. This side of the island didn't have sharks.

Jellyfish.

One had stung my left arm, but the way he panicked I could tell many more had gotten to him. I panicked too, knowing I had only one good arm. Now we both were fleeing the sea and her creatures, my effort pained and slow. I lost sight of him, struggled with making it back to shore, that shore no more than twenty yards away, that twenty yards feeling like twenty miles. The last few feet were impossible; a wave crashed over me and regurgitated me from the ocean back to the damp sand.

The red-haired man was already there.

I had to get up. Had to. I made it to my knee and saw him, in the sand, writhing in pain, holding his face with one hand and reaching for his lower back with the other. The jellyfish had gotten to him first and wounded him. His face, his back, his neck had been attacked, stung. There had been more than one of the sea creatures, more than one finding him before finding me. He was struggling to get up. Exhausted. Waterlogged. Battered. The mirror of my existence.

Now a jellyfish sting had swollen his left eye.

My blows had swollen his right eye. He could barely see, if he could see at all.

He had panicked, had taken in water as he fled the ocean.

He was fucked-up.

By the time he made it to one knee I had staggered his way, was standing over him.

The thirty-pound rock he had tried to bash my head with, it was in my trembling, aching hands. I struggled to raise it over my head. Left arm distressed, body shaking, I held it high.

The red-haired man turned his wounded face and looked up at me. Looked at the rock. Tried to crawl away, the sand keeping him where he was as I struggled to hold the rock higher.

He realized there was nowhere to run. The red-haired man looked back. Frowned in my direction, his swollen left eye closed as he searched for me, struggled to see me with his right eye. Again, that frown vanished for a moment. The man behind the demon shone through.

Respect stared up at regret.

I paused. This was not his war.

No referees. No one to throw the towel in. Unless one of us simply decided to walk away. I was about to drop the rock but his expression changed, the deep-set frown returned, a look of nonconcession that told me he would never stop coming at me, that this would never end.

Until the contract had been fulfilled.

His expression told me he was used to winning, would never concede defeat.

The same as Detroit, a woman who wouldn't let go; stubborn, irrational, and power hungry.

London. Cayman Islands. Huntsville. Now here in the white sands of Antigua.

And she had hired a man who had an unshakeable, bedrock commitment to facilitating my murder.

The same man who had used that knife and murdered two innocent women in London.

He had butchered Catherine's friends.

What had to be done was both regrettable and inescapable.

I brought the rock down on his face as hard as I could. His head opened in a gash. His blood poured into the gorgeous white sand as he continued to crawl away. Then I picked the rock up again. Brought it down on his head again. Another wound opened. His skin moved away from the bone on his head. Doing to him what he wanted to do to me moments before. Again I picked up the bloody rock.

I brought it down on his head again.

He stopped crawling.

But his hand was still twitching.

I bludgeoned him until he stopped moving.

Then I gritted my teeth and continued to bludgeon him.

I hit him with that jagged rock until his blood and brains mixed with the beautiful white sand.

I collapsed into the gritty sand, fell to my knees, struggled to breathe as I grabbed a handful of wet sand, rubbed that on my left arm where one of the jellyfish had stung me. I had no idea what type of jellyfish had attacked us, didn't know if it was a Portuguese man-of-war or a common jellyfish.

Hawks. Had to get to Hawks.

It took all I had to stand up again, and when I made it to my feet I kept rocking side to side, unable to move in a straight line. I had taken a handful of steps when I saw her.

She was limping toward me, her steps uneven. It wasn't Hawks.

Without looking up, I knew from the expensive shoes it was the strawberry blonde.

She took a step and paused, bent like she was in pain, then straightened back up.

She fired at me, her bullet finding a new home in the sand near my feet.

She bent over again, the gun at her side, her eyes on me.

She came closer, walked my death toward me one step at a time.

Her partner was five feet away from me, a bloodied rock resting near his head, the waves washing up to his motionless feet. I couldn't move, not the way I needed to if I was going to be able to escape. But I tried and slipped, pulled a groin muscle, the abrupt pain severe and crippling, making me want to howl, gripping my body and sending me to the sand, throwing me to the ground once again.

It was the accumulation of injuries, not just one, that took me down. Shoulder shot and swollen. Exhausted from the fight. Clothes weighed down by sand and water. Lungs on fire. Loss of blood from the gunshot. Dehydration. My last pain was the one that brought them all together. In chorus they sang the same song, told me I wasn't going anywhere. I battled my injuries. Tried to get up, refused to give up my life, never surrendering, moved the same way the dead man next to me had moved moments ago. In desperation. In vain.

I looked up, saw her bent over, hands on her knees, struggling to breathe.

Without warning she gagged, vomited, coughed over and over, began choking.

Her choking was violent. She was hurting. And she was hurting bad.

The gun wasn't pointing at me, not while she was doubled over, giving her insides to the sand.

I sucked in the agony, had almost made it up on one knee, only to have the groin injury spread like a powerful fire, the pain the most intense pain I'd ever felt, an agony that yanked me back to the sand. That was more than the time she needed to look at the lifeless body a few feet away from me, enough time to see her partner in crime had died an unkind death, time for her to close the gap that existed between us.

The strawberry blonde. She was in front of me. Her face covered with sweat. Blinking her eyes over and over, in time with her pain. Her hair was braided. Made her look Puerto Rican. Maybe from Spain.

That thought passed in the blink of an eye. The West Indies breeze on high, her exotic clothing fluttering as multimillion-dollar holiday homes and a tropical paradise framed her body.

A gun was in her right hand; her left hand came up; I saw her take deep breaths, cringe as she struggled to hold her death maker steady. She trembled, fought her agony. I saw the rage and coldness in her eyes as I gave her the rage and coldness in mine.

Unable to move, plagued by pain, I was helpless and hors de combat.

I had become a soldier out of the fight.

Stars over our heads, that beautiful assassin stood at point-blank range.

Thirty-three

brutal

Death's harbinger stood over me, frozen, gun aimed at the center of my head.

Her eyes opened and closed over and over, sweat pouring from her forehead.

Then she grabbed her stomach like she had the bends, her stilettos sinking in the sand.

She twitched and lost her balance, her face tense as she lowered the gun and looked down.

My eyes did the same.

Her white jeans turned pink at her crotch; that pinkness moved down her inner thigh.

She was wounded.

She wobbled, grabbed her stomach, gagged, regurgitated again, bent over, kept giving her insides to the sand, didn't let go of the gun as she staggered backward, lost her footing, and collapsed.

She fell like she had been shot, her impact causing a whirlwind of sand to cover her body.

Sand that made her close her eyes. Sand that had her temporarily blinded.

I made it to my knee again, grunted and pushed up, made it to my feet, took steps that made me want to howl, steps so short they were baby steps, moved toward her, eyed the property, expected more of them to come out gunning. The strawberry blonde, her face was dusted with sand. Her eyes were closed. The female assassin rocked and held her gut as if she had been shot in her belly with a .45.

She moved her legs, her shoes digging into the sand, slipping off one at a time. She couldn't stand up, wore a horrible expression that let me know her pain wasn't fake. The pinkness between her legs turned red. The gun she had pointed at my head was near her in the sand.

I struggled, couldn't bend over, the ache and fire in my groin severe. I fell to the sand again, dropped next to that gun. She panicked, struggled for the weapon, both of us grabbing the gun. I had the business end but she had her finger locked on the trigger. I tried to push that business end toward her head. Her expression was one of both pain and panic, a glare that told me she wanted to do the same thing to me. The silenced gun fired twice, bullets projected into the sky, then the gun fired over and over until the clip was empty. That was what she wanted to do, empty the gun and keep me from putting a bullet inside her head. She loosened her grip and I yanked the empty gun away from her.

Her eyes met mine, swollen eyes, redness invading the pupils.

She was suffering. Beyond ill. I'd seen that look on the faces of a few people.

It was the look of someone poisoned and dying.

In this world dying wasn't dead.

My mind told me to crawl on her, choke the life out of her. But the sting from the jellyfish, followed by lifting that rock up over my head and taking out the man with the red hair, had damaged my already-wounded shoulder, had left my arm in too much pain to make what I needed to do to that female assassin a reality. The gun I had in my hand, it was empty but hard enough to bludgeon her.

Not that long ago I had left one enemy alive, had done that and my life had become a living hell.

Never again.

I crawled over her, grabbed at her clothing as she tried to roll away, pulled her back, used my weight to hold her down. She tried to push me away, tried to beat me away, but she wasn't a physically strong woman. I crawled over her leg, crawled up to her breasts, crawled until

I was eye to eye with the agony in her face, my ragged breathing on her skin, her desperate breathing mixed with my exhales.

The gun was raised up as high as I could raise it, ready to come down into her skull.

The fear in her face was as deep as the hurting in her eyes.

She jerked, regurgitated over and over, turned her face away from me.

Her bile came fast, stained me, surprised me, and I tried to cover her mouth, tried to force her to choke and drown in her heated vomit. But I lost my grip and she turned her head, moved away from me. I rolled away from her and the grunts that came from her misery, left her gagging; that urgent move I made magnified all the agony I felt in an exponential fashion. Hands soiled with sand and bile, I didn't let go of that gun. Kept that unloaded weapon in my hand, made sure it was out of her reach in case she tried to take it, in case she had bullets nearby and tried to reload it.

I reached for her, did my best to grab her with my good arm, that movement giving me anguish.

She rolled over in the sand, moved out of my reach. She struggled to get ahold of herself, failed, eyes glazed over, her expression miserable, her breathing sharp and sudden. The blood between her legs spread as sand and sea washed across her face and into her braided hair. Her mouth opened but no words came out. The strawberry blonde's shoes had been kicked off her feet, were in the sand, on their sides like capsized ships. Her eyes searched for mine, her pain so deep and severe that it had stolen her ability to breathe, and without breath there was no sound, no cry for help, no warning others.

Jaw tight, I gritted my teeth, shook my head, every inhale a curse, every exhale the same.

Hawks. Had to get to Hawks.

No noises came from the main house, none I could hear over the sea and the singing frogs.

That was terrifying.

If Hawks was dead, I'd come back to the beach. If I had to crawl down the tile and drag myself across broken glass to get back to the white sands, I'd do that. My glare back told the strawberry blonde she didn't want to see me again. If I came back I would drag her out into the sea. I'd put a plastic bag over her head. I'd do whatever I could do to kill her on these shores. I struggled to my feet, left the strawberry blonde gagging, dealing with her own agony, trying to get up and unable to shake away her pain.

She bled like she had been shot. Like she was dying. But dying wasn't dead.

I moved by the woman, limped in the direction of the main house, clothes soaked and covered in sand, my weight tons, sweating profusely. I raised my leg to move up the tiled steps that led past the infinity pool, a pool that had a dead body floating in its deep end.

I limped into broken darkness . . . unarmed . . . the tile damp . . . sticky . . . pools of liquor on the floor . . . silhouettes down on the tile . . . not moving . . . not moaning . . . stilled bodies . . . clicked a light on . . . looked for Hawks . . . it was a gruesome sight . . . a sight that would've made a weaker man scream . . . blood by the gallon . . . more broken glass . . . pots and pans turned over . . . every concoction that had been made stained the floors and walls . . . most was on the floor in the kitchen . . . three bodyguards . . . steak knives in their throats . . . butcher knives in their chests . . . mixtures of boiled honey, broken glass, poison fruit, and hot sauce in two of their faces . . . faces that were no longer recognizable . . . silenced guns at their sides . . . red rivers came together and created crimson ponds around the weapons they had brought to this battle.

None of these corpses was the shell that had contained Hawks.

Not too far away from them was one boot.

It was Hawks's boot.

Something inside of me sank, sank hard and fast.

I swallowed, prepared for a new surge of misery, agony that almost pulled me down to the floor. I struggled. Managed to pick up two nine-millimeters, both loaded, not fully, at least six shots spent between the two. Six shots meant Hawks could've been hit six times. From a glance I couldn't tell if those shots had been put in the walls.

My heart ached. Didn't know if one of those shots had been a kill shot. Didn't know if this was it, the last of that killing crew, or if there were a dozen more hired killers waiting in the wings. As long as Detroit was alive, there would always be someone.

This property had become a tropical graveyard.

I dropped the unloaded .22, let it crash to the tile.

Hawks. Had to find her.

During my next heartbeat, left arm tender and unusable, I used my right arm, stuffed one of the loaded guns inside the waist of my wet pants. I couldn't open and close my left hand, not the way I wanted to, but it was good enough to pull the trigger on a gun. My left arm might have been out of commission, but my left hand would have to stay in this fight. It wasn't until then that I paused. Not until then did I realize how much noise I had made, how much my panic had taken over.

Looking for movement, I listened for any noise, hobbled. Water dripped from my clothing, each drop as loud as a gong, each granule of sand the same; my shoes squeaked. I moved at a snail's pace across the tiled floor, a second silenced gun in my right hand, the business end pointed straight ahead. I followed a trail of blood, the pain in my heart a thousand times stronger than a jellyfish sting.

There was movement. A struggle in the darkness. Someone was a few feet away from me; the roar from the waves no longer swallowed that faint sound. Gripping the wall to maintain my balance, I rounded the corner, the gun leading the way. Two wide-brimmed hats were in the hallway. Another man was on the ground. His legs kicked in slow motion, white tennis shoes scrapping the tile, running in place, trying to get away from this firefight, or maybe he was chasing his dreams. A gun was in his right hand, a weapon I stepped on. My weight crushed his fingers, made him cringe, then I held the wall and kicked the gun away. That sound betrayed my position to whoever was waiting up ahead.

The man on the ground, he reached for me, tried to grab my ankle.

With a silenced *pop* I stilled his movement the same way he would have stilled mine.

I looked back, expected to see the strawberry blonde. Gun in hand,

I *wanted* to see the strawberry blonde, *wanted* her to come after me, *wanted* to pull the trigger and finish her before she could regroup.

No one was there. Not yet.

In front of the dead man were bloody footsteps, a thin trail that led to the next corner.

Someone around that corner was breathing hard, trying not to be heard.

Could be one person lying in wait. Could be many.

I took the second gun out, held it in my left hand, a hand that didn't want to work but had no choice. I leaned against the wall, let the wall hold me up as I inched toward that breathing, guns leading the way, spied back as I inched forward, my mind on the assassin I had left on the beach, knew she could rise up from the sands and come back inside this compound.

I had to move forward. I rounded that corner.

That was where I found Hawks.

In agony.

She was down. Her long hair was loose, as if it had been pulled free in a fight. Her blouse was ripped. A gun in each hand, both guns pointed at me, waiting, as soon as I turned that corner.

The jellyfish sting ached, the pain excruciating, but I was still moving.

She trembled, her eyes focused, relaxing when she saw it was me. Her guns lowered but weren't put away. Hawks was anxious, her haunting eyes telling me she remained in battle mode.

I lowered my guns, my left arm appreciating that moment of rest. My right hand, that gun remained in shooting position while I glanced behind me. Nothing was there.

I limped closer to Hawks.

I was relieved. It didn't show, my every movement frantic and agonizing, but that was how I felt.

Her eyes told me she felt the same way.

I held up one finger. That told her that at least one was left. I pointed back toward the beach, back in the direction I had left the strawberry blonde. Hawks nodded, then pulled her hair from her face.

Hawks grimaced; her agony showed in her sweaty face as she held up a fist.

That fist meant zero; none were left that she knew of.

We knew that didn't mean all were disposed of, that we were out of trouble.

More could be on the way. More could be here.

Hawks had on one boot. The other foot was bloodied. One glance at her, remembering all the downed soldiers I had passed, told me all I needed to know. They had come and tried to catch her off guard. Maybe they saw a wounded woman, underestimated her. Or had demanded to know where I was, then fucked up and took their eyes off her for one deadly moment. She had stepped on glass during her battle. As long as we were trapped, the details of what had happened were irrelevant.

I gave Hawks my hand, tried to pull her to her feet, but my shoulder wouldn't let me do that. Her belt was at her side. She tossed me the end with the buckle, wrapped the other end around her wrist, and I used my weight, found leverage, grimaced with agony, and pulled her back up to her foot. Her boot almost slipped from underneath her, and that simple move almost pulled me down to the tiled floor. A rush of agony made me stumble, but I held on, my groin on fire, flames erupting from my shoulder.

We took our wounds down the hallway, Hawks with a gun in each hand, hopping on one foot, me with a gun in each hand, groin ablaze, using the wall to stay upright. Two crippled soldiers on the move.

Had to get Hawks situated. I poured alcohol over her bloodied foot, her muffled curses and tense face screaming that it burned like hell. Then I found rags and struggled to help her wrap her foot.

Hawks was taken care of for the moment, but she was in too much pain to move.

I struggled, pulled my shirt open, exposed my left forearm, where the jellyfish had attacked me, hoped it wasn't a Portuguese man-of-war—if it was there was nothing I'd be able to do to stay alive long enough to make a difference. Hawks held her guns, became my guard as I moved as fast as I could, tried to move without panicking, had to move and watch out for the enemy.

The jellyfish sting, adrenaline couldn't mask its pain.

Couldn't use fresh water; the change in pH could release more venom. I searched, looked at all the shit we had pulled out of the cabinets. The wound begged me to rub it, but I didn't. Alcohol. Spirits. Ammonia. Urine. If it wasn't a common jellyfish sting any of those remedies would make the venom release and do what others had failed to do.

A jellyfish sting could finish what Detroit had started.

Shivered. Had to deal with this now. One pot was left on the stove. The one I had put on the stove. The one that didn't have broken glass and honey and poisonous fruit. Water still boiling. I made my way to the pot, poured that boiling water on my wound, water that felt like liquid fire, wanted to scream, teeth tight, trying not to black out, felt as if I was going into shock.

I took a few deep breaths. Poured the rest of the hot water on the injury. The wound had to be neutralized before I went on. And the tentacles had to be removed. Had to keep my good hand from touching the tentacles or that would be like getting stung again. I refused to let the agony from the hot water slow me down. The empty pot dropped on a dead man. His body stole the noise before it rolled away to the tile. I grabbed a fork. Dug the tentacles out of my body the best I could. Then I dropped the fork and picked up a steak knife, used its edges to dig in my skin and remove any leftover nematocysts.

Sweat rained from my forehead; my own salt blinded me until I wiped it all away.

Tried not to panic. I needed baking soda, needed ice, needed antihistamines, something in the diphenhydramine family, the irritation strong and demanding, but I'd have to let my skin remain irritated until I could find something on the level of Benadryl. In this moment my dying was nothing.

With that done, I was going to hobble back to the beach.

The woman with the strawberry blonde hair, I had a bullet with her name on it.

But when I made it to the back door and limped to the end of the infinity pool, she was gone.

The footprints in the sand showed me her escape route, showed me she had stumbled, fallen, crawled, made it to her feet, stumbled again, did what she had to do to get back toward the waters.

More weapons or people could be in the direction she had gone.

I backed away, used a column as a shield as I searched for her in the night.

I didn't see her. Her capsized shoes were no longer in the sand.

I waited. Listened.

Not too far out I heard the rumble of a motor. She had made her way to a dinghy—not the one we had stolen, that one was in the opposite direction. The stars above highlighted her escape. The waters rocked her, made her a bobbing and moving target. I raised the gun at an angle, above the dinghy, fired until it was empty. With the second gun, I did the same. Fired up at an angle, tried to make bullets rain down on her. The kick from the gun gave me agony, but I didn't stop shooting, hoped to hit her with a lucky shot. The wind, the distance, the movement of the dinghy, each shot had a one-in-a-million chance of being pulled downward by gravity and finding a target made of flesh and blood.

Still, I tried.

If I didn't hit that runaway assassin I wanted to wound the dinghy, pierce that floating inner tube, kill her horse, make it sink into the bowels of Davy Jones's locker. On the main island she would call for backup. Or people were there, stationed at that post, waiting just in case I was chased back to the docks.

Clouds moved in, stood between me and the stars, a new level of darkness arriving abruptly. With darkness came rain that was as warm as piss.

I hobbled back to the main house, found Hawks hopping around on one foot, using counters and bar stools to keep her balance, her broken-hearted belt back on, that belt now a holster for both of her guns.

Hawks had been busy. She had gone through the liquor and found bottles of Bacardi 151, was pouring a river of alcohol all over the crime scene, over the men on the floor, but most importantly all over the blood and DNA trail we had created. The scent of Bacardi 151 filled the room and the hallway, back down to where I had found Hawks hiding, had been splashed on the walls, gave moisture to any place she had touched, any place I had touched. Any alcohol over one hundred proof was better than gasoline.

A microwave was on the counter. I put cans, metal, and aluminum foil inside the microwave, filled it with things that would create sparks—sparks that would start a fire and make friends with the flammable river. Hawks and I limped and hobbled by each other, once again moving in concert, trained by Konstantin.

The homes were made of cinder blocks—no dry walls for flames to burn through—with sturdy roofs made of concrete and tile; impossible for a flame to leap from one section of the compound to another.

Once started the blaze would remain contained and burn until its conclusion.

I set the microwave to three hours, knowing that was overkill.

Hawks bent and picked up her stray boot, limped, opening shutters, letting Caribbean air inside.

Fire needed oxygen, had to breathe so it could spread and become a living and roaring beast.

We limped away, moved through the rain, rain that would make trekking across sand a little easier. We passed the dead man in the infinity pool, raindrops splashing around his body. After that I picked up my backpack, let it hang from my right shoulder, the same shoulder Hawks used as a crutch. The rain came down harder, the winds picked up. Not long after, our wounded strides took us to where I had left the red-haired man in the sand. Hawks cringed when she caught a glimpse of that horror. Every pain told me I was the one who was still living. What I had done to him was what he would have done to me. That was what Detroit would have loved to have heard had happened to me. The red-haired man was dead but my deep-rooted fears were alive. Moved over my skin like a million lizards.

Powder Springs. They will die.

We hobbled to the water. Hawks cringed, was stopped by the

extreme pain when the salty water licked her injured foot. When the pain subsided and she was able to go on, we crawled over rocks, made it to where I had left the dinghy. We fell inside, winded and wounded, the rain coming down as hard as a shower. Hawks slid toward the back of the dinghy, pulled the crank, started the motor on the third try.

I adjusted, felt my iPhone in my back pocket. Knew it was waterlogged and useless.

A new frustration mounted. No way to get in contact with Catherine and the kid.

No way to try to get in contact with Alvin White. No way to call Konstantin.

For a moment, a small, *small* moment, I thought of Arizona, wished for her help as well.

Hawks looked at me, her expression the same as mine, laced with a deep hurting and aggravation. She maneuvered, pulled herself up on the edge of the dinghy, positioned a gun in each hand, her eyes on the shores and sand behind us, guns aimed the same way, on full alert. I moved us out into the sea. It was the thick of the night. Darkness across the waters was deep, appeared bottomless. If someone was in the water waiting, we wouldn't see them until it was too late.

The waves slapped into the dinghy, rocked us; the motor hummed like a dying old man.

The world stretched out; the mainland looked like it was a hundred miles away from where we were.

I looked in the direction the strawberry blonde had fled, back toward the Beachcomber Hotel.

Thought I saw flashes on the dock. Muzzle flashes. At least a dozen. Maybe more.

If they were shooting at us, unless they were using a cannon, we were too far away.

Just the same, I kept my eyes that way.

If they had regrouped, if they had another dinghy, or a boat by now, we were fucked.

I couldn't go back. And I knew we wouldn't survive a shoot-out on the seas.

We kept moving, fought the waves, looked to see what was coming from that direction.

In the distance, headlights came on inside the same parking lot where we had left our stolen ride.

They were there.

Detroit was there.

The dark skies made those headlights light up like stars, probably visible for miles.

I didn't have binoculars; no way could I see that far, but my guess was the strawberry blonde had made it to shore. Someone was there waiting for her. Didn't know how many, maybe dozens.

Hawks stared at me, her haunting eyes powerful as she wiped sweat, seawater, and rain from her face. A downpour and harsh winds assaulted us, waves rose and sprayed us by the gallon. Seawater burned and cauterized my injuries, gave the same unbiased and needed pain to Hawks's wounds.

I had no idea if they were speeding after us, the darkness too complete.

Our engine moved us forward as the sea did its best to flip us over.

Hawks pointed; that motion told me to look back and to my right.

It pained me to do so, but I shifted, frowned in that direction, ready for the worst to happen.

There were lights back at Jumby Bay, the ferry leaving the docks for Antigua.

They couldn't see us from where they were, riding waves in darkness.

I sped us toward the docks at Parham Town, the oldest town on the island, storm harsh, the gentle flames from a burning two-million-dollar vacation home glowing, reddening the night behind us.

Again I grimaced in the direction the strawberry blonde had fled, searched for people in pursuit.

In the distance, once again, gunshots lit up the night.

Thirty-four

target of an assassin

Hawks hot-wired a twenty-year-old four-door Nissan and crawled into the backseat.

I sideswiped three parked cars before I controlled my anguish and adjusted my one-handed driving. Right arm ached as much as the gunshot wound in the left. My steering and braking and abrupt turns tossed Hawks around. Everything on my body ached. I broke all traffic laws and drove a stolen car through Parham Town, streets wet, the rain no longer coming down. I slowed down, drove empty roads back toward St. John's, almost ran off the road a few times, pain continuous and undefeatable. Elbows. Knees. Jaw. Shins. Wrists. Hands. Every part of my body felt swollen. Hawks grunted, her pain deep, looked behind us, both of the guns in her hands.

I drove around, made sure we weren't followed, took High Street, Corn Alley, Nevis, then Independence Avenue back over to Redcliffe Street, cruised until the road ended at St. John's Harbour. The streets were clear. The city naked and quiet. I backed up and parked outside Vendors Mall and Kalabashe restaurant. I had circled the block to check it out, had seen unarmed security guards around the corner at St. Marys and Thames streets, guards who sat outside of Antigua Commercial Bank and Bank of Antigua. Those guards didn't stray from their posts, looked like they were in a battle to stay awake all night. The town was asleep. Unaware of the fire back at Jumby Bay. Unaware of the dead bodies left behind. Unaware that two people who were on the run like outlaws were hiding in Antigua's shadows. We reeked of violence. The stench of alcohol had covered our soiled and bloodied clothing.

City Pharmacy was on St. Marys, close to Best of Books, below Hemingways.

This stop wasn't random. I'd brought us there for a reason.

We had open wounds; last thing we needed was infections.

Hawks picked the locks to the pharmacy and I crept inside, panted and dripped water and sand. I pulled things from shelves in the darkness, collected medical supplies, grabbed a few bottles of water, wanted more, but this wasn't a casual shopping day at Epicurean. I grabbed candy bars, PowerBars, stuffed them inside my wet shirt, didn't worry about fingerprints. By the time I finished shopping Hawks had broken into the store next door, was limping out with T-shirts.

The wet clothes would be a problem too.

I drove the stolen car down Popeshead, slipped through the congestion in the red-light district, then turned left at Percival Texaco, drove to the beach down at Fort James, that area dark and empty.

Not until then did I exhale. When I stopped, the ache didn't do the same.

Under the moon and stars we tended to our wounds, then got back inside our hot ride.

We sipped water, ate candy, chewed on PowerBars.

Hawks was in the backseat, her leg elevated.

I was in the front, aching like hell. I was still alive. For now.

I was the one who could hear the sounds of the sea crashing into the shores.

I was the one who could look up at the dark skies and see a million constellations.

I was the one who would live to die another day.

Detroit.

She was out there. She was close.

She had been dying for her chance at retribution.

I felt the same way.

I needed the same thing.

Retribution.

I shifted, ached, frowned, swallowed curses laced with pain, felt the same fucking way.

Hawks asked, "Anywhere to get any real food?"

"Not until morning."

"I've been hungrier. Need to lose a few pounds anyway."

"Water okay?"

"I could use one bourbon, one scotch, and one beer."

"I could go for a Jack and Coke."

Hawks shifted, let out a sound of pain. "How we looking on weapons?"

"Not as good as they'll be looking."

"Wonder how many more she'll send after you."

"I want to put you on a plane in the morning. The first flight to anywhere."

"You going?"

"Just you. I want you to get to another island, then catch a flight back to America."

"I don't think so."

"Hawks."

"If I didn't know any better I would think you were trying to get rid of me."

"Hawks, you only have one good leg."

"You have a thing against one-legged women?"

"Hawks."

"And you have one good arm."

"Hawks."

"But do you hear me discriminating against you?"

We went back to silent mode, looking out, expecting to be found, waiting for another attack.

I said, "She knows about my family."

"You have a family?"

"The woman who raised me. And her son."

"The wonderful mother who nurtured you and taught you to kill people to make lunch money."

"Yeah. Her."

"And she has another son?"

"Long story about me and her. One I want to live to see to its end."

"Think Detroit is going to go after them?"

I didn't answer. Something told me she already had.

Detroit wasn't done. I was alive and she wasn't done. Like a gambler who was losing all of his money, she would keep playing, keep gambling until she won, until she hit blackjack.

I wasn't done either.

We drove back into St. John's and abandoned the third stolen car before sunrise revealed us, slipped out into the maze of one-way streets as soon as delivery vehicles came toward Redcliffe Quay. New T-shirts on, pants still wet and covered in mud, sand, and blood. Hawks limped on her sprained ankle and wounded foot. My face was beaten, arm shot and stung. We looked like we had been pulled from under debris after a hurricane. We needed to blend in; what we had on wasn't doing the trick.

No way could we show up at V. C. International Airport looking like battle-weary refugees.

Detroit would have more assassins guarding the routes to the airport, I knew that.

But I didn't have a choice. I needed to get back to North America.

Even if I had to shoot my way into the airport and steal a plane.

A Cessna could get me to another island.

I remained anxious, expected the shoot-out to resume at any moment.

Soon we were on the move. I wanted to move faster but the ache in my groin controlled my stride; the muscle was a fiery knot. We mixed with droves of people that came from the east and west bus stations. First the crowd wearing jeans and T-shirts showed up, along with older women in modest dresses and sandals. Farmers brought in fresh produce and filled bins by five in the morning. We bought bananas, mangoes, coconut water. The vendors who sold arts and crafts, beaded and shell jewelry, and other goods arrived and set up before darkness ended. After eight or nine the sun would be high, streets filled with men in dark suits and women in low heels and colorful bank uniforms. And killers in search of a man and woman who had killed more than a few of their coworkers, the reward on my head probably doubled by now. Wouldn't surprise me if a bonus had been offered to take out Hawks. We had to keep moving, no matter how exhausted. Couldn't chance getting caught out in the open, clothes covered in evidence.

We limped down Redcliffe Quay, followed a pathway that took us back into the heart of Heritage Quay, searched until we found the public toilets. I stood guard as she washed her face and cleaned up the best she could. Then she stood guard while I did the same. My left arm wouldn't cooperate, the pain back. I popped more pills, antibiotics and Benadryl we had stolen. Didn't want drugs in my system, but didn't have much of a choice, not with the jellyfish sting. Not with the chance of infection. If I ended up in the same condition I was in when I had flown that Cessna from Alabama to Georgia, I would be no good to anybody. With sunup we had a new enemy. Heat assaulted me, beat me down like I was an unworthy opponent, made me sweat and kept me dehydrated, kept me light-headed, drained what energy hadn't been drained by the blood loss and battle at Jumby Bay. A roadside vendor was out selling home-cooked food and beverages, the back of her van crowded with early morning customers. I stood in the crowd, my body starved, still thirsty, tried to keep my balance, and when it was my turn the vendor looked at me. I ordered two sandwiches. The bruises on my face, Hawks's injuries, the crowd took them all in as the woman made the food. The first sandwich was ling fish with eggplant, spinach, okra, and sweet plantain. The other was bread and salt fish, eggs, crushed eggplant, lettuce, cucumber, tomato.

Hawks bit both, kept the one with the sweet plantain.

We sat down long enough to eat and sip water, then we limped over to Market Street, bought more clothes, dry backpacks, wide-lensed sunglasses, and nondescript baseball caps, then hurried inside a hardware store, picked up over-the-counter weapons. We had guns but the guns had only so many bullets before they became useless.

I called Konstantin. He was on the way down. He was glad to hear my voice.

He asked, "What happened?"

"Hell broke loose."

"You in a safe place?"

"We're safe enough."

He told me he was on the way to the islands.

I said, "I'm about to try to get to the airport."

"Getting yourself killed won't do anybody any good."

"Same for you."

"Just do this one thing for me. Sit tight for a little while."

I took a breath. "Okay."

"Go to the Anchorage Inn."

"Not going anywhere I might end up boxed up in a room."

"You're injured."

"Nothing I can't handle."

"Just don't go near the airport. That would be a death trap."

I didn't argue. Just hoped I lived to see him again.

Hawks followed me and we went inside Ceco Pharmacy on High Street. We came across a pair of crutches for Hawks. Then we went into Digicel, Hawks on lookout while I bought a phone. I still wanted to drop Hawks off at Holberton Hospital, but she still refused to go unless I was planning to do the same. I couldn't go. I repeated that one look at the gunshot wound in my arm would have them calling the police. We had left more bodies in the sand than were buried on Cemetery Road.

We argued over that as we hobbled. The island's heat was a growling beast.

Just like Detroit. This heat was her breath on my neck.

We spied the road, looked at the faces in cars that passed, both of us on edge.

Hawks said, "Where we going?"

"Time to get off the streets."

"They have Starbucks?"

"Afraid not."

"Find a place where we can change and get some air-conditioning."

I nodded.

She said, "What's that all about?"

I looked down the road and saw a group of people coming our way, all in red shirts.

Hawks asked, "That a gang?"

"Political party."

"Got worried. Thought it was the Bloods for a minute."

"Antigua Labour Party protesting the United Progressive Party."

"They get up early to start a ruckus."

"I would rather deal with this one than the one we had last night."

Protesters held signs, marched up the center of the road, the heart of town.

CRIMINALS RAPING OUR WOMEN
AND SPENCER RAPING OUR COUNTRY.

UNDER UPP EVERYTHING RISING;
TAXES, UTILITIES, CRIME.

WET YOUR HAND AND WAIT FOR ME.

Hawks pointed at the last sign as it passed by, asked, "What does that mean?"

"It's from a song. An old calypso from King Obstinate."

"Uh-huh."

"Means always be prepared because I'm going to come at you at some point. In the song, from what I remember, two women were cursing, one told the other, 'Wet your hand and wait for me.'"

"Retribution."

I nodded. "Lot of that going around."

We mixed in with the political parade, used it as a shield, and made it to the KFC across the street. Again we took turns, went to the bathrooms, separated and tended to our wounds again, changed and dumped our damp, sandy, and torn clothes in the eatery's rubbish.

We took a table where we could rest with guns in our laps, found a spot where we saw anyone who came inside before they saw us. Another crowd headed up the road. The second wave of red shirts. Different signs with basically the same messages we had seen before.

By then the news media had pulled up the narrow street, cameras being set up, people being interviewed. A few police officers arrived, stood to the side, made sure nothing got out of control.

Police officers. Media. Witnesses. That made this the safest spot on the island.

Hawks said, "So they don't have Republicans down here?"

"Nope."

"Must be nice."

"No Democrats either."

"Well, the world ain't perfect."

Hawks groaned, moved like her pain was equal to mine.

In the middle of grimaces and grunts, I called Catherine and the kid.

The phone rang. Nobody answered.

I called Alvin White. On the second ring he picked up.

He said, "I didn't answer because I didn't recognize this number, area code 268."

I said, "Where are you?"

"Powder Springs. I tried to call you all night. The number you gave me, called it all night."

"Shit. iPhone died."

"You okay? You sounding sick."

"I've been calling you since yesterday afternoon."

"Well, my phone was on silent. Sorry about that. Was busy looking out and didn't want to get distracted by my wife calling. Well, to tell the truth, got tied up with Bunny for a little while, then—"

"Bunny?"

"Girl that work for Mr. Kagamaster."

"The young girl with the big mouth."

"She might be young in years, but she ain't young in all ways. She kept me company for a while."

"This is important." I rubbed my eyes. "See any trouble in Powder Springs?"

"Was some. Another reason I didn't have time to be on the phone."

"What happened?"

"Some people came by."

"The woman and the kid, they okay?"

"Ain't seen them."

"I need you to knock on the door."

"The people who came by, they were spying on the house, tried to break in."

"What happened?"

"I think you need to get back here."

"I'm not in America right now."

"I really need you to get back here as soon as you can."

"There was trouble."

"Some."

"Did you handle it?"

"We don't need to get into that kinda conversation over the phone."

I shifted, grunted, got comfortable, ready for bad news. "What happened?"

"Can't say certain things about certain situations over the phone."

"You haven't seen the woman and the kid at all?"

"Not at all. There was a situation."

"How bad?"

"Bad enough for me to have to go inside my trunk."

"Go to the door."

"I went up two or three times. There was a FedEx package."

"That's mine." What had been urgent didn't seem as important now. "Something for me."

"Kinda figured it would be."

"Where is that package?"

"I got that with me. Did like you told me and picked it up as soon as they left it."

"Was it opened?"

"Wasn't opened."

"Go back to the door." I took a hard breath. "If nobody answers, break into the house."

"Around back?"

"Around back. Look in the windows. See what you can see before you do."

"What you think I might see?"

"See if anybody is in the house."

"There is a car in the garage. I saw that when I tiptoed and looked in."

"What kind of car?"

"One of those little bitty ones."

Catherine's car was in the garage. No answer at the door.

My insides dropped.

I knew the house being locked from the inside meant nothing, not in my trade.

That was when I looked up, looked toward Hawks, expected her to be watching me.

Hawks was distracted, her face painted with a deep frown.

She touched my shoulder and pointed up.

That was when I saw my enemy. I looked up and saw my problem from Detroit.

The woman who wanted me dead smiled in my face.

Thirty-five

the manipulator

She fled Long Island, strawberry blonde braids caked with white sand, clothes soaked with salty seawater. Her blouse torn, practically ripped away in the fight. Skin bruised. Her face scratched.

She trembled, rode from the island in terror. Whispered Matthew's name over and over.

Matthew, now the name of a dead man, a name that put more tears in her eyes than stars on a clear night. This night no longer clear. Rain. Wind. The waves steady and powerful.

The waters that had been so affable were now filled with wickedness and anger.

As if the waves had been possessed by the devil himself.

Discombobulated. Wounded from fighting a madman. In shock. Grief-stricken.

She was a widow. A widow in severe pain. A widow who ached like she was about to join her dead husband. The life inside her refused to let go of her, refused to leave without a battle. A stubborn sentient being refusing to go away without erasing her in the process.

Ten minutes ago she had almost been killed. Gideon tried to slay her. Almost succeeded. He had killed her husband and tried to destroy her as wicked pills tried to terminate what grew inside of her. An unborn child as stubborn as its mother.

White pants soiled, blood between her legs spreading, moving with gravity. She could hardly shift, the aching so bottomless, the contractions in her gut deepening with every passing second.

Then.

Something fell from the sky and hit the dinghy, opened a hole in the rubber.

The dinghy was sinking. The floating balloon lost air, gained water. Then.

Another hole opened in the rubber craft.

Panic rose. Her husband was dead, his head caved in, the man she loved no longer recognizable. El Matador no more. She did her best to look back, see if she was being chased, afraid that she'd see Matthew's crushed head. Saw the silhouette of a man on the shores. Gideon. He was shooting at her. Another bullet fell from the sky and punctured the dinghy, its impact like an explosion. She didn't see the bullet, impossible to hear it fall, just realized the dinghy had opened up in a new spot.

Winds were strong. Rain came down hard. The dinghy, losing air fast.

She crawled, put her hand over one of the holes, did her best to steer the craft and stay afloat.

There wasn't enough air in the craft to try an evasive maneuver, not enough to zigzag.

She had to travel the shortest distance between two points, had to go in a straight line.

The sinking dinghy hit a wave and she slipped, was thrown, lost her balance, almost flipped into the Caribbean Sea. She wasn't strong enough to struggle, unable to scream, a rag doll being tossed overboard, but another wave knocked her back inside the dinghy, flat on her backside.

Ahead of her, lights from the people they had left at the shore.

The woman who financed this horrific mission and the bodyguards she kept at her side.

Salty seawater and sand draining from her strawberry blond hair, she kept the dinghy going in a straight line, had to make it back to the dock. She needed to get to the hospital, give them a phony name, be up-front and tell the nurse or the doctor or whoever the fuck showed up that she had taken an abortion pill, had taken ecstasy the day before, didn't know if there was enough E and marijuana left in her system for the drugs to mix, throw them cash, and get rushed to be seen by a doctor, get painkillers.

The hospital. There was only one. On the other side of the island.

The other side of the island might as well have been on the far side of the moon.

The roughness of the waters had added to her swelling sickness on the way over.

Now.

The Caribbean Sea did the same damage ten times over as she fled.

The E she had taken, angry at herself for taking the E, realized she had no idea where it had come from, had no idea where the boy from Swetes had picked up the drugs. Maybe her dead lover had given her some bad shit, had done to her what she had done to him, sex for sex, death for death.

The morning-after pill, she wondered if it was a *true* morning-after pill or just some poison, maybe a devout Christian had poisoned her and did to her what she was trying to do to her unborn child.

Matthew.

This had to be Matthew's arrogant spirit refusing to leave this world without her.

'Til death do us part.

She held her head over the side of the deflating piece of rubber, regurgitating, dry-heaving, suffocating, nothing came up, just gagged.

She was covered in seawater. Sand. Bleeding. Decorated in her own vomit.

Rain came down hard, the heavens trying to drown her.

Like the child inside her belly, she was dying.

Like the dinghy she was in, she was sinking.

She had to swim or drown.

Blahniks in hand, she crawled out of the Caribbean Sea like a baby leaving a womb.

Not crying, unable to scream, struggling for air. Struggling to stay alive.

Little fish were stuck to her skin, fish shorter than her baby finger.

The two men with the Lady from Detroit saw her, her dinghy almost making it to the dock before it was submerged in water. She called out for help. Called out in the rain. Called out against the sound of the waves. One of the men held on to his hat and ran to the edge of the water to help her, didn't come all the way in, did that like he didn't want to get his designer clothes wet. She was drowning and a man was worried about his wardrobe. She gagged and looked at the man. Capas hat. His face was filled with disgust at what he saw.

She made it to the parking lot, the ground rough under her feet as the bodyguard pulled her to shore. She dropped her Blahniks, put a foot inside each one, caught her breath, adjusted to being back on firm ground, looked back toward Long Island, saw no one following, limped toward the parked cars.

Detroit was there, waiting, large purse on her shoulder, the second bodyguard holding an umbrella over her head. Chic hat on his head, a nine-millimeter in his other hand. The politician looked anxious, angry, terrified. Her hair, dark and shoulder-length, parted on the left side, was dry, not covered in rainwater, not soaked in seawater, not caked with white sand. Unsoiled and unspoiled.

The Lady from Detroit hurried toward her and asked, "Is it done?"

Blouse damn near ripped away. Her skin black and blue.

She faced the woman who had no respect for her existence, the woman who saw her as the weak link. The bodyguard next to the Lady from Detroit held a nine-millimeter in his hand, pointed at the ground. The other, the one who had helped her out of the sea, he held the same type of gun, an SR9.

Two SR9s. Seventeen plus one times two. Thirty-six shots between them. No choice.

She looked at the Lady from Detroit, cringed, panted, answered the question: "It's done."

"Gideon is dead."

She nodded. "Gideon is dead."

"Where is his body?"

She motioned. "Back there. On the beach."

"Why didn't you bring me his body?"

She grimaced. "Do I look like I'm in the condition to carry around a dead man?"

Her eyes went to the shoes on the politician's feet. The Bottega Veneta shoes. A different pair. She had changed shoes since they were at the Sticky Wicket. While people were dying, she had been changing shoes, like she was Patti LaBelle between songs, this night her concert.

The Lady from Detroit turned toward her, yelled, "I need to see his body!"

"We need to get away from here!" she yelled back, energy low, pain high. "Before the ferry comes back. If the ferry comes back you'll have to take out whoever is on the ferry, workers and civilians. The damage has been done. The target is dead. Let's leave before we get careless and sloppy."

The Lady from Detroit frowned out into the darkness, toward Long Island, paced the edges of the jetty as if getting two feet closer would give her a better view of what hostilities had happened over a mile away, moved back and forth, an umbrella-and-gun-carrying bodyguard moving back and forth with her, doing his best to keep her dry; he didn't do a good job. The politician's posh heels clicked and clacked across the concrete and wood, then she paused, stood in profile, stood akimbo, her hands on her hips as if she had super-vision. Pain in the core of her being, she frowned up at the politician, saw the way she looked into the blackness, wrath and panic in her face. She stared into the wind and rain.

When the politician turned and walked back toward her, she saw unadulterated anger and fear.

The politician shook her head, angst and fury unbridled. "I have to see that son of a bitch dead."

"Matthew stabbed him. But he got to Matthew and killed him."

The fury washed away, replaced by disbelief. "Matthew is dead?"

She nodded. "Then I shot Gideon."

"Where?"

"Twice in the head. On the beach."

The politician paused, her eyes wide. "Matthew failed."

"But I didn't."

"You're one hundred percent sure he's dead."

"Two bullets in the head. The rest of my clip unloaded in his body. Seventeen plus one."

The Lady from Detroit whispered, "And you are sure . . . Matthew is dead as well?"

"He's gone. My husband is gone."

The politician swallowed. "How?"

"Just told you. Gideon killed him."

"I mean . . . how?"

"He's dead. That's all you need to know."

"The others?"

"They won't be coming back."

"All of them are dead?"

"All of them."

"You are the only one who made it out alive."

"I'm the only one."

"Impossible."

"Get me to a doctor."

Detroit didn't move from where she stood. "The woman with Gideon?"

Pain hit her. She panted. Cringed. "She's dead."

"Who killed her?"

"One of your men."

"Who was she?"

"I have no idea."

"Where did she come from?"

"I don't know."

"Was she on the plane or already here?"

"Didn't I just fucking say that I didn't know?"

"You're sure they're dead."

"I need to get to a hospital."

"You're wounded."

"Are you listening to me? This is done. It's over. I need to get to an emergency room."

"Where are you wounded?"

"I'm bleeding between my goddamn legs."

"Why? Why are you bleeding?"

"Don't worry about it." Pain hit her again. "*Get me to a fucking doctor.*"

"I'll take you to a doctor I know at Devil's Bridge. A friend at a resort, the Veranda."

"Take me now. I've lost a lot of blood."

"After confirmation."

"I just confirmed the kill. *So get me to Devil's Bridge.*"

The politician shook her head in disagreement. "After I see Gideon's dead body."

"There is only one way to see his body. Wait. You're going back over there?"

"We're going."

"Don't you see me bleeding to death? I can't handle another ride across those waves."

"All of us are going. I want to see his head hanging from its neck. I want to cut his nuts off."

Agony growing, she shook her head, snapped, "I need a medic. I need a fucking medic *now*."

"We see Gideon first. Then we get you medical attention."

"No."

"You don't have a choice."

Detroit stared at her, the cold-blooded eyes of a wayward politician locked on the eyes of an assassin. An assassin in pain, without weapons. An assassin who'd just seen her husband slaughtered.

She fought her pain, said, "Gideon is dead."

The politician nodded and said, her voice cracking, "Then we should have nothing to worry about."

"The authorities. Going back to the scene of a crime, only a fool would do that."

"It will take them a while. We have time. After confirmation, we get you a medic."

She struggled to breathe.

The politician was unfazed. "I see his body; you get the rest of the money I owe Matthew."

"I don't care about the money. You see me bleeding? I'm injured. I'm seasick."

"It's a ten-minute trip to get there. You show me Gideon, we come back. Twenty-minute trip."

"What kind of fool are you? You're going back to the crime scene."

"Because you failed to deliver what I asked and paid for. Gideon's dead body."

"I'm not a mortician."

"No, but if Gideon isn't dead, you will be a corpse."

Her eyes went to the politician, to the lunacy and determination in her eyes.

Then she looked at the politician's bodyguards.

Two guns were pointed at her, the two bodyguards with nine-millimeters in their hands. Men with unfriendly faces. She shivered and stood at point-blank range in front of men who were armed and dangerous. Faced a woman who wouldn't stop at anything to see Gideon dead.

She growled, damn near yelled, "I'm not going back to a fucking crime scene."

"*We're going back*. My children have to be safe."

"*The man is dead.*"

The politician shouted, her voice trembling, "*I want to see his head hanging from his neck!*"

Wounded, she struggled to breathe, shook her head. "I'm going to the hospital."

"*We're* going back, bitch. I paid a lot of fucking money and *we're going back.*"

A big hand grabbed the assassin's arm, pulled her toward another dinghy. She stumbled; her left shoe came off. The big man never let her go as he picked up the shoe and handed it to her. She held her Blahnik in her hand, hobbled with one shoe on, one shoe off.

She snapped at the politician, "Whatever you say. Bitch."

"Matthew said you were slipping."

"He told me a few things about you as well."

The politician's voice cracked. "He's dead."

"You're going back to the island, in this rain, after a shoot-out, to see Gideon or Matthew?"

"While we were here last week, Matthew said you were a fuckup."

"My husband wasn't here last week."

"Oh, he was here."

"He was in South America, then he went back to North America."

"No. He was . . . meeting with me."

"Meeting with you."

"Stupid bitch."

"He said he used to fuck you when you were married. Before you had your husband killed."

"Is that what he said? That he *used to* fuck me?"

"Was my husband . . . was Matthew with you last night?"

"I don't want to see Matthew. Not dead. But I do need to see Gideon's body."

"Why was my husband here *meeting* with you?"

"I need to see Gideon's body. I want the devil decapitated."

"How long had you been fucking my husband?"

The politician's voice cracked again, sounded like tears. "Shut her up."

"How long?"

"Shut that incompetent bitch up."

A large hand smacked her face, stunned her, bloodied her mouth. A light show went off inside her head, reds and yellows surrounded by an electrical storm. The light show gave way to the darkness of the ocean. Her face felt numb from the blow. The numbness faded and the sting spread from her lips to her neck. She stumbled, fight or flight became flight, but a big hand grabbed her and yanked her up from her fall. Again she dropped her desecrated Blahnik. She tried to pull away from the abusive bodyguard, a bodyguard who was arrogant now that Matthew was dead. She reached for her fallen Blahnik. Burgundy and topaz patent leather damaged by seawater and sand. Crisscross vamp broken when she had struggled with Gideon. Stiletto covered with grit and sand. Unable to grab her possession by its four-inch heel, that bend magnified her misery. Again she stumbled, gravity pulled her toward the concrete. The bodyguard grabbed her, shook her like she was a rag doll, shook her hard enough to rattle her brain and give her shaken baby syndrome, then manhandled her, forced her to face Detroit.

She tried to spit on her employer, her bloody spew getting lost in the pouring rain, not making it to its target.

"*You fucking whore.* You fucked my husband when you were married. And you fucked him while he was married. You're nothing more than a whore in a nice dress. *You fucking embezzling coward.* Hiding and running from the man who has you pissing in your panties. *You are the incompetent one.* You are the incompetent bitch. You had to get your husband killed so you could get some fucking attention."

The Lady from Detroit faced her, tears in her eyes. Grieving for another woman's husband.

"Shut up, shut up, shut up."

"Living in a city that used to be great but now ain't shit. What have you done to make it better? Nothing. You're part of the problem. More people are leaving than moving in. Because of corrupt motherfuckers like you. Stealing taxpayers' money is the same as stealing jobs from the people. Embezzling, then smiling on television and ripping the fucking city off every chance you get."

Detroit slapped her, growled and hit her hard, again in the mouth, hit her over and over.

She yelled, "You have spent how much, have tried how long to kill Gideon?"

"Shut your goddamn mouth."

"You fucking incompetent embezzling corrupt hypocritical cocksucking whore."

The Lady from Detroit lashed out, hit her over and over, each smack harder than the one before.

She cringed, took every hysterical blow the politician had to give, unable to strike back because the guard held her hands, unable to kick because of the pain in her gut.

The Lady from Detroit had attacked her face, clawed her, made her less beautiful.

Her face was stinging, felt swollen; the scratches ached like ditches had been dug in her face. Then the Lady from Detroit walked away, cringing and holding her hand like it was in severe pain.

She spat at the politician. "Incompetent embezzling corrupt hypocritical cocksucking whore."

"Keep talking."

"You need me held so you can hit me. You fucking coward."

The Lady from Detroit took the nine-millimeter from her bodyguard.

She smiled at the politician, smiled despite the pain and nausea, the gun pointed at the center of her head. The politician held the gun wrong, almost held it sideways, like in the movies.

She didn't say anything, just waited for the politician to pull the trigger.

She stared in her eyes, saw inside a woman who had paid for death but had never killed before.

She allowed the politician to see inside a woman who had killed many.

She saw the politician's hand tremble. Saw her eyes widen.

She waited for the coward to find her courage.

Her heart raced as she waited for total blackness.

The politician handed the gun back to the bodyguard, panting, her chest swollen with anger.

She growled at the politician. "Incompetent embezzling hypocritical cocksucking coward."

"You want to know who is incompetent?"

"Cocksucking bitch."

"Matthew came to see me. While you slept alone he was with me. He told me you were incompetent. That you couldn't be trusted, not as a wife. He was going to put you in therapy here. Crossroads. *My suggestion.* He tell you that? If you made it through this contract alive. You surprised him. You surprised me. We expected you to get killed before this was over. Didn't expect this."

"Don't put that lie on my dead husband."

"Be real. Do you really think he went to Barbados? Do you?"

"Don't you dare lie about my husband."

"If he's dead, then he's dead because of you."

"You're the one who sent him after the man you were afraid to go after your damn self."

"You were his goddamn partner."

"Fucking coward."

"You were the worst decision he ever made. That's what he told me. You were his one regret."

"You fucking bitch."

"From the mouth of an incompetent cunt."

"What did you call me?"

"A *cunt.* An incompetent *cunt.*"

She screamed at the politician. And as she did a wave of nausea hit, she vomited, gagged, struggled to pull herself together, looked up and saw her employer frowning down on her.

Again her Blahnik was picked up and shoved back inside her hand, a shove that almost knocked her over. The big hands gripped her shoulders, her body being yanked, forced toward the dinghy.

The Lady from Detroit shook her head and said, "You fucked up in London. This could've been over with. And you expect to get paid more money. To get rewarded for incompetence."

"I. Don't. Care. About. The. Money."

"Bitch, please.

Now she was a prisoner. They would kill her, leave her on Long Island, next to Matthew.

If they took her that far. If they didn't throw her into the sea halfway between the islands.

She held her damaged Blahnik to her chest; the men overpowered her, led her to the dinghy.

Unbearable pain clutching her gut. Nauseated. Head aching. Barely able to stand.

Her blurry eyes on their weapons. Seventeen plus one times two.

Weapons they held close to them at all times.

Fear. She was the epitome of fear. This trip her sojourn to death row.

A bodyguard stepped down into the dinghy, reached back for the Lady from Detroit.

The politician stared at the dinghy, paused as if she were terrified to get on board, as if she wondered if Gideon was really dead, the look back exposing a new level of fear, a new level of doubt. Then she took the bodyguard's hand, stepped down into a floating inner tube.

That was when she noticed that the bodyguard who was assisting the politician was trembling too, afraid to go to Long Island. Afraid because that had been a one-way trip for his coworkers.

Doubt was in his face. He wasn't sure the boogey man was dead either.

She spat out more blood. Her face ached, the raindrops making her wounds sing.

They were going to kill her on that island. She would die on the white sands of Antigua.

Then the bodyguard leading her pointed out toward Long Island, beyond Jumby Bay.

Startled, he pointed out into the rain, uttered one terrifying word. "Fire."

Everyone looked toward Long Island, startled, mouths wide open.

The beautiful flames from a luxurious vacation home barely visible, but luminous.

A fire had been started. A fire that obviously had been ignited *after* she had fled.

A fire that couldn't be blamed on Mrs. O'Leary's cow.

Something else was seen in the distance, in the glow, moving out over the rough waves.

Another dinghy was leaving Long Island, the dark shores of hell.

A dinghy fled what looked like a swelling conflagration, moved toward Antigua, sped away from the fire, didn't come toward them, moved in another direction, toward another dock that was unseen.

Panic rose, her chest tightened, her heart beat loud and strong, drowned out all sounds.

Those were the flames of the truth. They knew someone had been left alive.

She knew that was the moment they knew Gideon wasn't dead.

Thirty-six

murder and betrayal

Blahniks.

One damaged work of art on her foot. One damaged masterpiece in her hand.

She felt as if she were dying, flooded with hormones, frightened, heartbeat so fast she knew that she was about to have a heart attack, about to pass out, faint, nauseous, everything flashing.

She looked down at what was in her hand. It was no longer a Blahnik. It was her last hope. She sucked in the pain, grunted.

She gripped her Blahnik, pulled it back, swung hard, did that with all the strength she had.

The bodyguard was turning, about to reach and grab her.

But it was too late.

She swung the Blahnik and the four-inch stiletto heel led the way, like a knife.

The four-inch stiletto went directly into the bodyguard's eye, sank deep.

Like a blade going into a ripe plum or sinking inside a ripe grapefruit.

She hit him hard enough for the stiletto to come to rest in the back of his cranium.

The bodyguard roared, set free a scream the sounded like it had come from the basement of hell.

Driven by the pain, the bodyguard reached for his face.

He reached for his face with a nine-millimeter in his hand.

His fingers bending to grab the pain in his face.

His gun discharged. Shot himself in the head before he reached the Blahnik.

He shot himself in the head, blew his hat into the air, and silenced his own screams.

The bullet found a new home above his wounded eye, his head opened like a trapdoor.

Small hole in the front of his head. Big hole in the back.

Instant death.

His huge body collapsed, started to fall forward, his momentum taking him toward the dinghy.

The female assassin grabbed the bodyguard's arm, struggled with the dead weight, held on to his muscular arm and pulled hard, grunted and struggled to get the body to fall backward, land on the dock.

The Lady from Detroit screamed. The other bodyguard aimed his nine-millimeter.

He began shooting. Shooting and missing.

Four shots. Four near hits. Four misses. Seventeen plus one now down to thirteen plus one.

He had fourteen more bullets. Fourteen more chances.

Rain fell hard and the wind blew, clouds overhead blocking stars and moon.

The bodyguard struggled to find his balance in the rocking dinghy.

The Lady from Detroit ducked inside the dinghy, screamed into the rain, terrified.

So close to death right now.

The politician had a gunman.

And she had no one.

Like it had been most of her life.

Just her against the world.

She fell down on the rugged landing, dropped next to the dead man, a man who had a hole in his head and a stiletto heel in one of his eyes. The concrete scratched her, opened a wound on her skin, hurt her elbow, her right elbow, the elbow on her shooting hand. Her elbow smashed into the concrete and made her want to howl, made her want to grab her arm and hold it, rock until the pain went away. But she didn't have time for that. There was no time for recovery. She had been shot three times in the past, that pain always on her mind. Her insides were on fire as she scampered for the gun, as she battled pain and nausea, as she felt blood between her thighs, as she hurried after the smoking gun, a gun that was lodged inside the dead man's hand. The grip of death held it in place, his finger still on the trigger. Bullets hit the dead man. Bullets that were meant for her. Bullets that were too close to finding their target. Three shots from a gun that held seventeen plus one. Eleven shots left in that SR9. Two more shots cried out. Nine shots remained. That dead man rested between her and a promised death.

The bodyguard tried to get out of the dinghy, get back to steady ground for a better shot.

She saw him come her way.

Two more gunshots rang out as she struggled to pry the gun out of the dead man's hand.

Seven bullets left in that nine-millimeter. That was seven too many.

Her heart pumped fast enough to explode in her chest.

Another shot.

Six chances to send her on the express train to hell left inside his gun.

Heard him stepping back up on the landing.

The motor on the dinghy, she heard it try to start. The Lady from Detroit was trying to start the engine. While she screamed for the big man with the small gun to *blow her fucking brains out*.

Here.

Now.

Nausea gripped her, forced her to dry-heave again.

Saw him. Coming through the rain. Gun in one hand, pointing at her.

She was on her side, snuggled up to a dead man, that man her shield, closer to him than a bulletproof vest. That same rain falling into her face. Huge drops of water splashing into her eyes. Rain that was washing sand out of her braids, sand that tried to slip inside her eyes and blind her.

The dead man's gun was in her hand.

She fired three times. Her shots missed. Down to fifteen chances to live to see another day.

He fired twice.

Down to four.

She fired once. Fourteen.

He fired twice, one bullet hitting concrete next to her head, his shots getting closer.

She fired once. Thirteen.

He fired twice.

Then he got in range, she saw he had a clear shot, a kill shot, and he fired at her again.

The last shot did nothing but make a click, that sound of emptiness swallowed by the storm.

His gun was empty. Seventeen plus one down to zero.

He reached inside his pocket, reached for a fresh clip.

She didn't expect him to have a refill.

She sat up, gun in right hand, leaned over the dead body, elbow aching, left hand holding the weapon steady. She saw the man with the empty gun staring at her, an *oh shit* expression on his face.

An empty gun in one hand, a full clip in the other.

Being at the business end of a nine-millimeter made him hesitate.

Made him rethink his life in a flash.

Made him focus on what was important.

That look that said *No, I have family, I have kids, I have a mother, bills and taxes to pay,* his begging for sympathy, empathy, life. The three things they didn't give her when she had come out of the water bleeding, wounded, cramping, dying. No sympathy, no empathy. No chance at life.

She fired. Missed. Adjusted for her pain. Fired again.

The second shot created a moon roof in the bodyguard's head. His face remained painted with surprise and terror. Not ready for death. He had things to do. Places to go. People to see.

Not in this lifetime.

The lifeless body fell backward. Dropped into the dinghy. Dropped hard.

There was another urgent scream, the cry for help stolen by the storm.

Her body felt heated. Emotional. Her stomach like someone was blowing a balloon up inside.

That heat traveled upward to her throat.

She closed her eyes and retched, gave in to the nausea, again choking, again gagging.

When she finished she heard the motor on the dinghy struggling to start.

Eleven rounds left. Eleven chances to stay alive. Eleven chances to be free.

Could barely lift the light gun in her hand. Eyes clouded with tears and rain.

She looked toward the parking lot, toward the empty cars and trucks. Each looked like freedom.

But she had to go the other way, toward the sea, toward the dinghy.

She took two uneven steps, stopped, bent with the pain, kicked off her shoe, let her foot move across the rugged concrete. Then the pain returned, a great pain that sent her down on the concrete.

The motor started as she struggled back to her feet, made it to her knees, crawled, scratched up her knees and the palms of her hands, did that until she made it to the edge, to where she could see the Lady from Detroit. The woman who had slept with her husband.

The woman who had insulted her and called her a cunt.

The motor to the dinghy was on. The engine strained. But the dinghy hadn't been untied from the dock. It was anchored, struggled against a rope that wouldn't break. Maybe the Lady from Detroit had expected the bodyguard to be victorious, to kill her seventeen-plus-one times, then return.

His dead body was inside the dinghy, had dropped and blocked her from getting to the rope.

Detroit looked up at her.

Saw a woman battered and bruised. A woman with a scratched, bloody face.

She looked down at Detroit.

Saw a woman in expensive jewelry and top-shelf clothing, a woman who would be queen.

Detroit stood up. She expected the politician to surrender, to concede, to beg, to apologize.

The Lady from Detroit surprised her.

She raised her right hand and pointed an SR9 at her. She had a goddamn gun. The Lady from Detroit had stashed one of the goddamn guns that had come from the Punjabi girl on her person; maybe the bitch had kept it inside her purse, didn't pull it out until now, didn't show her hand until she had to.

The politician fired the gun without hesitating. Fired as the dinghy struggled against the docks, fired as she struggled to keep her balance. Fired seventeen plus one times.

Missed seventeen plus one times.

The gun was light, but the trigger weight was too much for her to handle. And they were separated by more than point-blank range. At this distance, skill was more important than luck.

The dinghy struggled against the rope, struggled to get free, strained and went nowhere.

The female assassin stared at the politician who held an empty gun like it was an empty threat. A woman who had fucked her husband, had beaten her, then tried to kill her.

She raised her gun. All bullets, no words. All the talking had been done.

The politician scampered, moved like she was about to dive into the sea.

Then she stopped. Came to an abrupt halt like she was trapped.

The reason she had stopped became apparent.

The Lady from Detroit looked down at the water, terrified.

She couldn't swim. The fear of drowning lit up her eyes.

The assassin found strength, stood in the proper firing stance. Feet shoulder-width apart, the elbow of her dominant hand almost completely straight. Aligned the front sight with the rear sight.

Aimed for center mass. Then readjusted for the target she wanted the most.

The first shot hit Detroit in the front of her head. The next two opened a wound in her heart.

She ruptured her beauty. The same way that bitch had tried to claw away hers.

Well-placed shots. Like on a professional job. She was good. Had always been good.

But this wasn't a professional job. Not a contract. This had become personal.

Her gun fired five more times. Crime of passion. A pissed-off woman.

Detroit was stilled. No insults, no treachery came from the dead.

Gun in hand, in pain, she stumbled toward the parking lot, but once again she turned around. She went back to the dinghy, pulled the rope free, let the rubber raft and her cargo head out to sea.

The dinghy went against the waves, rose and fell with each crash.

She mumbled, "Now who's incompetent, cunt?"

As the rubber raft sped out to sea she grimaced, fired her final three shots, each hitting the dinghy. The dinghy would get swallowed by the Caribbean Sea, dragged down by its heavy motor.

Five seconds of agony went by underneath dark skies and rain. Felt like five eternities.

She stood there, panting, aching, made sure they were dead. No one came out of the water.

She wanted no errors. Not like the man who had followed her down Rhodes Lane.

The dinghy vanished into the Caribbean Sea, a buffet for the bottom-feeders.

The Lady from Detroit didn't leap out of the waters like a creature in a horror film.

Didn't rise up and come after her like the man had done at All Saints Road.

Still.

She waited, smoking gun in one hand.

Made sure she wasn't slipping. Wasn't incompetent.

Off in the distance she saw lights, the ferry leaving Jumby Bay, ten minutes away.

The fire at Long Island, it radiated a beautiful, hypnotic glow.

The fire at the luxurious home would be seen by whoever was on the ferry.

She had ten minutes to get away, ten minutes before she'd have more collateral damage.

But.

The gun was empty. She'd become angry, used every bullet.

The weapon was useless.

The gun in her hand, she tossed it into the Caribbean Sea.

She bent over and picked up her Blahnik, the other one inside the eye of the bodyguard.

She pulled that stiletto out of its resting place.

Never leave evidence behind.

Never abandon a wounded Blahnik.

Another wave of nausea surged, attacked her hard, came fast.

Took her to the ground.

She dropped her Blahniks.

More nausea as the rain tried to drown her as she stood on land.

She was being attacked by the skies.

And she was being assaulted from the inside, from the womb.

This attack, the final battle.

A battle she knew she couldn't win.

Darkness covered her.

Consciousness faded as the ferry came closer.

Thirty-seven
beyond justice

My enemy was on television, a small thirteen-inch number, her image in black and white.

My stomach tried to eat itself up from the inside, her image disrupting my digestive system.

I'd been obsessed, watched the same news over and over, never leaving the television.

She had been on the news all day. Today she had been *the* news. Since early morning when Hawks and I were in St. John's hiding out at KFC. When I'd looked up and seen her on the small television screen. First her photograph had appeared next to a news reporter. That was followed by footage of her in the world of politics and religion. Picture of her with her kids. Picture of her with her late husband. People being interviewed followed those images. People who had tears in their eyes. I'd sat there with Hawks, no sound on the television, tried to figure out what the fuck was going on.

Below those images were what was the most important.

The date she was born. And today. The day she had died.

The next morning.

The Daily Observer had black-and-white photos, the story on its front page. Had pictures of her body being fished out of the Caribbean Sea. So did the *Antigua Sun*. Their photos in color, pictures of Detroit. More photos of people on the dock behind the Beachcomber Hotel.

The papers said she had died a horrible death, multiple gunshot wounds, body dumped at sea. The same fate had befallen her army of nameless bodyguards.

The news that she had come to her homeland to attend a friend's wedding at Holy Family Cathedral Church. On the eve of the wedding, she and her employees had been robbed at gunpoint, kidnapped, taken down to the docks behind the Beachcomber Hotel. They were killed by gunfire.

There was no mention of Jumby Bay. No talk of dead bodies. No talk of the fire.

I doubted if Jumby Bay wanted to have a reputation that would keep them from moving two-million-dollar properties. It was news. They fed the people the news they wanted printed. I didn't trust any of those articles. I got online and went to Wikipedia.com. Checked to see if they had taken down the information they had posted about my enemy's death. They had been wrong before. They'd killed off the comedian Sinbad and Sinbad was still aboveground telling jokes. Photos of my death in London had been sent out before, photos from a death that didn't stick. Anything was possible. Her page on Wikipedia hadn't changed. Said my enemy's body had been found in the early morning hours in Antigua, not clear if it was a robbery gone badly or an assassination of one of the key political figures in the Midwest.

She was dead on Wikipedia. But that didn't mean shit.

Anybody could post lies and bullshit out there.

Alvin White.

He'd broken into the house in Powder Springs. He went in through the back door, the boot on his foot the key to get it open. Breaking a window would've made the alarm go off. Breaking in the front or back door made the counter kick in, gave him sixty seconds of beeping before the alarm sounded and the phone started ringing. But the alarm didn't go off. I'd given him the code to disable the alarm. Shotgun in hand he walked the house, top to bottom. No one was there. No buckets of blood painting the walls. I had him go to the bedroom, to the closets, then had him go down inside the basement.

Dying for Revenge   413

He told me what he found. What was more important was what he didn't find.

My heart sank so fast it hurt.

He said, "There is a note here."

"What does it say?"

He paused.

I repeated, "What does the note say?"

He hesitated. "I can't say."

"What do you mean you can't say? Say it."

"Well, it's like this. To be honest . . . I can't read too good."

I paused.

"You can't read."

"I never have been able to read too good."

"You're telling me . . . you're telling me you can't read?"

Again he hesitated. "That's what I'm telling you."

I groaned, rubbed my eyes.

I thought back to when I was at the hotel on Metropolitan, when Alvin had come in and Kagamaster, the owner, had put the newspaper in Alvin's face. I remembered how Alvin had shied away from the newspaper when Kagamaster asked him to read the article about Sir Paul McCartney.

He said, "Might as well tell you this now."

"I'm listening."

"Was hoping you'd come back sooner than later. Didn't want to say over the phone."

"What is it, Alvin?"

He told me two people were inside the trunk of his orange taxicab.

Early evening.

We were at the two-level Antiguan house, the one we had passed up before, on Old Parham Road behind the eatery called Vigi's. We were upstairs in the two-story, hiding out. Three men were outside. One man was inside, his attention on Hawks. He was a doctor who had come up from Devil's Bridge. A man who did work off the books, work paid for in cash, British pounds preferred in this market, but the

American dollar accepted. Another man was posted across the street at the *tyre* shop.

The doctor looked like Morgan Freeman. Couldn't help but think that as I paid him, then shook his hand. He left, got in his black Mercedes, and drove off. Traffic on Old Parham Road was backed up but drivers let him in right away. I stayed at the window. Hawks was in the squeaky and worn bed, her foot elevated, doctor's orders. My shift to be on lookout. Her turn to rest and try to sleep a few minutes.

No air conditioner. The place was hot, ceiling fans circulating warm air.

Ten minutes later a taxi pulled up in front of Vigi's. A man wearing white shoes got out. He had on black pants, white shirt and jacket. A man who thought he looked like Archibald Leach, but I thought he looked like an aged George Clooney. It was too hot for the jacket he had on but I knew he had it on to shelter the nine-millimeter hidden underneath. The men he had stationed downstairs waved at him. He nodded his head and moved on. Konstantin had left with a driver and came back in a taxi. I guessed he had sent the driver on an errand. All I knew was he looked like a tourist, sunglasses on and a Nikon camera at his side. He had landed, gotten me and Hawks situated, then gone on an errand while the doctor patched me and Hawks up.

Konstantin hurried up the stairs and came inside.

He asked, "Package I ordered get delivered yet?"

"Not yet."

"Sure you need it?"

"Not going to the airport without it."

"Understood."

I cleared my throat. "Any problem getting into the hospital to see the body?"

Konstantin took off his jacket. "Your problem is officially in the ground."

"Sure it was her?"

"Word on the street was that she took two of her bodyguards with her."

"Just her and two bodyguards were found."

"Detroit and two bodyguards, both men. Both died from lead poisoning."

"No woman with strawberry blond hair."

"Only one woman."

"Her braids made her look Puerto Rican. Color of her hair, could've been Scandinavian."

He shook his head. "Two bodyguards. One on the pier. One in the water. That was all they found at that location. But people on the ferry had seen the bodies. No way to cover it up."

"Makes no sense."

"Not much in life does."

"Show me what you have."

He turned on the Nikon. Showed me the pictures he'd taken. A dozen pictures of Detroit, bullet hole between her eyes. Bullet holes in her chest. Beautiful woman who had died an ugly death. And they had done an autopsy. Didn't matter if there was a hole in her head. He showed me photos of her cut open. Pictures were worth a thousand words. But not one word came from my mouth.

That could've been me. A dead body with no identification, unclaimed and dissected.

Konstantin said, "Satisfied?"

It took me a long while, but I nodded. It was her. My hands trembled. Hate. Fear. Wasn't sure.

Konstantin said, "You didn't get to put a bullet in her head."

"She has two kids. Kids who go to a Christian school."

"You okay with that?"

"Don't have a choice. Have to be okay with that."

"If it would make you feel any better, I can give you my gun with a full clip and arrange for you to get some alone time with her at her next destination. Either Barnes or Straffie's Funeral Home."

"That won't be necessary."

Konstantin asked, "You said another woman was working for her?"

"Strawberry blonde. She was at Jumby. Same one from London. Had braided her hair."

"So she got away."

"If she didn't turn up in the morgue, she's still out there."

"She's probably off the island. Probably took the first flight they had to get out of here."

I asked, "Was the red-haired man in the funeral home?"

"Didn't go through all they had. Just her. In and out. Had to rush. They ship the bodies from there to Holberton for autopsy. And it looked like they have had a busy week down here."

"If Detroit had had it her way, there would've only been one body bag."

Konstantin patted me on the back. "But she didn't have it her way."

"So you don't know if the strawberry blonde was in one of those other bags."

"Only one woman. Was taken to the woman."

"She was injured. The strawberry blonde was injured."

Konstantin asked, "Shot?"

"Looked like a gut shot. She was hurting."

"But she got up and walked away."

I rubbed my eyes, unsure. Was in so much pain last night, could've been delusional.

I said, "If she was shot she would've died before she made it to the hospital."

"Gunshot to her gut."

"She would've bled out before she made it to Holberton."

"But you didn't shoot her?"

"Wasn't me."

"Hawks get to her?"

I shook my head.

"You thinking whoever shot down Detroit and her men shot down the strawberry blonde?"

"Looking for facts. Not much making sense right now."

He pointed at the center of his head. "That was a fact for your problem."

I nodded. "Just need to make sure I don't have another one out there."

"An assassin who would fulfill her obligation even when the issuer had been terminated."

"Some people have a strong code of ethics."

"She wouldn't get the rest of her fee."

"She might not care."

"Like the psycho in *No Country for Old Men*."

I nodded. "The guy had a strong code of ethics."

"So you think Detroit being in the ground might not be the end of it."

"Can't let my guard down. Can't assume that was the epilogue to my situation."

He asked, "What's happening in Powder Springs?"

I took a breath. "It got pretty bad."

"Who covered?"

"Guy working for me. Heavyweight boxer. Think he's good with guns too."

"You get the details from your guy?"

"Will find out when I get back."

I remained uneasy. Living in caution mode. My gut told me this wasn't done. I had a presentiment that something extremely brutal was going to happen, more violence, more tragedy.

Konstantin said, "Catherine and the kid?"

That paused me. Magnified my aches. I said, "They're gone."

"What happened?"

"I happened."

I went to the window and looked down on Old Parham Road. Catherine and the kid weren't at the house. Detroit had sent people to come after them, but they weren't there when the assassins had arrived. Catherine had taken the kid, packed up, taken her passport, taken all the money out of the account I had set up for her, and left the country. I'd gone after the truth and she'd run away. Running away had saved her life. Had saved the kid's life. The reason why she had left, it was still back at Powder Springs.

Her fears were inside a FedEx package. Answers from DNA Solutions. The answer to X. Y. Z.

Konstantin said, "You're strong. Smart. Relentless. Shrewd and cunning. A powerful fighter."

I nodded at his assessment. Still, that wasn't enough.

Hawks came into the front room, foot wrapped, on crutches. Cowboy boots replaced with sandals. Jeans replaced with linen pants. Antigua T-shirt. No bra. Her face was bruised but looked better than it had earlier. The baseball cap and wide lenses on her sunglasses hid most of the damage.

She asked, "How are you feeling?"

"The strawberry blonde. She's out there."

Hawks said, "The game isn't over until the last man is out."

I nodded, stepped away from the tinted window but went right back.

It wouldn't be over until the fat lady sang. And she wasn't singing. I couldn't hear an aria being belted out by a heavyset woman dressed like a valkyrie. This was intermission, not the final curtain.

Left shoulder ached. Had been tended to by the doc from Devil's Bridge. Would take a while to heal. Just like the rest of my body. I wasn't in any shape to fight again, not like that. Could barely move.

Ten minutes later a car pulled up and parked next to Vigi's, close to the bus stop. Two people got out, a male and a female, college students, both in worn shorts and inexpensive sandals, both wearing AUA T-shirts. They laughed as they opened the trunk of their ride, took out a box, and came upstairs.

The girl was Punjabi. Her friend was silent, didn't know if he was European or American.

Konstantin opened the door, his hand behind his back, nine-millimeter in his hand.

With a congenial smile he asked, "Can I help you?"

She smiled. "This heat is a *killer* today."

Konstantin nodded. Her tall companion handed Konstantin the box.

The girl said, "You're Russian."

Konstantin nodded.

He handed the girl an envelope filled with enough money to cover the transaction.

She said, "These sell for five but I'm letting them go for half that. Need the cash. Fees at the university are kicking my butt. And the gas prices. I saw on CNN that back in the States people are stealing gas by drilling into gas tanks. Crazy. You caught me on a good day. Need the fast cash."

I asked, "Did you sell any hardware to a man with red hair?"

She evaluated me and my injuries, my arm in a sling, my aching walk, then she shook her head.

"Revealing my customers, not good for business. Just like if anybody asked me if I sold some merchandise to you, I'd say no. If I see you on the street, I don't know you. That's how I roll."

We stared at each other.

I nodded.

She did the same.

That gunrunner turned around, walked back down the stairs a few dollars richer.

They got inside their old car and made a left on Old Parham Road, blended with traffic going back toward St. John's and Friars Hill Road. Konstantin opened the box, my left arm in a sling and no good. Four SR9s were in the package. Along with eight clips.

The airport was ten minutes away, but we weren't riding naked.

I took two of the nine-millimeters. The light metal feeling heavy in my hands. A small piece of lead had been the end of so many. A small piece of lead had taken down many Goliaths.

Hawks took the other two nines, inspected them, popped the clips in, nodded.

Konstantin was already strapped. He opened his jacket and took out our new fake passports.

He said, "Ready to get the hell out of here?"

"Yeah. I better get you back to the States before your wife gets worried."

"I'm more worried about your condition and state of mind than she is about me."

"I'm good to go."

"You're pacing, tense, fidgety, like you're suffering from PTSD."

"I'm not traumatized. I'm alert. I'm ready."

Konstantin backed off.

He said, "We'll all be at the airport at the same time. We'll sit near each other, but we don't know each other. Different airlines. Sorry about the long layovers, but that's the best I can do."

I stared at Hawks. She looked guilty. She used her crutches and came over to me. Kissed me.

I asked Hawks, "What was that for?"

"Worried about you, that's all."

"I'm not traumatized."

Hawks smiled at me. Tried to get me to smile. I searched deep but couldn't find a smile to give.

I frowned down at the local newspapers, the pictures of Detroit being fished out of the Caribbean Sea. Her death. I had died in London. Hunted down in the Cayman Islands. Ambushed in Huntsville.

Her death was nothing more than a Pyrrhic victory. And a Pyrrhic victory was no victory at all.

I went to the window, looked down on the men who were looking out for us.

I asked, "Why didn't she let it go?"

Konstantin said, "Because for some it's easier to reach a consensus for war than to reach a consensus for peace. Some people are made that way. If she was still alive, what had started between you and her might've lasted longer than the civil war in Colombia. That's been going on four decades."

I searched the Caribbean landscape, that foreboding sensation refusing to wane and let me go.

I should've felt vindicated, but that victorious sensation eluded me.

I had taken out the red-haired man, had done to him what I had wanted to do to the man who had killed me in London. I hadn't taken this war to my enemy. She had outsmarted me, lured me here. It was done. Done in my favor. But I felt so motherfucking hollow. I should've felt good, should've felt relieved, but I felt empty. If I had killed her myself, that same vacant feeling would have consumed me.

Killing never felt good, never felt like a victory.

Even when I killed the man with the red hair, that action was born out of necessity. So I would have to deal with that hollowness. An empty space that was being filled with a different anger, a different fear. Catherine and the kid were gone. That canceled everything out. I sat down for a hot minute, took a few deep breaths. When I looked up Hawks and Konstantin were watching me.

Hawks asked, "What's the problem?"

"I made too many fucking mistakes. Too many blunders."

"What blunders?"

"Almost got you killed."

"I didn't see it as blunders."

"Left you in the house alone."

"You had to hide the dinghy, cover our tracks. Just part of what we do."

Konstantin stepped up, said, "Think about what you did right. You were trapped. You had been outmaneuvered, outnumbered, and outgunned. Yet you managed to flip the script on whoever was attacking you."

"I did things wrong."

"I have done things wrong. You can and will do things wrong. You're an assassin, not James Bond or Jason Bourne. Those motherfuckers have stunt doubles and have never been in a real gun battle in their lives. This was the real world. You're used to being the hunter, not the one being hunted."

I lowered my head, rubbed my eyes, angry at myself.

Konstantin said, "You had no weapons, had to be creative. They had guns and you had bottles of liquor. Look at you. You can barely move. Your injuries are severe. Fighting with elbows and fists, that shit hurts. That's why you should always grab something, or use brass knuckles. The body is a delicate thing, no matter how strong you are."

I didn't say anything.

Hawks came over and hugged me. "You've been shot in the arm. Stung by jellyfish in the same arm. Beaten. Almost drowned. Probably swallowed God knows how much seawater. But you swam back to shore with one arm. Not to mention the blood you lost from being shot. And a groin injury."

Konstantin said, "Groin injuries can sideline the biggest player, take them out of a football game, send a big man out on a stretcher with tears in his eyes. And you're still moving around on yours. The two of you worked like a team. You worked how I taught you to fight. Both of you survived."

I pushed my lips up into an overwrought smile, told them I was ready to get out of there.

I said, "The strawberry blonde."

Hawks said, "Don't worry about her."

"Let me get you out of this country." That was Konstantin. "Time to move."

We took to the stairs. Konstantin went first, then me. Hawks wanted to come down last. Which was fine. I wanted to have her covered. A van with tinted windows waited for us down below.

I doubted we would need the guns, but I wanted them with me, my nine-millimeter pacifiers. Would carry mine until I made it to the airport. Not until then would I give my guns to my escorts, men who would walk with us and stick around while we went to three different counters to check in. Tickets had been bought online, but we still had to go to the counter, checking in still old-fashioned down here, couldn't walk up to a machine and have it spit out an E-ticket like in the U.K. or the States. We'd go up to the counters one by one while our escorts made sure we made it inside the airport without trouble.

Hawks and I had backpacks as well. CDs, credit cards, pens, belts, and pencils inside.

This was my life. This was my world.

Hawks said, "I'm taking the other van."

I looked at the van with darkened windows. A second van was next to that one.

I said, "That wasn't the plan."

Hawks said, "Plans have changed."

Konstantin nodded in agreement. "Don't want all of us in the same van. If they came at us on the road, they wouldn't know which van to hit. And we could have firepower coming from two directions."

I nodded. His strategy seemed flawed, but at the same time it made sense.

Had too much on my mind to debate that issue.

Again, Hawks came over and kissed me.

I said, "See you at the airport."

She nodded. "See you later."

I hopped inside the van with Konstantin, and the driver made a right, jumped into traffic, and headed toward Airport Road. I looked back, saw Hawks getting into the other van. Her arms weren't injured. Both of her shooting hands were 100 percent. She was bruised, but she was functional.

Konstantin had his gun at his side. I rode the same way.

Sleep-deprived. On medication. Groin on fire. Aching to my bone marrow. Mind ablaze. Kept wondering how in the fuck I ended up here. I wondered who in heaven decided I would be the son of a whore and a whore-fucking mercenary. I pondered who I was and how I had come to be.

Maybe this was all I deserved. Maybe I was dead and already in hell.

But I knew. I reminded myself of what I already knew, reminded myself of my faults.

My inability to let things go. My inability to let go of things that I needed to let go.

I had done a job for Detroit a while ago, a job that had almost gone bad because the target had access to a weapon that I didn't know anything about. His profile had painted him as peaceful and passive, a large man who had never lifted a hand to hurt anyone. That target had ended up being more gangster than the Kray brothers, came at me shooting, tried to put me in the ground. He had tried and he had failed. At that moment it had felt like I had been set up to fail. And in that angry moment I had called her, told her there was a penalty, had demanded a fee for not providing me with adequate information. I was angry. I had almost been killed and I was angry. Maybe she was afraid

I would blackmail her. Either way it was a fee that Detroit had paid; then when the time was right, the last time I was in London, she had sent an assassin to track me down. An assassin who had trapped and killed me.

This was my error. My bad judgment had gotten the best of me.

I had died a slow and torturous death in London, but on that menacing day I didn't stay dead.

Someone else had killed my assassin on my behalf. Someone had stolen my victory.

Maybe this was the life I had earned. I had killed my father when I was seven years old. I didn't think about that often, had some sort of dissociative, almost amnesiac state when it came to that moment.

The moment that had defined me. The moment that had created me.

The Grim Reaper had followed me ever since, always with a different face.

Now Death might be an assassin with strawberry blond hair, wearing high heels.

The driver passed by the American counter, did that at a casual speed. I had come full circle, back to the airport; madness and murder had taken root. The gravel parking lot where we had left a few dead bodyguards, no sign of any wrongdoing, business as usual. We spied out the entire route from Airport Road, passed the printing shop, passed the airport once and then the Sticky Wicket, looped back before we parked. No one stood out. No one looked anxious. I stuffed my guns inside a backpack I had brought along. Had the backpack positioned so I could get to the nine if I needed to. Only problem was my left hand was no good, could hit somebody only from point-blank. And my right hand was swollen. Could barely open and close my hands. Konstantin watched me, saw me struggling, but didn't say anything for a few seconds.

He said, "Your hands are swollen."

I nodded.

"Can you pull a trigger on those guns?"

"If I have to."

"But can you hit a target?"

"If I have to."

"Do this." Konstantin opened and closed his hands. "Let me see you do this."

I tried. Barely could.

He said, "I didn't think you could."

"I'm fine. Won't be making any more mistakes."

"Think about who's alive and who's dead. It's not about all the mistakes you make, it's about who makes the *last* mistake. You only fuck up if you make the *last* mistake. And you are the one alive."

"This isn't over."

"I know it's not over. I know."

I looked back, searched for the van that carried Hawks.

Konstantin said, "Don't worry. Hawks is fine."

"There wasn't any traffic. She should be right behind us."

"You have different flights anyway."

I nodded.

"Hurry." Konstantin looked at his watch. "You have just enough time to check in and get on the flight."

"What time is your flight?"

"I have time."

Konstantin stayed in sight but wasn't with me as I waited in line and got my ticket. He did the same as I took out twenty dollars in U.S. money and moved to another line to pay the departure tax. Free to get into the country. Had to pay to leave. Lots of people were out. If trouble was there it was well-hidden. I made it to the door that led to customs, took one last look, searched for that woman with the strawberry blond hair, made sure she wasn't in sight before I handed my backpack to Konstantin.

He said, "Keep your guard up."

I nodded, once again feeling vulnerable, unable to move with any real speed.

He said, "I'm going to check in at Carib and get rid of this hardware."

"Where's Hawks?"

"Her driver pulled into Texaco to get gas."

"Bad move. We should've stopped with them. Easy to get blocked in at a gas station."

"Everything is under control. Relax."

I nodded, then moved on, went inside, past customs and through metal detectors, sat inside with my back to the wall, sat where I could see every face that came in, saw every face that came toward me.

By the time I went to board my flight, Konstantin hadn't made it through security.

I waited, was at the end of the line, the last one, searching for Konstantin. And Hawks.

If something had happened to Hawks on the road, I didn't know.

If Konstantin had gone to help Hawks, or if something had happened to Konstantin outside . . .

I didn't hear gunshots, sirens, or screams. But a silencer created death with a sweet whisper. Done right, a hit could happen in public, the body left sitting, or leaning against a wall, death unnoticed.

I stood up, racked with pain, almost went back, almost hurried out into the mouth of danger.

Unarmed and wounded from head to toe, I was ready to hobble back onto the battlefield.

I stopped my frantic rush to the door, paused, on the verge of a panic attack.

Catherine and the kid. They were on the opposite side of the scale, that scale almost balanced.

I looked back at the gate, heard the announcement being made for final boarding.

Thirty-eight

the dying and the dead

Queen Elizabeth Highway.

Mouth ached, tasted blood from where she had been hit by the bodyguard turned assassin.

In darkness, she drove toward Holberton Hospital. The main hospital on the island of Antigua. She had driven in panic, had sped away from the docks, made it to the car as the ferry arrived, as the people on the ferry pointed at the fire on Jumby Bay, unaware they had run over bodies in the sea. As she started her car, she heard someone yelling in dialect. They had found the dead bodyguard on the docks. She sped into the darkness having visions of her own death, struggled to keep control.

The road going into the hospital was smooth, a few streetlights, enough brilliance to show her that pathology was to the left, admissions, emergency, and everything else to the right, and, when she turned in to a circular driveway, enough light to see no one had followed her.

She struggled to park her damaged rental, wires hanging where a side mirror used to be.

Forever went by before she made it out of the car.

A hotel towel was on the front seat. She wrapped it around her waist, let it hide her mess.

She staggered in cramping, bleeding, the scent of cordite on her sweaty and sandy flesh, expected to walk in and someone would rush to her with a wheelchair, make her top priority and hurry her to a private room, like in the movies, get hooked to an IV. No one rushed to help her.

People sat around on wooden benches and makeshift furniture in a room that had no air-conditioning. Sweaty children huddled in parents' laps. Crying babies. Long, sad faces. Heat exacerbating sickness and anger. Outbursts and accusations of favoritism among the Cuban nurses and the Spanish patients. An ailing woman scowled at her, at her braids, frowned at her as if she thought she were Spanish. A man came in doubled over, moaning that his appendix was about to rupture.

Darkness had become daylight. Hours of pain and suffering. Her body her own hell.

She stood, throat dry, staggered, holding the towel, found water. When she returned her seat had been stolen. All seats had been taken. Forced to stand, leaned against the wall, staring at the citizens.

Mouth ached. Lips felt swollen. Tired of tasting blood.

She wanted to slide to the ground, sit back against the wall, but if she sat down she wouldn't be able to get up, wouldn't be able to move if the man who had slaughtered her husband rushed into the emergency room, guns blazing. There was security, but not the kind of security she wanted to see.

She wanted gun-carrying security like at the airports in Brazil and in Cabo San Lucas.

Then. Finally. When she felt Death was standing next to her. Her turn.

They asked her what she used. Wanted to know why she was bleeding. She told them about the morning-after pill. They wanted to know where she got it from. She just said another tourist gave it to her. Some woman. Name unknown. She asked what was going to happen, scared. They said if they ended up admitting her they would take her blood, if needed, and determine her blood type and blood count. They told her that if she needed a transfusion, she would have to get relatives to come in and donate blood. She told them that she had no relatives. Depending on the situation, they told her they might have to take her to the operating theater to have a D and C, where they scraped out the womb.

Questions. They asked so many questions. Wanted to know who brought her to Holberton.

Her lie. Was late-night skinny dipping, out at Half Moon Bay, had just left her date, was going to the hotel to wash away the water and sand, and that was when the illness came on, that was her story.

She waited. In pain, she waited. Each minute felt like an hour of being kicked in the gut.

In the end they came and took her temperature, checked her heartbeat.

They told her there was nothing to treat. She had to ride it out. She had to bleed until the embryo was gone. They gave her a prescription for the nausea, Phenergan. Aspirin for the pain.

She wanted Vicodin. Percocet. Morphine. For the pain to be surgically removed.

And security.

Her mind was on the battlefield she had escaped.

She was injured. *Gideon* knew she was injured. He had stumbled away from her as she lay terrified in the sand. He was walking. He was mobile. He'd gone inside that section of the compound. Heard sounds. Like he was on a killing rampage. She had willed herself to her feet, saw the horror, Matthew's crushed skull, and fled. Then bullets rained down and destroyed the dinghy as she fled.

The hospital. That would've been the first place Gideon would've looked for her.

Like gang members knew the wounded from the rival gangs had to find medical attention. And they followed blood trails, followed ambulances, swarmed to the hospitals with a vengeance. Gideon had seen her wounded. There was only one hospital here.

Matthew was dead.

The nurses saw her crying. But the nurses thought the tears were because of the pain.

Or because she had chosen not to have a baby.

She wiped her eyes and dealt with it. Foster home kid. Only the weak cried. Only the weak showed emotion. Showing emotion in this world would get you trampled. No respect for the weak.

Death was part of the business.

Death was inevitable. Death, prison, and taxes, the inevitabilities of life and the occupation.

She nodded, took a deep breath, ready to move on before the panic attack returned.

The nurses were kind enough to find her some clothing. An old cotton dress that was clean, folded, had hundreds of wrinkles. Probably a dress someone had worn before she died. They took her to a room, let her clean herself up some and rest. The meds kicked in and the pain lessened. With the pills she had been given, the nausea was controllable. She put on the dress. It was tight, especially around her butt, pink with big flowers from the collar to where it hung below her knees, a cotton dress from two generations back, but it was good enough, considering the circumstances. She sat and groaned as she put on the sullied Blahniks, one with a heel stained with blood, a redness no one had noticed.

She went to a pay phone, tried to call her handler, the one Matthew had used to lure Gideon to this island. Needed his assistance getting off the island. The phone rang and rang and rang.

Her head ached, the pain of dehydration. She had to get out of here.

She stepped out of the hospital at the same moment five vans came up the road. All pulled into the hospital. Vans that contained dead bodies that had been picked up from an overnight melee.

A parade of death in the afternoon sun, passing by people who didn't look twice.

She wondered which van held her husband, a man she would never be able to say good-bye to.

The shortness of breath tried to come back; her heartbeat sped up.

Deep breaths. She took deep breaths. Breathing helped with the pain.

She had to keep moving. Had to erase anything she had that connected her to Matthew.

He had no fingerprints on file; there would be no photo of him on this island.

The Lady from Detroit now rested inside that hospital. She wondered if her husband was already inside there. They would have to bring the bodies from Jumby Bay on a boat, that island a crime scene.

She looked at the white building, its foundation painted a light green.

Fear. Anger.

She had almost ended up inside that place. Along with her husband.

Along with a boy named Anthony Johnson, a boy who had been autopsied and moved on to a funeral home on Newgate, a conversation she had overheard as she lay on a gurney in severe pain.

Anthony Johnson. A boy who had lived in Swetes on Matthew Road.

A lover so wicked he would never be forgotten.

She wished she hadn't killed him.

Sadness.

While she was standing there, an older gentleman had passed by her. A man who could've been British. The older gentleman walked with purpose, in a rush, side by side with two swarthy men, men who looked Antiguan. The older man was handsome, extremely, the face of an aged movie star.

The man passed her, carrying a Nikon camera. He had to be with *The Daily Observer* or the *Antigua Sun*. A professional photographer. Or with the police department, the type of guy who might show up and document a crime scene. Something about that older man had a policeman's edge. That was what she thought. Shoes. Women always noticed a man's shoes. His were not policeman's shoes.

The handsome older man had to be a photographer. A photographer who wore white shoes.

She looked down at his shoes as he looked down at her.

He smiled at her and nodded. She wiped tears from her eyes.

She ignored the old man, figured he was captivated by the way the tight dress clung to her body.

He looked like an older well-to-do man. Classy. Like a man who ate caviar and owned yachts.

Bad day for him to be staring at her.

Real bad day for him to have his eyes on a brand-new widow.

Maybe when she was done grieving. Maybe when it was time to not be alone.

Maybe an older man then. Someone less sexual and more respectful.

Not now, not when she was experiencing two deaths. Matthew. And what was inside her.

Not now.

Not when she was in trouble.

First a deeper sadness.

Then a rising fear. A rush of adrenaline. Once again, in fight-or-flight mode.

Every step of the way, from hospital to parking lot, she paused, searched for Gideon.

She stood next to her rental car, its side-view mirror yanked off, wires hanging.

A long scratch down the side.

Another dent on the driver's side, a crash she'd had when she fled the docks.

None of that mattered as she scanned the parking lot.

If Gideon was smart, he'd be at the airport. On a plane. Where she needed to be.

He would be a fool to stay. Too many dead bodies.

She told herself that she had nothing to worry about as she stood there in a tight dress and a bloodied Blahnik, standing with a scalpel in each hand, scalpels she had stolen from inside the hospital.

The village of Swetes was off All Saints Road, her route back to Antigua Yacht Club. Right before the speed bump at Our Lady of Perpetual Help in the village of Tyrells. Maybe it was seeing the church in the distance. Maybe it was the pain, the cramps. She had to get back to the hotel, had to find out why her handler wasn't answering, but she turned right, went into the villages, the roads in that area not paved like the main roads, that ruggedness not bothering her, a deeper mission on her mind.

She had about six thousand dollars in American money on her. All large bills.

Walking-around money she had brought on the trip with her, just in case. Cash for tickets, cash for rental cars, cash for emergency shopping, cash for everything, no credit cards, no paper trail.

Swetes. A village where everyone knew everyone.

Two girls walked her way, teenagers, jeans, sandals, low-cut sleeveless blouses.

She slowed down the car, dust kicking up, waved for the girls to stop.

The sweaty girls stared at her, both wearing baby powder on their chests, more than likely heading to the bus stop, on their way to town to pay bills for their parents, maybe heading to the market to buy food. They stopped, stared at the face of a stranger, a snowy-faced tourist.

Both girls said, "Hello, good day."

"Anthony Johnson, the boy who was killed on the beach, can you take me to his house?"

The girls nodded at the same time. Both came to the car and got in the backseat.

They lived where they helped people they knew and helped people they didn't know.

One of the girls pointed up the road. She drove that way, turned where the girl said turn, stopped in front of a yellow and red house. It wasn't Jumby Bay. Or Hodges Bay. Or that area with the golf courses. The opposite of all of that. Small home. Situated on cinder blocks. Big black thing that collected water on the side. Maybe four rooms, bedrooms included. Where Anthony Johnson had lived.

She reached into the glove compartment, found an envelope, stuffed the money inside.

Six thousand American dollars. Somewhere between fifteen and sixteen thousand E.C.

She told the girls, "Take this envelope. Tell his family I heard about the boy being killed. I was at the hospital just now and heard about it. Had actually gone to the benefit they had for Anthony Johnson at Abracadabra. Saw the flyer there. Wanted to help. Some. Tell them . . . tell the boy's wife . . . tell her that I lost my . . . that my husband died not too long ago. I'm a widow . . . like her. And I wanted to help."

One of the girls said, "A we brother."

"Your brother?"

The other girl said, "That's our brother."

"He was your brother?"

Both girls nodded.

She stammered; that response created unexpected, exponential sadness. "How is his wife?"

"She was pregnant. Three months. Baby die when she heard the news."

"How old is she?"

"She seventeen."

Tears sprang up in everyone's eyes. Antigua. Small island. One big family.

She handed the girls the envelope. Told them to take that to Anthony's wife.

When the girls went inside the home, she drove away wrapped in tears, guilt, and sadness.

She drove to the airport. Still in pain, the ache not as deep, no longer debilitating.

Parked in the roundabout where she could spy on the terminal, almost in front of the Sticky Wicket. Made it there just in time. Gideon. She saw him. He was alone. In line at the American counter, limping, backpack on his arm. She watched him limp to the front of the line and get his ticket. Then he vanished, went to the other side of the wall where people went to pay the departure tax. When he reappeared he didn't have his backpack. It had vanished. Maybe he had checked the bag and she had missed that part, the distance at least fifty yards. What was important was he limped inside the terminal.

She waited.

Gideon had gone to the American Airlines counter. Only one flight on that airline.

The American Airlines flight took off.

She waited another hour. The traffic in front of the small airport thinned out.

Gideon never reappeared. He was gone. Gideon was off the island.

She took a deep breath, tossed the scalpels in the glove compartment, and left.

Falmouth Harbour.

She parked in a space in front of Sunseakers, below the rooms at the yacht club.

Lip swollen; she saw that in the rearview mirror. Hurt worse than it looked.

Lots of traffic was in both English and Falmouth harbors. More snowy faces by the hour. Stanford Antigua Sailing Week approaching. Everybody arriving. More yachts every day. Dockside supermarket crowded, surrounded by dinghies, parking lot packed. People from the superyachts and others who had winter homes had arrived. Shorts and sandals. Sipping tea. Coffee. Buying provisions. Seabreeze Café, Slipway Chandlery, Lord Jim's Locker, that place that sold yachts, Jo and Judy's Delightful Bookstore, all crowded with the pale and privileged. The world belonged to them, the rich and beautiful.

Colonists pretending not to be colonists.

She glanced out toward the *Alfa Nero*, then toward the yacht she had visited days ago.

One day she would fit in. She wouldn't have to wear Blahniks to look like she belonged.

One more night here. She would pack and leave now, but she needed one more night.

The loss of blood. The medication. The pain remained, slowed her down too much.

One more guilty night.

Let the meds do what they were supposed to do. Let the bleeding stop.

She stood next to her battered rental car and called her handler again.

The phone rang and rang and rang. No answer. Concerned, but not too concerned.

Her mind on Anthony Johnson. Her heart on Matthew.

When she made it back home, if the neighbors asked, she would tell them Matthew had met another woman, an island girl, and left her to be with him. He'd moved out of the country. Matthew would've said the same if she had died on the job. A conversation they had had, half-serious, never thought that plan of action would ever be needed. But they had already worked it out, talked about that possibility when they first married, when they moved into a home and tried to live like normal people.

Across the nameless road, by the Skullduggery Café, she saw the man she had seen at the hospital. The man who looked like an aged movie star. The man who wore the white shoes. He was taking pictures of the yachts with his expensive camera. Maybe, like everyone else, he was in town for sailing week. George Clooney. The man looked like an older version of George Clooney. The man turned. In profile he looked more like Cary Grant. Looked better than Cary Grant, actually.

Room 29.

Matthew's things were still there. As if Matthew would return at any moment.

Sadness came and she allowed the grief to do what it wanted to do.

She undressed and went to the shower, sat on the tile floor, let the water wash over her, and cried. Then she stood up, still crying, reached for the shampoo, and washed her hair.

She told herself that she didn't have to leave Antigua. She had nowhere to go. Not right away. Their home was secure. A home that would have to get put on the market.

No way could she stay there, not in that big house, not without Matthew.

Six bedrooms. Four vehicles. Eight bathrooms.

She wondered if she could stay here. Rent a Caribbean-style home. Or lease a place back at Harbour View Apartments. Live where the locals worked hard all week, got paid on Friday, went to town on Saturday to pay their bills, and then went to church on Sunday. Or to one of the 365 beaches. She loved the weather, was on an island that had 365 beaches, and she wanted to skinny dip in each. She could let that be part of her therapy, giving her tears to the sea each day.

She missed Matthew. His voice still in her ears. His scent all over the room.

She didn't care if he didn't go to Barbados. Or if he had slept with Detroit.

Let he who is without sin . . .

At the end of the day, he was her husband.

She was going to do like Matthew had wanted. The things he had said were for her own good. She was going to lose some weight. Would diet after she went to the *Sex and the City* premiere.

Marriage was about compromise. Check into Crossroads after one last hurrah in New York.

She had to get a new I.D., become a new person.

She could take contracts and work from the West Indies. Have her broker find her when work was available, maybe do wetwork only in the islands, or travel to South America, always a death needed in Brazil, maybe even pick up a few jobs in the more exciting parts of Europe, pop in and out of London, Paris, and places like Florence, places with great shoes, clothes, and wonderful shopping.

When she needed to dance and party, when her mind was in that mode again, she could get a direct flight into Miami, dress in her beautiful Blahniks, get all sexy and party until dawn. She could go to South Beach and party and have fun, a widow in a single woman's clothing, could drive down to Haulover Beach Park, trek down to the nude section of the beach, tan naked whenever she wanted.

That would be her new life. A widow. Living in Antigua. Traveling the world.

Once again she would rise up. Like a phoenix.

But first she had to cry. Let the tears dry on their own.

She finished washing her hair, dried off, looked at her mosquito bites, then put on lotion.

The television on CNN. Breaking news about a murder in Antigua.

The Lady from Detroit.

Another part of her pushed through the sadness.

Her instinct.

She paused where she was.

Something wasn't right. She sensed it.

The man with the Nikon. The man in the white shoes. She had stepped out on the balcony with a towel wrapped around her body, and there he was, one story down, standing in the narrow, curved driveway. He was looking down at the brick design as if he were an architect. Then he looked up at her. He'd been everywhere she had been. He took several steps up the hill, that camera in his hand.

His jacket slipped open. She saw that he was carrying a holstered gun.

The man in the white shoes knew she had seen his weapon, simply nodded at her.

He wasn't with the police. Wasn't one of the four policemen of the apocalypse.

Her heart raced and she turned around, held her towel tight, hurried back inside her room.

Television still on CNN. Murder in Antigua. The Lady from Detroit.

She was startled. A woman was inside her room. Standing by the door, near the small kitchen.

A woman with hypnotic green eyes, eyes that startled her, made her pause.

A woman who supported herself with crutches. Her hair long, braided, hanging below her waist. Her dress long, sandals on her feet. More like a sandal on one foot. The other, wounded. She held an SR9 in each hand. Seventeen plus one times two.

There was no look of anger, no look of revenge in the woman's bruised face. It was the look of a professional at work. All business. She wanted to tell her that it was over, that Detroit was dead, the woman who was sleeping with her husband, she was dead, had been killed by her. Wanted to tell her that she missed her husband, he was dead, killed in the line of duty, so to speak, that she was sad and angry but she accepted that as part of the trade they were in, part of the business, no hard feelings, no intention to come after anyone or harbor a grudge like Detroit had done, wanted to say that her grief was her own and she had no problem with being a widow, and that unlike Detroit she understood that when you followed hatred, you turned blind, everybody died, that maybe they could talk this out, maybe they could—

The first bullet hit her between the eyes.

The next four she didn't feel.

Thirty-nine

sins of the mother

Hartsfield-Jackson Atlanta International Airport.

A mountain waited for me, stood in the middle of the anxious crowd. I had just hobbled off the train at the baggage claim exit and made it to the top of the escalator. That mountain's name was Alvin White. He saw my arm in the sling, saw my injured face that was covered in shades, nodded, and handed me a backpack. I took it and nodded in return. The backpack had the weight of a loaded .38.

I said, "You still have that other package?"

"The FedEx or the other thing I told you about?"

"Both."

He nodded.

We headed past baggage claim and stepped out into the weather. Dark clouds. Rain coming down harder by the second. The muscle in my groin had become a tight knot, couldn't walk too fast.

He said, "Looks like you had a little fun wherever you went."

"Little bit."

"Next time, take me along with you. I could help you out."

"You have a passport?"

"I can get me one."

It hurt me to ease down inside Alvin's taxi, black vinyl seats cracking under my weight. The inside of the taxi still smelled like cigarettes and old socks. Once again I sat up front, watched him maneuver his mountain of muscles, stuff his right leg in first, then bring his body inside before he worked his left leg inside. His seat was all the way back. His head touched the roof of the car.

I said, "You ever thought about getting a bigger vehicle?"

"With these gas prices?" He shook his head. "They say gas might go up as high as seven dollars a gallon. Hard times all over. They about to shut down over six hundred Starbucks, heard that this morning. No matter what kinda job, on the top floor or in the basement, people getting let go."

He reached into the backseat, moved old Starbucks cups and older Krispy Kreme boxes out of the way, grabbed a FedEx box, and handed it to me. I handed him money to pay the toll to get out of the parking garage and he eased his taxi out into the bad weather, windshield wipers working overtime.

Jewell Stewark smiled at me from a billboard, the rain giving her face tears.

For a moment I smelled her on my hands. Then that one-night stand was in the rearview.

Alvin said, "Hope you don't mind, but I spent a little of that money you asked me to hold."

"How much?"

"Was a little behind on my rent."

"No problem."

"Spent about five hundred. Can run and get the rest if you want it right now."

"We can take care of that later. Get me to Powder Springs."

I stared at the package from FedEx, the label from DNA Solutions.

The answer to my fears, doubts, and obsession was in my hand.

I asked, "Where is the note you found at the house?"

"Left it at the house. Didn't think to bring it."

Something was down by my feet, didn't want to kick it around, so I picked it up. It was a pair of black, French-cut panties. A matching bra was down on the floor too.

Alvin took those out of my hand. "I think those belong to Bunny. That girl something else."

He left Hartsfield, took Camp Creek Parkway, the rain coming down hard enough to make the streets become red rivers. Some of the soil had a reddish color, the rain making it look like blood was running into the street, that redness in the soil caused by iron oxides. Blood everywhere I looked.

I said, "Those two problems you found . . . ?"

"They in the trunk. Keeping each other company."

"They're awfully quiet."

"Yup."

"They dead?"

"They wasn't the last time I checked."

"When was the last time you checked?"

"Yesterday. Might've been day before."

"You feed 'em?"

"Food cost too much."

"You give 'em water?"

"There is a drought here. No extra water to go around."

"Good man."

"Cramped up like that with no food or water. They should be pretty weak. They was tiptoeing around the house. At first I thought they was stealing gas. Lot of that going 'round now. People siphoning gas like they did back in the seventies. Not only that but people are drilling into the gas tanks on the SUVs and Hummers and stealing gas. Stealing gas and messing up people's gas tanks. Bad enough all your gas is gone, but now you have to get your gas tank repaired."

I said, "You said they were tiptoeing around the house."

"Yeah. I snuck up on 'em."

"You hit them?"

"Left hook dead square on the chin."

"Knockout punch."

"He was knocked out like Suge Knight. Did the same to his buddy. Knocked 'im out too."

"Way to go."

"Fellows in the trunk. Both of 'em had guns. I threw the guns away. They hog-tied."

"Alvin."

"Yes, sir."

"Alvin, I think this is the beginning of a beautiful friendship."

About eleven miles out, Camp Creek turned into Thornton Road. Twelve miles after that Thornton Road ran into Richard D. Sailors Parkway. I had been on the cellular the entire ride. Called Hawks a dozen times, tried Konstantin just as many. A new level of stress erupted as we approached Macland Road. Stress magnified as we turned on Gus Robinson Road and found our way to the section of Powder Springs where I had bought the three-level house for Catherine and the kid.

Thirty-two miles and a little over an hour later we had pulled up on Double Creek Drive.

It was raining pretty hard. Skies as dark as midnight.

Midnight. I thought about the man they had called Midnight.

When Alvin pulled up in the driveway, I had him get out of his taxi.

Told him to toss me his keys, and I told that huge man to go wait inside until I got back.

He nodded.

I took off in his orange taxi, moved through rain and winds, tornado warnings on the radio.

When I made it back, I was up to my ankles in soil that looked like diluted blood.

Once again the Creature from the Black Lagoon.

The taxi was about four hundred pounds lighter when I returned.

Alvin's trunk was empty.

As empty as the smoking .38 I had wiped down and tossed into the Chattahoochee River.

I stood and looked up the street, searched for more of Detroit's men.

A strawberry blonde was on my mind; leaving her aboveground gnawed at me.

A lot of things gnawed at me.

I took the FedEx package off the front seat and headed for the house.

The note Alvin had found inside the house.

It was in Catherine's beautiful handwriting. In cursive writing that looked like art.

What she had to say had been left on a sheet of printer paper.

In blue ink, she had written the note in French, her native tongue.

It said that she and the boy were leaving America.

They had packed as much as they could and had gone back to Europe.

That hurt me more than the gunshot wound and the jellyfish sting.

Didn't take many words to shatter a fragile heart.

Hawks and Konstantin.

I heard from them the next day. I was resetting the system in the house. Lightning had knocked the system offline. Had to reboot so I could look at the cameras.

Konstantin had made it back home, was with his wife and kids.

He had left madness and gone back to normalcy.

Hawks came to Georgia, called me when she was at Atlanta Harts-field.

I took the Mini Cooper I had bought for Catherine and picked Hawks up from the lower level. Hawks was back in jeans, still on crutches, wore one cowboy boot, a backpack on her arm. When she got inside the car she kissed me so long I had to pull away from her.

She said, "Don't be mad at me, okay?"

"Why would I be mad?"

She showed me pictures she had on her cellular phone.

The strawberry blonde. Naked. A hole in her head. Pretty shoes at her side.

The opera was over. The fat lady had sung.

I asked, "Did you have to go do that?"

"You're one ungrateful jerk. You are really disappointing me right now."

"I'm surprised you didn't drown her and make it look like an accident."

"Was going to. Her suite didn't have a bathtub."

"How much I owe you?"

"Oh, please."

"Thanks, Hawks."

"Thank me when you take me where you promised to take me."

"Where was that?"

"Puerto Rico. Did you forget?"

"Puerto Rico. Right. I'll take you."

"Promise?"

"Promise."

"Pinky-swear promise."

"Hawks."

"Pinky-swear promise."

"Okay. Pinky-swear promise."

Newspapers were on the dining room table. Mostly *USA Today*.

ANTIGUA FINDS 11 DEAD IN THREE DAYS. Men from Oakland, New York, Memphis, Miami, Cleveland, Compton, and Detroit were in that lot of the dead. All had entered the country on forged documents. Assumed to be drug-related. Not one of the men was connected to my enemy. The hardworking locals wondered how the deaths would impact tourism and sailing week. Hard times were all over. Everybody was suffering. Somehow I doubted that series of murders would be noticed beyond the shores of Antigua. Most of the dead were of the wrong complexion to have a meaningful impact on tourism. It was blamed on the Jamaicans. Everything was always blamed on the Jamaicans.

I wondered who the Jamaicans blamed their problems on.

Next to that were dozens of pages that had been downloaded from the Web site for the *Detroit Free Press*. That paper ran the story on the front page. Had more details. The death. The funeral. Pictures of grieving politicians, relatives, and friends. Enemies were there too. Posted were words from people she had wronged, people who were glad she was dead, the talk of her death being a hit in retaliation for all the wrong she had done over the years. She was called a narcissist with a bottomless ego. Said she knew where the bodies were buried. And they repeated they believed that she had hired a hit man to kill her husband. Others speculated she was about to expose the elected official who had killed her husband, that was why she had been silenced. Another story said that over the last few days hundreds of thousands of dollars had been found missing, money misappropriated from the city she claimed to love so much. She was dead and the FBI was investigating her legacy as well as council members. Bribes for approving a sludge-removal contract. Forty-seven-million-dollar sludge contract in exchange for kickbacks. A morning news anchorwoman was involved. My enemy was dead but much was being said. Her being confirmed dead had left a lot of intimidated people unafraid to speak their minds. A lot of the negative shit was posted where people went to post negative shit and remain anonymous, on the Internet. They hadn't found any incriminating text messages. At least not yet.

I read the papers not to confirm her death, but to see if she had stashed evidence of her crime anywhere, if she had left behind anything that would lead the law to me. Nothing popped up in the newspapers. Nothing popped up on the Internet. I had Google alerts set on *Gideon* and *Detroit*. The only thing that popped up was a Baptist Church in Warren, Michigan, and a guy named Gideon who had graduated from Syracuse with a degree in finance. No one came banging on the door.

The Daily Mirror. Daily Star. The Independent. The Daily Telegraph. Daily Express. The Sun. London Lite. News of the World. Those were the newspapers in London and Britain. I searched them online, went back to the day I had last been there. Not one word about two women being found butchered on Berwick Street. They had died the way they had lived, unimportant to the important.

Two weeks went by.

Two weeks of me and Hawks taking meds, icing down injuries, taking warm baths, recuperating. Fourteen days of a mesomorphic man and a woman with an ectomorphic body playing Scrabble and unloading wagons before she had to leave. Hawks said she would call me soon. She promised.

She was going back to work. Had bills to pay and a condo to keep from sliding into foreclosure.

I bought her a present before she left. Something for Puerto Rico. A pair of Italian-made pink open-toe stilettos with a rhinestone brooch as an accent piece. She loved those shoes. Took off her cowboy boots and sashayed around in five-inch heels, loved the ribbons that tied across her ankles.

I sat up in the bed and asked, "Still think I'm a jerk?"

She looked stunned, whispered, "Good Lord, these are *gorgeous*."

I laughed as she hurried to stand in front of a full-length mirror.

"Good Lord. They make my calves look beautiful. Look at my butt."

I laughed. "How do they feel?"

"Supercalifragilisticexpialidocious."

Hawks took off everything except for the shoes. Modeled naked in heels. Her body unbelievable.

"They look good on you."

"Good Lord. These heels are so high I might get a nosebleed."

I stared at the shoes, shoes that led to smooth and sexy legs, a road to ecstasy in five-inch heels. She sat down on the bed, touched the Italian leather, ran her fingers across the design, then she stared at me.

Her haunting eyes locked on me.

Hawks touched the shoes and trembled, stared at me, her expression intense.

I asked, "Why are you looking at me like that?"

"These shoes . . . got me all tingly . . . made me a little excited."

She let her hair down, her highlighted mane flowing down her back, hanging below her waist.

Hawks came to me, undressed me, mounted me, kissed me, took me to a wonderful place.

Days passed before I heard from Catherine.

A few days of not knowing where the kid was had felt like one hundred years of solitude.

She had gone to claim Nusaybah's body. And she had done the same for the Yugoslavian named Ivanka. The money I had given her, she had taken that with her to make sure her friends had proper funerals and proper burials. Nusaybah had no relatives. Ivanka's people wanted nothing to do with a whore, shunned her even in death. Catherine paid for them both to have services at a Catholic church. And she paid for them to be buried in a decent cemetery, side by side, both in graves that had tombstones. Tombstones where friends could visit and leave prayers and flowers. She didn't leave them to be claimed by the government and disposed of like they were animals. She made sure they left this world with some sense of dignity. And she had taken Steven, the boy who used to be called Sven, the X in our algebraic equation, had taken the kid to help her find Nusaybah's son, if he was still alive.

I asked, "Are you and the kid coming back?"

"Nusaybah's son is missing."

"No one has seen him?"

"Not since the day his mother was murdered."

"What now?"

"I am going to the morgues. I am going to look at the unclaimed bodies of children."

Silence and grief sat between us.

She asked, "Did your package come?"

"It came."

Two weeks moved by on the back of a snail.

When Catherine's taxi pulled up in the driveway at the house in Powder Springs I was downstairs in the basement. In jeans, T-shirt, and steel-toe work shoes. Sling off my arm. Groin no longer on fire. Dust mask on. Tools all over. Knives, cornering tools, electric drywall saw, scissors, sanding sponge, stainless-steel mud bucket, keyhole saw, utility knife, solid large sheets of drywall, a few sheets damaged.

There were also cinder blocks, the kind used in the islands to hurricane-proof a home.

When we were done, this basement would be more than just a basement.

Alvin White had just left to run to Home Depot, then he had to go by his apartment in Lithia Springs, see his wife and kids for a while before he came back to work a few more hours. He'd been there every day for the last twelve days, almost twelve hours each day. Showed up at seven in the morning with a cup of something from Starbucks in his hand. I had told him he could keep the rest of that money I had given him. Between fifty and sixty thousand dollars. Told him the money was his. Hard times were all over and maybe that money that had been paid to put me in the ground could do him some good. Do his family some good. Or his girlfriends. I joked and told him that I hoped the one who could cook would start a chicken soup business over in Buckhead. In exchange for that wad of cash he was helping me finish the basement. I was taking up a new hobby with Alvin White as my teacher. Most of the walls were up. Soon we'd install a toilet, paint, put up fixtures, then put down carpet and tile. He'd just left to make that run to Home Depot when Catherine and the kid came inside the house.

Steven came downstairs, happy to see me. I'd never imagined he'd be happy to see me. He had on his yellow and green footballer jersey, the number 10 and the name RONALDINHO across the back.

He came down and gave me some dap. I wanted to hug him, but I didn't.

Behind him was a dark-skinned boy who had on new jeans and dark trainers, a new blue and white footballer jersey, the colors of Chelsea, the number 8 and the name LAMBARD across the shoulders. A worn soccer ball was under his right arm. The same soccer ball he used to kick on Berwick Street.

Nusaybah's son. The boy whose mother was from Vanrhynsdorp was there. The son of a woman who had come from a peaceful town in the folds of the Matsikamma and Gifberg mountains was there. He was alive. They had found him.

He paused when he saw me. He knew me. He would always remember me.

I wanted to tell him that the man who had murdered his mother was dead. Wanted to tell the boy that I had killed the man with my own hands. Wanted to fall on my knees and tell the kid that his mother had died because of my obsession and fears, that she had died a senseless death.

I swallowed, nervous, and with a kind smile I asked, "How are you?"

"I am fine."

"I am sorry . . . what happened to Nusaybah . . . I am sorry."

He nodded at me, held on to his worn European football.

He said, "It was a man with red hair."

"You saw him."

He nodded.

I swallowed.

He asked me, "Will I stay here in America?"

"Do you want to stay here in America?"

"My new mum said that I can stay here in America if you say I can stay here in America."

I nodded.

Catherine had brought home the child of another murdered prostitute. The child of a murdered friend. They were called whores, prostitutes, sluts, but they all had been somebody's child. Like the boy. His mother was dead because of me. Catherine had rescued him from the system.

Maybe the problem was that she had changed and I hadn't.

I looked at Nusaybah's son, said, "I forgot your name."

The boy smiled. "I want to be called Robert now."

I nodded. His accent was more British than African, like his mother's had been.

Then I looked at Steven.

I asked the kid, "Where is your mother?"

Steven pointed up, meaning Catherine was upstairs.

I said, "Show Robert the backyard. Kick the ball around a bit."

"May I show him the bedrooms when we are done?"

"Sure."

Steven smiled. "Robert, Mum said you can pick out your own bedroom."

The boys took to the stairs in a hurry.

Upstairs I heard Catherine's voice, that Parisian accent that would never get tamed.

She yelled, "No running in the house."

"Okay, Mum."

"Okay, Mum. Sorry."

I walked up behind them. It was time to sit down with Catherine.

Catherine had on worn jeans and low-heeled shoes. She wore a red T-shirt that had UNITED KINGDOM across its front in blue and white lettering. She was in front of the dining room table, her hands on the back of a chair, her grip tight, stress rearing its head as she stared down at the FedEx, the label from DNA Solutions in her eyes. Tears formed in her eyes as she stared at the answers to X. Y. Z.

She asked, "Did you open it?"

"No."

She turned and saw me. Her eyes widened a little.

She came to me and put the palms of her hands on my wounded face.

I looked in her soft brown eyes. Her fingernails were a little long, in need of a manicure, eyebrows needed to be arched again; her motherly and chic bob needed trimming but still looked nice.

She had had a busy and hard month, an emotional and rough time in Europe.

She asked, "Are you okay?"

"I should ask you the same."

"You changed the front doors. You changed the back doors too."

I nodded. "Better locking system."

"They're heavier."

I nodded. "They're solid."

She pulled out a chair, sat down. The television was on. A small one on the counter. Looked like something about a movie premiere in New York, *Sex and the City*. I turned that off, took a seat.

I told Catherine, "What you did was brave."

"I am not brave. I have never been brave."

"Going back there and finding her son. That was brave."

"I only did what was right."

"You did for them what you did for my mother."

"I only did what was right. I just want to do what is right."

I nodded.

She motioned at the FedEx.

She said, "Open it."

"It can wait."

"You've come this far. My friends have died because of this."

"Because of me."

"No, because of me. Because of what I am ashamed of. Because of what I am afraid of. I have to be strong and face this as much as you have to face this. Open it and know what you must know."

"About the kid."

"No. About you." She swallowed. "About Margaret. About the lie I put on Margaret."

"What about my mother?"

She wiped her eyes. "Margaret was not your mother."

I swallowed.

She shook her head. "Open it. Open it so I can take that lie off my friend's memory."

"Was there a Margaret?"

"Yes. I had a friend who was murdered. My best friend in life. She had a horrible death."

"She was left dead in a Dumpster in Alabama. In Opelika, Alabama."

"The story about Margaret is true. But Margaret . . . she was not your mother."

"What are you telling me?" My voice softened. "Who was my mother?"

Her bottom lip trembled. "Open it."

Killed in London. Attacked in the Cayman Islands. Ambushed in Huntsville. Then there was Antigua; I would rather have redone all of that one hundred times than suffer through this moment.

Shouts interrupted us. The yells of two boys having a ball playing soccer. Steven jumping up and down in victory, like he was Beckham, made a score over his best friend. They were reunited.

We watched them for a few moments. Our focus on the new kid.

I asked, "Will he be okay?"

"I'll know in time. He cries at night. He has had a tough life."

Our eyes went back to the FedEx. To the truth that had separated us for so long.

I said, "The kid. I've been jealous of the kid."

"You're jealous of Steven?"

"You're good with him. Cook for him. A real mother with him. You never were like that with me."

"I did my best with you. Do not be jealous of him. He is but a child."

"I know."

"When you were born . . . your mother was young. And afraid. She had had a hard life."

I nodded. My mind on the FedEx, on Margaret, avoiding the truth I had searched for.

She hesitated. "When I went back to London, when I went to where I used to live, saw how I used to live, I can't do that again. I can't go back to being that person. Not with Steven."

I swallowed my thoughts. "Where did you find Nusaybah's son?"

"Outside Charing Cross. I cried my heart out. Robert was dirty, a child doing soccer ball tricks, walking London alone, sleeping on the concrete, begging strangers for scraps of food at tube stations."

"Robert."

"He wants his name to be Robert. He wants to fit in. We just want to fit in this world."

"He doesn't like me."

"He's afraid of you. What you did in London, when you attacked me, he remembers that."

"I have a habit of making people not like me."

"Play soccer with him. Ask him to teach you how to play. He loves soccer."

"Maybe after we've done what we have to do."

We sat there with the FedEx between us.

She whispered, "In London . . . when you came to kill . . . I lied to save my own life. If I had not lied, if I had died that day, then my friends would still be alive. This . . . all of this . . . this is my fault. I thought it would last forever, but a lie can only last so long. The truth will always find you. In time the truth arrives."

Outside I saw two of the happiest kids I had ever seen in my life.

In the end we chose what battles we fought. We chose our wars.

We chose what we clung to. And we chose what we let go.

I picked the FedEx up and walked into the kitchen. I dropped my obsession, stuffed my fears inside the trash can. Did the same with the stacks of papers I had on my deceased problem from Detroit. Let that go as well. I looked back at Catherine. She was on her feet, wiping her palms on her sides.

I said, "Steven and Robert, the way they're playing, they'll be hungry soon."

She spoke in a nervous tone, said, "I'm going to clean up the kitchen. Cook a big dinner."

"You might have to drive to Publix and food-shop. Not much here."

"Okay."

I nodded. "I have a friend coming back."

"You have a friend."

"Guy named Alvin. We're going to finish the basement. He's a good carpenter."

"You never had a friend before."

"I know."

"Will you stay here with us?"

"Until the basement is done. If that's okay. After that, I'll visit. But I won't stay here."

"Where will you go?"

"Promised a friend I would take her to Puerto Rico. Have to keep my word. Not sure where I'll end up after that. Maybe go back to where they measure their weight in stones and their money in pounds. I'm more comfortable there. Haven't really put that much thought into it. Day by day. For now."

"So you will leave North America."

I nodded.

"Europe is very expensive. Much cheaper to live here in America."

"I'll keep that in mind."

"Would be nice if you were close." She paused. "Steven would like that."

I nodded.

She said, "I would like that too."

Again I nodded.

"You are always welcome here." She choked on her tears. "Son, you are always welcome here."

A moment rested between us.

I asked, "What do you want me to tell people I am to Steven?"

"Tell them . . . tell them he's your brother."

I nodded. "I'll tell them the other kid is my brother too."

"He would like that."

Steven and Robert were having a good time chasing each other around the backyard.

I said, "The man who killed your friends, the man who killed Ivanka and Nusaybah, I killed him."

"You murdered him?"

"I killed him."

"How did you find him?"

"I killed him. That's all that matters."

"You still . . . you are still working. You are still in that horrible business."

We stared at each other a long while.

"Good." She nodded. "Some people deserve to die."

I nodded. Catherine did the same. She saw who I was. I saw corners of who she used to be.

Even the righteous wanted revenge.

I said, "Some people deserve to live."

She wiped her eyes and nodded.

She went to the trash, moved the printer pages to the side, took out the FedEx box.

She held it in her hand. X. Y. Z.

She said, "I will keep this. For you. For Steven. In case either of you ever want to see what's inside. He should know. And you should be certain. Whenever one of you wants this, it will be here."

I nodded.

She wiped her eyes, wiped that vengeance from her face, took a deep breath before she looked around, saw the dishes in the sink, the carpet that needed vacuuming, and said, "This house is a mess."

"Some. Sorry I'm not as tidy as I used to be."

"And don't wear those shoes on the carpet, Jean-Claude. This is nice carpet."

I headed down to the basement, dug inside my back pocket, and took out a B.C. Powder, took that and went back to working on their house. Their house. One day I'd get my own. One day.

I'd figure out a way to get my own house again. And I'd get a dog. Never had a dog.

No matter how I got there, this was who I was.

I could pretend to be Jean-Claude. Pretend to be Jean-Claude the same way Batman pretended to be Bruce Wayne. I could pretend that there wasn't a demon inside me, that I wasn't part Golgo 13.

Soon the phone would ring and Konstantin would be on the other end.

And once again I would be on a plane, or in a car, going to do someone else's dirty work.

That was what I did.

It took money to raise a family. Cost money to stay alive in this world.

Konstantin was back at work too. Cost the man over a hundred dollars a day to stay on top of the soil. He had to put men under so he could stay on top. I hoped I didn't end up in his ironic situation.

The boys kicked the ball and it hit the basement door.

I went to the basement door and looked out in the backyard. Watched them run and play.

My name is Gideon. But before I became Gideon I was a child.

A child who grew up in red-light districts, a child who had been hardened by heinous things.

Like the two boys playing soccer in the backyard.

Never had a house like this to live in. Or a backyard to play in. Or a friend.

I had killed a man when I was seven years old.

Killed a man who was trying to murder my mother.

He was choking her to death. I shot that man with his own gun.

That man was my father.

Steven told me he had shot a man. A man who had attacked his mother.

He had shot that man before they moved to London. He had killed a man in Germany.

I wondered if Nusaybah's son had done the same.

I wondered that as I stepped into the backyard and they kicked me the ball.

They laughed at the way I kicked the ball back.

I went after them, did an easy jog into the quarter acre behind the house.

We set up a triangle and kicked the ball to one another.

Robert came over to me. "I can teach you, help you get better."

"Remind me of the rules."

"Football is played—"

"Soccer. Your football is called soccer in America."

"Soccer is played with one goalkeeper and ten field players."

"Okay."

Steven, the boy who used to be Andrew-Sven, said, "And there are three positions."

"What are those?"

"Defenders, the midfield players, and forwards."

They told me more of the rules, told me about basic formations, like four-four-two and three-five-two.

I paused, stared out at the grounds, at the neighbors' homes, looked for trouble, expected to see a sniper on one of the roofs, in one of the windows, a rifle aimed in my direction with my core or head in its crosshairs. My life had been filled with mystery and death, every breath closer to being my last.

Detroit was dead. The death verified. I hoped my problem was dead as well.

The winds were calm, the air balmy, birds flying overhead.

Nothing was there. No one was there. Today trouble had taken a holiday.

We all needed rest. A short break from the rainy season. A *petit carême*.

Today was calm. Tomorrow would bring whatever tomorrow would bring.

Once I started playing soccer and laughing, pains went away and every fear was put on hold. I became a kid having fun with his brothers. I was playing with them, but in the back of my mind I was doing something else, working them out, making them strong enough to survive a hard world.

My problem in Detroit had spent a lot of money to find me.

I know someone who can find you.

He will find you.

I needed to reverse-engineer that paper trail. If that was possible.

And there was only one person I knew who could do that.

Only one woman. A grifter named Arizona. Soon it would be time to go back to that well.

Whoever Detroit had financed to track me in London, to find me in Huntsville, to get information about Powder Springs, whoever she had paid for that information, they knew about me as well.

They probably knew more about me than Detroit did, only passed her what she paid for.

I had to protect Catherine and the kids. Once a man had a family he was never safe.

They would never be out of harm's way, not as long as they lived under my shadow.

That was why the basement was being built with impenetrable doors and cinder-block walls.

That was why I had twelve cameras inside and around the house.

That was why as I had fun kicking the soccer ball, a nine rested in the small of my back.

Maybe it was done.

Maybe it wasn't.

I'd fooled myself into thinking it was done before.

I just knew that today I was still alive. And I knew life was a temporary state of being.

This was my season between storms. I was waiting. Waiting for my *petit carême* to end.

We chose our wars.

But sometimes our wars chose us.

Revenge is a confession of pain.

—Latin proverb

Acknowledgments

I went to Antigua, West Indies, the land of 365 beaches.

I made friends and chatted at the Antigua and Barbuda Literary Festival.

I stayed.

I went to Antigua for the book festival, fell in love with the beaches, the people, the weather, and the next thing you know there were EJD sightings all over the island, at movie premieres, at Best of Books, shopping on Market Street, at poetry readings at Funky Buddha on Redcliffe, eating at KFC, working out at Sandals, liming and writing and pigging out at Big Banana in town, doing more of the same at the Sticky Wicket. Man, in the name of research, I was all over the place. Old Road. Doing the zip line. Devil's Bridge. Betty's Hope. Learning the history of the island. Every day a new experience.

Every day I looked for something new to give the characters.

I was practically an Antiguan. Well, in my mind. You know how fiction writers are. ☺

I guess when you go to a place that seems like heaven's waiting room, you want to belong. Four trips in a few months. So I guess I had become a fan of Antigua, a *Fan*tiguan.

It was impossible not to become smitten with a tropical island that stimulated me in so many ways and allowed my creative juices to flow, an island that gave me a much needed setting for my writing. Caribbean people are beautiful, delighted me with their charm and warmth every day I was on the island.

Before I arrived I had heard there were 365 beaches, but since I didn't see any of the beaches numbered, I guess I'll have to take the tourism peeps' word on that one. Dickenson Bay. Coconut Grove. The view is outrageous. Like stepping inside someone else's fantasy. Wonderful stretch of white sand. Half Moon Bay. Simply beautiful. Rendezvous Bay. If you want some privacy, you have to go there. If you drive to Hawksbill, make your way to the *third* beach. No clothing required, no cameras allowed.

And that's all I'm gonna say.

It may not be a big thing for the people on the island, but I learned to drive on the opposite side of the road. Inside a small rental car with the steering wheel on the opposite side. Granted, I probably scared the hell out of a couple hundred people in town when my brain had me on the American side of the road for a moment. A thousand apologies for any heart attacks I may have caused.

I enjoyed Sailing Week, enjoyed cricket matches at the stadium, got caught up in J'ouvert, went to house parties with the staff at Antigua Yacht Club, had fun at many other wonderful events.

I'm coming back. This Fantiguan is coming back.

And I am going to make a point of bringing a Sharpie so I can number the beaches.

Until then, let me thank a few people for helping me create the novel you have in your hands.

To my wonderful people in Falmouth Harbour at Antigua Yacht Club, my Caribbean family who took great care of me from the moment my plane landed until I headed back to the airport. Eloise, Everlie, Devin, Beverley, Sean, Foster, Iris, Esther, Nakisha, Bernadette, Samantha, Gailann, Vendella, Jackie, Ms. Morrell, Kerry-Ann, Ranny. I hope I spelled all of your names correctly. If it's wrong, blame Devin.

To everyone at Siboney Beach Club and Coconut Grove, thanks for the wonderful hospitality.

Maria Pentkovski in San Francisco, thanks for the wonderful Russian lingo. It was great meeting and chatting with you up in the Bay.

Christina Pattyn and Club Bleu in Detroit, thanks for everything Mo-town. LOL. Hope you enjoy the book. Asami King in Chi-town, my MySpace homie, thanks for allowing me to pop in your screen for some English-to-Japanese translation. Most of it wasn't used, things changed along the way, but the character stayed in the book, her role small but meaningful. ☺

Nerissa Percival in Antigua, West Indies, thanks for the dialect and the information. LOL.

Susan Noyce in Antigua, West Indies, thanks for helping with the same.

Nadine Greenaway, thanks for showing me around Sandals.

Now let's recruit some of my fans at Christ the King to help me count the beaches.

And to the founders of the Antigua and Barbuda Literary Festival, Pam Arthurton and Joy Bramble, thanks for everything. K. C. Nash, you are the best. Thanks for taking me all over the island. Your new home rocks! And shout-outs (do people still say *shout-out*?) to Barbara Arrindell and Treasa James. Troy Byrne of Digicel, thanks for the kind words you said at the festival. Man, that caught me off guard.

Before I go on, I *love* classic noir. I love the darkness, the danger, the duplicity, the desperation . . . the list of what I love about that genre is endless. While I was working on this novel I paused to watch *Du Rififi Chez les Hommes*. Loved what they did to it on the big screen. Loved it so much I had my characters pause in the middle of this novel and watch it with me. In the film there is a wonderful twenty- to thirty-minute sequence that has no dialogue, no score. Suspense and tension. And some damn good acting. It is mesmerizing and simply brilliant. I won't spoil it for anyone who might love classic noir and missed that one. But the ride is worth the ticket. At least it was for me. Somewhere in this book you're holding is a small tribute to what made that section of the film work: tension, and at times silence.

And now to thank the people back home.

Denea Marcel McBroom, thanks for reading this as I worked and reworked the pages.

I have to thank a few of the people who drove me around on the

Pleasure book tour, people who allowed me to ask them a ton of questions as I traveled from city to city, working on the novel you have in your hands. I made it up as I went along, and I couldn't have done it without you. Nashville—Michele Buc. Huntsville—Shawana Ariel. Atlanta—Robert Fisher. Pittsburgh—Sandi Kopler. Dallas—Linda Veteto.

Now, I have to thank the people behind the man who writes the books.

Always wanted to say that. ROFL. ☺

Sara Camilli, my wonderful agent, the journey continues. How many more books to go?

Lisa Johnson, Beth Parker, Stacy Noble, and all the peeps in publicity at Dutton, thanks for the continued hard work and support. Couldn't do it without you and everybody back there in NYC.

And special thanks to Brian Tart. Hope you enjoy this installment of Gideon.

John Paine, thanks for looking this over in its early stages. Your input was invaluable.

Thanks to Erika Imranyi. Welcome aboard and I look forward to working with you.

Last but not least, to my fantastic editor, Julie Doughty, thanks! You are the best of the best!

In case I left a few peeps out, quit complaining; scribble in your name and keep it moving. ☺

Me wan' fu tank _____ fu all the help s/he min give me when me min all ova de place, and dung dey inna Antigua. If you no min help me out wid all de so-and-so and so-and-so, me couldnta write dis book ya.

Oh? You didn't understand a word I just said? ☺ Well, neither did I.

I want to thank _____ for all of his/her help while I was all over the country and down in Antigua working on this project. Without your help, insight, and wisdom there is no way I would have been able to write this book.

Gray sweats, white T, Nike cap on, about to go find some lunch at Baja Fresh.

See ya!

Eric Jerome Dickey

July 22, 2008
11:44 A.M.
Latitude: 33.99 N, Longitude: 118.35 W
80°F. Sunny. Humidity: 48% Winds: SW at 7 mph

www.ericjeromedickey.com
www.myspace.com/ericjeromedickey
Facebook

About the Author

Originally from Memphis, Tennessee, Eric Jerome Dickey is the author of sixteen novels, including the *New York Times* bestsellers *Pleasure Waking with Enemies, Sleeping with Strangers, Chasing Destiny, Genevieve, Drive Me Crazy, Naughty or Nice, The Other Woman,* and *Thieves' Paradise.* He is also the author of a six-issue miniseries of comic books for Marvel Enterprises featuring Storm (X-Men) and the Black Panther. He lives on the road and rests in Southern California.

www.ericjeromedickey.com